VIOLET MOON

KAYLA MAURAIS

Also by Kayla Maurais
Soul Sucker

ISBN: 979-8-9929665-0-3 (Paperback)

ISBN: 979-8-9929665-2-7 (Hardcover)

ISBN: 979-8-9929665-3-4 (Ebook)

First Edition, May 2025

Edited by Jennifer Lindsay

Proofread by Claire Olivia Golden

Cover Art by Allison Li

Map Art by Shepengul (@shepengul)

Playlist Art by Nikkita Bell

For all the stories that sat on shelves collecting dust, waiting for their time to shine. This book sat for six long years. Now, its journey begins.

"People like us, who believe in physics, know that the distinction between past, present and future is only a stubbornly persistent illusion." — Albert Einstein

TIMBER'S VILLAGE

NORTH WOODS

BIG OCEAN

CODING OF ELDER HUTS

JON'S HUT

THE INN

DUNES

M'AKER'S MARKET

TIMBER DWELLING

MINES

SOUTH WOODS

VIOLET MOON

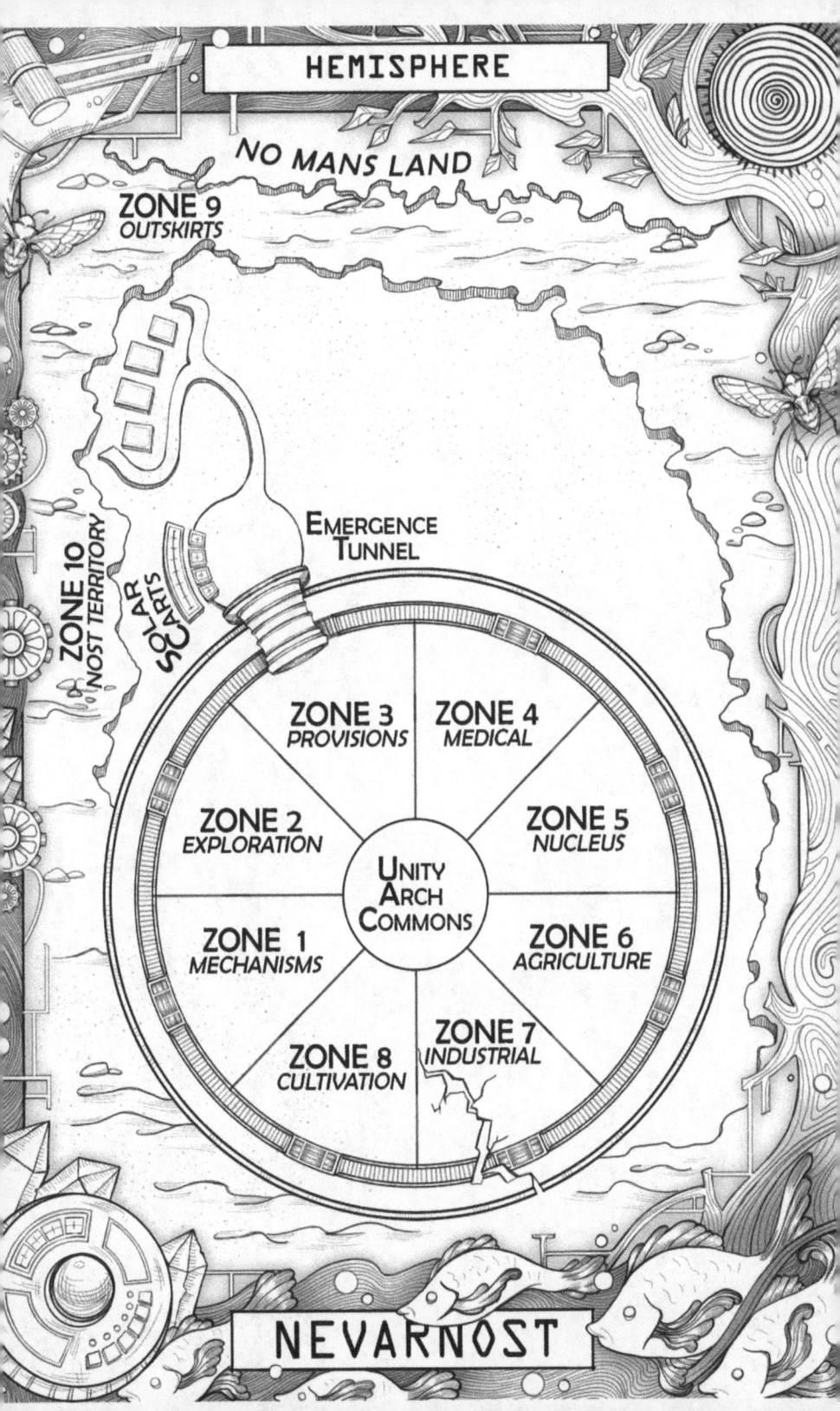

HEMISPHERE

NO MANS LAND

ZONE 9
OUTSKIRTS

EMERGENCE
TUNNEL

ZONE 3 | ZONE 4
PROVISIONS | MEDICAL

ZONE 5
NUCLEUS

ZONE 2
EXPLORATION

UNITY
ARCH
COMMONS

ZONE 6
AGRICULTURE

ZONE 1
MECHANARIUM

ZONE 7

ZONE 8 INDUSTRIAL
CULTIVATION

NEVARNOST

You are about to embark on an adventure through time and space, one that has been my passion project for the last six years. Throughout this journey, music became a big source of inspiration for me as I drafted and edited this book. Sometimes, I'd hear a song while driving and play it on repeat, choreographing the scene over and over until I could finally put the words onto the page.

As part of this book's release, I've included a playlist of my favorite songs and instrumental pieces that inspired the scenes you're about to read. If you'd like to join my musical journey, you'll find the playlist along with the corresponding page numbers for each scene it influenced, plus a scannable QR code linking to the Spotify version on the next page. I hope you enjoy the words playing out like a film inside your head, just as I did, as you read while listening to the music.

Before you dive in, note that this book contains references to sex, an unplanned pregnancy, drug use, a natural disaster, violence, blood, death of a parent/grandparent, grief, and anxiety, as well as some explicit language. Please consider this information, along with your own reading preferences and/or comfort levels, before moving forward.

VIOLET MOON

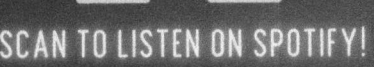

SCAN TO LISTEN ON SPOTIFY!

OFFICIAL PLAYLIST

KAYLA MAURAIS

1: VAIDA

Planet Nevarnost: Year 3051

Today, the chancellor dies.

I wipe sweat from my brow and tighten my grip on my brother's old hunting knife, its worn hilt heavy against my palm. A gift from our father on his eleventh birthday, it's one of the only pieces of him left. It was once intended for cracking open desert melons and spearing the sand lizards that invade our sleeping quarters, but now, it craves blood.

A drop of cool liquid splashes my cheek, and the nectar bats roosting in the stalactites hanging overhead chitter in my presence. One flaps its greasy wings at me before fleeing into a hollow groove coated in red lichen. If they weren't so sacred to the Nost, I'd scare the lot of them off. But they play their role in the underground ecosystem like everything else. Perched in tangles of plump saccharine roots until they molt and spurn sharper teeth. They tear away the tap points so the roots will leak sugar water, which the Nost then collect for remedial use.

Nia, who walks beside me on her four tentacle-like legs, is used to them. Having worked in these caves for years, she doesn't think twice before taking me through their nesting tunnels. I, on the other hand, can't stand the smell. Cloyingly sweet, it carries in the cool air current, and nausea rolls through me with each breath.

I consider putting on the carbon filtration mask I stole for today's quest but leave it hanging loose around my neck. Even if I have to stop and ralph up the questionable porridge I ate this morning in the Hub, it's still better than using anything manufactured by the enemy.

That would be a shame, though. Cook's porridge is the only thing I've eaten in days.

Nia picks up her pace as we approach a fork in the tunnel we've been following for the last hour. My two human legs don't stand a chance against her lofty four, but I push myself harder, reclaiming the lead. Humans are rarely welcome in the labyrinth of underground passageways connecting the Outskirts to our rival's dome-like fortress, but there's no way in hell I'm letting a little thing like this mess up my opportunity to face the chancellor.

We slow beneath a curve of mossy stalactites at the fork. Nia guides the oozing orb of light clutched in her right tentacle along the serrated rock walls.

I immediately head left. "This way is faster."

"I have to disagree," she says, remaining where she stands.

But I'm already in the dark, swallowed by the shadows.

"You don't have to come," I call back with a shrug.

Moments later, her light follows, its shine hitting the back of my neck. "Why is it you insist you know Nost Territory better than a Nost? I will never understand."

I sweep a low-hanging stone spider's web out of my face with the tip of my brother's blade and clean it on my khaki green cargo pants. "Look, I appreciate you getting me past the guard, but I don't need a babysitter. I do this all the time. I don't need help—"

Nia's free tentacle shoots out, stopping me short. A horde of nectar bats scatter, wafting the sickening odor of hardened sap up my nose. She lifts her glowing orb, revealing the edge of a gaping half-crystallized pit overlayed in a shimmering mist.

She raises a crooked brow. "You were saying . . ."

I roll my eyes, swallow the dry heave threatening to climb my throat, and spin on my heels, knocking gravel into the pit as I turn back the way we came. "If we'd taken the southeast path like I originally wanted to, we wouldn't be here."

"A simple thank you would have sufficed," she says flatly.

Of course, she wants me to thank her. And maybe she did just save me from falling to my own death, but who's to say I would have died? I would've found a way out like I always do.

Plunging into a bottomless pit of discarded sugar wouldn't have been *that* big of a deal.

When Nia moves back in step beside me, her orb illuminates the intricate patterns and decorative swirls covering her body from the shoulders down. Dark brown ink blends seamlessly into her slippery skin, my favorite being a set of ornate wildflowers that twine around her left tentacle and weave in between the eight suckers at the end.

It's how I tell Nia apart from the others. Nost markings are unique to each of them. Otherwise, they all look similar, towering a foot above the rest of us with hairless, oblong heads and two wide eyes that radiate an ethereal gray-blue hue.

We reach the fork once more and veer right this time

against my own free will.

About halfway down the passage, Nia whispers, "We are getting close."

Before I can ask how she knows, bits of stone and dirt rattle around us. A resounding shriek whizzes by as the solar train passes above ground overhead.

Dammit. She was right. This *was* the correct tunnel.

Nia hands me her glow orb, and I cradle the bright, sticky blob, savoring its raw heat in my palm. A gust of air ruffles the tattered drapes of brown cloth swaddling her slim frame. In one motion, she reaches upward. Her tentacle stretches twice its length, snapping as she yanks down a rope ladder with wooden rungs.

A ripple courses through my gut. *Soon, Chancellor. Soon.*

She swings the ladder toward me. I catch it, then hand her back the orb.

She affixes it to the cavern wall, where it settles into a groove.

"What is your plan if the chancellor refuses to give you what you want?" Nia asks, holding the ladder steady so I can climb. "The likelihood is high he won't concede, and you are not a killer, Vaida. Whether your urgency for revenge makes you believe you are or not."

I ignore the possible truth in her words. The Nost aren't always right, despite what they think. Anyone is capable of anything if the timing is right. I've learned that the hard way.

My fingers curl around a rung. "You don't know what I'm capable of. I can be whatever I want to be. Just—let *me* worry about it. You're always up in my business."

"It is not that I am 'up in your business' . . . whatever that means." Her voice follows me as I climb. "Humans are creatures of habit. You are no exception. You get impulsive

4

ideas."

"You don't know everything about us, okay? Or me. So stop."

"Fair enough. But what about the last ridiculous infiltration you attempted? You told me you were going to Nucleus to get close to the chancellor's son, gain his trust, and convince him to help you attack the chancellor in his sleep with a paperweight if he refused to back down and hand over the Hemisphere. Which, if I recall, was another unsuccessful endeavor."

"It was unsuccessful because talking to the chancellor's son made me want to rip my hair out." I grit my teeth and continue climbing. "Obviously, I'm not going to move forward with a serious plan if a guy has zero personality or capability. Soren couldn't handle it."

I reach for the thick, metal-plated hatch above my head and lock a steady hold around the wheel handle. "I could have sworn I told you all that."

"All I know is you were gone for almost a week."

I ignore her comment because I don't owe her anything, and I twist the wheel. It pops, releasing the seal with a deflated hiss. Stale air catches in my lungs, but at least it isn't laced with the sickly-sweet stench of nectar and ground water.

"I do not believe we ever had a *real* conversation about it all," Nia adds.

I peer down at her. I know she knows I'm lying. The downfall of having a Nost best friend. Their species reads minds and emotions with a single touch of their tentacle, but everything is so black-and-white with them. *Normal human tendencies included.*

Probably not the greatest foundation for friendship, or

whatever it is we have, but Nia's been in my life since the day the Unity Arch fell. She was there in the medic tents, bandaging the injured. She comforted me when they found my mother's and brother's bodies in the rubble. And every day, whether I like it or not, she sticks by my side.

She's the only friend who's ever stuck around. Which is why I've learned to put up with her nagging, steer clear of her suckers, and get really good at lying. Or at least try to.

Nia wouldn't understand what really happened with Soren Bay. I've done a lot of shitty things in my short nineteen years, but even after two months, I still wake up haunted by those four days. Maybe someday I'll tell Nia, but for now, it's my secret.

And I won't let her close enough to read it off my psyche, either.

"If you must know, my plan is to break into the chancellor's office, find something worthy of blackmail, and force him to back down." I slip on the carbon filtration mask still hanging around my neck. "And if he doesn't, then he dies. It's really that simple."

Nia reaches up and pushes open the hatch, leaving enough space for me to climb through. "I think you'll make it halfway and turn around before anything comes of it."

Oof. I might be a liar, but she never fails to give it to me straight.

I tuck my knife into the sewn-in loop in my sleeve. "Then I hope I prove you wrong."

"Me too," she says with a grin. "May Goddess Cassia be with you."

The hatch delivers me to an empty alleyway across the street from the solar train station, at the outer edge of Zone 6: Agriculture, a border zone to the forgotten Zone 7.

My vision adjusts to the haze, taking in the thick dust hanging in the air.

We didn't always wear masks. But we learned fast: our bodies can't filter the Nevarnost dust that catches in our lungs. Not like the Nost, with their throat slits that flutter open and shut like petals—a natural filtration system. Their slime-coated, rust-tinted skin also protects them from the harsh ultraviolet rays of Nevarnost's two scalding suns.

The Nost were born on this planet. They belong here. We humans just burn.

I climb a flight of bowed stairs with broken rails. Ahead of me, littered streets and skeletal buildings cut stark silhouettes against a backdrop of gray. I dodge a few sweepers, the flying bots programmed to spot-clean the air. Nothing more than nuisances if you ask me.

The everlasting hue in the sky space won't fade, no matter how much dust they filter and suck up. Surprisingly, it's still an upgrade compared to living in the Outskirts.

I merge into a sea of olive-green uniforms and carbon masks on the walkway. A myriad of wandering eyes in every shade pass me. You can tell a lot about someone from their eyes. The nebulous silvers meeting mine before darting away? *He wants to be left alone.* The glittering blues sneaking a peek at me over the bridge of her nose? *She thinks she's better than me.*

Any other day, I'd indulge in the rush of sizing people up. But today, I need to go unseen. Today, I'm the heavier-set girl with downcast eyes nobody bothers to notice. I like my size and own it proudly, but sometimes blending in is easier when you're me.

You can't stop what you don't see coming.

I approach the far end of the street, stepping into Unity

7

Commons, the public courtyard where the remnants of the Unity Arch still stand. Each zone is separated by 30-foot metallic pillars, linked by a hexagonal grid-like energy field that can be turned on or off as needed. The solar train and patrol officers who regulate the connecting walkways hold special pass keys, making them the only ones able to cross with ease. This central courtyard, once meant to be a communal gathering place, now fades into patches of dirty artificial grass, decaying ironwood trees, and crumbling stone ruins. The entrance to Zone 7: Industrial is so tightly boarded up with panels and scrap metal that even the solar train doesn't pass through it anymore.

I pull up my hood, avoiding the attention of a small gathering of people and Nost clustered in the fallout's remains. For years, this place was a dead zone. But with the 10-year anniversary of the tragedy approaching, Unity is just itching to make its comeback.

Old members hand out flyers. Others chat with bystanders. A Nost perches on a rotting crate, waving a brightly colored banner stamped with the image of a budding oak tree.

The Unity symbol—the artistic brainchild of my mother and her best friend, Billy Hale—was meant to represent peace and harmony. But for me, and the many others who lost loved ones the day the Arch fell, the tree is a painful reminder.

Everyone claimed I was lying when I said it was Billy Hale who blew up our arch. Nobody could fathom how our former chancellor, someone so devoted to humanity and his so-called peace project, could commit a crime that wiped out an entire zone. I was only nine, but I remember seeing him standing amid the smoke and wreckage, a weapon in his hand.

These reconcilers plant themselves on the graves of our loved ones, pretending it's in their honor rather than heaping on insult to injustice. They parade around their symbols and ideals of the past, preaching forgiveness, as if that will bring back jamborees, unification, and our families.

But I know better. I know the truth.

Nothing will bring back my mother and Ethan. Nothing can undo what happened here. Some say we should be over it, let the past be the past, but even if we could go back in time and stop Billy Hale from doing what I *know* he did, it wouldn't change anything.

The Arch falling wasn't even the worst thing that happened to us. It was Chancellor Bay taking over as leader of the Hemisphere. Still, I can't imagine why anyone would want to revive a forbidden organization that divided us and sparked a greater struggle for power.

A whistle blows. I slip between two old Arch posts, out of sight, before patrol officers storm in and break up the fallout assembly. The few remaining are hauled off in electric cuffs.

Thankful for the chaos, I jog toward the high rises in the distance, drawn to the towering building where our current chancellor sits on his inherited throne.

Zone 5: Nucleus.

My fingers curl around the weighted identification card in my pocket. I take the front steps with ease, scanning in at the double doors as if I do this every day. Acting like I belong. Downcast eyes are useless here. Self-assurance is the key. I keep my focus forward, locked on the mirrored lift ahead, passing through the vast lobby.

Around the sandstone columns are a scattering of plush,

misshapen love seats and artificial desert plants in clay pots begging to be dusted. In the corner, a blender bot whirls as a barista prepares beverages at a small refreshment cart.

The barista holds up a steaming tin mug. "For . . . Annie?"

At the front desk, the receptionist stands, and I pause to let her pass. In response, she flashes me her pearly-white veneers. For a moment I let myself imagine the luxury of working a day job with not just fancy drinks but proper indoor air filtration too. We can get away without wearing a mask inside the Hub or in our dwellings on a good day, but too many nights, I've fallen asleep with the blankets up to my nose and a heaviness in my lungs. And some Outskirters don't even know what real boxed milk tastes like, let alone a cup of herbal tea that hasn't been brewed using the same tea bag as the person before them. A casual smile like *Annie's* isn't a comfort I know, and it unsettles me more than it should.

I press the call button on the lift, catching my reflection in the glossy doors. My carbon mask silences me, but my brown waves with violet-tipped ends frame my round face boldly.

My lurid hazel eyes, however, give me away.

You're not a killer, Vaida.

But I'll be anything if I have to be.

I clench my fists at my side, ready to board, finding comfort in the cool touch of my brother's knife against my wrist beneath my sleeve. I imagine the look on the chancellor's face when I waltz into his quarters like the scorch beast of his nightmares. So many have suffered because of this man and his commands. What will it feel like to watch him suffer?

10

The lift arrives. A ding fills the silence. The doors glide open.

"Vaida Marie Wardell," Dad says, and the blood surging through my veins freezes over. "What in Nevarnost are you doing here?"

My heart thunders as I realize he isn't alone. Behind him, Matron Nost Far steps forward, clutching the woven cords dangling with crystals and bones around her slim neck. And then, emerging like a haunt, the heinous ruler himself—Chancellor Ezra Bay.

I force my hands to stay relaxed at my side, though they long to curl around his neck. This man exploited our greatest tragedy, dismantled Billy Hale's remediation plans, and exiled *my* people from the Hemisphere. All to conserve air for his precious few. And Dad stands next to him like they've just been playing a friendly game of virtual disc golf.

"Steven, you didn't tell me your daughter would be joining us today," Chancellor Bay says, raising a neatly trimmed brow.

This has to be a mistake. I checked Dad's calendar before I left the Outskirts. This wasn't scheduled. He's supposed to be laying boundary markers at the quicksand pits right now.

Dad's expression twists. "I am terribly sorry about this, Ezra. I had no idea she was here in the Hemisphere. Especially when she isn't supposed to be . . ."

"Surely she must have a good reason," Matron Nost Far says, clutching the bone talisman with a spiral sun carved in its center. "An emergency, perhaps?"

Her gaze is light but knowing. *She's helping me.*

"Yes," I say quickly. "There was a fire in the Hub. We put it out."

From behind his mask, Dad crow's feet crinkle. *He doesn't buy a word I'm saying.* Like with Nia, I've never been able to lie to him either. At least not to his face.

"I think if everyone is safe, this could have waited until I got back," he says.

"Don't stress, Commander." Chancellor Bay straightens the collar of his plum-colored suit, not a lock of quaffed, ashy gray hair falling out of place. "It's no big deal. It happens."

It happens, I mimic in my head. He probably thinks dooming young children to a life of lung sickness just happens, too. Or sentencing adults to poverty and weekly ration tokens. I fix my gaze on a candelabra on the nearby wall. Forget the blackmail. Forget demanding surrender and knives. One good swing to the back of his head, and the chancellor would be out like a light.

Oh, you know, it happens, I'd say, if there were any repercussions left to face.

Dad clenches his jaw, the straps of his mask going taut. "Again, I apologize."

"Much obliged," Chancellor Bay says, returning to the lift. "It was nice seeing you again, Miss Wardell. I look forward to working with the Outskirts. A brighter future is ahead."

That's it. I let out a growl and lunge forward just as the lift snaps shut.

Dad jerks me back, and he and Far drag me away like they do to the Hub thieves who steal rations while the night watch take their piss breaks. Soon we're out of the building and down the front steps, back onto the streets of Zone 5: Nucleus, and I've never felt more on edge.

I was *so* close this time.

Dad's voice cuts into me. "What has gotten into you?"

"You acted like a rabid animal," Far adds, not bothering to look at me.

I shake off their arms and storm ahead, pushing past surprised pedestrians who quickly give me space to pass through. I don't care what Dad or Far think. They weren't even supposed to be here. I tear off my carbon mask because the privileged act is over and dig into my pocket for my normal face covering, a worn galaxy-speckled rag with stars.

Infiltrating the chancellor's high castle was a bust. No need to play Hemisphere girl any longer than I have to. Even if their masks are 99.9% more effective, I'd rather get lung sickness than admit anyone beneath this stupid dome did something right.

Far's tentacle loops around my arm from behind, stopping me in my tracks.

"If only you knew the cost of carrying that much rage in your heart, child." She reads me and whips me around to face Dad. "Your father was talking to you."

I roll my eyes. Curse the Nost and their cat-like reflexes. And I don't care what she feels or hears coming from my body. I don't need a lecture. Not from her. Not from him.

Dad's face, what little I can see around his mask, is beet red. More from hauling ass to catch up with me than anything else.

"I will not have you jeopardize the progress we've made with the Hemisphere, young lady. We've worked too hard convincing Chancellor Bay to join our merger."

"Your father is right," Far says. "Calm yourself if you can."

Calm myself? They don't get it. They've fallen for a monster's wit and charm.

"Didn't you see the look on his face?" I look straight into

Dad's eyes. "Chancellor Bay doesn't want to help us. He's manipulating you. He's manipulating us all. That's what he does."

"I've heard enough." Dad adjusts his mask. His eyes quickly scan left and right, as if looking for eavesdroppers. "Our people have been without clean water for months. I'm done justifying myself because you can't let go of the past."

Naïve. He's so naïve.

I cross my arms over my chest. "It's not about letting go of the past. It's about trust. Having a meeting with the chancellor means nothing. He's never agreed to anything before."

"He's had a change of heart," Far says evenly, taking the lead to guide us toward the solar train pulling up to the platform.

I scoff. "He doesn't have a heart."

"The damage in Zone 7 has gotten worse. Air quality in the Hemisphere is dropping," Dad says. "It needs to be mended. In return for sending us the mechanism specialists we need to repair our irrigation grids, we'll send him laborers to reinforce the crack."

I let out a bitter laugh. "You can't be serious. At least they have air quality inside the Hemisphere. We can't let these people into our home. They won't respect us."

"My word is final." Dad ushers me into the nearest solar train compartment. "And do you have any idea how humiliating it was for me to be escorted into the Hemisphere because I didn't have my scanner card this afternoon? Hand it over. Now."

Ugh. I dig into my pocket.

Dad swipes his Nucleus-issued identification card from my hand and scans us into a double seat. Far sits across from us, expressionless. Our compartment could be on fire and it wouldn't faze her. Nothing ever fazes the Nost. I slam into the seat and press my head against the window, letting the lurch of the train's motion roll through me.

"Trusting him is a mistake," I say. "He'll just use us. And if you won't help our people or stand up for the change we deserve, then I will. Even if I have to do it alone."

"No, you won't." Dad straightens his glasses and sighs. "I know this is hard for you, Vaida, but need I remind you, this isn't a war. Violence isn't the answer. Sometimes, a calculated approach alongside those who share our goals is a better long-term solution. That's what Far and I are doing here. We can't force others to change. We have to work together."

I let out a sniff of disgust. Before Mom died, he wanted nothing to do with community meetings and unification strategies. He claims violence isn't the answer, but peace isn't either. Peace didn't help Mom or Ethan, or anyone forced to leave when Zone 7 was boarded up to preserve air quality. And working with other like-minded individuals? That wouldn't work either.

Nobody hates the chancellor as much as I do.

I won't give up. I'll try again. Billy Hale may have caused this mess ten years ago, but instead of fixing his mistake, Chancellor Bay took Hale's place and sentenced us all to a life of suffering. He uses people. He pretends to build them up, only to discard them when he gets what he wants.

I would know.

His son did the same thing to me.

2: KEVIN

Planet Nevarnost: Year 3051

~~snacks~~
~~regulate motion sensors~~
~~replace aerogarden pump filter~~
~~nana's vitamins~~
~~review nucleus comm systems~~
~~find misplaced baby doll~~
roakes

H eat cables are fried. *Again.*

Third time this month. Every time I think I've mastered proper levels, I'm wrong. Which makes no sense. Bulbs are intact. Coils are charged.

So what am I missing?

I change out my latex gloves, disturbing the nine roakes basking in the terrarium before me. Similar in form to scorpions, their telsons buzz and pincers rise in warning. They scatter, tearing through the silky webs they spun overnight. Overheat a roake, and they reduce themselves to venomous stardust. Freeze them, and their complex minds become hostile. Find that perfect temperature, and they release a hallucinogenic poison twice as potent as they would in the wild.

Get stung too many times, though, and you're dead.

If it weren't for the latter, I don't think I'd be sitting here with a hand lens and a thermal thermometer, poking at the beasts that claimed both my parents' lives. I never knew them. They were both gone before I turned three. Yet, understanding roakes feels like understanding the reasons why my mother became so dependent on them.

So far, my understanding has been inconclusive.

"Hey, Lux?" My digiband picks up on my voice recognition. "Add 'rewire the terrarium mechanisms' to my to-do list for tomorrow. I want to change out the bulbs."

The monitors on display at my workstation whirl to life.

Luxframe wakes and starts her daily syncs between devices, projecting without delay. *"Adding to the list now."*

Scouring the broken slabs of red rock, I pluck a roake up by the tip of its tail, just beneath its stinger so it can't sting me. It writhes, then settles in the glass dish beneath my macroscope.

As I adjust the focus for a better look at the silver scaling along the roake's abdomen and thorax, I call out, "Lux, read me the daily report, please?"

"Of course, sir." My robotic companion's words fill the small but quaint loft. *"Nevarnost continues to rotate at 1,000 miles per hour. There is another lightning storm due north, coming off the rings of planet Horn, but it will bypass us altogether."*

I peer through the ocular lens. Prod the roake to flash its six tiny sharp teeth and the twenty-seven orange spikes splayed along its back. "What about air quality?"

"Nevarnost air quality is down by 40% since the last scan."

"That's strange. A massive decrease?" Nah, that can't be right.

I set down my dissecting forceps, toss my goggles aside, then gently return the roake to its rock in the terrarium. As it offers me another hiss, I swivel my chair past my secondary workspace, where my latest tinker project sits in pieces waiting for my next day off, and then beyond the vertical 53-gallon column fish tank, home to my late uncle's two pet glowfish, Galileo and Puck. On the other side of that, I pull up to the dual screens and control panel, where an array of stats and geographical charts update on the display.

I zoom in on the exosphere tracker. "Lux, what is the reason for quality decline?"

"Dust increases in the desertscape and overall humidity," she replies. *"Would you like to send an updated report to ISR Headquarters? You are overdue for a video conference."*

The message board pops up, cursor blinking, ready for me to type.

A meeting with the highest-ranking authority in the galaxy, who doesn't know I've been impersonating my uncle—their former agent—for the last ten years? I'll respectfully pass.

I run a hand through my scraggly brown hair and quickly minimize the attachment.

"Put off the video conference for another month. Tell them I've been busy with Hemisphere affairs. And calculate the number of decades left until exospheric suffocation."

"It is less than a month, sir."

My heart flutters.

I skim the codes once more to make sure Lux hasn't completely gone off her circuits. It's happened before. More than once. But the data bar confirms her report—less than a month.

"Air quality on Nevarnost has never been this bad," I say to Lux as if she's sitting right next to me in human form. I'll admit, sometimes I imagine her that way. But only when it gets *really* lonely. Otherwise, I risk going off my circuits, too. Compatible friends my age are hard enough to find, let alone keep. "Run a Hemisphere capacity sequence just to be safe."

"Scanning and sending the report now," Lux says. *"I am also getting an exterior alert. Motion sensors have been triggered on level 1. It appears you have visitors. How fun!"*

"Lux, is this your way of telling me you don't enjoy my company?"

"I am not sure what you mean. Would you like me to send them away?"

I draw my lips into a line. "No, no. Let me see who it is, please."

As Lux brings up the external camera feed, I tap the image and wait for it to load. I rub my temples, trying to fend off the tension headache creeping in. Maybe I could write Lux a new AI code that includes witty banter. I managed to program enthusiasm. Though, considering I'm not so good at banter myself, it'd probably just end up being embarrassing for both of us.

When the image sharpens, two familiar silhouettes appear, and my skin crawls. *Shoot.* That time of the week already? Thought I had more time.

I get up, and a roake hisses at me. Only when I adjust the heat lamp, just enough to cover the entire basking rock, does it settle into a curl, content. A smirk tugs at my lips.

Roakes are smarter than we give them credit for.

I get up and leave the loft. Down the ladder, into the hallway. My pace quickens at the sight of Nana, peering through the window beside the entrance.

"They're here for me, Nana." I steady her as she clings to me, letting me guide her back to her bedroom off the entryway. "Maybe you'd be comfortable in your chair?"

She tugs at my ear with delicate fingers. "My—my baby."

"Oh, you lost your baby again?" The knocks at the door come faster, sharper. I tense. Waiting for a few seconds more won't kill them. "It's okay. I'll find your baby for you."

I leave her standing and drop to the floor. Search on my hands and knees. Pull away decorative cushions. Fumble under the metal dressing cabinet. I check behind the woven baskets heaped with yarn, a lifelong hobby Nana will never touch again because her fingers don't work quite the way they used to. The box of knitted masks in the loft crosses my mind, but then I spot the pink ruffles tucked in the folds of her chair.

Relief spreads through me. The last time I couldn't find her baby doll, Nana had an episode that took hours to calm.

She holds out her hands. "Oh, my Quinny girl."

I place the baby doll in her arms and brush a thick lock of gray hair away from her wrinkled, mossy-green eyes, which glisten a shade brighter than my own.

"Yes, here's your baby. She isn't lost. Everything is going to be okay now. Go sit, and I'll make breakfast soon."

"You found my girl." Her hand finds my cheek. "Thank you, Billy."

I remind myself it's the sickness that makes her forget who I am. The sickness that makes her think the baby doll she named after my late mother is a replacement for the daughter she lost.

"Kevin, Nana." My tone softens. "Remember? Kevin."

Her response is barely audible. "Oh yes . . . Kevin."

Outside the bedroom, I lean my head against the wall. Close my eyes. *Breathe.* In for four. Hold for four. Out for four. And then again . . . as many times as I need to.

Box breathing. Uncle Billy taught me.

I first caught him doing it one morning after breakfast when I was seven. He was up in the loft, settled on a yoga mat with his legs crossed. Uncle Billy was big on meditation and spirituality, despite his love for science and inventing. He used box breathing to calm his nervous system before heading off to work as our chancellor.

He was against outright confrontation—we have that in common—but he also taught me that being passive and being assertive are two very different things. You can keep the peace and still speak your truth. You can stand up for what you believe in without being cruel.

If I need to cope, I box breathe. Four counts before making any decision or reacting emotionally. That's key. Uncle Billy drilled that into me during the last conversation we had before everything changed.

It was the morning of the Unity rally. I'd just thrown a tantrum because he had to leave early, and I wasn't allowed to go with him. Instead, for some reason, I had to go with Nana to pick up new guitar strings. On his way out, with his half-strung guitar slung over one shoulder, Uncle Billy knelt down on my level, wiped a tear off my cheek, and said—

Listen, Kev, you're emotionally led like me, which means sometimes you'll feel things stronger than most. When that happens, take a moment to breathe before you react. Count to four. It'll help you calm down. Always let yourself feel and choose kindness, but make all decisions when you're level-headed. I gotta head out now. Remember what we talked about. I love you, and I'll see you at the rally later, okay?

Then he left for the rally.

The Unity Arch blew up.

And I never saw him again.

It doesn't matter how many times I box breathe; I still haven't figured out how to stop his death from consuming me. My parents' deaths have become a scientific exploration, something I mourn because I didn't really know them, because it feels like what a parentless child is *supposed* to do. But Billy was more than an uncle. He was a father, a brother, and a best friend.

I don't know what I'll do when I lose Nana, too.

The knocks at the door grow rougher now, a reminder that someone is still waiting, that life goes on regardless of the past.

I take one final breath. Open the door.

Chancellor Bay and his son, Soren, stand at the threshold.

Soren enters first. "Took you long enough."

The chancellor lingers at the doormat. "Mr. Hale, mind if we have a little chat before you and my son play *Starships and Spacespirits*, or whatever the hell it's called?"

Starships and Spacespirits? That's what Soren tells his father we do here every week? He could've mentioned any number of skill-building games—Holoblocks, draughts, metal cards.

Instead, he went with the one that's all about improvisation and character play.

"I suppose that's . . . somewhat of an accurate description of what we do here."

Chancellor Bay raises an eyebrow but follows me into the sitting room. Soren pushes past him, making a dive for the daybed I sleep on every night. Muddy boots and all.

He fluffs my pillow before sprawling out. Funny enough, that used to be one of my triggers. I'd tried to tell him how much it bothered me, but he met my discomfort with carefully crafted insults. So I adapted. Let it go.

Now his weekly visits just so happen to fall on my laundry day.

Soren notices the box of freeze-dried cheese curds on the bedside table. As he helps himself, I hold back a smirk. I'd picked those up last night from a ration shop and placed them there this morning. *Another adaptation.* If snacks aren't accessible, he'll raid the refrigerator, including Nana's meals, and leave the place a mess.

Chancellor Bay lets out a long, drawn-out sigh, the kind that drips with disappointment, before turning to me. "Imagine my dismay when your name came up this morning during my conference with Commander Wardell and the Nost leader, Far."

"You mean Matron Nost Far?"

"I don't care what they call her, but they requested you personally represent the Hemisphere in our merger." He steps closer, and I take a step back. His cologne is overpowering, and so is his arrogance. "A very specific request, if you ask me."

I keep my expression neutral, not allowing him to bait me. "As someone who aced their tech exams, sir, my name is one of the first on the mechanism ledger. Commander Wardell probably reviewed it and made his choice accordingly."

Chancellor Bay drifts to a shelf lined with hand-blown

glass cats—Nana's collection, before she got sick. He runs a finger along the edge, catching a layer of dust.

"You think highly of yourself, don't you, Mr. Hale?"

I cross my arms. "I know my worth. Yes."

"Seems egotism runs in your family." He picks up one of the last known paperback books on Nevarnost, flips through it with a scowl, then sets it back down. "For the life of me, I'll never quite understand why that is. Especially since you Hales are nothing but trouble."

If he knew I knew his history with my uncle, he'd take that back.

If he knew I knew, he'd also be mortified.

My attention drops to Chancellor Bay's hands, now fiddling with a silver fidget ring etched with evil eyes. Years ago, I found a hard drive filled with digital scans of my uncle's journals. In one of them, he mentioned that ring, a gift he'd given the chancellor.

I know what happened before and after that gift was given. The sequence of events, the choices made, the heartbreak. If he despises my uncle so much, why does he still wear it?

I could make an educated guess. But if I spoke that truth aloud, Chancellor Bay would likely have me banished. Or worse.

Instead, I say, "My uncle had every right to think highly of himself."

Chancellor Bay's nostrils flare. "Your uncle was a pacifist know-it-all who didn't have the guts to do what was best for our people. He was impulsive, flighty, and he made a pre-existing issue much worse when he decided to blow up that damn arch. Hardly someone I'd look up to."

I suppress the fire building inside me. I don't usually care what people assume, but when they blame my uncle for a tragedy that destroyed everything he loved most, I wonder if box breathing will be enough.

Uncle Billy didn't do what they say he did. I'd swear my life on it.

I bite my tongue. "Just tell me what you want me to do."

Soren snickers from his spot on the daybed, but Chancellor Bay silences him and turns back to me. "You will go to the Outskirts and play your part in this merger the commander and Far so desperately want."

"What else?" I ask. There's always something else.

"You'll let them believe you're there to help them with their irrigation system, but under no circumstance are you to complete the task. We will not waste our supplies on them." He closes the gap between us. "Got it? Or shall I remind you what happens if you don't comply?"

His presence stirs insults inside me I'll never say. At least not to his face. Not when I'm holding on like a failing air filter just to keep a roof over my grandmother's head.

"You don't need to remind me," I say evenly. "I get it. I'll do it."

"Wonderful." Chancellor Bay's lips curl with satisfaction as he leans closer. I turn my cheek, focusing on anything but him. *Box breathing. Thoughts of baby dolls. Angry roakes.*

"Let your time in the Outskirts enlighten you. Galaxies know you need it."

He smooths a hand over the curve of his hair, then flicks soot off his cuff.

My pulse settles. I keep my head down until the front door slams shut.

I won't react. Not emotionally. Not outwardly. But, *man*, it's hard.

Like Uncle Billy used to say—karma will handle him instead.

"Fuuuuck. What a drag that was." Soren's voice startles me. He lets out a deep breath, refreshed from his laze. "So, do you have my weekly order ready or what?"

I'm *this* close to crossing everything off my to-do list.

"You sure you don't want to play *Starships and Spacespirits* instead?" I furrow my brows. "We could act out one heck of a galactic adventure through time and space."

Soren flushes a deep red, the same shade as his bloodshot eyes. "I had to tell my father something, okay? Give me a fucking break. All that matters is that he bought it."

I grimace at the way he chews his nails.

His greasy blonde hair looks like it hasn't been washed in weeks. Judging by the dark circles under his eyes, I doubt he remembers what sleep feels like.

"Look, maybe you should . . . skip this week."

"Why?" He springs off the daybed. "You don't have them?" His body trembles. I reach out to steady him.

"You better have them. You promised me."

Promises. Soren's all about promises.

"Okay," I assure him. "You can have them."

Minutes later, we're up in the loft, sweating in the artificial heat, bathed in the violet luminescence from the tank where Galileo and Puck swim.

Soren leans over the terrarium and admires the roakes burrowing in the sand.

Most days, I can't stand Chancellor Bay or his son. But during Soren's weekly visit, that feeling fades, and dread takes over. I watch him roll up his sleeve. Cringe at the inflamed welts trailing up his arm. A routine I now know all too well. One sting here. The rest to go.

26

Without gloves, Soren reaches into the terrarium and picks his poison.

My throat thickens as the roake writhes between his fingers. He presses it to his arm. In defense, it stings. A welt forms. Then, as always, the creature curls in on itself and dies, spent from giving its venom away.

"There's fewer than last time." Soren speaks more steadily now, a completely different person, revived by a quick fix. "There should be fifteen."

"I lost a few." I grab a jar from the shelf beside the AeroGarden. "The cables overheated. I'm still working out the right levels. They're tricky."

"I can tell they're stronger than usual." He shoves his hands in his pockets and watches as I load the remaining roakes into the jar. "Means you're finally doing something right for once."

"Nothing about this is right." I screw on the lid and hand him the jar. "And if I say I'll do something, I'll do it. I always keep my word. But I won't have more until I rig the cables."

"Rig the cables, then." He gives the jar a little shake, prompting the roakes to hiss.

The *right* thing to do would be to stop enabling him altogether, but like his father, Soren's got his hooks in me too.

He turns to leave, pointing to the old Unity poster pinned to the bulletin board above my workstation. "FYI. My father's arresting anyone associated with that peace group now."

"No crime in hanging up a poster. But thanks."

"Whatever." He scoffs, nudging me on his way out.

After he's gone, the tension in the air deflates.

I tap my digiband. "Lux, cross roakes off my to-do list."

"I have crossed off roakes."

I breathe in through my nose, count to four, and exhale slowly. Recollecting myself, I grab the photo of Uncle Billy and me from my desk. In the picture, we're in his lab over in Zone 2: Explorations. I'm holding a beaker, bubbling over with some elixir he taught me to make during an enrichment craft. He's leaning against a secondary glowfish tank, his grin wide.

A moment frozen in time. It was taken the same year the Unity Arch fell.

Billy was still physically twenty-six then, preserved by years of cryosleep and space travel for ISR before settling on Nevarnost to become our chancellor. Some believe he destroyed our community, but others remember him like this—young, wise, a visionary.

Nana says I'm the spitting image of her son, which is why she mixes us up.

And I'd have to agree. We're nearly identical.

But Billy wore black-rimmed glasses, knew how to grow decent facial hair while I work hard to maintain my stubble, and his fascination with the metaphysical far surpasses mine.

I set the photo back on my desk, brushing off the dust that had collected on the frame. After everything we've been through, I'm not sure I fully believe in an otherworldly power. If something else *is* out there watching us, beyond what we already know of magic and other planetary beings, it feels cruel to think it would allow so much death and loss.

And like so many others, Uncle Billy's body was never found.

I've held onto the smallest sliver of hope that he's still out there somewhere. But if he is, if he survived, then maybe he really did betray everything he once stood for when he became chancellor. Something deep inside kicks back at the thought. My uncle was the one who taught me right from wrong. He lived with integrity even when no one was watching.

He wouldn't just abandon his passion project.

He certainly wouldn't have abandoned me.

3: TIMBER

Planet Violet Moon: Year 3083

M y heart beats in double time when Head Elder Cyan's voice pierces the air, causing a stir in the Council of Elders' hut. "Timber Dean Hale."

As I rise from the defendant's bench, the jute bindings at my wrists chafe against my skin. I clench my fists, encouraging warmth and circulation back into my hands. The watcher who tied them left little room for movement. And if I don't tend to them soon, they'll bruise.

At the same time, I welcome the pain. It distracts me from my throbbing temples and the overwhelming amount of people awaiting my sentence.

I approach the half-moon-shaped table carved from indigo wood, where the eight elders of our village sit in high-backed chairs forged from the same violet-silver grain.

If tonight were a full moon, the indigo wood table and chairs would glimmer. The wood is a rare, natural material. So rare that when a child is born, a section is cut from our tallest indigo tree and carved by the maker of the family's choice into a talisman meant to be given to the child following their Coming of Age ceremony.

My own talisman remains tucked away in Mother's cloak. I've never seen it. Only she and the maker who carved it have. And given what I've failed to do, it's likely I never will.

Mother's easy to spot in the crowd, seated in a sea of colorful tunics and cloaks that fill in the tiered viewing area behind the council's table. Her long chestnut locks fall in waves around her round face. Strands catch the ebbing light, while her ivory skin gleams beneath them. She offers me a forced smile, but it doesn't settle me like it normally does.

Head Elder Cyan strikes the edge of a bronze singing bowl.

I take in the resonating tone, its reverberations intensifying my headache. The incense wafting from the two herbal torches on either side of the space isn't helping either.

As I tuck my nose against my shoulder to avoid the smoke, the other elders rise, including Father, the Head of Transmissions, who sits at the far end, fiddling with his digiband.

I'm surprised he's here in general.

For the past few moons, all he's cared about is work. Even at home. Coding on tablets at the dinner table. Skipping morning playtime with my toddler-aged brothers to sketch blueprints and run diagnostics. The only real conversation we've had in weeks was the night I stumbled into the sustenance chamber for water and found him hunched over the counter, electric wire-cutter in hand, working on some futuristic-looking device hooked up to the generator.

"What's he doing out there in the Dunes all night?" I'd asked Mother.

"Planning something important," was all she said.

But Father's barely looked at me since the trial started.

I've committed treason, the worst thing an elder's son can do, and all he cares about is his virtual to-do list.

Head Elder Cyan beckons me forward.

His long beige cloak, which swathes his hefty frame, tangles as he rounds the table, prompting a watcher to fluff out his train. He lowers his fur-lined hood, revealing his balding head, and dips a hand into the leather satchel at his waist.

This is the part of tonight I've been dreading the most. Head Elders are also Ritual Masters. They always carry crystals and herbs soaked in ceremonial oils. It's customary for him to anoint those he counsels, but the thought of anyone touching me makes my entire body tense.

I'd rather they lock me in the holding pit with a red-eyed flare cat.

I fixate on Cyan's oiled thumb, internally begging my shaking body to stay still. But I can't control the trembling when it happens. I can't control any of my natural body responses at all. I've been known to pass out in moments like these. *Gods, I hope that doesn't happen.*

Head Elder Cyan raises his hand to my forehead. I keep my sweat-soaked body tight.

All I can do is hope he makes this quick.

He runs his thumb across both my cheeks, and my knees go weak. He re-saturates his fingers and finishes the anointing by drawing a spiral on my forehead, all while the smell of sage and vervain grips the back of my tongue.

I know what comes next. The result of another's touch is something I have zero control over, and as expected, Head Elder Cyan's true thoughts and emotions pulse into my mind like an amplified, fractured whisper. *What an odd boy. Why couldn't he just kill the worm? Why did it have to be an elder's son? Such a disappointment. If he were smart, he'd reconsider.*

With a wince, I shove the message away, but it echoes in my head like shouts trapped in the South Woods. Sweat drips from my hair as his judgment lashes through me, while his disappointment settles into the soles of my feet. Not every feeling carries the same weight. Happiness and joy are high-speed whirlwinds that make it hard to breathe. Sadness is like a knife, stabbed right in the heart. Desire is an insatiable hunger, relentless until it's fed.

But judgment and disappointment? They're parasites.

They gnaw at my bones, burrow their way in, and make permanent homes.

This is exactly the kind of situation I go out of my way to avoid each day. A curse I never asked for, a secret I've harbored since the first time it happened as a Seven. Whether it's a handshake, a hug, a simple tap on the shoulder, or someone accidentally brushing past me—every time someone touches me, the unfiltered feeling comes rushing in against my will.

And this is the toll it takes on my body.

I am only minimally good at hiding it.

The wrinkles in Head Elder Cyan's forehead deepen. "*U evere u lefere*, Timber."

We're taught traditional Vio at a young age. I'm fluent enough to hold a conversation, join in hymns, and translate his words: *We've given you life, Timber.*

I swallow the bile threatening to rise long enough to respond, "*I know.*"

"You have refused to sacrifice a moon worm in the name of ceremony," he continues in modern Vio. "Rarely do we find ourselves in such a predicament. Why do you refuse?"

Now every eye in the village is on me, including Raine's, who sits a row away from Mother. Other than his talisman, he wears only a simple pair of tan pants, and his dark shoulder-length hair is braided back at the nape of his neck. When his encouraging brown eyes catch mine, my shoulders relax. Only a little. He requested the night off from his watcher duties so he could offer his support. I don't know what he sees in me. Or why he sticks around. Anyone else would have shunned me the moment I set down the knife last night, but Raine doesn't rattle that easily, and I certainly don't deserve his kind of loyalty.

I still haven't told him the truth about why I didn't kill the worm or of the curse that wreaks havoc on me. For some reason, I can't muster the courage to share that part of myself with him. I know he wouldn't judge me. It's just easier for me to ignore it all.

The council, the village—they all want answers. But I can't tell them either.

I didn't experience the relief of a mercy killing they all speak of in Violet Moon lore when I plucked a moon worm from the barrel last night. The innocent creatures we harvest from the Dunes as a rite of passage—who are said to exist for this purpose—instead radiated pure fear, pain, and, most surprisingly, disappointment in us Vio for not valuing their lives as we do other living things on this planet. For that alone, I couldn't do it.

I couldn't cause them or myself any more suffering.

Head Elder Cyan speaks again. "Well?"

The pulsing in my head returns. "I don't . . . I don't know."

"You don't know?" The Head of Knowledge pushes her glasses up the bridge of her nose and leans forward in her chair. "This is a serious matter. You'd better know."

"I just—"

"You just what?" she presses.

"Go easy on him," Raine's grandmother, our Head Healer, says.

The Head Watcher slaps a hand on the table and stands. "If he isn't going to speak, let's give him his sentence. We're only prolonging the inevitable because he's an elder's son."

I jerk my head toward Father, still seated at the end of the table with reverence, but at the mention of our familial connection, he stops messing with his digiband.

My mouth goes dry. I think if I look up again, I might vomit.

His lips draw into a line. "Sentence him to the mines—"

"Oh, *William*," Raine's grandmother blurts out. "Have a heart."

"You didn't let me finish," Father says calmly. "Sentence him to the mines if you must, but I would like to make a motion that falls in line with village rule first, if I may."

Head Maker folds his arms across his chest. "Oh, this shall be good."

Father ignores him and stands, his broad shoulders relaxed as he presses his palms against the table for support. "My son is an Eighteen, as his educational year states, yes, but he won't officially be eighteen years of age for another seventy-two hours."

The murmuring crowd picks up once more as Father continues, "My motion is to release him under my care until then, a short-term rehabilitation. On his formal eighteenth birthday, we allow him one more chance to complete his ceremonial act, or his sentence to the mines is final."

"It's a *worm*," Head Maker reminds us. "A sacred but measly worm. If he can't knife it down now, what difference will three days make?"

"I second Elder Hale's motion," Raine's grandmother says.

Head Maker laughs. "Yet *another* conflict of interest—"

Another murmur erupts in the crowd, and Head Elder Cyan silences them with a strike of his singing bowl. Its pitch echoes in the circular space, fizzling out in the thatched roof above.

Gods, it's worse than the screech of slate scraping stone.

"I've heard enough, and I've made my decision." Head Elder Cyan sets down his leather-wrapped mallet. "If you'd all care to stop bickering and listen . . ."

A smirk forms on Father's face, but my expression twists. He's too calm. Why isn't he more worried about this? Any other father would be irate. And I should feel grateful for his consideration. Another three days to right my wrongs. But I'm not going to change my mind. Not even the horror stories I've heard about the luster dust, shadow beasts, and bottomless pits in the mines could change my mind. They might as well send me now. I'd lose everything for the duration of my sentence, but I wouldn't have to touch another human being ever again.

And maybe I'm better off that way.

An outcast in the most undesirable place.

Head Elder Cyan motions for a watcher. "Three days, Timber," he says while the watcher cuts my bindings. "I'm granting your father's request. But in three days, you'll be back here to complete your ritual, or you will spend the rest of your days in the mines with no future pardon."

The remaining frayed material from my wrists falls into the dry dirt at my bare feet. I rub the raw skin and calluses that are close to bone. The first thing I'll do when I get back to our dwelling is slather them in ointment or give them a good herbal soak. I can't mine for crystal or fend for myself underground in isolation without steady hands.

As villagers file out of the hut around me, they throw me dagger glares and looks of disappointment. Mother pulls her hood up before she leaves. Raine lingers a moment, like he might come over to me, but the Head Watcher gestures for him to follow the others.

They'll mock him, no doubt. He'll find some way to defend me. He shouldn't, but he will. Because that's who he is. What he should do is call me what I am—a coward, afraid of the silly little voices in his own head and the pain they bring.

I stay behind, tending to my wrists and the pounding in my chest to keep my thoughts sane. The soft ping of a digiband redirects my attention. I force myself to look up.

The council's hut is empty now, except for two of us. Father and me.

I brace myself. Physical affection isn't something we display often in our family. Neither of my parents have put their hands on me unprompted since I was a young child needing general care, but the only rational explanation I can conjure for Father's indifference during my trial is that he was saving his anger for now, when no one else is around.

"I'm—I'm sorry," I stammer.

He runs his hand through his graying brown hair. "It doesn't matter. It's alright. I don't care about the ceremony or the moon worm. I just needed to buy us more time . . ."

I frown. "What do you mean?"

He ushers us out of the Council of Elders' Hut and into nighttime air. Firebugs crackle and scatter in our presence, taking off into the moonlit canopies above. A breeze washes over my clammy skin, and I stagger to the railing of the landing where a drinking stream trickles down the mountainside, next to the stairs that descend into the village. I ditch the metal drinking cup. Scooping water with my hands, I gulp it down greedily and splash a handful over my head.

Father waits patiently for me to have my fill. The warm air shifts, growing heavier, like it does right before a torrential downpour. I dry my mouth on my arm, biting back the sting of one blister in particular on my wrist where the skin has peeled completely.

He waits until the last few villagers disappear around the bend, silences a notification on his digiband, and then says, "We need to talk about something serious."

Gods, here we go. "Alright."

"You've probably noticed my absence lately."

"You've been working in the Dunes all night. We've all noticed." I hold pressure to my aching wrists to ease the throbbing. "Mother said you were busy planning something."

"I have been," he says. "I've been preparing for a rescue mission. A mission to save two people from a planet that was obliterated by a geographical storm 32 years ago."

Suddenly, the momentary relief the fresh water gave me is gone.

"What?" I say.

"You heard me."

"I don't understand—"

"It's okay. You will." He closes in on me, and the uneasiness returns. "I needed to buy you more time with the council because the final phase of my plan involves a team going back in time to ensure the targets board an aircraft and escape the storm."

My entire body goes rigid. "And what does this have to do with me?"

"Because, Timber—" he says. "You're the one going back to save them."

4: KEVIN

Planet Nevarnost: Year 3051

~~rewire terrarium mechanisms~~
~~laundry~~
meet with commander w.
~~pick up supplies from ed~~
~~pretend to~~ help those in need

The station platform outside Zone 1: Mechanisms is more crowded than usual.

An unbearable heat clings to the air. Overhead fans whir and creak, struggling to circulate. Another reminder of Lux's planetary warnings from yesterday morning.

I unwrap the last aqua orb from my pack, lower my mask just enough, and pop it into my mouth. Cool against my tongue, the orb releases a smooth liquid that soothes my throat. Once the edible membrane dissolves, I spit the residual goop that always leaves a bad taste in my mouth into a nearby trash bot, still charging on its dock.

A whistle blows, signaling the incoming solar train. The crowd surges around me, readying to board. My boots graze the platform's edge.

As the tracks start to shake, a green paint pod rolls to a stop at my heels. I bend down, pick it up, and slip it into my pocket, scanning the sea of color-coded uniforms for the culprit.

If I had any sense, I'd toss the pod in the trash bot too. Paint pods are considered contraband. Officially, they're banned to prevent graffiti in solar train stations. But we all know the truth: Chancellor Bay can't stand anything resembling artistic expression. It reminds him of the Unity rebels, those who dream of bringing back jamborees.

And anything tied to Unity inevitably leads back to my uncle.

Another paint pod rolls into view. I sling my pack fully over my shoulder and step onto the ledge for a better view of the station. Below, the crowd is a jumble of movement and color. A cluster of Zone 4: Medical staff in crisp white scrubs; aquaponic farmers from Zone 6: Agriculture in olive-green overalls, lugging worm farms; a huddle of young businesswomen from Zone 5: Nucleus in purple slacks, scrolling through news projections on their wrists.

I recognize a few of them from my housing unit, Earhart Residential, including a nurse who delivers Nana's medication. The rest live nearby, scattered across neighboring residential blocks. Beneath the Hemisphere, we wear the color of our home zone until we join a career field. If our work takes us elsewhere, we trade those colors in for the ones of our assigned zone.

I've been wearing gray since I was born, and I don't see that changing anytime soon.

As the solar train nears, the sea of color shifts again. Educators from Zone 8: Cultivation, dressed in tan suits and dresses, press toward the front—probably heading to a summer training or one of the many meetings attempting to restructure our education system. More gray jackets like mine, worn by other specialists from Zone 1: Mechanisms, fill in the gaps, waiting to board.

It's not uncommon for mech techs like me to travel between zones for tune-ups or system checks. Sometimes it's routine work. A factory reset, software updates. Most days, though, I'm behind a desk running programs or tinkering in the mechanics' lab. I prefer it that way.

But today, I'm looking forward to making a difference for those who need it.

Then I spot her.

A woman in a navy-blue dress, standing across the tracks. Navy blue was the color of Zone 7: Industrial, a zone that no longer exists. I can't believe she hasn't been spotted yet, especially with an automatic airbrush in hand.

Our eyes meet briefly as two male patrol officers, jolt sticks charged, circle the platform on their rounds. The woman waits for them to disappear behind a stone pillar before moving.

Green stains her nimble fingers. Dark brown drips from her knuckles. Tan splashes streak her dress. *She wouldn't.* Not here. Not *now.*

Roots take form along the grimy silver tile. A single leaf multiplies into twenty more. By the time the patrol officers sound their sirens, she's already gone. But her mark remains, just as the solar train barrels full force into the station.

"It's another Unity tree," one officer barks into his digiband. "Call in a clean-up crew. Paint pods. Fast-drying type."

The second officer grumbles as he manages the rush of people boarding. "When are these people going to let the past go? This isn't the year 3041 anymore. What's done is done."

"What's done is never done," I say as I step onto the train. The doors slide shut before the officer can argue.

Behind my carbon mask, I allow myself a smile. I sway with the train's motion as I scan the compartment. Six rows in, a familiar mess of bouncy, bright orange curls catches my eye. My co-worker, Graham, motions me over with a pasty, freckled hand and scoots aside to make room. If this is Chancellor Bay's petty way of proving a point, he's made it.

I was top of my class. Graham barely scraped by on his mechanism exams.

This should be . . . . fun.

As I remove my pack and take a seat, Graham plucks at the frayed end of a curl and tucks it behind his ear. "This is humiliating. All the other mechanism specialists are being promoted, and we're being sent to the Outskirts."

I press my lips into a line. "Water is essential for survival and for cultivating crops. The Outskirts need this way more than you need bragging rights in our division."

"Uh, tell me you know we're not actually supposed to help these people." He untangles his sunspecs and tries to put them on properly, but they snap back against his head.

"AH—"

My grin returns. *Yeah.* Saw that one coming.

Graham finally untangles them. "All I'm saying is, I downloaded the new issue of my favorite holocomic, and I plan on catching up on my reading while I'm there."

"Reading on the clock? Really?"

He slumps against his seat. "Don't act like you've never done it."

"Nope. When I'm at work, I work."

"Even during breaks?" he asks.

"I like to optimize my time."

"Then I'd say you work too much and need a life. You're nineteen. Not ninety. What, did you pack your hover walker and bone density injections too?" He tugs down the window screen as we pass through another zone wall. It glitches on contact, and the lights flicker.

My uncle deactivated all the zone walls when he was chancellor for this reason. He wanted people to feel united, not boxed into color-coded factions.

Now patrol mans every boundary line and reports daily to Nucleus.

"Besides," Graham adds, "it's not like we're actually working in the Outskirts anyway."

"How would you feel if you were them?" I ask, and he squirms. "Would you want someone to visit your home, lie to you, and watch holocomics on your dime?"

"What are you even talking about?" He kicks his feet up and blows out a puff of air behind his mask. "The guys back at the office were right. You are weird."

"Didn't realize I was such a topic of conversation," I say.

"You're a Hale. Your whole family is a topic of conversation."

With an eye roll, I tap comms on my digiband. "Lux, add 'visit the office' to my to-do list for Monday. Ed still needs to—"

"See. Right there." Graham sits up abruptly. "Who *does* that? Nobody does that. Stop."

"I'm utilizing my digiband's organization features. There's

nothing wrong with that."

He shoots me a look. "If you say so, weirdo."

I'm the weirdo? *Me*?

We near the Emergence Tunnel, and the solar train slows.

I open my canvas backpack, pulling out my sunspecs and my Hemisphere-issued, light-brown flexi-skin jacket. It hugs my muscular frame, blending in with the suns-kissed tint of my skin. And the green pigment pellet sinks heavily in my pocket. The woman in navy blue. The Unity symbol. Patrol. Their images are now cataloged in my memory. I know what Chancellor Bay will do if I don't obey him. But I also know what will happen if I do.

Neither outcome is good.

The glass-paneled curve of the Hemisphere becomes visible above us as Graham and I exit the solar train. He stops short, barely dodging two Nost carrying crates.

"Thinking about Zone 9 always gives me the creepy crawlies," he says, nearly knocking into someone else. "And we're risking our lung health for this. I have so many . . . thoughts."

I switch my digiband into power-saving mode. "Yeah? Keep them to yourself."

At the end of the paneled wind tunnel separating the Hemisphere from the outside, a set of wide, iron-plated gates creaks open. A swish of dusty wind rushes in. The crowd proceeds forward automatically, and Graham and I funnel into the filtration vents.

The system hums, scrubbing the air behind us as we step through.

Rays of pure sunlight hit me. Even through my sunspecs, the scorch stings.

Few humans travel outside the Hemisphere during the day. One searing sun is harsh enough. Two is inhumane. Inside the Hemisphere, we regulate our temperature, air quality, and light exposure. Out here? People don't have a choice.

The suns alone are the reason I only hunt roakes during our brief night hours.

Mere minutes have passed since we exited the Emergence Tunnel, and my gray T-shirt is already soaked through beneath my flexi-skin jacket. The reluctant thud of Graham's footfall follows me down the sandstone steps that wrap around the hill. At the bottom, a makeshift port houses a row of solar carts parked beneath a worn, stretched nylon tarp. Like the solar train, they charge up during the day and run for a week.

They're also entertaining. Probably the only *good* thing about hunting for roakes.

"My skin is going to crisp up," Graham complains, trying to keep his hands in his pockets and out of the suns. "And Ed didn't give us any shielding gloves."

I approach the revving vehicles. "We should keep watch for Commander Wardell."

Graham looks up at me. "How can you be so calm? We're going to bake out here like thick-skinned hot potatoes, and not the good kind."

"I'm going to pretend you didn't say that," I say, surveying the port.

Commander Wardell's drab khaki uniform sticks out mid-center, behind a wheel.

"Boys," the commander says gruffly as we approach. He nudges his wire-rimmed glasses up his button nose, leaving red marks where they pinch too tight. "I was beginning to wonder if you got lost. Welcome to Zone 9: Outskirts."

We get into the solar cart, and I shake his hand. "Good to be here, sir."

"Matron Nost Far and I are thrilled that Chancellor Bay was able to accommodate us." He switches gears, quieting the sputtering engine as he backs out of the port. "We wanted the best mechanism specialists the Hemisphere had to offer."

"Well, you got us," Graham exclaims, nudging me. "Hear that? We're the *best* the Hemisphere has to offer."

I wipe sweat off my brow. Eh, I'll let him believe that.

"We've had a few of our own take a look at the system," Commander Wardell continues, accelerating over a massive speed bump, "but so far we haven't made much progress."

The solar cart dips and jerks us around. Sandy gales lash against the windshield. Tiny pebbles whiz by the side mirrors, a few grazing through my windswept hair.

Graham grips my arm. "I think he's trying to kill us."

"You'll want to grab onto those side bars if you can," Commander Wardell hollers over his shoulder, his voice muffled by his blue pinstriped face rag.

He takes an incline at full speed. The cart catapults into the air, hovering for a split second before slamming back down. We skid sideways, and my stomach drops.

Gritty clouds form around us. Graham yelps, but a deep chuckle rises in my chest, building into a full-blown, red-faced coughing fit.

The Commander joins in.

Graham glares. "Are you two *laughing?*"

It's the simple thrills.

"You'll have to forgive me, boys." Commander Wardell

glances at us through the rearview mirror, finally slowing to a steady crawl. The engine lurches and adjusts to the shift. "Far drives us when we travel back and forth between zones. She insists on it."

"Gee. I wonder why," Graham says.

I counter, "It's alright. I haven't laughed that hard in a long time."

"You clearly need to get out more. Both of you." Graham shakes sand out of his knotted curls. "And you snort when you laugh, Kevin. Like a dust hog."

"You were just screaming like a child, and I said nothing," I fire back.

That shuts him up.

As we crest the hill, a shantytown of huts and slanted dwellings comes into view. Even though I've passed the Outskirts many times, the sight hits me harder than the two blaring suns overhead. *Tragic* is the kindest word I can think of for the crumbling shelters that barely stand and hordes of people packed beneath tarps and layers of canvas.

While they seek solace from the relentless heat, I'm starkly reminded of how divided we've become. How divided we've always been. The Outskirts have nothing. They endure the worst of it while we sit comfortably, assured of a brighter future. Chancellor Bay made this decision without hesitation. The Unity Arch fell, the Hemisphere cracked, and he exiled an entire portion of his people without looking back.

If Uncle Billy could see this, he'd be irate. He would've found a way, despite the wreckage, despite the tragedy, to care for everyone equally.

Commander Wardell parks the solar cart and rubs a thick layer of dust off his glasses. "I've had Madame O'Hair prepare a hut for you both to rest and wait out the heat."

"We'd be happy to take our supplies and get started right away," Graham insists. "I'd like to *access* the grid and make it back to Zone 1 for dinner."

Subtlety isn't in Graham Foster's vocabulary.

Commander Wardell raises a brow. "Unfortunately, we don't work that strenuously during the day out here. It's not safe with the conditions. Night hours are best."

Someone didn't read his briefing very well. But by all means, if Graham wants to risk heatstroke . . .

I clear my throat and nod toward the still-present suns. "We'll get started at sunsdown."

"That's perfect." Before the commander turns to go, he gives me another glance. "Are we still meeting later? I'd like to sit down with you and discuss the grid in more detail."

"Yes, sir," I say.

"Very well." Then he strides off, heading toward two women and a man struggling with a metal washtub full of sweat-soaked clothes and soiled drapes.

For a moment, I consider helping too, but before I can move, murky water sloshes into the sand as the commander lifts the basin into the back of a solar cart parked out front.

Graham steps up beside me. "What the hell are we supposed to do for eleven whole hours? Sunsdown isn't until 1:00 AM. As if Ed sent us here this early. I could be feet up in my gaming chair playing *Holoblocks: Lost Crusade 53*, or hanging out with my girlfriend."

"We'll get settled, pick up our kits, and sleep a bit so we're rested for tonight." I start walking toward our hut. "And you don't have a girlfriend."

He scoffs. "*You* don't have a girlfriend."

"I never said I did. Unlike you."

"I could have one if I wanted one." He kicks an old rubber shoe where sand mice have gnawed at the soles. "Also, there was nothing in the briefing about an extra meeting with the commander. What was that all about?"

I spot our hut a few dwellings down and quicken my pace. "Just a rundown for the irrigation grid. You won't need to be there. I'll relay the information to you."

"I don't care, as long as it gets us out of here faster."

I glance at one of the other huts, where a group of dust-covered children kick around a dried tumbleweed beneath the overhang. They chase it back and forth until it falls apart.

"You know, it's not their fault they were forced to leave the Hemisphere," I say. "Maybe we should try to understand how they feel."

Graham catches up to me. "Try to understand? Are you saying you *want* to help these people? They've never done anything but cause trouble."

"We kicked them out of the Hemisphere," I say as calmly as I can. "Things were going well before the Arch fell. They didn't deserve any of this. It was a fluke."

"It wasn't a fluke," he argues. "Air quality was an issue before the crack, and everyone knows your uncle set off that bomb to try and get rid of Chancellor Bay because Bay was the only one willing to do something about it. Your uncle was a crappy chancellor. No offense."

I shake my head. "You weren't even old enough to remember what the Hemisphere was like when he was in charge. You're just basing all your opinions on what you hear." I exhale sharply, my patience wearing thin. "And you know what? I'm tired of people throwing Billy under the solar cart because they believe rumors like that."

"People *saw* him do it," Graham insists, sucking his teeth. "If he'd just stepped down like everyone wanted, the Hemisphere wouldn't have cracked, and we wouldn't be suffering."

I can't believe what I'm hearing. He has to know this is wrong. He can't be this uninformed. Or that self-absorbed. Can he?

"We're not suffering." I motion to the dilapidated buildings around us. "*They* are. We have it easy. What about that do you not understand?"

"Hell, Hale. You're starting to sound just like the unifiers." He puffs out his chest, a poor attempt at intimidation that almost never works on anyone. "My cousin is a patrol officer, and he says it's out of control. How much you wanna bet you're one of them?"

He takes a step closer, but I hold my ground. I'm not scared of him like he thinks I am. I *choose* to regulate my emotions. Doesn't mean I don't know how to throw a decent punch.

"*Are* you one of them?" Graham asks. "Is that why you care so much?"

Heat rises in my cheeks. *Breathe. Let it go.* Now isn't the time to argue over this.

I raise a brow. "We can agree to disagree on a lot of things, but human decency and ending perpetual suffering isn't one of them. That's all I'm going to say about it."

Graham scoffs. "Fine. Let's just do what we came here to do then."

His eyes stay on mine for a second longer before he steps inside our hut.

"Yeah. I plan on it," I mutter under my breath.

5: TIMBER

Planet Violet Moon: Year 3083

I twirl a lavender sprig between my fingers, while the others that float around me in the water basin soothe my raw wrists. Floral steam rises from the surface. It carries up and fills my lungs with each inhale. All the while, Father's words from outside the council's hut last night swirl in my head: *Because, Timber. You're the one going back to save them.*

As if the confession that time travel is real wasn't cryptic enough, Father escorted me back to our family's dwelling and sent me to sleep with the promise of telling me more the following day.

A restful slumber was out of the question. Instead I tossed and turned, nearly sweating a hole in my sleeping mat. Any semblance of a dream became nightmares filled with endless cramped and jagged routes lined with tracks, where those sentenced to a life of prying raw aura quartz from pure stone spend their days shoveling it into carts to be sent up a shaft and tumbled.

How could Father's plan to change the fate of another planet in the past possibly save me from such a future? He made it clear he doesn't care about worms, the mines, or my wrongdoings, but I do. And what if I don't *want* to accept his so-called mission?

I lean back against the basin, knocking the linens and daily vitamins left for me off the side stool. The pills roll away beneath the open arched window at the front of the washroom, where glints of morning sun peek over the coastline, offering their warmth.

I listen to the waves crashing against rock and the mangrove trees swaying in the breeze.

One way or another, this is one of the last times I'll get to enjoy it.

"Timber! You're going to be late!" My sister, Marlowe, raps on the door. "Mother says I'm allowed to pull you from that tub if you don't get out in the next three seconds."

The threat of her possibly laying a hand on me is more than enough to motivate me. I lean over the basin for the larger square of linen that lies on the floor. Water seeps into the patterned beige tile, but I manage to get out and wrap myself up before the door whips open and Marlowe leans in against the frame.

"What are you doing in here?" She steps over a puddle and tips a basket of soaking salts upright. "I know you're going through something, big brother, but no need to mess up the place."

I grab my clean off-white tunic from the hook on the wall. "It was an accident. I'm fine."

She brushes a strand of long brown hair out of her face. "Well, I find your fate utterly mortifying. If only it could be avoided by you completing a simple task. Oh wait . . ."

I say nothing, grabbing the healing kit from the bench.

Killing a moon worm will be easy for Marlowe next lunar year. She'll tackle it with vigor like she embraces everything else. She has Mother's confidence. Father's tenacity and brains. All qualities I don't think I fully inherited.

She watches as I smear chamomile salve over my wrists and says, "You think I'm being harsh, but I love you. I want you to have a good life."

The phrase *I love you* always rubs me the wrong way. Not because I hate it. Out of all the feelings one can have, love can be pleasant, just not when you feel it tenfold. It's desire's more emotionally expressive twin. Instead of a gnawing hunger, love is a constant swell, starting small and gradually expanding with unpredictable highs and lows. One minute it's calm; the next it flips and crescendos, leaving an impact that lingers long after the initial touch.

As I slip on my tunic and pull on my pants beneath my linen wrap, Marlowe adds, "I brought home papaya and bread from the market if you're hungry."

"I appreciate it," I say.

She stands there quietly while I run my bamboo brush through my sandy-blonde hair, pop an anti-tooth decay tablet in my mouth, and tilt my head beneath the washbasin faucet to rinse my mouth out. All while I watch her tapping foot from the corner of my eye.

Finally, I let out a sigh. "What, Marlowe."

She throws her hands out. "Why can't you just kill the worm!"

"Because I don't want to."

"Will you in three days?"

"No," I say. "This is my choice."

"But you'll go to the mines."

"I'm aware."

We stare at one another the way we used to when we'd play the blinking game as children, but this isn't a game anymore.

Her eyes glisten, wet with tears. "It's like you don't care."

I don't respond.

By the time I put on my boots, she's fled. The front door slams, and through the window, I watch her disappear down the path outside our dwelling.

And this is why I don't tell her about the whispers either.

I, alone, am upsetting enough.

I exit the washroom and enter the sustenance chamber where Mother sits in a rocking chair by the hearth. She keeps watch over two of my younger brothers, Micah and Oak, playing—well, wrestling—with wooden blocks beneath the bay window.

Our home is small but comfortable. Jars of dried herbs line the countertops. Potted plants hang above the mahogany table Father built himself. The everlasting smell of baked pastries clings to the faded wood walls as do the oils Mother slathers all over the babies after she bathes them. She is a nursing mother and has been for as long as I can remember. Outsiders bring their babies when they can't provide for them. Mother supplements for the orphaned few and cares for the others because she is selfless in ways I cannot fathom.

The Vio are her people, her community, and she'd do anything for them.

"Hit your brother, and you'll never see those blocks again," she snaps at Micah, a rebellious Three with chubby cheeks that rise with an impish grin each time he's caught.

He holds a block over Oak's head—an innocent One—nonetheless, then screams when Mother rocks back and kicks it out of his hand. I dodge the block. It strikes an old, bronze music box adorned with a mermaid set up on the hutch. The entire shelf collapses, and Mother ignores it, guiding my third and youngest brother, Nash, to her breast until he latches.

"Goddesses, give me strength." She uses the same foot she kicked the block with to pull up a stool for me. "Alright, you. Tell me what you said to your sister that upset her like that."

"Nothing." I sit, keeping careful watch of everyone's hands. "She asked why I couldn't kill the worm, and she didn't like my answer. I'm just—I'm not doing it. I'm sorry."

"You don't have to apologize, Timber. Not to me, at least."

"Who should I apologize to, then? It's my fate. I've accepted it."

She gently sweeps her fingers through Nash's hair as he feeds, and for a brief moment, I remember the days she'd do the same to me. Before the whispers, I didn't understand feelings, but comfort came easy. Now it's a prison, an emotional overwhelm bringing pain and suffering.

"People are disappointed. People are sad. Everyone cares about you is all."

I pick up one of my brother's blocks, turning it over in my hand. They once belonged to me, but the painted image of a sundial is now worn and faded. "Are you . . . disappointed?"

Mother pats Nash's bum so he'll focus on feeding and not the decorative tree inked on her chest. A sign of commitment, all those who are partnered wear tattooed symbols for one another above their hearts. Raine talks about the gesture all the time, how excited he is for ceremonial partnership someday and for spending life wrapped in the arms of someone else.

Even though I've indulged in the idea of partnership, I

know I wouldn't survive it.

"I'm not disappointed, Timber. Life is hard enough," she finally says, once Nash is settled again. "I will always support you, no matter where you land. If that means sending you care packages down a hole in the mines and biting my tongue when other villagers comment, so be it. But if, in the next three days, you find another path, that would be welcomed too."

I stand and toss the block into the toy crate. "Maybe if we're lucky, I'll get sucked into Father's time warp, and then instead of judgmental comments, you'll receive condolences."

"Rest assured I've gotten plenty of both already, and none of it fazes me. I don't fear the judgment of others, and neither should you. Nobody is perfect. You ought to be careful about falling into time warps, though." Mother points to the cotton rag Oak's sucking on like a pacifier. "Hand me that burping cloth before you go, will you?"

I retrieve the rag for her. "It amazes me you know all of Father's secrets and still stand by him."

"We all have secrets. We've all done things we aren't proud of, and we all hide parts of ourselves we aren't sure others would accept." She pulls her dress back up and dabs Nash's mouth. "But there comes a point where we must embrace who we are, even the flaws we wish we could change. A life without self-acceptance is already a miserable sentence."

I admire the way my brother watches our mother, the innocence glazed over in his bright green eyes. She pinches his cheeks lovingly and gives him a kiss on the forehead as I'm sure she did with me when I was his age. I know Mother's right about self-acceptance, but would she say the same about my curse?

Should I accept and embrace it, too?

Part of me believes Mother would understand if I told her the truth. But like with Raine, I can't bring myself to say the words aloud. The people close to me just think I like my personal space. Sharing my curse with others would mean they'd feel obligated to keep themselves distant from me. They might worry about overwhelming me or triggering intense pain, and I can't bear to see their faces as they calculate every move or advance toward me.

It's better to keep this burden to myself.

Micah swats Oak across the head with another block. The innocent One's cries wake the other babies that are sleeping in the cradles near the hearth.

"That's it," Mother harps, rising from her chair.

Both toddlers' eyes go wide.

"Pack 'em up. Into the ocean they go."

T he Dunes are on the east side of the island, reached by a steep hike up curving trails and hills that rise above the valley where the village rests.

Closed canopies overhead cast the path in a shadow, where jungle bells and heliconia flowers tangle in the over-grown flora. I'm careful to avoid tripping over roots zigzag-ging along the dirt beneath my feet, but the low-hanging ferns are equally as unpredictable.

Father says his trek to the Dunes is his favorite part of each morning because he gets the privilege of enjoying fresh, clean air and a kaleidoscope of colorful plant life along the way. I can't say I disagree. I often find it ironic that my name refers to the trees because nature is where I'm most at peace and where my mind seems most clear.

I could spend hours out here, alone, with nothing but the silence in my head.

When I reach the bridge, I wipe my sweaty palms on my pants and gaze at the giant water lilies drifting along the stream. As children, Marlowe and I dared one another to cross the river, hopping from one pad to the next until they sank beneath our weight. My sister was always faster, and I always ended up trekking home drenched.

That is the version of me I hope she remembers most when I'm gone.

Humidity soaks into my skin, dampening the underarms of my tunic. Once I reach the summit, I stand at the edge of the drop-off and admire the expanse of our planet. Dirt paths entwine clusters of bamboo and planked dwellings with thatched roofs. Beyond the crowded Makers Market and the flourishing coastline lies a sparkling ocean that goes on for miles. To the left are the South Woods and to the right, the North Woods. Shifts of movement slither in the sway of the shade, and though I can't see them, I know the watchers are stationed at the boundary lines. Hidden in tree stands and tucked in caves, they are there when we need them.

Violet Moon is a safe haven. I've never known anything else.

As I keep walking, a stretch of desert mounds guides me into the Dunes. Coarse black sand with a hint of iridescence cakes the undergrooves of my boots. About a mile out lies the galactic graveyard, where Father's old aircraft sits parked alongside melted space metal and fragments of machinery. Beyond that, past the solar glares on the horizon, I imagine the entrance to the mines, and a chill slinks over the surface of my skin.

The *Iris* is on the smaller side and has seen better days. Tarnished patches of metal connect misshapen solder lines. A crack has widened in the rear viewport. My favorite part is the faded symbol of a tree painted on her underside. In another life, I'm sure she flew elegantly. But Father has since grounded her, built around her, and now uses her as a command center in direct contact with Intergalactic Space Relations, the highest-ranking authority in all galaxies.

I duck under the left thruster and follow the curve to the other side, spotting him immediately where he works in a pod connected to the hull. My mouth becomes dry and my lungs feel like clay, pinching and flattening with each breath.

Even if Father's been working long nights preparing for some rescue mission through time, he can't expect me to save anyone. I know nothing about a doomed planet or its people. And are we really just going to forget that, in three short days, I'm back on trial?

"There you are. I was beginning to wonder if you'd run off." Father slings a grease rag over his shoulder. "My assistant is waiting for you inside the *Iris*."

I furrow my brows. "Wait. You're not the one briefing me on this mission?"

Father slips on his goggles and fires up his solder gun. "My assistant's been working closely with me for moons. He'll fill you in. I've got some last-minute prepping to do."

"Forgive me—" The whirl of his machine drowns me out. "But you seem outwardly calm. About the trial, the mention of time travel, *and* my sentence!"

Father dodges rogue sparks and yells back, "It's all going to be okay!"

I clench my jaw, swallowing the urge to retort.

Moments like this make me wish I could wield my curse to my advantage. What good is the ability to sense someone's true feelings and thoughts if it comes with such harsh consequences? Why couldn't it have been as simple as reading minds? Did I really have to embody their emotional state, too?

As sparks continue to fly, I let out a long sigh and relent.

6: TIMBER

Planet Violet Moon: Year 3083

The *Iris* drones beneath my feet as I step up onto the entry ramp of the aircraft.

Automatic lights buzz on, revealing dust-covered equipment along either side of the adjoining chamber. I have to remind myself that the Council of Elders respect Father because they themselves have no interest in intergalactic relations, and he's doing them a favor—not because he's yet to utilize his inventing skills to build a good grime bot.

I stride further up the incline, triggering another sensor.

The automatic doors glide open.

A familiar girl about my age, wearing nothing but lacy silk underclothes and a thin, translucent shawl, appears in front of me.

I look away, out of respect. "Oh. Sorry, I was just—"

"Wait here on the mat," she says, wrapping herself up. "I'll let him know you're here."

I do recognize her, I realize. Rosanna Ralor, but she goes by Rose. She was in Raine's cycle. They became watchers together. Only he works in defense, and she's in the response sector, handling emergency situations like banishments and mine matters.

The way Father spoke, he made it sound like he had one assistant, so what is she doing here? Why isn't she dressed? And why doesn't it feel like *anyone* is taking my current situation seriously?

Moments later, Rose returns in a different robe, a satiny bronze color that complements her delicate brown skin and her long raven-black hair.

She leads me to the lift and presses her palm into the scanner. "Take it all the way to the top. He's waiting for you on the flight deck."

I straighten. "Thank you."

Once the lift doors close, I wring my hands.

A green light glisters on the pad. The lift rises, then stops. The doors open, and I step out onto an open flight deck with a large control panel at the front and two revolving, curved leather seats. Beneath one sleeps a full-grown flare cat. Larger than the jungle leopards that stalk the boundary lines, it's curled up with its massive paws tucked under its head.

Resting, flare cats are harmless. But awake, they tend to be violent. You can always tell their intent by their eyes. They change color depending on their mood—purple when content, green when envious, red when hungry or riled. They can change moods in an instant, which is also why they're not supposed to be kept as pets.

Seems I'm not the only one breaking village rules after all.

"Wake Ere, and we'll have bigger problems on our hands," a gruff voice says to my left.

It belongs to a young man sitting behind a second control board. He crosses one muscular arm over the other. As he looks me over, a lock of shaggy red-and-black hair from his fade cut falls in his face.

He blows it away. "Are you coming in or not? I haven't got all day."

Another familiar face. Maybe even more threatening than a moody flare cat.

Delorean Mars is Father's assistant?

As in, the former Head Elder's son? As in, one of the babies Mother nursed after said elder and his partner succumbed to violet fever in a surge that decimated nearly half our village years ago? Mars' parents were highly respected. They selflessly put others before themselves.

Mars' reputation was built on that foundation.

When I was a Fifteen, Raine dragged me to a renewed energy demonstration led by Mars, who was a skilled Sixteen at the time. We sat in a large crowd, mostly made up of his admirers, and he showed us how to harness a glowfish's glow without getting electrocuted, using a mechanism my own father had invented for the village years prior.

When I wasn't hyperventilating from being squished between the girls who whispered about how handsome he was, I found myself amazed at how easy harvesting energy came to Mars. His movements were swift, almost like a dance. A burst of violet light enveloped him as he held the glowfish's power in his palms.

When it came time for us to try, I was the only Fifteen who got stung because at the last minute, I froze, backing away just before his hand could come up on mine to guide the pole.

The girls were jealous that Mars fished my limp body out of the sea, but I was just happy to be alive. I spent the rest of the afternoon in Raine's grandmother's healing hut.

Since that day, I ignore the unprompted flutters I get when Mars comes around. Because as he tossed me onto the shore and called for the healers that day, his hand touched mine anyway, prompting one emotional burst connected to one phrase that's kept me away from him since: *you really are daft, aren't you?*

Long story short—I know Mars hates me.

I didn't just almost drown. I ruined his entire presentation.

And now we have to work together?

After a stilling silence, I ask, *"You're* my father's assistant?"

He stares at me blankly. No emotion. Nothing.

"I mean—that came out wrong. I'm sorry."

Again, Mars says nothing. My pulse soars.

What is he even doing here? Last I knew, he was working in the mines. We're given a handful of placement options to choose from based on aptitudes and skills following our Coming of Age ceremonies. I know for a fact Mars was offered an apprenticeship with the Council of Elders. He still chose digging for crystal. Nobody in their right mind chooses the mines.

Not unless they have a death wish.

But he's here now. And he's still not saying anything.

"Well, uh, I think we should—"

"Stop talking." Mars glares at me as if I'm a sand grub stuck under his boot. He kicks a spare chair near the control panel. "And sit down. Hovering irritates the living bugs out of me."

I scramble forward. "Oh. Okay. Sorry."

Nausea creeps in. For some reason the image of giggling girls in the presentation crowd, trying to guess what Mars' kisses might taste like, flashes in my mind.

I push it away.

"Are you blushing?" Mars asks.

I rip my focus away from his lips and study the blinking lights on the control panel. When I take a step forward, my foot knocks a stack of canisters, sending them across the floor. Heat surges up my neck and spreads into a splotchy patch of red on my chest.

Oh, Gods and Goddesses. Make it stop.

I slam down into the spare chair, not daring to look back at Mars or Ere. Awakened, the flare cat lets out a growl, and her fierce red eyes hunger for blood.

If I'm lucky, she'll kill me. Then nobody has to sentence me anywhere.

"You cosmic slug." Mars springs up and intercepts Ere before she pounces. *"Learee deree, Ere."* He wrestles with her, calm but firm, speaking to her in Vio because that's the only language flare cats understand. At least that's what Raine told me. *"Sture deree. Nu keare."*

Ere lets out an exasperated huff until her eyes slowly fade to a vibrant shade of purple. She saunters back to her resting place and collapses in a heap.

Mars glowers at me.

"I'm—I'm sorry." I pick at the skin around my nail bed. "I didn't mean—"

"No offense, but I don't think you're right for this mission." He turns back to the control panel, shuffling through pieces of stacked parchment.

We're not off to a good start. "Well, I only just—"

"You're not trained," he continues. "Your refusal to kill a moon worm deems you a wild card when it comes to authority. That tells me you aren't ready to take on this responsibility."

"My father only told me about this last night." Blood sticks between my fingertips as they throb, raw from picking at a hangnail. They'll need a good salt rinse and a wrap if I keep this up. "He said you're supposed to brief me. I didn't have much of a choice."

Mars' striking, smoky gray eyes dart elsewhere. "You've always got a choice. And by all means, choose wisely," he says, shoving a heap of parchment under his arm. "This job isn't for the faint of heart. Once you're in, you're in deep, and there's no going back."

I'm worried I may already be in too deep.

He crosses the room and flips a switch, lighting up the screens floating above the main control panel. Ere purrs at him, and he bends down to give her soft tufts of white fur a pat before logging into the system. As he runs his thumb up the keypad, I notice the calloused scars that snake from his thumb to his wrist, a clear contrast against the brown of his skin. The excess scar tissue tells me they were wounds that weren't stitched properly when they were first tended to.

But it's really none of my business.

A speckled galaxy fills each monitor, rapidly moving until it stops on a dusty taupe planet with black smoke billowing in its exosphere.

Mars swivels in his chair. "How much did your father tell you?"

"Not—not much. Just about a storm and two targets."

He grabs one of the parchment folders off the dash, opens it, and thrusts it at me. My trembling hands grip the file. Coordinates and meteorological stats for a planet two travel years away, a redacted planet called Nevarnost, are on top. It's been deemed uninhabitable since 3051.

"Kevin Hale and Vaida Wardell. Both are Nineteens," Mars says, flipping a paper to reveal their two profiles.

"One of them is your father's nephew, your cousin. The other is the daughter of your father's former best friend. Apparently, before he came here, your father had a whole other life on planet Nevarnost, working as a field agent and chancellor for ISR."

My fingers coil. Mars knows more about Father than I do, it seems.

I had no idea he worked on other planets. I knew he'd done some prior work for ISR before I was born, but I guess I always thought he'd done it here, while building a life with Mother. Suddenly my chest hitches. What else has he neglected to tell me about his past?

I hand the file back to Mars. "Why now? And why . . . me?"

"*Us*," he corrects me. "As if we'd let you go alone."

He crosses the flight deck and triggers a compartment in the wall. A deep drawer slides out with a click. "And how much do you know about time travel?"

Is *nothing* an appropriate answer? "I didn't even know it existed before last night."

"Right. Well, for starters, everything I'm about to tell you is classified. Not even the Council of Elders knows about this. Given what your father told me, neither does ISR."

I chew the inside of my cheek. "Okay . . ."

"We're going now because the timing is right. When your father was a graduate at the Academy on their homebase *Ophelia*, a briefcase appeared outside his lab. Inside was a note from his future-self, regarding the unfolding of the events that took place on Nevarnost and these—" He pulls out a circular device. Its touchscreens curve along two crescent-shaped sides, and a small, purple crystal glisters faintly in the middle.

"This," he says, holding it closer to my face, "is a transporter. Your father invented them. Programmed correctly, they can be used for traveling through time."

"Why doesn't he go back, then? Why do we have to go?" I ask.

"The note from his future-self stated that you and I are the ones who go back."

I sway slightly and steady myself against the wall to keep from passing out. Like Father did last night, Mars is throwing a lot of necessary information at me, but all I can think about is the overwhelming amount of energy I'll be exposed to on this mission—people in turmoil, the pressure to keep them safe, a mix of emotions as they realize their home is about to be destroyed.

Mars is right. I don't think I'm right for this mission.

I don't care if my name was on some note from the future.

"Forgive me . . . I'm still . . . trying to take this all in."

As I continue analyzing the device in Mars' hand, Ere rises, her sparkling eyes now a deep shade of green. She circles him once before resettling at his feet.

"I'm as thrilled we're being paired up as you are," he says flatly. "I've been training for this mission for several full moons. As far as I'm concerned, you'll just get in my way."

"At least you're honest." I rub the back of my neck. "I mean, I agree—it'd be best if you went alone. What are the odds I stay behind and log files or do busy work while you're gone?"

Mars scoffs. "Don't spend your last three days as a free villager logging paperwork. Go back to your dwelling, spend time with your mother, and gather your bearings before they send you down the hole." He collects all the folders. "Trust me. You'll need the mental clarity."

It takes everything in me not to ask if gathering his bearings worked for him. Judging by his defensive nature, I'm going to assume it didn't.

"My father expects me to be a part of this, so logging paperwork is a compromise." I pick my nail bed again and smear crusted blood onto my pants. "You get what you want, the mission goes smoothly, and I spend the next three days with him off my back."

It's the least I can do. We don't need a repeat of the glowfish presentation.

Mars watches me as he thinks. "It could work. I leave for Nevarnost tomorrow morning. Come by first thing, and I'll set you up at the dashboard to track my route."

I nod, and that's the extent of our conversation.

As I head for the lift to exit, Mars returns to the main control panel. He sits, back turned away from me, and I linger a moment, admiring the bond between a boy and his flare.

He calls for Ere, who rests her head on his lap. He strokes her between the ears.

As cubs, flare cats are gentle. Most fear them when they age because that's when their eyes start to change. That's when they turn. Wrangling one in the wild is nearly impossible. I know this because Raine has come back from shifts with horror stories and bruises.

Watching Mars with Ere now is like watching two rogue flares together.

One wrong move, and they'll tear me apart.

Both of them.

7: MARS

Planet Violet Moon: Year 3083

The lips are always the hardest feature to draw on a person. Whether it be subtle curves or precise shading, every angle demands accuracy.

All in pursuit of capturing the likeness of my muse.

Rose's bare skin glistens in the late morning light, gold shimmering through the strands of her long hair. She sips her tea on the stool by the viewing window at the far end of our sleeping room. As she tucks one leg beneath the other, the silk wrap draped around her upper body slips slightly, revealing the vibrant planet Mars inked just above her left breast.

I chew my lip, reaching for a slice of blood orange from the wooden bowl resting beside me in the folds of linen. I pop it into my mouth. Tart-sweet juice bursts on my tongue. Sucking it dry, I smear the uneven lines on the sketchpad resting in my lap.

Ere stretches out beside me. She lets out a yawn and licks her paws. I lean back into the warmth of her fur, then pluck the dark brown wax stick from behind my ear and drag my thumb along all the harsh graphite lines to smooth them out some more.

I carefully shade the arch of Rose's back where the light gathers brightest.

Defined curves. Delicate folds of silk. Skin dewy with the sheer salve she slathered on after her bath. The shimmer on her skin composes her like music written on fresh parchment.

A flutter of wings crosses the air in front of me, and a zinc moth lands on the edge of my sketchpad. Their name comes from the bluish-gray color of their wings, but Rose calls them Confess Me Moths because they keep secrets. In truth, the watchers use them to relay messages during shifts. Nothing is more sacred than the conversations between our village protectors, especially since once a Confess Me Moth delivers its message, that message vanishes forever.

The moth rests on my shoulder.

Rose's allure lulls off its two fuzzy antennae, into my ear. *"I know you're drawing me."*

"Vain of you to think such a thing," I speak, releasing the moth.

I follow its flight, narrowing in on my commitment partner's smirk as the delicate creature relays my retort.

Rose rises from her stool and saunters into the sustenance chamber out of sight.

Her moth flutters back to me.

"You liar," it sings in my ear.

She returns moments later with another blood orange, half-peeled, and joins me on our sleeping mat, trying to sneak a peek at the unfinished drawing.

"Can I see it? You have such a talent for—"

"No." I shut my sketch pad. "There's nothing to see."

"You let the miners see your art. Why can't I?"

72

"Because there's a difference between a horde of sweaty people stumbling upon the chalk scrawls I plastered all over the cave walls to keep me sane and this," I say.

Her smile fades, and it breaks me in a way. My words always come out harsher than I mean them to. I owe Rose everything right now, but there are parts of me I still can't open up to her. Not yet. Not until I make amends for everything I've done.

"At least tell me how your proposal is coming along," Rose urges.

I glance at the scroll resting on the side table. My proposal to rewrite village rules has been finished for at least three full moons, but I still haven't submitted it.

As a Nineteen, I lack the experience and influence to convince the Council of Elders that our traditions are outdated. Binding practices like commitment partners, placements, and ceremonies need more flexibility. We still tie stones to wrongdoers' feet and toss them into the sea, for Goddess-sake. I was lucky to escape my own trial with only a pardon and a slap on the wrist. Bearing my late father's name and Elder Hale vouching for me helped, too.

Rose traces the outline of my jaw with her finger. "I'll admit, I read the first couple lines. Ere knocked it off the table the other day, and when I went to pick it up, I caught a glimpse."

I open my sketchbook and continue shading. "And . . ."

"Is that really how you feel about Vio tradition?"

My graphite stick snaps, some cheap, crummy version from the Makers Market. I swipe away the dust. "I have a problem with others telling me what to do or how to think."

"Clearly," she says. "But I'm proud of who I am. Proud of my life."

"You're proud because you were taught to be proud."

She straightens. "I'm proud because it's an honor to be a watcher. To be committed to you. To have a roof over my head, and all that comes with it."

"Come on, Rosanna." I set my sketchbook aside and pull away from our covers. "You're not proud to be committed to me. This partnership is a complete—"

"I care about you," she says, grabbing my arm. "That's enough for me."

I know better than to start this argument with her. Rose doesn't think like I do, so it'll always be a constant struggle. She's okay with following whatever rules and norms are set into place for her. She's okay with being committed to a man who stopped loving her properly a long time ago, a man she doesn't see that way anymore either.

But we're both stuck now. Commitment is until we return to Ether, as the Vio say. We'll both die never knowing what it's like to be truly aligned with someone who shares our values, perspectives, and overall goals in life. She'll agree to her fate, blindly taking on the duty of making our commitment work for the rest of her life. No matter how miserable she is. And I'll carry the resentment of being the reason we're stuck in this mess.

I care about Rose. Love her, even, in the way you love a friend who's become one of your closest confidants. I can even turn off my brain in those lonely moments when we both crave physical touch. But neither of us can be what the other needs. Adaptation and acceptance may make Rose a great watcher, but she deserves better.

I lean back into the folds of the soft linens bunched up on our sleeping mat. "Forget it. It doesn't matter. I'll probably never submit the proposal anyway."

"At least you got your thoughts out on parchment," Rose muses, nudging me playfully between nibbles on blood orange slices. I ignore her, but she's persistent. "But if I can't see your artwork or the rest of your proposal, then you've given me no choice."

Her fingers graze my torso.

"Don't," I warn.

"So serious all the time," she teases, mimicking my scowl.

I know what she's doing. She's the keeper of my secrets and the only living soul who knows I'm ticklish—her weapon against my attitude. Her fingers find my sweet spot, and she pounces. A flurry of plush linens and pillows surrounds us as she tackles me.

"Stop fighting it," Rose squeals as I squirm out of her reach only to be captured again.

I will never stop fighting it.

She wraps her arms around me, and I hide my face, wrestling with her until I can't breathe from laughter. Her giggles ring out, echoing through the chamber.

"Enough," I say, out of breath. "That's enough."

Rose rolls off me. We lie side by side.

Her umber eyes sweep every inch of me. "Feel better yet, oh Grumpy One? Or shall we give it another go?"

"You're not funny." I get up and tuck my sketchpad and proposal scroll under my arm. "Don't you have somewhere to be? With what's-his-name or something?"

"You know his name is Julian."

Honestly, I can't bring myself to remember.

"He's very kind," Rose continues, picking herself up and following me into the sustenance chamber. "We're going on a walk by the water to find rare shells."

"Sounds like a date."

"It isn't a date." She crosses her arms. "And don't get defensive. You're the one who told me to go find other people to do all the things you won't do with me. I'd rather it be you."

"You know what I mean." I slide my sketchpad and scroll across the counter, ignoring the knot in my stomach. "What will the Elders think if they see you with him? You think that just because I'm a legacy, they won't hesitate to banish us both for commitment treason?"

Tears well in her eyes. She blinks them away.

"Forget I ever said anything. Forget I even brought him up in the first place." She heads for the washroom, but not before adding, "You know, at least I try to make the best of what we have here. You just mope around, angry at life."

The door hisses shut behind her, sealing the space between us.

When the entryway scanner beeps a moment later, I half expect Rose to be there again. Then the archway pings open and Elder William Hale appears, of all the people to stop by right now.

He lets himself in. "Morning, Mars."

I let out a sigh. "Now really isn't a good time."

"I'll be quick, then." He scours the metallic counter dividing the sleeping room from the mess and helps himself to a cup of tea. "We need to talk about my son. You leave for Nevarnost tomorrow morning, but I didn't see his name on the mission ledger."

"He's staying back. He'll sort through ISR files and enter logs."

Elder Hale grabs a tea bag off the rack. "That wasn't our agreement."

He's right. It wasn't. But I'm not dragging some timid,

sheltered slug into this.

"No offense, but he wouldn't last out there. Not where I'm going."

The rack spins under Elder Hale's hand, and he catches a mug before it clatters. "I've pulled a lot of strings to get you where you are. I let you live in the *Iris*. I stood up for you at your trial following the incident in the mines. In return, you're taking my son."

"You never told me he was incompetent. I heard about the moon worm—"

"We can't mess with time." His voice hardens. "According to the note and instructions I left myself, you *both* show up on my nephew's doorstop. So, you're *both* going."

Another thing I didn't ask for. Being tangled in Elder Hale's time travel schemes.

"Yeah, according to your notes, a lot of things happen, don't they?"

"I told you. I can't tell you more than you're supposed to know—"

"Or we disrupt the timeline and cause a chain reaction. Yeah, yeah. I get it." I grit my teeth. "But what's in it for me? You've been training me to risk my life on some doomed planet to save your nephew and some random girl, and you haven't even told me what *I* get out of it."

This time, he raises his tone. "You were pardoned! Isn't that enough?"

"They would've pardoned me, anyway, out of respect for my father." I cross my arms. "And don't give me that speech about how 'honorable' it is to work for ISR. This mission doesn't affect me. I already exist. It's not my family on that planet. I gain nothing here."

"Funny." Elder Hale's grip tightens around the mug. "You

seemed eager enough to join ISR's long-standing ranks until I told you Timber was coming along."

I scoff. "Yeah, because he's dead weight."

Elder Hale lifts a brow. "You sure that's the only reason?"

"What the stars else would it be?" I bite. "Are you daft?"

"You've attended every trial with Rose since the two of you committed, but for some reason, you refused to attend his last night. Any particular reason why?"

I tense. "I was *busy*. That's literally it."

"Ah, I see."

"Don't try to intimate me or manipulate me by reading into things that aren't there," I say, squaring my shoulders against him, holding my ground. "Your son's not coming with me."

"Unfortunately, I'm the Elder here. Not you." Elder Hale abandons his tea, the crinkles in his forehead deepening. "So, if I say you're taking my son with you, you're taking him."

I don't bugging think so. "He stays here. That's what's best for us all."

"Unbelievable." Elder Hale exhales sharply and heads for the entryway.

My father might have vouched for him when he was alive, and sure, Elder Hale might be the reason our village runs on glowfish energy along with all the other convenience mechanisms he's in charge of, but I'm not budging. Not on this. Timber Hale is *not* coming to Nevarnost.

I don't care what happened in the past.

As I move to set Elder Hale's mug in the wash basin, the distant rush of water sounds from the washroom where Rose readies for her shell-hunting 'not date' with Julian.

My eyes draw to my proposal scroll on the counter. She

claims she'd rather it be me walking the beach with her today, but I know part of her is screaming for freedom, just like I am.

Maybe there is a way I could use this situation to my advantage.

"Wait—" I grab the proposal scroll and catch Elder Hale before he disappears down the ramp. He turns back, expression bright with such hopeful promise, it's cringeworthy. "I might be able to work something out with you. A way for us both to get what we want."

He nudges his glasses up his nose. "Fine. Let's hear it."

"I'll take your son on the Nevarnost mission." I let the words really sink in because they taste bitter rolling off my tongue. "*If* you back my proposal for traditional change to the Council of Elders. I need a higher-up on my side. They respect you, for reasons I'll never understand, so if you support me, they'll listen."

Elder Hale takes a moment, his eyes following the scroll in my hand.

"You enjoy being difficult, don't you?" he mutters.

"What can I say? It's a cherished pastime."

"Fine," he says, jaw tight. "I'll bring your proposal to the council *after* you complete this mission with my son." He unsheathes a crystal blade from his belt. "I want a blood promise."

Of course he does. Another Vio tradition I'll gladly do away with when this is over.

As if blood and words could bind anything real.

But I'll play along. For now.

"Anything that helps you sleep better at night," I say with snark.

Ignoring my comment, Elder Hale drags the sharp point

across his palm.

The luster of his aura quartz blade takes me back to the mines for a single second. Raw stone dust under my nails. Fingers numb. Blisters splitting just below my knuckles. Violet blood wells up on his hand, sticky and slow, just like mine, a side effect of surviving violet fever the year the surge gutted half our village. Including both my mother and father.

He wipes the blade and holds it out.

I set my scroll down on the entryway ledge, slice the thickest part of my palm, and offer him my hand. We lock hands and recite the words all blood promises on Violet Moon warrant together: *"U promerre u leye u mere soere buun fere."*

I promise you my loyalty or may my soul be bound in fire.

I pull back and wipe my bloody hand on my tunic.

"Give Timber the brief sooner than later," Elder Hale says, grabbing my proposal scroll on his way out. "He's easily flustered. He'll need the whole night to read everything through."

"Will do," is all I say.

The archway closes behind him, leaving only his footsteps fading down the ramp.

As I return to the main level, the washroom scanner beeps, and Rose appears with that doe-eyed look that always makes my knees weak. She knows what I need before I do. No matter the chaos we go through or how much we bicker, she is the one constant in my life.

"Apologize to me," she says, tempting me like a siren in low tide. "And I'll forgive you."

It kills me to say it. To anyone, really. But for her, I make an exception. Always.

My voice is so smooth, it's bugging celestial. *"Sorry."*

She approaches me, her fingers stroking my chin, then my lips. I pretend to bite her, and she smirks, giving me that silent nod. We're okay again. For now.

As her hand drops, I leave her side and glance out the large round window overlooking the old training pit. A square of roped-off black dune sand brings me back to days training with Elder Hale and sparring with Rose between watcher shifts.

"What is it?" she asks, joining me.

I keep my eyes on the pit. "I've been training for moons. Timber isn't going to be ready overnight." I fiddle with the amethyst-plated bracelet around my wrist, the one with the Head Elder spiral engraved on it. Gifted to me by Head Elder Cyan when I became a Thirteen, it was my own father's, and I haven't taken it off since.

"Someone is going to get hurt," I utter. "It'll be him."

Rose puts a hand on my shoulder. "I know that bothers you."

Feaukere. I let it slip once that a student getting stung at a survival lesson three lunar cycles ago because of my simple mistakes had put me on edge. Now Rose thinks I care about some incompetent slug, and she's convinced Elder Hale I'm too shaken to attend a trial.

Why assume anything when they couldn't be more wrong?

It's the mission, the one thing I've worked toward, that matters most.

I shrug Rose away and lean against the window instead. "If I want this mission to succeed, he can't get in my way. Otherwise we could mess it up. I'll have to train him myself."

Rose chuckles. "In one day? We train our watchers for

seasons before we let them take a shift. You can't train him in a day. It's bad enough he has to read an entire briefing tonight."

"If you come up with a better idea, let me know."

"You wouldn't listen even if I did," she says.

I push down all the frustration bubbling up inside me. Rose does have a point. A day is nothing compared to the time I've put in.

But failure isn't an option. Too much depends on this task. As head of this mission, it is my duty to prepare. That includes training someone who's never faced a real struggle.

Even if I teach Timber *one* thing before we leave—a defense move, a strategy, or how to simply stay out of my way without getting caught in the crossfire.

That's still better than nothing.

8: VAIDA

Planet Nevarnost: Year 3051

After an hour of waiting for an available healer, my name is finally called.

A perky Nost attendant with periwinkle eyes guides me along a backline of canvas tents nestled against the red rock.

We're at the boundary line of Zone 9: Outskirts. To the right lies the Hemisphere, its domed curve aglow beneath the Nevarnost suns. And to the left stretches an endless desert, fading into No Man's Land. The dusty horizon makes my head spin if I look too long.

I'm led to the very last tent, which I'm okay with. The more discreet I can be about this, the better. That's why I chose a Nost healer over one of the few medics in the Hub. When the Unity Arch fell, Chancellor Bay kept the best of us and left the rest of us to fend for ourselves. Besides, the Nost have a more holistic approach.

They focus on the root cause rather than the surface details.

"You'll be with Zee," the attendant tells me with a smile.

She pulls back the drawn curtain, and I step into a cool, dark space. The earthy smell greets me instantly, the same smell that always finds me in the underground tunnels of Zone 10: Nost Territory when I travel with Nia. Like underground, the air in this tent is pure and breathable because of the prickly vines snaking along the canvas walls. They curl around the wooden poles that hold the structure in place. I don't even need my face rag.

Zee waits for me by candlelight, standing next to an oval slab of stone draped in a downy, beige blanket that looks like it took someone hours to weave. Shelves of strange desert flora surround her. Apothecary jars filled with herbs shine, almost as if they have a life of their own. Suspended in the center of the tent is an upside-down, triangular mound of porous rock.

"Please, take off your jacket and lie down," Zee instructs me.

I do as I'm told, shrugging out of my sleeves. My brother's hunting knife clatters to the ground, and I quickly scoop it up and set it aside before hoisting myself onto the table.

Zee's ink markings remind me of Nia's, though she has fewer of them, and a sinking feeling takes hold. I told Nia I was coming here to get lunar root for heavy bleeding and cramps. She believed me, and somehow that makes me feel even worse about lying.

Light dances in Zee's dappled eyes. "The Specters will tell us what you need."

Nia's told me countless stories about the Specters. They're the light spirits that dwell in the Hallow, a sacred underground space where the Nost are born. All Nost are female, each one eternally connected through the sacred gift of feeling. The Hallow isn't just the origin of their Goddess, Cassia, but it's *the* source of guidance, healing, and knowledge.

How the Specters are supposed to help a human like me, I don't know.

"Should I stay still or—"

"You must remain quiet." Zee raises a tentacle. "You must focus your mind. Focus on the Specters and the warmth that radiates from them."

The candles dim on their own, leaving us completely in the dark.

My heart batters in my chest as Zee continues, "You must let them read you."

I hold my breath, waiting for something—anything—to happen. The silence is suffocating. Maybe a generic Hub medic would have been a better choice after all.

Then I see them.

From the porous rock hanging above us emerges a flurry of glowing orbs. Drifting through the air, they fall like gentle ash, multiplying until there are hundreds. They radiate a warmth unlike the blistering Nevarnost suns. This warmth is comforting instead.

One settles in Zee's cupped tentacle. She lets it drift free. The orbs continue to surround me, flitting the wisps of purple and brown hair that frame my round face. I watch in awe as they trace the curves of my body and hover over my lower half.

Before I realize what's happening, Zee pulls back the brown overshirt covering my belly. She begins to recite a Nost invocation under her breath and places a slimy tentacle at my navel. The Specters grow brighter. One by one they sink into me, into my abdomen, and light up my womb like a molten ember. A chill washes over my entire body, quick like shifting sand.

The Specters dive deeper, brighter, until an array of images floods my mind.

Soren Bay's large four-poster bed, bathed in red sky light. Bits of dust dancing in the glister above. A stack of herbal smokes in the ashtray by his bedside. The smell of whiskey and skullcap. Silky sheets wrapping around me. His touch—caressing, tempting, luring me in.

"Stop," I gasp, springing upright into a seated position.

As I wobble, Zee supports my back. The Specters are gone like they were never here to begin with. The candles reignite. Goosebumps prickle my skin.

"What just happened?"

Zee runs a tentacle along the curve of my belly. "The Specters are drawn to life most of all. They protect it at all costs," she explains. "They have confirmed you are with child."

With child. Does she really have to say it like that?

I wipe away the moisture in my eyes, frustrated at myself for wanting to cry in the first place. This is such a bullshit reason to cry. Dad always says I'm free to make my own decisions but I'm not free from the consequences. I used to mock him when he said it, but he was right—I was the one who let my guard down and gave away my trust like it was nothing.

One time. Two months ago. That was all it took.

I really did think Soren was the perfect play. We knew one another from grade school, so it wasn't that hard to strike up conversation. Getting close to him meant access to the chancellor. And we bonded over hating his father. Mutual disgust turned into playing Holoblocks all night. Gaming turned into laughter and deeper conversations. For once, I didn't feel so . . . alone.

But all Soren's compliments, his flattery, his gentle

touch—it was a lie. He confided in me, and I made the mistake of letting my guard down. He got what he wanted and moved on. He used me. Which makes him no better than his tyrant father.

In some ways, it makes him worse.

Zee's tentacle continues to move, poking and prodding me. "Your child is strong," she says. "They have been touched by the Hallow and will remain connected to its source."

"Good to know," I mumble, pulling my shirt back down.

"Take this to any Nost working the ration shed." She hands me a thin square of bark, its back marked with sketched symbols. "They will give you what you need."

"Thanks." But what I really need is a way to turn back time.

I swing my legs around and stand.

"You are not happy with Cassia's blessing," Zee observes, walking me out.

"I'm still . . . processing." Bright light blinds me as she pulls back the tent flap. I secure my face rag at the first glimpse of dust. "Because I'm not sure if it's a blessing or a curse."

N ia waits for me outside the Hub.

It's a massive gray blob of a building, its teal beacon towering above the others. Easily visible from miles away, it's the perfect marker of home if you get caught in a sand-storm.

She rises from the crate she's sitting on. "Did you get the lunar root you needed?"

I wish I'd left with lunar root. Dealing with a period right now would be a hell of a lot easier. But I'm not ready to tell her the truth. She wouldn't judge me. She'd just speak her mind, sparing no feelings out of blunt honesty. Like the first time I stole Dad's scanner card. Or the times I snuck out past curfew and she caught me wandering in the middle of the desert. Or when I got a nose ring. Or when I dyed the tips of my hair with Essence of Mauve for the first time.

The color is semi-permanent and will fade unless reapplied. Are you sure you can afford the upkeep? she'd asked. She'd hovered while I ground the seeds into powder, questioned me as the pigment set in, and pressed me when I rinsed it clean with a bucket of murk water.

Was it a fair point at the time? Sure. Do I now spend more than half of my monthly tokens on Essence of Mauve because my hair is a part of me that I really like? Absolutely.

Still not going to admit it was a careless decision.

A fresh wave of emotions flood through my belly and my fingers instinctively press against it. I will admit, though, getting involved with Soren Bay was probably the worst decision I've ever made. No amount of dye or tokens can change that. But if I wanted a lecture on getting knocked up at nineteen, I'd visit Dad. Which is also not happening.

I tuck the bark list Zee gave me into my back pocket and force a nod to Nia's question. "I got everything I need, but I have to go to the ration shed anyway. Can I catch up with you later?"

"Oh, I'll go with you."

My muscles tense. As much as I want her to come with me, she can't.

My naturally larger size will hide this pregnancy for a while, but one look at the Nost items I'm given and Nia will know I'm *with child*.

"Actually, I'm going to go take a nap after I stop by the shed. Maybe we can meet in the Hub later and talk about our next attempt at breaking into Nucleus?"

Nia offers me a slack expression. "Sure. I shall meet you in the Hub after your nap."

She takes off, leaving me alone and feeling like the worst friend ever.

After taking a stifling breath to settle my nerves, I continue on. The mass of crooked shacks and slanted huts draped in layers of cloth sway with each gust of wind. I pass a few of Dad's men reinforcing shelters, working together to move faster against the airborne grit. Further down, a group of teenagers my age huddle beneath a canopy, tinkering with the engine of a solar cart I know damn well they plan on using for late-night sand drifting and roake hunting.

One of the girls, a slender redhead with a pointed nose and a hollow stare, locks onto me immediately. Recognition dawns on her face. Her eyes widen for a split second before she looks away, just as the boy beside her rolls out from under the cart to grab a rag. A couple others join them, laughing as they pass around cloudy bottles of water.

I keep moving. I don't need to revisit my past or the hollow eyes of a girl who once called me a friend at thirteen, only to spread rumors for clout and ditch me the moment something better came along. We don't have the luxury of being picky out here when it comes to friends, but I thought it was real. She even had the audacity to blame me for our fallout.

The ration shed sits at the edge of the last row, right at the center of everything, its shadow cast by the Hub behind it. The ever-present queue waits silently, and I fall in place behind a woman balancing her son on one hip. The child looks up at me, sullen, and hacks behind his face rag. Bits of blood seep through the cloth covering his mouth, and his mother rubs his back. I can't help but picture myself in the mother's place if I choose to have this baby.

Before the Arch fell, there was a birth control mandate because population numbers were growing too rapidly. The old men in the Hub still bitch and moan about it from time to time in the evenings when they play their own version of draughts they call Stone and Teeth. They line up their rotted teeth and collected stones in place of board pawns, talking about how the one good thing Chancellor Bay did was veto the mandate for a lottery to decide who gets the contraceptive implant. Women were the first ones to be suggested, naturally. But Billy Hale shot it down because he believed that nobody should be forced to do anything like that.

When they couldn't come to an agreement, Billy then proposed they bring the issues to the community, hoping a collective discussion would encourage 'mindfulness.' His idea was met with laughter, but he still refused to let the burden fall solely on the people with wombs. Instead he pushed for a lottery system, ensuring no one suffered more than another. The plan passed and hormonal implants were prepared for distribution, but then the Unity Arch fell, Billy Hale disappeared, and Chancellor Bay stepped in to override it all. Now, the mandate only applies to people born with wombs beneath the Hemisphere, following their first bleed.

The Outskirts isn't regulated. But it's instances like children soaking their face rags in blood from coughing fits that make us do our best not to bring children into this world. Lung sickness. Sleepless nights. Gasping for every breath. A lackluster childhood. Or none at all.

A child doesn't deserve this. And the question isn't *could* I carry this pregnancy to term. It's *should* I? Because what kind of life could an innocent baby have in a world like this?

I'm only nineteen. I live in the Outskirts. I take care of myself because I have to.

I've heard stories, whispers of communities beneath the Hemisphere where babies are hidden, protected, even when the implants should've prevented them. They come together. People take care of each other. It sounds like another one of Dad's delusions. Even if places like that exist, I don't have that security out here. If I keep this baby, I'm on my own.

When it's her turn, the woman with the sullen child in line ahead of me steps up to the counter and speaks hoarsely. "Soothing syrup please."

A Nost, Ama, is working today. She presents the woman a glass bottle filled with a foaming green liquid. "That'll be three tokens."

The child coughs deeply, and blood dribbles down his neck. As he screams in pain, his mother rocks him, searching her pockets with her free hand. Shakily, she draws up two tokens, and they clatter down onto the wooden counter.

"That's all I have," she confesses. "Please. He won't be able to sleep. He needs rest."

"I'm sorry. The Hemisphere hasn't given us any more in the last few weeks. Our supply is running low, but perhaps there's something from the Nost healers that might help?"

"Your herbal remedies aren't strong enough," the woman says.

91

The child's shrieks grow louder, broken by gasping breaths and another mouthful of blood. I don't know how much more I can handle.

"Here." I reach into my own pocket and toss one of my last tokens of the week onto the counter. "Give her the syrup."

Ama nods and hands over the bottle.

"Thank you. Thank you," the woman says. "You are sent from the heavens."

I wouldn't go that far. She hurries off, and I sigh.

Pulling out the bark list, I hand it to Ama.

"Goddess Cassia has blessed you," she says. "I will prepare your list."

"How much?" I ask, thinking of the two measly tokens left in my pocket.

Can I even afford to be so blessed?

"From Zee, your order is taken care of."

The weight that's been pressing on me since leaving the tent lightens just a fraction. Maybe Goddess Cassia is watching over me after all.

Moments later, Ama has gathered the items on Zee's list and laid them out on the counter for me: three containers and a dainty, over-the-shoulder brown leather satchel to keep them in. I recognize the drawstring canvas pouch of supplemental vitamins, but the glass dropper bottle and small, oval-shaped box are unfamiliar. I unscrew the top, hit first with floral notes, then citrus.

"A drop under your tongue will help with fatigue," Ama instructs. "And if you feel nauseated at any time, place a spore on your wrist, and they will relieve you."

She wedges her tentacle beneath the lid of the wooden box, revealing four fleshy, puff-like creatures with suction cups. They squirm in a thick coating of exo-slime, rising and sinking with each breath. I go to touch one and it tries to latch onto me, so Ama shuts the lid.

"Nost remedy is strange," I comment, at which Ama smiles.

I load up my new satchel and fumble with the latch. As I turn, I collide with someone, and two sturdy hands come up to catch me before I topple over.

My stare locks with a pair of kind emerald-green eyes, wide with the same surprise.

A chiseled jaw. Scruff, well-grown in. Tousled brown locks that complement his suns-kissed skin. Objectively handsome. But then I notice his mask—black, carbon, issued by Zone 3: Provisions—and an all-encompassing hatred fills me up.

He's from the Hemisphere.

"I'm so sorry," the boy says. "Are you okay?"

"Gee, Kev. Walk much?" another boy with blinding ringlet curls jeers. He adjusts his fancy Hemisphere-issued jacket. "That's what you get for talking to your digiband like it's your girlfriend all the time."

"Graham, go pick up our tool kits. I'll be there in a second." Mr. Green Eyes releases me, and I put distance between us immediately. I want nothing to do with him.

"Wait," he says as I take off. "You're Commander Wardell's daughter, right? My colleague and I are here for the merger."

"I know why you're here," I bite.

Graham leans over the ration counter. "Kevin, come over here. They've got Nost working their supply. A mix of modern and holistic medicine. You'll love this. Seriously."

Mr. Green Eyes, otherwise known as Kevin, sighs. "You'll

have to forgive my co-worker. He has no sense of—"

"Respect? Boundaries? Common sense?" I cross my arms. "Shall I keep going?"

Kevin's brows rise, and I can tell he's smiling behind his mask. "Uh, yeah." He chuckles and runs a hand through his hair. "That's exactly how I would describe him. That's funny."

Funny isn't the term I'd use.

"Here are your kits," Ama says, handing Graham two steel toolboxes. "I'm also supposed to tell you that if we have an acid storm, you should head inside immediately."

"We don't have acid rain in the Hemisphere," Graham says.

Well, no shit, genius. You live underneath a giant dome.

"How often does that happen?" Kevin asks me.

I shrug. Maybe a little acid rain would do them some good.

"Every few days," Ama answers. "Just a precaution."

Kevin thanks Ama, and I continue on my way, no longer wanting to be part of this conversation. Even when Kevin calls out, "It was nice to finally meet you!" I don't look back.

Now is the time to plan my next move. Now is not the time to dwell on mechanism specialists or Hemisphere boys in general. If we don't take back what's ours, it's not just my people who will keep suffering now, it's the unborn child I'm carrying too. And I'll be damned if I don't do everything I can to give it a chance at life, should I choose to keep it.

Nia's right. These empty infiltration attempts are getting me nowhere.

Forcing a surrender isn't good enough anymore. I'm just going to have to storm into Nucleus, unsheathe my brother's blade, and drive it straight into the chancellor's chest.

9: TIMBER

Planet Violet Moon: Year 3083

T hat afternoon, I search for Raine in the Makers Market.

Navigating the array of vendor carts, booths, and displays is something I usually avoid at all costs. The natural chaos sends my pulse into overdrive, a world away from the sanctuary of solitude I find in the trees. I imagine I come off as odd to anyone watching me skittering between canvas tents and drapes of colored cloth to avoid the rush, but I don't care. My reputation in the village is already tarnished, and crowds mean more chances to brush elbows or arms with others.

I check Raine's favorite fruit stand, the one he stops at every afternoon before his night watch. The seller usually hands him a sack of quinn fruit free of charge; an offering of thanks for all the watchers do. But today, he isn't here. And the only other place to search is through another tightly packed mass of people as they await the fisherman restocking the fresh catch of the day. I barely glance at the striped fish and urchins with curved needles, which seamstresses will refurbish and use in their work, as I press ahead.

Is braving the crowd really worth the pain? Maybe I should just go home.

But just as I back away from the crowd, Raine comes to mind again, and I realize if we don't talk now, we might not get the chance to say goodbye before I leave for the mines.

I tense my shoulders.

Up on my toes, I'm quick, avoiding every glare aimed at me and the murmurs that filter into my head as I race through the crowd. A woman juggling two burlap sacks of seasoned octopus nudges against me by accident, and I grit my teeth.

I can't escape the whispers, and the hollowness in my abdomen, that follow.

What a privileged, disrespectful child, she thinks. *I'd be ashamed if he were my son.*

The tremor in her words travels through me, slowing me down.

As the market starts to spin, I spot the boardwalk, but not before a fellow Eighteen—one who completed his cere-mony without hesitation—and his blacksmith father knock into me while trying to maneuver their cart:

He's always been a coward.

I hope the mines toughen him up. He deserves it.

An elder's son? Ugh. More like a disgrace.

Disgust. Disappointment. Dismay. They're always a treat.

I push through the sudden headache and break into open air at the edge of the boardwalk, shakily letting my hands rest on the railing. As I breathe through it, I shift my weight and watch the horizon, where the sea waves are steady and the gatherers digging for clams whistle old folk songs. Songs Mother sometimes sings to the babies she nurses.

"Timber?"

Raine's voice pulls me out of my daze.

I swallow the burn, rub off sweat from my brow, and straighten. Head held high, Raine stands to my right, ready for his shift. His slate gray tunic is pressed and clean, his supple knee-high boots and leather breastplate polished. The true mark of a watcher—a thick, leafy crossbody sash—must be earned, and he sports his with honor.

"Are you alright?" He peels the periwinkle skin off a quinn fruit, pops it into his mouth, sucks on it for a few moments, then spits out the pink pit over the railing.

I take a few more deep breaths to calm my nerves. This is Raine. My best friend. The one who's been by my side since we were nervous Tens paired together during a diving lesson. If anyone is going to understand what I'm going through, it's him.

"I came to say goodbye," I say softly.

As he moves closer, he spits out another pit. "Don't talk like that. Everyone makes mistakes. Besides, the council's given you another chance. In three days, you'll make it right."

"I'm not making it right, Raine. I'm accepting my fate."

"That doesn't make any sense." He hucks the last pit out and wipes his hands on the paper sack his fruit came in. "I know you value life, but don't think of it that way. It's a simple moon worm plucked from the Dunes. Fishermen feed them to the squids in the port."

He faces me, and the disappointment has never been so clear. That and the dark circles.

He hasn't been sleeping. Without touching him I know that's my fault, too. I'm hurting the people I care about because I can't be honest.

Just tell him. Tell him the truth. Right now.

I take a breath. "Look, it's not just about valuing life—"

"I have something that might change your mind," he says. "Come on."

And I feel I have no choice but to follow him down a bamboo ladder into the cove, where his grandmother's dwelling comes into view. Clashing against the starkness of the rocky shore, her thatched roof is adorned with vibrantly colored flags that dance in the sea breeze. Herbal smoke wafts from her windows. Even with gusts of salty wind, the fresh lavender and sage fill my nose, a comfort that always soothes me.

"*Heioe*, Kiki!" Raine shouts to his grandmother.

The Head Healer flips her long gray braid over her shoulder and looks up from her spot on the dock, where she feeds the glowfish from a pouch at her waist. As we get closer I notice just how many there are. Twelve of them gather, waiting for the bits of brine shrimp and larvae she offers. Glowfish are among the most majestic of colossal beasts. They aren't native to this area, but they seem to congregate here. Their organs are slightly visible beneath their translucent skin as they squirm. It's their natural energy and long flowing fins, spread out like a veil, that give them their violet glow. Not to mention, they provide the energy that powers our village.

My failed attempt at harvesting comes to mind again, and the look on Mars' face when he stood over me, dripping wet, to see if I was breathing.

I'm sure he's sitting in the *Iris* right now, relieved he's going on this mission alone.

I will never be one of the daring who collects the electric currents generated by the seven subtle stingers rising up their smooth backs. Neither will Raine's grandmother, but for different reasons. Still, she spoils them. They respect her, and she respects them. Much like the motto of our people, that applies to all life on Violet Moon.

Except moon worms. They get sacrificed.

"My brave Raine." As he climbs onto the dock, Kiki pulls him into a tight embrace and straightens his sash. Then she flicks her eyes to me. "And gentle Timber. How are you feeling?"

"Mildly nauseated," I admit. "Thank you for backing me up at the trial."

"We all deserve grace." Kiki ties up her sack of food. "Alright, off with you all," she says, gesturing to the glowfish, who scatter with flopping tails.

Inside Kiki's dwelling, the comforting aroma of chamomile and lemon tea carries from a pot simmering on the hearth. Aside from her personal sleeping room, the dwelling is one large circle split into two spaces: one for entertaining and cooking, and another for her healing work. Above a canvas-stretched cot draped with flare cat pelts and hand-sewn throws, a wall of apothecary jars and homemade remedies towers from floor to rafter.

I've spent hours perusing her inventory, despite Raine's complaints, picking up little tips and tricks each time we visit his grandmother. The last time I was here, she taught me how to blend calendula flowers and violet leaves with clay using a mortar and pestle to make a poultice for a villager's rash. The time before that, it was an elderberry tincture to reduce inflammation.

Learning from Kiki has been an endless source of enjoyment, one I will miss most. Because healing is a passionate hobby of mine. If I weren't cursed and doomed to live in the mines beneath the Dunes for the next decade, I might have pursued it as a vocation.

She ushers us to her table and serves plates of oat bread spread with cocoa butter, plump berries, and kelp noodles dressed in garlic oil. Raine will happily devour it all if I let him, including the charred skewers of cuttlefish Kiki prepared just for him, since I don't consume anything that breathes, thinks, or feels.

It became my preference when I was a Nine, helping Father gather sand hen eggs in the coop behind our dwelling. As I reached beneath a hen to grab its egg, the whispers conveyed her fear: *Please don't make me anyone's supper.* It was my first wrestle with fear, wrapping around my heart like an icy pair of shackles. That night, I cried in Mother's arms because Father killed her anyway. I eventually forgave him, after learning about the sustenance cycle in survival studies and that nobody else seemed as bothered.

Kiki sets down a cup of steaming tea for each of us.

"Thank you." I pull my cup forward and enjoy its warmth. "Raine said he had something to show me. I'm assuming it's something you'd like to show me."

Raine's little smirk, just before he shoves another bite into his mouth, tells me I'm right.

"Rather, to *say* to you, Timber," Kiki replies, settling into her chair. "The fact of the matter is, I am going to die someday, and I will need someone to take over my duties."

I take a sip of tea, letting its heat coat the back of my throat. I know where this is going, and it confuses me because what she suggests would imply I'm not going to the mines.

"You're the ideal person to take her place," Raine says between mouthfuls of ripe punchberries that stain his lips a bright shade of red. "You're a natural healer. I've seen it."

The wrinkles around Kiki's warm brown eyes crease as her dimples deepen, and she motions to her apothecary shelves. "This will all be yours. The things I will teach you—"

"*Could* have . . . taught me," I correct her gently, placing my tea back on the table.

I dismiss the anxious ping in my chest, triggered at the thought of tending anyone's wounds but my own. "I'm flattered you'd consider me worthy of becoming your successor. But unfortunately, I've made my choice. I'll make the same choice again in three days."

Kiki tilts her head, as though I've just sworn crude words at her in Vio.

Raine stops chewing. "Why are you throwing away your potential? I've been supportive. I've been patient. This is the perfect role for you."

I slowly pull away from the table. "Raine, you have to accept this—"

"My grandmother wants you to be her apprentice."

I'm fully standing now, paces away from the exit. I can't believe I thought Raine would understand. And I'm throwing away my potential? Is that what he really thinks of me?

"I'll give you two a minute," Kiki says without prompting. As she crosses the room, she slows for a moment, very quietly near my ear, so I only hear. "You will be my successor. Just not now. Not until after you return from Nevarnost. And it will require a full surrender."

A chill runs down my spine and settles in my toes. My eyes lock with Kiki's. Mars said few knew about our mission, the one I'm *not* going on. And surrender? Surrender to what?

Before I can say anything more, Kiki nods and disappears

into her sleeping room.

The silence barely has time to sink in before Raine says, "Is a life spent with luster dust in your lungs and iridescent stains on your fingers, really what you want? You have to know how hard it is for me to sit back and watch you throw your whole life away because of one worm."

I let out a long sigh. "Raine. *Please.*"

But he isn't listening. Once he starts a tangent, he has to finish it.

"Do you remember when I told you about my first training session to become a watcher?" He stands and faces me. "There was that obstacle course up in the highest trees."

Of course I remember. He raced home afterward and practically beat down the door of my dwelling to tell me about it. "You did it even though you had a fear of heights."

"I was scared at first. But then the Head Watcher told me the things we don't think we can do or that scare us end up being the best things for us. They end up being our strengths."

He takes a step closer to me. "Now I'm the fastest night watcher, and when they need someone quick up in those trees to chart a checkpoint, they call *me.*"

My skin prickles in response to our nearness. I don't think he's ever been this close to me before, and I can't tell if I like it or not.

Rain's voice drops and creases form in the corners of his eyes. "The other watchers ridiculed me to no end after your trial, you know."

I close my eyes briefly and steel myself for the inevitable. "I know this isn't easy for you," I say as I open my eyes again. "I know my actions don't make sense, and I'm sorry for it. If it means you want nothing to do with me, I completely understand."

"No, it's—" He half-laughs, rubbing the back of his neck. "Timber, they teased me because they know I care for you. They don't see the potential I see. I think you could be the best healer we've had since Kiki. I really, from the bottom of my heart, mean it."

When our eyes meet, his ache with affection, deep bronzite crystals compared to my bright calcite blues. Without warning he reaches out and puts a hand on my arm, bringing forth what I expect to be the feeling of genuine concern, which is like wearing a sweater in the sweltering sun. But instead, desire and something I can only describe as romantic floods in.

I gasp as I pull away, shaking the ever-persistent tingling on the surface of my skin.

Raine steps into the streak of afternoon sun that filters through the window above Kiki's washbasin, its warmth brushing over his olive skin. "You okay? This happened last night, too."

"Yeah. Yeah. I'm fine." I clench my jaw, hoping for the sensation to fade as all others do moments after I reclaim my personal space again, but this time it doesn't.

It only intensifies.

Raine furrows his brows. "You're scaring me."

As he reaches out again, I bolt from Kiki's dwelling. I don't know what's going on, but I need the feeling to go away. I need to get away. From him. From *this*.

I hear Raine call my name, but I'm quicker than I look when I'm not walking by his side. I race along the shore, up the bamboo ladder. I don't stop until I'm out of breath, pacing outside my dwelling, resisting the urge to break down.

Breathe through it, Timber, my inner self tells me.

My lungs squeeze in my chest. I bend over to calm myself some more.

Deep breaths. One. Two. Three. Four.

Eventually, the heat in my body starts to subside.

"Dune skulls. You gonna make it or what?"

I spin around, finding Mars standing in the thicket, a smug look on his face. How long he's been there, I don't know. My luck, he's probably witnessed my entire fit. Because almost dying by means of perpetual desire is an entirely normal thing.

"Yea—Yeah?" I stammer.

Mars pulls a spiral-bound book out of his pack and tosses it toward me like a saucer. It hits me square in the chest, but I manage to catch it and keep steady.

"Read up. That's the history of Nevarnost, and some tech manuals. I need you to be prepped by tomorrow. Report to the Dunes at sunrise for some last-minute defensive training."

He turns to leave.

"Wait," I say.

He doesn't stop.

"Why do I—"

"I changed my mind. You're going to Nevarnost." Mars' words fade as he descends the hill. "Now read. And don't be late. Or I'll send Ere after you."

As the last glimpse of him disappears over the rise, I'm reminded of Kiki's words: *You will be my successor. Just not now. Not until after you return from Nevarnost*

Then she mentioned something about surrendering.

I turn Mars' book over in my hands.

Somehow, Kiki knew. She knew Mars would change his

mind. Does she have this curse too? And if time travel is real, is it so hard to believe my future could change?

Going on this mission doesn't mean I'm giving in.

I'll read Mars' book. I'll read all night if I have to.

But I won't go back on my decision.

This morning, I was sure I'd end up in the mines. But given what Kiki said, and Mars' sudden change of heart, maybe that's not my fate after all.

One thing I do know. I'm not killing a moon worm.

10: KEVIN

Planet Nevarnost: Year 3051

~~knock some sense into graham~~ {redacted}
meet with commander w.
check in with nana

"The Outskirt irrigation grid runs on a controller. PVC pipe connects the water meter, the system itself, general filtration, and the backflow valves. I'm going to resource the controller—"

"Here we go again with the digital diary," Graham remarks.

I ignore him and continue speaking into my digiband. "—and scan the mechanisms to get it up and running. Of course, that won't work if the grid is faulty to begin with."

"Log recorded," Lux confirms.

The regulator is corroded shut. I flip on my beamer, which is nothing more than a high-tech headlamp, then pry off the front panel with an extractor from my tool kit.

"Why are you even bothering?" Graham shoves another handful of freeze-dried protein gobs into his mouth. "We're not actually making repairs. What's the point?"

Nevarnost only gives us about five hours of darkness each morning, and we've already been out here for nearly that long. So far, he's done nothing but lounge in the sand, eat our rations, and scroll through graphic novels on the tablet propped in his lap.

A notification goes off. I check my messages.

SOREN: Need more . . .

Graham brushes crumbs from his mouth. "Who else is up at this hour? Is it Ed?"

I silence my digiband and connect my reader to the regulator. "You do know protein gobs are meant to be rehydrated and used as a meat substitute, right? That bag could feed ten people."

"There's nothing else to do! The sticky sweets are gone. I sucked down the last fruit squeeze pouch." He gathers his trash and stuffs it into his bag. "Besides, I need sustenance."

"You need to learn to ration." I start the coding sequence for the controller that regulates the whole system. "Imagine having to live on a strict root diet and whatever Nost vegetation manages to grow out here in the Outskirts."

"Judging by the size of the chancellor's daughter, the Outskirts are being fed plenty."

My thumb slips on the keypad, and three lines of code disappear.

Crap.

I grit my teeth. "Judging by the marks on your mechanics exam, you shouldn't even be here right now."

Graham sets aside his tablet. "Hey, man. Don't be so cocky."

"I'm not." I pull the regulator off the converter and start

over. "I'm proving how ignorant you sound half the time. You don't know anything about the Outskirts or the commander's daughter." I plug back into the system. "Lux, re-code and regulate, please."

"Regulating now."

"Ah, I know what this is about." Graham pulls himself up and strolls toward me. "You've got a crush on the commander's daughter."

"People of the Outskirts are human beings. They deserve respect like everyone else." Sweat prickles the back of my neck, and I turn to face him. "And so what if I do?"

"Whoa. Like actually?" Graham smirks. "Like a 'hit it' kind of crush or a real crush?"

A *'hit it'* crush? I'm starting to realize there's more than one reason he's single, too.

I narrow my gaze. "Don't talk about women that way. Of course it's real. I think she's funny and interesting. Unlike you, I know what it's like to admire someone genuinely."

My wrist vibrates again. I ignore it. Again.

Graham crosses his arms. "Oh, step down from your righteous pedestal, will you? You think you're *so* perfect. With your high test scores, luscious hair, and your savvy mainframe."

I blink. "Not sure what my hair or Lux has to do with anything, but I never said I was—" *You know what?* He isn't worth the energy. "Just make yourself useful. At least pretend to be doing something in case a guard or Commander Wardell checks on us."

"It's almost sunrise. Means I'm packing up."

"Great," I mutter. "Pack up then."

I turn my back on him, focusing on the control. One last code.

My fingers slide swiftly between numbers. All I need to know is whether this irrigation system is worth saving. I might not be able to make physical repairs, but at least I can tell the commander what's wrong with it.

Next to me, Graham shuffles, then attempts to jump over a trench. He becomes unsteady and slips, face-planting into a sand mound. I smile behind my mask. *Serves him right.*

My smirk is gone the moment he lets out a shriek that doesn't sound human.

I set down my regulator. "What is it?"

"Get them off me! Get them off me!"

I yank off my beamer and shine it in his direction. Twenty or more roakes pour out from the sunken hole he's flopped himself into. Wriggling up his boots. Tangled in his laces. Slithering up his pant legs. Pincers snapping. Telsons buzzing.

My mind races. *Do something, Kevin.*

"Do something, Kevin!" Graham screams.

"Stay still!" I wrench my backpack off my shoulders. "They're drawn to movement. If you don't bother them, they won't sting you."

Graham nods, his breath coming in sharp, anxious bursts. All I can think is that Soren might get what he wants after all. I paw through my pack, my fingers closing around a glass jar.

Tugging on my gloves, I scale a heap of sand and sweep my beamer over the trench.

"What are you doing!?" Graham barks. "This isn't some science experiment."

I ignore him, swiping away a rogue telson with my free hand. A roake sidles into my palm. Then another. Four

110

more. Two more. Until I've gathered at least ten.

How many does Soren want? *Correction.* How many should he have?

I pluck up five more, my fingertips tracing the grooves and divots for the familiar webs where they hide.

Graham winces. "How much longer?"

"You can back up. Slowly," I tell him. "They're distracted enough."

He pushes himself away, kicking up a cloud of dust. I hack behind my mask but manage to corral the last few roakes into my jar, nearly missing one furious, warbling telson.

They resist and hiss at me as I tighten the lid.

I've never been stung by a roake, but I know it only takes one to get you hooked. After that, they become something you can't live without.

"This wasn't in the job description. No freaking way," Graham exclaims, fetching his pack and toolkit. "I'm out. I'll see you back at the hut."

The irrigation and filtration grids sit about half a mile from Outskirt camp. Beyond them, masked slightly by the haze, the Hemisphere takes shape. Graham is already a dwindling speck on the horizon, trudging off without so much as a thank you for saving him from possible death or a lifetime of chasing the next numbing high.

I shouldn't be surprised.

This is the same boy who talks about women like they're inanimate objects, who believes the lies about my uncle, and who thinks I'm perfect. So, why am I letting his ignorant assumptions and perceptions trigger me like this? It'll be something to *reflect* on later.

I'm far from perfect, though. I'm aware enough to admit that right now.

Every roake I take back to my loft. Every heat mechanism I install to modify their strength. Every order, every jar, every high I supply for Soren Bay, week after week, in exchange for keeping my support for Unity a secret—I'm the opposite of perfect.

My grip tightens around the jar of roakes. I tuck it carefully into my pack, where I know it won't break. Back at the controller, I unhook my regulator and check the reading.

"Absolute Damage," Lux reports.

Great. Nothing's salvageable.

I return to our hut and drop my toolkit on the bare tarp rug beside the door, keeping my backpack strapped on so I can head out again.

"I'm wiped." Graham yawns from one of the two hammocks stretched across the tiny space. "Not sure how much sleep I'm going to get. It's hotter than hell in here."

Our rations, or what's left of them, sit in a crate near a barrel of murk water. Judging by the state of the irrigation grid, it's undrinkable. The only other features of our hut are two plank-boarded windows, meant to keep out the dust. In reality, they just block the suns.

Even that's a stretch of efficiency.

"I'm going to go find the commander." I take a swig from my canteen and toss it into my hammock. "And I need to call Nana. I didn't hear from her last night."

Graham lifts his head. "Tell the commander his grid is busted and we can't fix it. And while you're at it, tell him we're ready to leave. I have blisters the size of a quantum portal—that's a gaming reference for all us normal teens with social lives and hobbies."

Uncle Billy would argue it's also a literal portal, a divine one. But my guess is metaphysics, or anything that challenges Graham's scope of reality, is beyond his comprehension.

For the record, I have plenty of hobbies: making lists, deep cleaning, reading instruction manuals. Sometimes I even do a little meal prepping for Nana.

Not that Graham deserves to know any of that.

"I'm aware," I reply flatly to his first statement instead. "And I'll make it my top priority."

The muted sheen of a twin sunrise casts long streaks through the sand-filled streets as I weave through Outskirt camp.

Overhead, unnatural black veins slink in the clouds. And around me, people work and cough, moving through their routines. Some rebuild huts that have caved in. Launderers from yesterday string damp linens along a sagging rope. Others pass out rags and tin cups.

The Hub's rotating teal light cuts through the shantytown, drawing me in.

The mess hall is packed with sick and thirsty people, draped over one another like damp cloth. Women teach children how to turn fabric scraps into face rags. Elderly men sift through what is clearly debris from Hemisphere trash receptacles, salvaging broken sunspecs and cracked parts. Vile smells hit me in spurts. My nose scrunches. The potent stench of urine and sweat mixes with whatever is simmering on the counter in the provision line for breakfast.

And amid all of this, Commander Wardell is nowhere to be found.

I step off to the side, away from the rush. "Lux, connect me with Nana."

"Connecting."

My digiband processes. No answer.

I try again. "Check motion sensor logs. Where is she?"

"She is in Lower Earhart Unit, Bedroom 1."

Right where I left her. It's not uncommon for her to doze off, but still worrisome.

"Connect one more time if you can, Lux."

Lux obeys. Again, no answer.

Nana needs to be checked on. She forgets simple things like eating, going to the bathroom, and taking her medication. Sometimes she even forgets where she is. The last thing I need is her wandering the streets of Zone 1: Mechanisms, lost and afraid. I'm sure the commander won't mind if I make a quick trip back to the Hemisphere and return in time for our meeting.

Before I can move, a young girl with double braids, wearing a blue dress, steps into my path. She holds out a tray of pale amber snake eggs nestled on a bed of wilted herbs.

"You buying?" she asks.

Most of the eggs are cracked, flecked with mold. Far from appetizing.

"Uh . . . well, let's see here."

The least I can do is offer her a few tokens. As my fingers scrape the bottom of my empty pockets, my heart sinks. They're in my toolkit, back in the hut with Graham.

The girl shakes her collection cup. "Only half a token. Two for one."

"You know what, I'm all set, but—"

"Don't bother with him, Lucy." Vaida steps forward, drawing the girl's attention.

I straighten. I didn't expect to see her here.

"He gets Hemisphere rations," she says. "Nutrient pods. Protein gobs. ISR-issued meals in tin cans. You wouldn't believe it."

She's right. It isn't fair.

Lucy scurries away. Vaida side-eyes me.

I've never cared what someone thinks of me before, but suddenly I'm hyperaware of the sweat clinging to my underarms, the dirt on my clothes, the way I might say something offensive. It's normal to feel this way when you find someone intriguing. Not that now is the time for *that* kind of thing, but still—I want to make a good impression.

And she might know where her father is.

"I would have gladly taken a share and donated tokens so others could eat instead." I move with her down the line of tables, trying to lighten the mood. "I understand it's not—"

"Ah, a real humanitarian we've got here." Vaida's laugh rings out in the mess hall as she lowers her face rag and steps onto a bench. "Gather round, everyone! The Hemisphere boy would like to make a very generous donation."

My stomach hardens as all eyes turn to Vaida.

Oh. "Geez. No. That's . . . not what I meant."

But Vaida isn't deterred. "He would like to donate his tokens so that we can eat."

The Outskirters clap, provoking her. They cheer. Some rise to their feet.

"Now, let's tell him how we really feel about that."

All at once, a great resounding, "No thank you!" booms in unison.

The roars die down. Vaida jumps off the bench in one swift motion, landing directly in front of me. "See? I can make grand gestures for the sake of nothing, too."

Trust me. I noticed.

She takes off into the crowd without a single look back, shoulders stiff and a sharpness to her stride.

I chew my bottom lip, then jog to catch up with her at the back of the provision line. "Uh, I was wondering if I could—"

"Stop following me."

"I'm not following you. That would be a complete invasion of your space," I say, running a hand through my hair. "I just need to talk to the commander. Do you know where he is?"

She crosses her arms, eyes still fixed on the line ahead. "I have no idea."

"It's okay."

I hesitate, then hold out a hand. Vaida catches the motion in her periphery, scrunches her nose, and grabs a tray from the stack. *God, is a handshake really that weird?*

"I didn't get to formally introduce myself outside the ration shed—"

"I know who you are."

"Right." We inch forward in line. When I realize my hand is still outstretched, the gesture ignored, I quickly put it down. "My uncle was Billy Hale. He knew your mother—"

Vaida spins around, her hazel eyes sharp. "What do you think you're doing?"

"I'm sorry. I just thought—"

"You thought what? That because your uncle and my mother sang peace songs together back in the day, we should do the same? I don't think so."

She snatches a set of half-rusted silverware from the tin pail at the counter.

"Those involved in the original peace efforts are dead. The Hemisphere is to thank for that. *Your* uncle is to thank for that. Get where I'm going with this?"

What is it with people and these false theories today?

Does anyone even remember the kind of person my uncle was?

"I know you think that, but blowing up the Arch would have gone against everything Billy believed in. He spent months planning that rally. Your mother, Blithe, was his best friend. He cared about her and everyone else who lost their lives that day."

"I was there. I saw him. Clearly, you didn't know your uncle as well as you thought," she says, her voice razor sharp. "And don't talk to me about my mother. You don't get to do that."

Wait. She saw him? I try to piece together this new information, but it refuses to compute. She must be remembering it wrong. She couldn't have been older than nine or ten at the time like I was, and when you mix that with a traumatic event, it's easy to think you saw something when really it's just your brain filling in the gaps.

I tap my fingers against my legs. Maybe Vaida truly believes she saw him. It doesn't make me think any less of her, but it does make earning her trust that much harder.

We reach the front of the breakfast line.

They're serving watery porridge speckled with green leaves and some kind of red seed. Likely Nost vegetation meant to supplement the lack of nutrition out here.

Vaida slams her tray onto the serving counter.

Alright. Obviously, we aren't getting anywhere today.

But you know what? She isn't the only one who lost someone that day.

I might live beneath the dome, and I might not go around slamming trays when I'm upset, but I do know what it's like to feel angry. To be frustrated by the way our two worlds are divided.

Grief is the common factor here.

"You can hate my uncle if you want, okay?" I start as her fingers curl around her tray. "You can hate the chancellor, the Hemisphere—you can even hate me if you want to. But I promise you, there are efforts in the works to make things right again. You just have to be patient. Trust me."

"You're right," she says easily. "I do hate you. You, your people, and your damn chancellor don't deserve that Hemisphere." She turns to me properly for the first time since we met outside the ration shed. "And I would never trust you. Or your false promises."

Her words are like a cup of suns-scorched water to the face.

"I think maybe we've gotten off on the wrong foot," I say as she plops a wheat wafer onto her tray from the basket at the end of the line. "I'm sorry if I said something—"

"You are not sorry. Don't even."

"I am," I repeat, meaning it. "You'd be surprised at how many people beneath the Hemisphere don't agree with Chancellor Bay."

She chuckles. "Let me guess, you're one of them?"

"Absolutely. I think the best way to approach this is peacefully."

"Now you sound like my father."

She leaves the line, searching for a seat in the mess.

I follow her.

"What would you have then?" I ask. "A war? That wouldn't make sense. More people would suffer. We'd be undoing all the progress we've made."

She stops short, and I nearly collide with her. "If you think we've made progress, then you're not as smart as your job title suggests—you're in my way. *Move*."

I hold my ground for a moment. She raises a brow.

Then I let her pass. But I don't give up.

"Planet conditions are getting worse." I join her at her chosen table, where she sets down her tray and sits. "We should all be living in the Hemisphere like we used to. It shouldn't be one way or the other. You of all people should know that."

"Why? Because of my mom?" She takes a bite of her porridge. "Apparently, you're not *just* a humanitarian but also a comedian. When's your next show? Sunsdown in No Man's Land?"

I stop myself from smiling. And the answer to the first question is yes.

But I also know it's more complicated than that.

"Vaida, the chancellor is a wicked man. You're right," I say quickly, because I'm losing her interest fast. She won't even look at me anymore. "He needs . . . "

Her eyes rise as she waits for me to finish. I know telling her the truth is a risk, but she needs to know she can trust me. That we're on the same side.

"This merger is a joke, okay? Chancellor Bay needs the Outskirts to help him reinforce the crack in the Hemisphere, but he doesn't plan on offering anything in return."

Vaida drops her spoon.

"I *knew* it," she says. "You're using us . . ."

Her voice trails off as a blood-curdling screams pierce the air.

In Vaida's rush away, she knocks over her tray. It clatters to the floor, splashing lukewarm porridge across the tiles and all over me. I grimace but don't hesitate, shoving through the crowd after her. By the time I reach the front of the Hub, a mass has already gathered.

A gust of frigid wind cuts the crowd like a blade.

Out in the shantytown, massive drops of black rain fall, sizzling as they hit. They eat through wood, canvas, metal beams—*everything*.

Including human flesh.

Those caught in the open sprint for cover. Some make it to the Hub. Some don't. Those who fall don't get back up. Steam rises from their pores as the rain carves into them, layer by layer, until they are nothing but heaps of flesh and bone.

I'm stuck still where I am. *Is this really happening?*

"Acid rain!" Commander Wardell bellows over the chaos.

The crowd parts as his guards haul him inside. He wipes himself down with a rag, shoving people away from the entrance.

"It's not the normal kind, sir," one of his men says. "It's taking down dwellings. Anything, or anyone, it touches."

The familiar bile burns in my mouth.

Graham.

He's still in our hut. In his hammock.

My head throbs as I struggle to stay calm.

"What should we do?" another guard asks.

Everyone turns to the commander.

"Get as many people into the Hub as you can," he orders, pointing in various directions. "Sound the alarm. Contact Matron Nost Far and the other Nost. Call the Hemisphere on whatever radio we have—I need to speak with Chancellor Bay. And until we confirm it's safe, Zone 9 is on

lockdown. Nobody leaves the Hub."
My mind glitches like an overloaded circuit board.
If I can't leave, I can't get to Nana.

11: TIMBER

Planet Violet Moon: Year 3083

The Dunes rise against the backdrop of an orange-and pink-swirled sky.

As I walk toward the *Iris*, I wonder if I'll see a sight like this again. Whether my fate is the mines or a mission in time, the moment of choice has come.

Behind the ship, Ere stretches out on a dune rock, basking in the morning sun. A few yards to her right lies a roped-off training pit, where the sand has been leveled and packed down.

The pit is about the size of the coral disc court the makers have set up on the shorefront. But instead of a hemp net stretched between two wooden stakes and a crate of dried and polished coral rounds, it's Mars and Rose in skin-tight, black leggings and matching sleeveless shirts. My guess is the outfits are ISR-issued. We don't have any synthetic materials on Violet Moon.

Everything sold in Makers Market is sustainably sourced.

"You look like someone roughed you up," is the first thing Mars says when he spots me.

"He looks exhausted." Rose puts a hand up to block the rising sun. "Did you get *any* rest last night, Timber?"

I place the book on top of a black storage container with a reinforced lid, set up just outside the entrance to the pit. "I was up all night studying the brief."

"Did you read it front to back, word for word?" Mars asks.

I swallow hard, clearing the phlegm. "Yes. I read it multiple times."

And when I wasn't reading, I was overthinking—about Raine, Kiki's offer to make me her successor, my near-death experience with desire, the fact that I'm going to be spending a lot of one-on-one time with Mars, and the mines summoning me like a malevolent spirit.

Mars crosses his arms. "Give me a rundown of the mission, then."

An all-too-familiar fatigue pulls at me. It seems every interaction we have is another opportunity for Mars to make me prove myself in some way. Still, I humor him because I know this. Mother and I made sure I knew this last night while she cluster-fed a starving infant who was sent to our dwelling right after midnight.

"At 10:00 today, we'll be traveling back in time to planet Nevarnost," I recite. "We'll arrive beneath the Hemisphere at exactly 2:00 PM on what they call Saturday, July 5th, 3051. From there, we will have approximately 45 hours to find Kevin Hale and Vaida Wardell."

Mars tilts his head, sizing me up. "Go on . . ."

"When we find them, we are to warn them of the storm, establish contact with ISR to request a rescue ship, and get them out of there. If time allows, we warn the others, too."

The thought of watching and possibly *feeling* hundreds perish makes my insides squirm.

"*If* time allows," Mars repeats, his tone growing terse. "Our mission is to ensure our targets survive so the greater timeline isn't altered. Everyone else is irrelevant."

I mess with the bandages around my wrists. "Nobody is irrelevant."

"You are. Right now." Mars steps closer, his arm muscles flexing as he tightens his fists. "Because now you're wasting training time. Let's not do that anymore. Got it?"

Wasting training time? He's the one who asked.

Mars strides to the center of the pit. "Now that you know the mission, Rose and I will show you some basic defense techniques and movements. Then you and I will have a go."

We will? Training, in my mind, meant learning to navigate comms, track someone, or read a holomap. Nobody mentioned anything about sparring.

Especially with Mars.

Mars kicks off his boots and takes his place opposite Rose in the sand.

"Watch carefully," he instructs me. "Observe Rose's technique."

"That almost sounds like a compliment," Rose teases, circling Mars. "Don't worry. I'll go easy on you."

The corners of Mars' mouth lift. "Don't flatter yourself."

He advances on his beloved. With elegance, she darts in front of him, flexing her wrist. Mars counters quickly, but Rose shifts in the sand at the last moment and jabs her palm upward towards his jugular. He blocks her just before impact, pulling her body close to his.

She grins.

"Nice try with the Derry Hook," I hear him breathe faintly in her ear. Then he looks over his shoulder at me. "Always read your opponent. Find their weak spot. Target pressure points."

Mars releases Rose, and she doubles back with a grunt.

He dodges her hit, tucks, and rolls in the sand. Back up faster than a flare cat.

Both Mars *and* Rose seem to move with a light-footedness I didn't realize was humanly possible. They don't spar, they dance. It's like watching Mars with the glowfish all over again. Rose is fierce and agile while Mars is grounded and strong. The two work together in perfect harmony, and for a moment, I forget that I'm watching a demonstration at all.

I'm supposed to mimic this? *Gods, I think I'm going to be sick.*

Confidence radiates from Mars as he evades Rose's next attempt. She glides through the sand, but Mars anticipates her wind-up and blocks another jab. Despite this, Rose is ready. Stabilizing herself, she alters her weight and kicks, sending Mars staggering back.

He manages his balance and bares his teeth.

"I thought you were going easy on me," he growls.

Rose shrugs. "I lied."

Mars lunges, wrapping his arms around her from behind and locking her in. She leers up at him, bending forward at the waist as she exhales hot air.

"Free yourself," Mars tempts her. "Show the slug how it's done."

They do enjoy this far too much. Rose giggles as she flails in his arms.

He adjusts his hold, and Ere sits up on her haunches across the pit.

The two careen to one side, and using the momentum of her weight, Rose whips herself around and aims for Mars' groin.

"Rosanna, don't you dare," he warns. "Don't—"

She knees him between the legs. They both stumble

back. Ere roars, but Mars puts up a hand to silence his flare while he catches his breath. "That was *not* part of the demonstration."

Rose curtsies at me. "When in doubt, knock 'em where it counts."

"Don't give him any ideas." Mars stifles a wince, and I don't have to touch him to feel the pain radiating through him. Then he gestures to me. "Alright, come on. Let's go. You're up."

My feet remain planted in the sand.

"Youuu can do it!" Rose cheers from the sideline.

But I don't know if I can.

Maybe I can tell him I'm ill. It always worked when I couldn't handle the stress of partner foraging in the woods or recreation lessons that involved team sports growing up.

"Any bugging day now," Mars says, his voice tight.

He stretches his neck. I still haven't moved.

"If you don't get over here, I'll drag you."

"Okay. Okay. I'm coming," I say quickly.

"Thank the Gods," he bites.

Despite every warning signal in my body telling me no, I force myself further into the training pit. Hot sun hits the back of my bare neck. My tunic clings to my skin, dampened from the sweat running down my shoulders. As my boots find their balance in the sand, I realize it's my Coming of Age Ceremony all over again. Anticipation torments me. Waiting for me is not a helpless moon worm but a headstrong boy whose energy both draws me in and terrifies me.

Mars lets out an impatient huff. We're facing one another now. Barely.

"Widen your stance," he instructs me. "Square your

shoulders. Fists up."

I do as I'm told, though none of it feels like me. My lanky arms are feeble compared to his sturdy build. And I've never fought anyone in my life. In moments of conflict, I prefer to walk away or accept the blame because it's easier that way. It makes the feelings go away.

As he advances, I inch back. "I can't do this."

"Do not tell me you can't do something. Try."

Sweat drips from his brow, the rising sun illuminating his form.

My heart beats wildly in my chest, so fast I can barely breathe. My muscles lock up. My knees won't bend. As he nears, I dart backward again. He grits his teeth, reaching out to knock me with his burly forearm, but I duck and slip under his swing without so much as grazing it.

A tightness persists. "I'm sorry—it's just—I have this *thing*—"

"Ditch the excuses. I don't care." He makes another advance, and in avoiding contact, my body falls back and collides with a heap of dune sand.

I bite back the sting in my tailbone.

A shadow crosses the sun.

Mars hovers over me. "On your feet. Now."

"I have to go get ready for a watch shift," Rose announces from the sideline.

"Then *go*," Mars spits without taking his eyes off me. "Take Ere with you."

Rose sighs and whistles for Ere. Together, they head into the *Iris*.

I put a hand up against the glare. "I'm—I'm not going to fight you."

"You're not going to fight me?" Mars cackles. "So, you're

saying that if and when we run into danger on this mission, I should leave you behind? That you won't have my back?"

I hadn't really thought of it like that. I hadn't really thought of anything.

"I get it. You want to protect me so I don't get hurt, but I—"

"You think I'm here to protect you?" He lets out a shallow breath. "Train you? Yeah, so you can pull your weight. But protect you? No bugging way. I couldn't care less if you get hurt or not—" He shakes his head, his scowl deepening. "We're done here. Be helpless for all I care. Don't come crying to me when you get yourself into a mess on Nevarnost."

As he storms off to the storage container, my chest burns heavy and hot.

Mars returns moments later, a handheld weapon with an interchangeable power cartridge in his hand. "Starting now, stop apologizing. It's redundant. Own who you are." He thrusts the device at me. "This is your glowbeam. If you won't engage physically, at least carry it with you."

I peer at the weapon in my hand. "There's no mention in the briefing of hostility. I don't really feel comfortable carrying a weapon. Is this really necessary to bring on the mission?"

He gapes at me. "I ask myself that about you."

A familiar ping draws our attention. We both look over to see Father approaching, carrying a medium-sized metal box in his hands.

"Training time is over," he says. "You'll be leaving soon."

"He isn't ready," Mars spits, sidestepping around me.

"I'll talk with him. Go change," Father tells Mars with a serious look.

Mars lets out another growl, kicks the sand, and storms

away into the *Iris.*

Father sets down the crate and kneels beside it, retrieving a transporter from a charging dock built into its interior. This is the first time I've been alone with him since the night of my trial. Even last night, he made himself scarce, avoiding all the questions I asked after we ate dinner, and dodging the ones I tried to sneak in while he was bathing my brothers before bed.

But he can't avoid me now. It's just the two of us, and I deserve answers.

He motions me forward. "Come here so we can program your transporter."

I do as he asks, setting my glowbeam on the crate. "Why didn't you tell me about this mission before today? Why was Mars the one to fill me in and not you?"

Father turns the transporter over, revealing the two crescent-shaped touchscreens. "Put your thumbs on the screens so the device can read your biometrics. It needs sixty seconds to fully sync with you. After that, I'll program it and have it ready for your departure."

My voice falters. "Father."

"I heard you." He motions again, his tone sterner. "But we don't have time for this right now. I will have a genuine conversation with you when you return, alright? I know this is a lot to take in, but my actions thus far have been guided by the very specific instructions I wrote to myself in the letter I found all those years ago. Deviating from the plan isn't an option."

I keep my hands stiff at my sides. "I'm going to the mines when I get back. There won't be time to have a genuine conversation."

"You aren't going to the mines." Father lets out a sigh.

129

"I'll deal with that too—*when* you get back. Now, come on. Please. You still need to get dressed."

With my lips pressed tight, I step forward and comply, placing my thumbs on the touchscreens. They glare green as they warm beneath my touch, reading my biometrics.

After a minute that feels like eternity, the device beeps. Father immediately takes it, then pops open the back compartment and begins fiddling with the inner wires and gears inside.

"Alright. All set." He shuts the back panel, sets the transporter away, and pulls a black canvas backpack from the crate. "A couple more things, then you can get ready. There's a set of mission clothes waiting for you in the latrine up on the bridge."

He hands me the backpack. "Inside, you've got a tablet connected to the *Iris*, a healer pack with basic first aid, two tactical shovel kits, and sunspecs to block out Nevarnost radiation. Mars' pack is full of rations, so you'll carry the holomap. It's preloaded with digital maps of the Hemisphere and the Outskirts, both of which you'll need to locate my nephew's residential unit."

Instead of talking at me, I wish he'd look at me and see that I'm not okay. But then the yearning goes away when I remember that comfort sometimes comes with hugs.

"You'll carry your breather with you and activate it when you arrive," he continues. "As you read in the briefing, the air conditions on Nevarnost are terrible. Before you leave, I'll give you a spritz of exo-skin to protect against acid rain or the harsh dust that precedes the storm."

"Got it."

"You're going to be fine. Don't let Mars intimidate you. If anything, I guarantee this will bring you closer." Before I have a moment to latch onto that statement, he adds, "Oh, I almost forgot. One last thing."

From the backpack's front pocket, he retrieves a tiny pouch and removes an antique brass column locket on waxen cord.

"What is it?" I ask.

Carefully, he slips it over my head. "This was originally in your healer pack, but I didn't want anything to happen to it."

He unscrews the pendant's top and tips a small purple pill into his palm.

"This is a venom neutralizer. Nevarnost is home to an invasive species called roakes. If you, or anyone else, get stung, use this pill immediately. Don't hesitate."

That doesn't sound ominous or anything. "Yes, I understand."

Father drops the pill back into the pendant and makes sure to tuck my glowbeam into the backpack's side strap. "Go get ready now. I'll be waiting near the mechanism pod."

I nod and walk off, the weight of what's being asked of me twisting my stomach into knots. I never wanted any of this. All I did was choose to spare a moon worm.

When I'm nearly at the *Iris*, I glance over my shoulder at Father once more.

He's looking at me the same way Mother did this morning before I left.

As if he may never lay eyes on me again.

12: MARS

Planet Violet Moon: Year 3083

I slam a palm against the cleansing stall door, and it swings back into the stark, silver tile.

Lightning bugs. Timber cannot be my mission partner. He'll ruin everything.

Condensation streaks heavily down the mirror in the washroom. Leftover steam rises, rolling off my pores and sizzling my blood with rage.

"I'm not going to fight you," I mimic him aloud, yanking a clean linen wrap off the rack and securing it around my waist. *"I don't feel comfortable carrying a weapon."*

Is that what he's going to say when his life is at stake? When there's a knife at his throat or a treacherous stretch ahead? *Oh, pardon me, sir. Please, put the knife away. We can all be friends here. You don't have to kill me.*

Nevarnost is unpredictable with its tyrant leader and unstable political climate. We're stepping into a battle that isn't ours. Not only must we convince them of a greater geographical threat, but we also have to ensure Vaida Wardell and Kevin Hale make it out alive. Some won't believe us. Others will reject us. And there *will* be violent encounters.

Now is not the time to plead pacifist.

I lean over the basin and splash cold water on my face from the spout. I glare at my reflection in the mirror above, at the black-inked rose on my chest. Then I uncap the metal tin of oakmoss-scented salve resting among Rose's essential oil perfumes.

Scooping out a bit, I massage the fragrant cream into the calluses on my left wrist, lingering over the deepest scar, healed but always there.

I've taught plenty of glowfish demonstrations. Up until my first run-in with Timber, I had never been so distracted that I failed to catch a harvesting rod if it slipped from a student's hand. But sometimes, late at night, I lie awake, replaying that moment over and over in my head.

What was it about *him* that threw me off?

And how could I have been so careless to put someone else's life in danger like that?

The minor sting Timber got was nothing compared to what it could have been. If I hadn't stepped in and taken a dorsal stinger to the hand, he'd be dead. These scars are my consolation. A reminder that it was a controlled failure. But we aren't in shallow water with a cluster of glowfish circling us anymore. Something will go awry on this mission if I'm not careful.

Timber *will* get hurt again.

What toll it will take on me this time is anyone's guess.

As I return the salve to the shelf, Rose's Confess Me Moth drifts into the washroom and lands on my shoulder.

"I have a secret," it croons in her voice.

"Do tell," I reply, sending it on its way.

While I clean my teeth, the same moth flutters back, landing on the tip of my brush.

"Come here and I'll tell you."

Without answering, I leave the washroom and step into the barrack off the bridge, the space Rose and I have long deemed our refuse room.

Most of the clutter gathering dust is hers. Stacks of fiction tales. Wax candles from the Makers Market. Glistening shell jewelry. Hand-woven bags spilling over with tinted solutions, dyed eye powders, and lip oils—the list goes on. Then there are the gifts she receives for watching. Gear piled in the corner. Her uniform crumpled on the one chair Ere hasn't clawed.

I nearly trip over a bucket of spearheads on my way to Rose's vanity.

"Another boring banishment. Nothing exciting ever happens around here." She sweeps a coat of charcoal balm onto her lashes. "Did the rest of training go well?"

"I'd rather not comment," I say. "And you're head of the watcher response division. If anything exciting happens, you're the first one they call. What more could you want?"

"So what. We banish people. Deal with the occasional flare cat attack. Toss someone out to sea once in a while, but nothing really exciting happens here, Mars. I want adventure. I want to be a part of something bigger. At least you get to time travel."

"If my deal with Elder Hale goes well, maybe you can."

I stumble over a hand-knitted rose plushie, a gift to Rose from someone in the village, and curse in Vio under my breath. "What is it you so desperately need to tell me? I'm running late, and I still need to get dressed."

"Good luck finding something clean to wear." She caps a mulberry gloss stick and files it away in her vanity. "You forgot to pick up the wash from the village again this morning."

I let out a growl. Ere echoes the sentiment from her perch.

"Not much of a secret." I dig through the clothing bin. "Besides, it wasn't my turn. Fifth Day is my day. First Day is yours."

Rose joins me in the mess. "First Day is not my day."

"*Yes*, it is."

"Well, regardless, I'm sure there's something for you to wear." She tugs on one side of a single boot as I pull on the other. "And that wasn't my secret, by the way."

"Julian better not be hiding in the *Iris* somewhere," I chide. She laughs and pulls out my other boot, which I snatch from her. "I mean it. This isn't a joke, Rosanna."

"Relax. Nobody's hiding in the *Iris*." She rummages deeper into the heap and holds up a black tunic, brown pants, and a leather jacket. "My secret is that I got you something."

I wrench the outfit out of her hands. "You knew these were here, didn't you?"

"Maaaaybe," she sings. Then she finds a small wooden box from the pile and offers it to me. "Just like I knew this was here, too."

"I don't have time for this." I start walking away.

She pulls me back. "Yes, you do. Open it."

I let out a long sigh.

"It's just a little something to celebrate your first mission. And to remind you I'll be thinking of you, and missing you, while you're gone."

I undo the latch on the box. "I'll only be gone a few hours your time."

As I lift the lid, Rose chews her bottom lip. Neatly fitted in silk cloth is a brand-new set of oil-based wax sticks—a myriad of vibrant colors, smooth and richly pigmented.

My fingers tingle, already imagining them streaked across blank parchment.

"The creatives were selling them at the Makers Market," Rose explains, buzzing with excitement. "They mixed and poured them right in front of me."

She lifts a bright starfish-yellow stick, turning it to show me an ombre fade into deep orange at the dual end. "Do you love them? I think they're perfect."

It's thoughtful. *Too* thoughtful.

I close the box and hand it back. "Return them."

Her smile falls. She trails after me until we reach the bridge. Then she cuts me off before I enter the washroom. "What do you mean? I thought you'd be happy."

She's always trying to make me happy. But that isn't her responsibility.

"It was a waste of crystal. I don't want them."

"That doesn't even make sense. I know you like them. I've seen you scour the creative carts on our weekly provision runs," Rose goes on. "You deserve these. You should enjoy them."

That's where she's wrong.

She tries placing the box back in my arms.

I don't take it. It slips, and wax sticks spill out onto the floor.

"Look what you've done now," she says.

"*Feaukere.* I didn't mean to!"

We drop to our knees, collecting the fallen sticks together. Ere sidles her way between us and prods at a coral pink with her paw, letting out a long mew.

"*U, Ere,*" I hiss, plucking the color from her fur. "*Gere ley dere.*"

"Can you just tell me why you don't want them?" Rose

asks, trembling. "Tell me what's wrong with them."

"Nothing is wrong with them."

"Is it because you think you don't deserve them?"

I freeze, a half-smooshed coral stick in my hand.

"You push me away on purpose." Her voice pinches. "The second I try to do something nice, you sabotage it. It's like you can't let yourself have anything good, and I don't get it."

She pauses a moment.

"I don't know if it's because you blame yourself for what happened in the mines or if you're holding onto this—"

"*Rosanna*," I growl.

"You need to forgive yourself!" she exclaims. "It wasn't your fault!"

But it was. All of it was.

"Just let me in. *Please*. I'm begging you." She dabs at her eyes and gathers the last of the wax sticks from the floor. "And if not me, then someone. Anyone. We can get you help. You don't have to go through this alone."

"You can't fix me!" I roar, and she flinches.

The motion scanner on the wall beeps.

I clench my jaw, steady my breath.

"Just . . . take them back."

I slip past her and swipe the screen.

The external camera zooms in on the gritty image of Timber waiting on the entry level. *Impeccable timing.* As always. I hit the button to let him in and turn back to Rose.

She tucks a wisp of raven hair behind her ear, her eyes red and swollen.

I hate upsetting her. I hate hurting her.

But all she has to do is hold on a little longer.

I rub the back of my neck. "I'm . . . I'm doing the best I can."

"No," she snaps before walking off. "You're choosing to let your mistakes define you."

Dune skulls. I slam my hand against the wall and let out a yell.

My clothes are crumpled at the base of the window overlooking the Dunes. I sling them over my shoulder, my eyes drawn to the horizon where the rocky edge meets the sky, knowing all too well the entrance to the mines is hidden somewhere out there, too.

Rose has always been perceptive. Another skill that makes her the best watcher in her league. And she's right. I don't think I deserve anything. Not after what I've done.

But maybe I can still make up for it.

Behind me, the lift splits open and spits Timber out.

He spots me and flushes immediately. Before he can apologize profusely for walking in on me half-naked, I head into the washroom and slam the door behind me.

Elder Hale waits for us by the mechanism pod at 9:50 AM sharp.

He stands by the transporter charging cell, which sits on a metal shelf jutting out from the *Iris*, eagerly checking his digipad and syncing devices for any last-minute adjustments.

A warm wind sweeps over us, picking up the sand and sending a slight metallic tang up my nose. My eyes water from the dry air. Hard to believe that in ten minutes, I'll be in a whole other ecosystem entirely. But the change of scenery will be good. It'll help me clear my head.

Rose is here, too.

I knew she would be. Even when she's angry, she shows up.

She lingers with another watcher by the *Iris'* left thruster. I don't know half the faces that tread the boundary lines, but I recognize Raine because he shadows trials from time to time.

Why he's here, I don't know. Nor do I care.

Then he says to me, "Is Timber around? I need to speak with him."

As if summoned, Timber exits the *Iris* behind us, now wearing a pair of dark purple pants, a dark blue tunic with leather neck details, and a gray weaponry belt. His supple leather boots catch a flicker of light, reflecting in the deep metallic black of his backpack.

Rose straightens. "Very handsome, Timber."

Her comment reddens his cheeks for the hundredth time since we've met.

I throw her a look, and she dusts a smidge of dirt off my black leather jacket. "A kind compliment, when deserved, is only right. You're handsome, too."

Instead of answering, I fold my arms tightly across my chest.

At the sight of Raine, Timber startles. "What—what are you doing here?"

He motions for the watcher to step aside, and their words trail off as they speak privately for a moment. I try not to stare, but I can't help it. The hush of their conversation carries.

Raine clutches his sash. "Did I do something back at Kiki's hut to upset you?"

Timber keeps his head down. "No. I'm fine. I promise."

"Please don't push me away."

"Raine, I'm not trying to."

Rose catches me listening in. I focus on making sure the cuffs of my jacket are tightly fastened until Raine murmurs something else that makes Timber tense. As I look up, he stalks off toward the path that'll lead him to the North Woods. I watch him until he's a speck on the horizon, silently wondering what anyone, especially a rugged watcher, would find appealing in a boy like Timber. I've only known him for a day and I'm ready to knock sense into him.

"There's an old ISR lodging unit in Zone 5 if you need a place to rest. I made sure to include extra tokens and IDs in your packs." Elder Hale sets down his tablet and fetches a chrome spray can from his kit. "Come on over, and I'll give you both a coating of exo-skin."

I leave Rose's side to get spritzed. A sticky mist falls over my entire body, setting in the next gust of wind. I flick it to make sure it's thick.

Elder Hale gives Timber the same dose, then speaks into his digiband. "Turn on the main charging cell. Log any glitches in transporter functions. Activate the trackers."

I notice Timber wringing his hands. *Is he always a nervous wreck?*

"There's still time for someone to back out and stay behind," I offer openly, despite my blood promise with Elder Hale. I mean really, it's a safety concern at this point. "There's a lot of logs to view and organize in the mainframe. Plenty of ISR missions to sort. Lots of busy work."

Timber glances between me and his father. "Is that an option?"

"No. It's not," Elder Hale replies flatly.

As his son sighs, Elder Hale opens the transporter charging cell, revealing the full set of transporters we have on hand. Six slots with two blinking lights at the bottom, one telling us the charge, and the other telling us which units are in active use.

He hands me mine. "I programmed Beta for you and Gamma for Timber."

"What happened to Alpha?" Timber asks, referring to the third empty slot.

"Alpha's been missing since the day I found the briefcase outside my lab," Elder Hale says, handing Timber his. "I have another screen set up in the *Iris*. I'll monitor you both."

I notice the way the slug analyzes the device in his palm and say, "They're good for one round trip to and from Nevarnost. When the return lights go off, you better have your thumbs on that scanner, or you'll be stuck in the year 3051 for good."

His lips draw into a thin line. "Got it."

"They're at full charge now. They should last the entire mission without issue." Elder Hale taps his digiband and brings it closer to his mouth. "Lux, activate Beta and Gamma."

"*Activating Beta and Gamma*," his AI confirms.

The transporters glow in our palms.

I position myself closer to Timber, bracing myself for the trip.

Rose steps forward and holds up a transparent sphere with a Confess Me Moth fluttering around inside. "This is in case you need a little encouragement."

Really? Has she learned nothing from our argument earlier?

She unzips my pack. I jerk away. "Oh, come on. Don't mess up the—"

She manages to stow the moth and plants a quick kiss on

my cheek. "Good luck to you both." I grimace and rub the lip gloss mark clean. Then she adds quietly, "Sounds like you and Timber might have more in common than you realize."

I roll my eyes. Leave it to Rose to say something outstandingly preposterous.

Elder Hale checks Timber's transporter one last time, then moves on to check mine.

"Don't forget," he says to me, nudging his glasses up his nose. "Vaida Wardell and Kevin Hale are your top priority. You cannot fail this mission. Your lives depend on it."

"Yep. I'm aware."

"Gather round." He invites Timber into our circle. "Press your thumbs into the scanners."

Mine lock into place with ease, riding the vibrations that confirm my prints. A green holographic light signals off the surface of Elder Hale's tablet as Timber does the same.

"Whenever you're ready," I say.

Sharp wind picks up around us as the crystals in the center of the transporters deepen their violet glow. The resounding hum intensifies, sending a pulse through my body.

More and more color drains from Timber's face with each whirl of sound. I glance beyond him for Rose, catching sight of her with Ere outside the *Iris*.

She offers me one last smile.

"Ready?" Elder Hale shouts over the roaring static trill.

"Ready!" I shout back.

The hum reaches its peak, and with a flash of violet light, we're gone.

13: KEVIN

Planet Nevarnost: Year 3051

. . . digital to-do list currently unavailable . . .

B odies lie in heaps inside the Hub.

Some moan in anguish. Others tend burns and patch wounds. More people whimper in pain, mourning loved ones who weren't fast enough to make it inside. There aren't enough able-bodied humans to help the fallen, so the Nost have stepped in.

My mask is strapped tight. Not because of dust, but because I can't stomach the stench of burnt flesh for more than a few seconds without blinking stars.

Hours have passed, and still, no one's given me any answers.

This is the Unity Arch tragedy all over again.

I wasn't there that day, but I remember racing through the aftermath like a virus in a corrupted hard drive, desperate to find my uncle. Nine-year-old me couldn't keep up with the medics as they pitched sickbay tents at every street corner between zones.

He isn't here, Kevin. Billy isn't here.

Nana dragged me home so fast, it felt like teleporting.

But he isn't gone, Nana. He can't be.

She held me for hours that night, running her fingers through my hair, whispering, *"Sometimes we lose people. That's just how life works."*

Apparently, she said the same thing the night my mother died. But instead of me, it was Billy she held. My mother was his twin, but since he was always off on ISR missions, she'd aged past him. By the time he woke up from cryosleep, she'd been dead for a year. He didn't even get to say goodbye. That was his last mission before he settled here to help take care of me.

Just let me see him. One last time. I need to find him.

An older man dips in front of me and projectile vomits all over the crossing table. I stop short to avoid the mess. He sputters, clutching his acid-burned throat. I force myself onward and rake the room for Graham's wild orange curls. We were both relocated here on assignment.

I have to make sure he's okay. It's the right thing to do.

Once I find him, though, my goal will be getting back to Nana.

The acid rain patters down on the Hub's concrete roof, a hollow, rhythmic sound beneath the hum of chatter and muffled sobs. It holds for now, but for how long? Even the commander, who's been trying to radio the Hemisphere since the fallout started, doesn't seem to know.

Across the room, he stands tense, soaked in sweat. Acid rain falls in short bursts all the time in the Outskirts. Sometimes it seeps into the Hemisphere's main sewer lines, causing temporary street closures. I once spent half a summer internship in hip waders underground, applying corrosion protectors to sanitation regulator boxes.

But this? This is different.

The suns that rose this morning have long since vanished in a sky that is now a muted gray with darker clouds rolling in from the horizon. Everything is changing too quickly.

We can't take it. They don't deserve it.

I approach one of the medics, dread filling me up as I ask about Graham.

"Graham Foster isn't here," she replies tersely, wiping her bile-covered hands on a rag.

"Please, just check again," I say, but she's already moved to the next Outskirter.

I steady myself against a wall, trying to box breathe the worry away.

"Water?" Lucy, the girl from before this disaster began, holds up a copper cup.

I shake my head, even though I'm thirsty, and she gives it to someone else instead.

I watch her move toward the back, where the Nost work frantically, stitching up gashes and rubbing ointment on burns. Even they know this is bad.

If the Hub is still standing, surely the Hemisphere is, too. Nana is safe for now.

But Graham. He's—He's—

A laugh cuts through the noise. It's faint, but I'd recognize it anywhere. Familiar. Obnoxious. Laced with sarcasm. I straighten, straining my ears, then trudge toward the sound.

"Graham!" I call out, picking up my pace.

Somehow I make it all the way to the back of the mess, where the Nost are crowded around the worst of the injured. I stumble forward and kneel next to—

Graham.

He's okay!

A breath rushes out of me, and I ruffle his curls.

He pulls back. "Why are you looking at me like that?"

An uneasy laugh escapes me. "No reason. Just happy you made it."

Graham adjusts the wrap on his burns.

"I would've been a dead man if a bunch of Nost hadn't come out of their hatches and dragged us inside." He nods toward a Nost tending to a young boy, a layer of skin hanging from his leg. My stomach rolls at the sight of bone. "I'm not saying I like the Nost now, but I wouldn't be alive if it weren't for them. It's bad out there, man. A lot of Outskirters didn't make it."

"I know. I'm just glad you're okay."

"My whole life flashed before my eyes. Scariest thing I've ever been through. Wait until I tell everyone back home. Cortés Residential is going to flip."

Graham keeps rambling, but I'm not listening anymore.

He's safe. That's what matters. But the relief is short-lived.

There's a bigger issue at hand: *I need to get home to Nana.*

She's been alone too long, and there's no telling how far this storm has spread. It may have reached the Hemisphere by now.

My attention lands on Commander Wardell, still in his corner, desperately trying the radio. It doesn't seem to be working. Acid rain probably took out the comm lines.

If that's the case, his efforts are useless.

As I watch, Vaida appears behind him. She waits until the commander is just distracted enough, then her fingers dart toward his pocket. In one smooth motion, she swipes his scanner card and scurries off toward the kitchen.

Commander Wardell doesn't notice. Neither do the guards.

A girl who can hold the attention of an entire room full of Outskirters mid-breakfast when a Hemisphere boy—AKA me—embarrasses himself, yet moves with such subtlety?

Now that's interesting.

Whatever her deal is, scanner cards mean Hemisphere access. And if she knows a way in amid the lockdown, I'll do whatever it takes to go with her.

"Do you think these will scar?" Graham's voice pulls me back.

He holds up his metal cup, squinting at his reflection as he prods the burns on his forehead. "Maybe they'll make me seem rough."

"You'll be fine," I tell him. "Stay here."

"Not like I was planning on going anywhere."

He keeps talking, but I'm already moving.

I press my shoulder against the swinging door near the provision line and slip into the kitchen. The faint stench of sour milk and overripe fruit guides me down the hall and into a supply room lined with barrels of bulk rations.

Through a gap in a curtained entryway, I catch a glimpse of purple-and-brown hair. Slowly, I pull back the curtain, careful not to startle her. But Vaida and the Nost she's with are locked in a practiced rhythm, shifting crates of rotting produce aside.

Every move is deliberate. One box against the wall, another stacked neatly on top. Eventually, a hidden compartment is revealed beneath the floor. Vaida hooks her fingers into the lock, but just before she heaves it open, she stops.

Her tone is sharp. "What part of 'leave me alone' don't

you understand?"

Add *extremely observant* to her list of admirable qualities.

I step into the room. "You're going to the Hemisphere, aren't you?"

This time, she looks back at me. "Why? Are you going to tell my father? Because, in case you weren't aware, he's a little preoccupied."

"That's why it was so easy for you to swipe his scanner card." I move closer, and she holds her ground. "Either he was too distracted, or you've done this plenty of times before."

Her eyes lift. "Oh, really. Is that so?"

Our last conversation didn't end as well as I'd hoped. She's already decided that because of my last name and home, I'm the enemy. I need to be careful—and honest—with my words.

"What you're doing is none of my business," I say, running a hand through my hair more than once. "My nana is home alone, and I need to get back to the Hemisphere to check on her."

Vaida crosses her arms. "Why? What's wrong with her?"

"A mid-to-late stage of Alzheimer's disease. I'm her caretaker."

My answer softens her expression, for only a moment. Then she catches herself and finds her scowl again.

"Perhaps we should let him come," her Nost friend says.

"Are you joking? He'll only get in our way."

"But he seems . . . . desperate."

"I am—" I say quickly. "I wouldn't ask if I wasn't."

Vaida's nostrils flare. "Obviously."

"I promise I won't get in your way," I assure her, though it doesn't change her expression at all. *I wish I knew what she was thinking.* "I've read a lot about Zone 10. I might be useful."

"You never stop trying to prove how much you think you know, do you?"

"I'm not trying to prove anything. I'm trying to have a conversation."

She doesn't respond. Instead, she bends and heaves open the floor compartment.

The panel slams against the grimy tile, stirring up a cloud of dust. I step beside them, and together we peer down a rope ladder that vanishes into the darkness below.

Vaida brushes past me, letting her friend go first. Then she grabs the rope and maneuvers her body through the gap. "If you slow us down, we're ditching your ass."

As she descends into the void, the tension in my shoulders fades.

"Does this mean I can come?" I call after them.

Vaida looks up, her silver nose ring catching the dim light. "What does it look like? Hurry the hell up, and close the hatch behind you."

I let out a laugh. "I won't slow you down."

Her voice rises from below. "Right, because you know all about Nost Territory. More than the actual Nost, even. How could I forget?"

A goofy grin spreads across my face, but it fades quickly.

All joking aside, I *do* know quite a bit about Nost Territory. Uncle Billy's journals made sure of that. Most Nost live among us peacefully, but some forbid us from invading their space. We may be free to inhabit the ground above, but the mazes, chasms, and tunnels below? Those belong to them.

My foot finds the first rung of the ladder. I loop my

fingers around the edge of the compartment door to swing it shut behind us. If we get caught, this could end badly. But this might be my one and only chance to get back to the Hemisphere.

To Nana.

14: TIMBER

Planet Nevarnost: Year 3051

A s the bright light dims, a thousand stars fade behind my eyes before my vision finally settles.

My boots find solid ground. We've landed in an alleyway of sorts as planned. I relax my thumbs, easing them off my transporter, and let the fleeting stillness in the air blow over.

Time travel. *I've just traveled through time.*

The thought barely sinks in as I desperately cling to my breather, struggling to activate its constriction. The briefing warned of poor breathing conditions, but nothing could have prepared me for a dust so thick it smothers the air. Each breath becomes more unbearable than the next.

I can't even imagine what it's like outside the Hemisphere.

Constriction still inactivated, I start coughing. Mars steps in to reach the control gauge for me, but I gesture him away, signaling I've got it.

"Sure. Because suffocating instead of letting me help you makes sense." He leans against the stone wall of a building to our right, arms crossed, while I struggle.

Through another fit of hacking, my fingers find the right

setting. The material stretches and forms tightly around my face. Filtered air pours into my lungs. I take an extra-deep breath to combat the lightheadedness and the shaking in my legs.

Mars peels away from the wall. "You really do have a thing, don't you?"

"It's a—" I cough one last time while my breather accommodates. "Sensory thing."

"I really don't care to know the details." He powers up his digiband. "Just don't let it get in the way of this mission. We'll need the holomap. Get it out and scope the area."

As I watch the holographic projection of our timer roll off Mars' digiband, a solid 45:00:00 kickstarting our pressuring countdown, I realize it doesn't matter what I say to him.

Before I left, Raine told me he needed honesty, communication, and vulnerability to continue our friendship, that it hurts him when I shut down every time he tries getting close. It stung when he said it. I'm not sure if we'll make amends, but Mars is different.

There's no expectation. I could tell Mars the truth about my curse, and it wouldn't faze him. In fact, he might be the only person I could tell at this point without fear of it causing a rift between us. He's already decided he hates me. He's been upfront about that since we met.

I have nothing to lose.

"If you're curious—"

"I'm not," he says, putting his transporter away. "I just want the holomap."

"I'm getting it." I open the side compartment in my pack and pull out the tablet Father gave us. "But it really isn't a sensory thing, it's more like a curse . . ."

He ignores my comment, his attention on the holomap

now hovering between us, which quickly becomes a full 3D projection of the Hemisphere—a dome sectioned into eight zones.

As he zooms in, our location trackers confirm we're in Zone 8: Cultivation, tucked between a learning center and a conservatory for spiritual development.

"It's a curse because when I physically connect with someone, I feel all their emotions and hear all their thoughts. Most of the time, it's painful and tormenting."

"We're two zones away from Kevin Hale's residential unit," Mars says, once again disregarding my words, which, surprisingly, settles me. "Let's cut through Unity Commons so we can avoid the trouble of patrol questioning us at each barrier."

As he starts walking, I stow the holomap and follow him toward the alleyway's exit. "But that's *why* I don't like to be touched, and why I like my personal space."

"I don't plan on touching you. Not now, not ever. So will you shut up?"

"Yes," I reply quickly. "I'll shut up."

Whether Mars fully understands the complexity of my confession or not, the tension in my body deflates. It doesn't change my curse or guarantee I won't be affected by it while I'm here, but it's a start.

Gods, I wish it were that easy with everyone else in my life.

At the edge of the building, the alleyway opens into a courtyard where old recreational equipment sits covered in a layer of red dust. Mars unsheathes his glowbeam, keeping it up and ready as we navigate the endless curves of roped climbing equipment.

A corkscrew slide made of hard, chipped plastic delivers

its sliders to a patch of worn artificial grass below. Hover swing sets, held in place by the magnetic pull of their metal frames, sway ever so slightly with the next cycle of simulated wind. Beneath my feet, old, faded chalk drawings litter the tar, permanent unless someone washes them away because it never rains.

I stare at a poorly drawn tree, which resembles the one painted beneath the *Iris'* hull.

It's hard to believe Father used to live here. I didn't expect much, given it's the warm season, lessons aren't in session, and even if they were, the population of children is practically nonexistent given Nevarnost's contraceptive mandate, but if this courtyard could tell me how it feels, I'd imagine it'd tell me it feels hollowed out and forgotten, too.

We reach the other side, and Mars slows when he spots the patrol officers in black face masks stationed at the entrance of Unity Commons. I'm drawn to the scattered piles of crumbled stone in the center of an otherwise industrial-style park. According to the briefing, that's what's left of their Unity Arch, which once symbolized a strength in community.

Now, its remains sit guarded by their version of watchers.

A group of teenagers crosses through the commons. The patrol officers stop them, check their IDs, and make them turn out their pockets before letting them pass through.

"If they catch us with ISR-issued tech, they'll alert someone." Mars' clench tightens on his glowbeam. "I'm going to go search the other side. See if there's another route. Stay here."

Before I can protest, he sprints off, leaving me hunched behind a climbing wall missing half its grips. His wisps of red and black disappear around the bend. I rest my head against the wall and close my eyes. It's probably better this way.

And he'll come back. *Right?*

"Hey, man! What's up?"

My eyes spring open.

I stiffen and straighten as the group of teenagers from earlier approaches.

As they get closer, a splotchy-faced boy in a dark purple sweatshirt says, "Oh, sorry, dude. From far away, you kind of looked like one of our friends. My bad."

A girl in a puffy maroon vest with auburn hair done up in two buns nudges the boy in purple. "Yeah. Couldn't tell behind the *mask*."

"That is a cool mask," the boy adds. "How many tokens did you pay for it?"

I can't actually tell them where I got it from. What am I supposed to say? That breathers won't be invented by ISR until several years from now? That I time-traveled here?

I look back in the direction Mars left, hoping any second now he'll return with a scowl and some rude comment to chase them off.

"I'm sorry. I'm just waiting for my friend."

The boy exchanges a look with the others. "You know, now that I think about it, I could use a new mask." He steps closer. "Or that fancy backpack you've got on."

"Well, these are mine but—"

He's already closed the space between us.

His friends follow, five against one. It would only take one to lock me in, another to put their sweaty hands on me, and I'd be a trembling mess. Left to ride out whatever feeling comes with malicious intent. The reality of everything I'd lose in the process starts to sink in, too. My transporter, healing kit, intel, holomap, protective gear—the list goes on.

I need to get out of here. *Now.*

"I don't want any trouble, okay?"

The boy laughs. By the time I've realized they've backed me in a corner between the climbing wall and an interactive puzzle display, it's too late.

My breath hitches. There's nowhere to run. One of the boys rolls up his sleeves, and I unsheathe my glowbeam as a last attempt.

It gets caught as I try and flip it around. "Please—"

The boy and his crew mock me, about as convinced of this empty threat as I am. I've no intention of pulling the trigger, and they know it.

The broadest of the bunch knocks my glowbeam out of my hands.

Two more grab my arms and whip me across the pavement like a sack of sand. Pain hits my ribs as I land. I curl up into myself and clutch my sore stomach while their sickening thoughts ring out:

What a loser.

God, this kid is such a wimp.

We're going to make bank on this one.

Once the nausea subsides, I try to block out what they're doing with my pack. They dump out my supplies, paw through emergency clothes, and unroll gauze from my kit. Worse, the boy in dark purple rips off my breather and sends toxic air into my lungs.

As the coughing takes over, a sliver of light grazes the top of his head.

Another shot explodes behind us, fracturing a grip from the climbing wall. When the dust settles, Mars rushes forward, glowbeam barrel up, ready for another go.

"Step away from the slug," he snaps. "Or else you'll wish you had."

The boy snorts. "Or *what?* You're gonna blast me?"

He passes over me, thumping my head, and I groan.

"I said or *what*," the boy repeats, tearing a double-pointed blade from his sleeve.

Mars cocks his weapon. "Blast. Stun. Obliterate. Whatever works."

The boy and his crew surround my mission partner. This could have been over in seconds. I could have stood up for myself earlier, but I didn't. Instead I let my curse win. Again.

Now Mars is going to suffer because of it.

All at once, the group of teenagers advance. In sync with the launch of the boy's blade, Mars fires a blast that strikes the boy square in the chest. The boy is thrown back in the air. Landing rigid, his body slams into a hover swing set and drapes across the middle seat.

Mars blows smoke off the barrel.

All eyes go wide. Including mine.

The posse scatters, taking the smoldering puff of sulfur-scented smoke from the blast with them. When they're gone, Mars stalks across the recreational yard, yanks my breather from the boy's front pocket, and returns to where I'm now seated.

He drops the breather in front of me. "Get up. Gather your stuff. We have to go."

"What—what have you—" I can barely get the words out. There's a subtle throb in my temples that won't go away, much like the pain in my gut. "What will happen to him?"

Mars sheathes his glowbeam. "Dunno. Don't care. Not my problem."

157

Not his problem? I force myself up slowly.

The ground is uneven, but it's more because I still can't see straight. "We should at least call a medic. It's the right thing to do."

"He just roughed you up, and you want to help him? Unbelievable."

As Mars turns to survey the mess, he clutches his shoulder, where a streak of violet blood gushes from a wound on his left bicep.

I gasp. "You were hit."

He wipes his bloody hands on his pants. "I'm fine. Pick up your stuff."

But I know for a fact it isn't fine from all the times I've watched Kiki stitch up Raine after a watch shift gone wrong, or when she speaks of proper cleaning methods. If Mars doesn't tend to that wound, he might lose too much blood or risk tissue damage and infection.

"I really think we should stop and take a look at it," I say.

"And I think you'd better drop it," he says back.

He bends over to pick up my pack.

Blood continues to drip down his sleeve, soaking his cuffs.

"It's not clotting, Mars. You need sutures."

"Seeing as I don't know how to do sutures, you're not touching me, and I'm not *letting* you touch me, we're going to forget about the—" He checks every pocket and zipper on my pack. "Where is your transporter? Do you have it on you? It isn't here."

"Oh, Gods." I struggle to get the words out. "There—there was a girl. She was going through my stuff. She must have taken it. She could be anywhere by now."

He drops my pack. "Dune skulls. This can't be happening."

"I'm sorry," I say quickly. "I'm so sorry."

"I told you not to say that anymore," he bites back.

"Okay. I know. I'm—what are we going to do now?"

Mars quickly repacks my gear and thrusts my bag into my arms. "We're going to go to the lodging unit in Zone 5 to figure this out," he states bluntly, walking on. "And you're going to do exactly as I say, because now we're behind schedule."

I follow, listening as he swears in Vio under his breath.

My entire body shakes. In less than 44 hours, a storm is going to wipe out all the structures, zones, and inhabitants of this planet.

Without my transporter, I'll die with them.

15: VAIDA

Planet Nevarnost: Year 3051

I'm not sure if I should appreciate or mock Kevin's reaction to the tunnels.

His eyes widen like a child witnessing their first solar flare show with every glimpse into the Nost world. I can't deny I share his admiration. Unlike the barren surface, each twist and turn down here reveals something new. Underground waterfalls where clear water tumbles over rocks and vibrant flora. Whole coves of sprouted herbs in neatly tended rows. Caverns of amethyst dreamer stones, dangling from stalactites, so Nost dreams will come true.

Even the vines growing in the stone walls bring Kevin to near tears.

"It's a whole ecosystem," he whispers as we pass through a flutter of six-winged moths, whose wings scatter trails of sparks through the air.

One lands on his shoulder, and I catch myself staring too long.

But the minute we start moving again, I remember who we are, where we come from, and how everything that happened an hour ago is yet another tragedy that could've been prevented had his uncle made a different choice.

My stomach sours at the memory of rotting flesh dripping from bone. Bodies facedown in the mud. Blood-chilling screams shaking the Hub. People I knew, fear-stricken with acid-stained hands—those images will haunt me until the day I die. There was nothing I could do for any of them.

And Kevin still claims he wants peace?

Funny how one trek through another species' world can bring out the illusion of innocence in someone. So much so that, for a fleeting moment, I imagine trusting Kevin and his intentions.

But Soren was someone I felt like I could trust at first, too.

He sat behind me in weekday lessons. He never gossiped behind my back like all the girls with enough tokens to buy a decent hairbrush. His father was always off negotiating Hemisphere affairs. His mother drifted in and out of his life. But I felt for him, and I'd watch him play Holoblocks by himself from my cramped third-story unit in the Angelou Residential block.

A part of me still sees Soren as that lonely seven-year-old, collecting holographic blocks from a projector cube. Then I remember people grow up and become the spitting image of those who raise them, whether they mean to or not. Soren may not be a ruthless dictator, but he knew exactly what he was doing when he lured me to his bed. I should've known when I woke up the morning after, and Chancellor Bay himself escorted me out of the building with distaste, that I'd indeed been played. Eliminated from Soren's metaphorical Holoblock game in the first round.

He scored. I took the penalty.

"I've never seen anything more beautiful," Kevin says in the darkness.

This sound of his voice makes my body stiffen. He

wouldn't be any different than Soren. Just another descendant of a leader who failed us. But when he mentioned his nana, home alone with the memory sickness that's taken so many of the older generations, Outskirters included, I caved—a moment of weakness.

It won't happen again.

"How are you not in complete awe of all this?"

"After the first time you've seen it, it loses its *awe*," I mutter.

Another moth lands on his hand before fluttering down the tunnel, triggering the glow orbs embedded in the grooves along the walls. They pulse to life around us, up into the cavern overhead, where thousands more blink on, secreting mucus as they awaken.

Kevin's breath hitches. "Oh, I very much disagree."

He pulls his mask down, revealing his full face for the first time. He grins as he plucks an orb from its groove and lets it pulse in his palm, the goopy residue slipping between his fingers.

Nia steps up beside me. "These orbs were your favorite the first time I brought you here."

"Well, yeah," I say under my breath. "But don't tell *him* that."

"They're ethereal like stars," Kevin says.

He's right. They shimmer in clusters like constellations I've only ever heard about. You can't see the stars from Nevarnost. The dust smothers the night. This is the closest we'll ever get.

As Kevin smiles again, I study the curve of his lips, not noticing Nia's tentacle resting flush against my arm. "Interesting," she murmurs. "You find his reaction to all this endearing."

I jerk away.

"I do not." Heat creeps up my neck, and I walk ahead. *I should've just come alone.* "We should keep moving. If we're going to make it to the Hemisphere in this century, that is."

"Right." Kevin hands the orb to Nia. "I need to get back to my grandmother."

"Relax. You'll get there," I say, picking up my pace.

Nia catches up to me and lifts the orb to light our way.

With Kevin trailing behind, she lowers her voice. "There's something I need to talk to you about." I keep my eyes pinned on the enveloping darkness ahead. "I spoke with Zee."

Fuck. Whatever happened to patient confidentiality?

I grit my teeth. "Nia, I don't want to talk about this right now."

I motion to Kevin, who's 'studying' Nost hieroglyphics behind us.

He clears his throat. "I can, uh, walk ahead a ways if you—"

Nia's left tentacle jets out in front of us, halting us both.

"Someone's coming," she says quickly. "You two must hide."

Before he can blow my cover, I grab a fistful of Kevin's flexi-skin jacket and yank him into a shadowy alcove. My body slams into place beside him, squishing us together.

A familiar Nost, Osa, wanders into the passageway and spots Nia.

"*Hyogg Nyogg,*" she says.

"*Ayogg,*" Nia replies.

Nost dialect was a required course back in grade school. I skipped most of those classes, and it's not often I regret it. But now is definitely one of those times.

Kevin leans forward, straining to listen.

"They're talking about the harvest," he mumbles. "She wants Nia to help."

Of course he speaks Nost. I shift so I'm not pressed against his chest. Which is annoyingly solid. And despite spending all day in the stifling desert heat, his cologne is still fresh.

"She's going with Osa. They're leaving right now." He peers down at me, and I ignore how close our faces are. "How are we going to get through Nost Territory without her?"

"We don't need her. I know these caverns—you're on my foot."

"What? I am not on your foot," he says.

I elbow him in the ribs. "Yes. You are."

He doubles over, stifling a groan. "Gah! What the heck was that for?"

We both lunge forward at the same time. I slam into him, and his arm catches me around the waist, stopping me from face-planting.

"Get. Your hand. Off me," I say, disregarding the way his touch sends my pulse soaring.

Kevin drops his hand. "Sorry, but I wasn't going to let you fall."

I push past him into the open. "I don't need you to catch me."

The last bits of Nia and Osa vanish around the corner, along with the glow orb's light. Darkness closes in around us. I can't believe she left me here. With . . . *him.*

"Can we just be honest for a second?" Kevin says. "You've had a problem with me since we met, and I don't get it. I haven't done anything to you."

Without answering, I start walking into the inky black. I

don't have to listen to him. Without Nia here, I'm running the show. And Kevin better shut up, or I'll ditch his ass.

"Oh, you're just going to ignore me?" He scrambles in behind me. "You're just going to walk off into the dark without a clue where you're going? That makes sense."

"For your information, I do know where I'm going."

"Great. That's great. You're still avoiding me, though."

I stare at my feet, though I can't see them in the dark, praying I don't lead us into a bottomless saccharine pit or a nectar bat nest. "Not everything is about you, Kevin."

"I know that." His chuckle echoes around us. "But I've been trying to be kind to you because you're interesting, and I don't meet a lot of interesting people around here. I just don't get the aversion. I can't help where or who I come from. I'm just a guy."

Just a guy. Soren was just a guy. The chancellor is just a guy. It's always *just a guy.*

"Maybe you just have to accept that I don't want anything to do with you, no matter how nice or kind you are. You should really work on handling rejection."

"Rejection? I'm not asking you out. I'm just trying to get to know you."

I whip around, hearing his boots scuff to a halt. "Why? We're not in this together. I only let you come because I felt bad about your grandmother. That's it. Literally."

There's a pause, then he says, "I'm sorry, but I really can't handle having a whole conversation in pitch-black darkness—Lux, activate illumination setting."

A sharp beam of light flares from his wrist for a split second, then dies.

"That's weird. Lux, activate illumination setting."

This time, nothing happens.

"Looks like your digiband doesn't work." I run my fingers along the rough stone walls, searching for a stray glow orb. Sometimes they bloom in random places. "Are you just going to stand there, or are you going to help me look for light?"

"The acid rain must've fried more than just the comm lines," he says from somewhere in the dark. "If Lux is down, that means anything connected to lower exospheric satellites is too."

My nails touch something sticky. The gooey glob pulsates with heat and skitters with smolder bugs. I grimace and wipe them away. They smear, leaving a smoky smell behind.

The orb awakens between us.

"If tech is down, that means anything connected to the main power source in the Hemisphere will lag," Kevin continues. "Including Nana's air filters."

"She's really important to you, isn't she?"

He nods. "She's all I have."

I know what that's like. And for a split second, I want to tell him that. I want to say I understand how he feels. But the last few times I've let someone in, it ended in nothing but hurt. I can't afford that kind of pain right now. Not when I'm so close to ending the chancellor. Not when I'm this close to securing a safe place for me, my people, and my unborn child.

"We'll figure it out," I say before walking on.

Kevin stays close as we navigate the winds and turns. Nothing looks familiar, but I rely on the intuition swirling inside me. I've traveled these tunnels with Nia hundreds of times.

Then we pass beneath a dripping arch of rock I've never

seen before.

The rational part of me says to turn back. But the pull in my belly urges me forward.

"Are we anywhere near the Hemisphere?" Kevin asks, following me up a set of stone steps that lead to a platform stretching into another network of tunnels.

I wish I knew. "I think so."

"Does anything look familiar?"

Not even a little. "Yes. Now please stop asking."

The walls taper on either side of us, and oval-shaped openings in varying sizes appear in the rock. They radiate a bluish-teal light, making the glow orb useless, so I ditch it.

My heart begins to pound. I have no idea where we are.

Why did I bring us here?

Ahead, the passageway dead-ends against a solid rock wall.

"Everything alright?" Kevin asks.

Silence settles between us as I look around at nothing but oval openings. Crouching, I peer through one into the cavern beyond. At the far end there's another path, a possible way out.

That's good enough for me.

"It's all coming back to me now." I brush myself off, forcing confidence into my words. "The Hemisphere is on the other side of this cavern."

Kevin glances around, brows furrowing. "I don't know, Vaida. Something about this place feels off. I vaguely remember reading about—"

"Yes, I know. You've read about everything."

"I'm just sharing my thoughts," he says calmly.

"And I'm sharing mine. This is the way out."

Kevin pats the top of the opening. "We'll have to crawl

through."

I take one look at the narrow space and immediately search for another.

His expression shifts. "What's wrong with this one?"

"Um, it's too small. Me and my fabulous fat self are not fitting through that."

A flush creeps up his neck. "Don't say that. You're not fat. You're . . . beautiful."

I laugh. "Where did you hear me say I wasn't beautiful?"

"Why are you laughing? I'm being serious."

"Yeah, me too. I'm not afraid of that word." I spot a more suitable gap farther down the wall. "People act like the worst thing you could be is fat. Beauty's subjective. I like who I am."

"I never said being fat is a bad thing, and I agree about beauty being subjective." He quickly runs a hand through his hair. "I mean, I'm too. . . tall, I guess? Nerdy? I don't know."

"But I'm beautiful? You mean it?" I tease, hoping he'll relax.

I only manage to deepen the shade in his cheeks.

"I mean . . . yeah." He looks away for a moment. "You are."

For a second, I almost give into the way my lips tug. *Almost.*

Then I stop myself and crawl through my chosen opening before Kevin can see the red creeping up my own neck. *It's a compliment.* It means nothing. *Soren called you beautiful, too.*

"I know I'm beautiful, Hale. I don't need a man to validate me." My feet hit the ground on the other side of the wall, and I bend down to peer at him. "Also, the flattery doesn't change my obvious aversion to you. Nice try, though."

His face appears in the gap. "I never once assumed you needed a man to validate you."

I step aside as he climbs through. "Now you're catching on. Good for you."

Once he finds his balance, he straightens his backpack, checks it like something might be out of place, then secures it again. "You can believe I have some ulterior motive all you want, but I meant what I said. I've meant everything I've said."

"I'll try remembering that—"

A giant glob of exo-slime drips from above and lands between us with a wet squelch, splattering gunk across our pants and boots.

I unsheathe my brother's knife from my sleeve so it's ready in case I need it.

Thick, writhing, goop-coated vines slither through the nooks and crannies of the domed, porous rock surrounding us. In our wake, they convulse like living organisms along the walls and stretch over every oval-shaped opening, sealing us in.

Including the shallow archway that was supposed to be our way out.

"Vaida," Kevin breathes, inching closer, putting his hand on my arm. "I know what this is. I remember reading about it in my uncle's journals."

I think I know what this is too.

Together, we look up into the vast, cavernous space above us.

Thousands of translucent, egg-shaped cocoons hang in glistening bunches. Each one cradles a squirming embryo, vaguely resembling a Nost.

And drifting among them—Specters.

But not the small, divine spirits Zee used on me back in the healing tent. These are massive. Brighter. Warmer. More powerful. The Nost may value life above all else. But they depend on the Specters to create it. And this? This is where that life comes to incubate.

If there's one place we didn't want to be caught, it's here. This is the Hallow.

16: MARS

Planet Nevarnost: Year 3051

"**M**ake sure you flush the wound thoroughly with the antiseptic," Timber tells me.

I grit my teeth, letting another blood-soaked linen square fall at my feet before I rinse the wound. Fumbling for the bottle of solution on the counter, I uncap it and spray the liquid onto my skin, wincing through the burn. Then I yank the sterile linen from my shoulder to pat it dry.

The washroom is barely big enough to fit the latrine, washbasin, and a cleansing stall with faded tiles. It wasn't my first choice, but neither was stopping to locate a transporter.

When I'm done, I exit the cramped room and step back into the communal space of the lodging unit. Timber hunches over the sleeping mat, carefully arranging a spread of healing supplies. A large, half-circular window spans the opposite wall, dimmed by a tinted privacy screen. It allows us a view of the Hemisphere and the desert beyond, while corkscrew lamps that hang from the ceiling overlay the space in a neon-purple diffusion.

A rickety air filter whirls overhead, providing enough clean air to go without our breathers, so I tuck mine into my pocket. The soft light illuminates Timber as he unwraps a fresh needle and lines it up next to a pair of tweezers, scissors, and a stack of gauze.

He glances up at me. "There's no numbing ointment. Or suture forceps."

"It's fine. I don't need them." I settle on the far side of the sleeping mat, just far enough to keep him quiet but close enough to follow his instructions. His so-called curse, whatever it really is, doesn't concern me.

Timber crosses his legs, facing me. "Okay. Here we go . . ."

I swallow hard and give him a curt nod.

"First, keep the wound as closed as possible. The smaller the gap, the tighter the stitch."

I pinch my skin, biting back the pain, ignoring the violet blood smearing my fingers.

"With the curved end of the needle, start at one edge of the wound, about two to three millimeters—"

"Don't make it complicated." I hover over the gash.

Timber leans in and watches my shaking hand. "I'm not trying to. Silkworm fiber is flexible. It knots easily. Keep it smooth as you pass the needle in and out."

I tense my jaw and drive the needle in. Trembling, I pull the fiber through.

"Use the gauze to control the bleeding. You need a tight enough knot—"

"Are you sure you can't do it?" I say through gritted teeth.

The needle slips from my fingers. I grasp the gauze, pressing hard to soak up the blood, and the searing pain simmers in my stomach more than I'd like to admit.

"Keep pressure on it for a moment," Timber says gently. He picks up the needle I just dropped. "And this isn't sterile anymore. You'll need a new one."

"*This* isn't working," I say, and the light in his eyes fades. "We all have strengths. Tending to wounds is one of yours. I saved your life back there. You need to pull your weight."

He hesitates before opening another needle. "I can't. I told you why."

"I really don't care." I ball up the bloody gauze in my fist and grab my tablet from the sleeping mat's side table. "You're the reason I'm here. These instructions are impossible. Suck it up and stitch me up so I can focus on finding your transporter in the meantime."

Timber goes pale. "You really want to risk me hearing and feeling everything going on inside your head? Because no offense, but you seem like someone who wouldn't like that."

The guys in the mines used to talk about people born with a sixth sense. I didn't buy into it then, and I'm not buying into it now. I'm half-convinced his curse is just a figment of his imagination, like all the other concerns rattling around inside his head.

"I'm not worried about it." I pull up the population manifest on my tablet. "What did the girl in the recreation yard look like?"

Timber exhales slowly. "I really don't want to feel your anger or judgment, Mars."

"And I really don't want stitches, but we don't always get our way—what did the girl look like? What color was she wearing? We can eliminate non-applicable zones."

Timber reluctantly gets up and moves to my side of the sleeping mat. New needle in hand, he grabs another square of gauze.

"She had reddish-brown hair," he says. "She was wearing

maroon."

"Alright. That puts her in Zone 3: Provisions. They wear maroon."

While I scroll the identification directory, Timber assesses my injury before his fingers graze my skin. A chill courses through my body, sending prickles across my arm. Though I can't see exactly what he's doing, I can imagine based on his movements: the mild pressure he applies, the sting that accompanies the needle's weave, the repetitive pull of soaked cotton squares, and the drops of violet blood trickling down my arm.

None of that bothers me. What bothers me is how *close* Timber is to me.

It was like this with Rose when we first met. It took time to get used to her always being around. Letting her into my personal space was a big step. Every time he nears. Each poke and prod. A closeness like this is different from sparring or training. It's . . . intimate.

A pained look crosses Timber's face, but he doesn't say anything.

His needle nicks raw skin, and I wince.

Dune skulls. Why does it hurt so much?

"Because the tissue and skin contain a lot of nerves that are sensitive, especially with the amount of swelling you have," he answers softly, using the upper part of his arm to soak up the sweat from his brow. "You're actually doing better than you think."

Did he really just answer a question I thought inside my head?

His hand shakes, but he steadies it. "Yes . . ."

"*Feaukere*," I say under my breath. "I'll quiet my thoughts then."

"Maybe reel in the anxiety, anger, frustration, and the . . . fear, too, if you can?"

"Oh, for Goddesssake. I am not feeling any of that—"

"And *please* don't move. Or we'll have to start again."

I freeze, tightening my body. I shut my mouth. Quiet my mind.

Anger? Maybe. Frustration? Always with him.

But anxiety and fear? He's reaching. *I am not afraid or . . . anxious.*

"Subconsciously, you are," Timber says, and I scoff. "Hey—I warned you."

Silence fills the air as he works. I scroll. All while fighting the urge to jerk my arm away or knock his teeth in. A strained expression overtakes him. There's skill in his hands now.

He's a completely different person when he heals. If he applied even an ounce of the effort he puts into healing, dare I say, he might actually be a decent mission partner.

I've obviously lost a lot of blood.

"How long?" I ask, trying to distract myself from thinking too loudly.

"How long what?"

"How long have you been able to mind-feel?"

"You mean read thoughts and emotions? Since I was a Seven."

I pull up a string of girls our age on the screen. "Oh . . ."

Then he grins.

"What?"

"Nothing. It's just . . . when I answered, your frustration became . . . empathy . . ." He removes an herbal adhesive from his healing pack and flattens the slimy, green bandage between his palms. "Which still feels like someone's press-

175

ing a hot iron to my chest. Incredibly forceful, but less excruciating than the frustration, anger, or disappointment. This finishing bandage is a poultice, by the way. When it dries, you shouldn't notice it."

I close my eyes. No thoughts are safe now. No feelings are safe now.

"Block it out," I tell him.

He hovers close again. "I can't."

"You haven't tried."

"I've tried. Trust me."

"Really? You've tried letting other people's emotions and thoughts flow through you instead of holding them in like a 'hot iron against your chest' or whatever you just said?"

He wraps the herbal adhesive around my bicep like a cuff. "Not exactly. No."

"Maybe consider it. That way you aren't holding onto crap that isn't yours."

"Actually, you talking to me helps. If you want to keep doing that." I try pulling away, but he latches onto my arm and holds me steady. "You forced me to do this. I'm finishing it."

Fidgeting with my amethyst-plated bracelet distracts me for a moment. Then I catch myself tapping my foot against the sleeping mat, the rush of overwhelm rising in my chest.

"You're tensing again," he says abruptly.

Dune skulls, I think it's him.

He's making me tense.

"Hurry up," I say quickly.

I need this to end.

"Talk. Please," he says.

"What do I even talk about, then?"

"What about the mines? You're the only person I've ever

met who's been there. Tell me what I have to look forward to."

"I'm not telling you about the mines," I say. "It'll just make you feel sicker."

He pauses a moment, his face turning paler. "What . . . happened down there?"

"Okay. We're done here." I quickly pull down my sleeve. The last thing I need is him digging around inside my head about the mines. "You know, you can't just read everyone you meet. Do you do this to your friends and family, too?"

"They don't know. You're the only one who does."

"It's incredibly invasive." I put on my jacket. "It makes it really hard to—"

"Hide your true self? Yeah, I know. I didn't ask for it."

He starts picking up supplies.

"What did you feel and see just now?" I press, watching the way he watches me.

"Nothing," he says. "I didn't see or feel anything you didn't want me to."

We linger in silence for a moment. I grab my tablet again.

"Here—" I thrust it into his hands. "Scroll through and see if you spot her."

While he swipes through potential transporter thieves, I turn away from him and plop down in a chair next to the window. I fiddle with my amethyst-plated bracelet once more and stare out at the view, counting air sweepers that zip and zoom past the glass.

I'm the only one that knows about his curse. *Me.*

What am I supposed to do with that information? Even Rose knows my deepest, darkest secret. Our commitment might be a sham at times, but at least she knows. And maybe that's its own burden. Maybe that's part of why I feel so indebted to make her life better.

I've dragged her into my darkness and made her an accomplice to my pain.

Perhaps I wouldn't feel as bad if she didn't know. But then again, not knowing would make the distance between us even more unbearable. Either way, someone suffers.

Feaukere. I'm nightmarish.

"I think this is her," Timber says.

I swivel the chair to face him. On the screen, the profile for Byatt Green is visible. A girl with auburn-colored hair and upturned eyes from Zone 3: Provisions.

If she's our only lead, we're not wasting any more time. "Address?"

"Dickinson Residential," he reads. "Unit 88."

D ickinson is as pathetically built as any other structure beneath the Hemisphere.

We tuck back against a tall half-finished building that looks like it was abandoned mid-construction. A dusty crane sits off to one side, clearly discarded, surrounded by mounds of fragmented stone and corroded scaffolding. As we approach, translucent blue light rolls off my wrist, and our countdown timer offers another reminder.

TIME LEFT: **40:06:76**

Timber gestures to the numbers. "Still plenty of time. Right?"

"For now," I counter. "But we can't afford to waste any more of it. We go in, get your transporter, and then get out. We'll be on our way to Kevin Hale's unit within the hour."

We climb a flight of stairs littered with rubbish.

"I just hope she gives it to us," Timber says, keeping his head down.

He's been acting weird since we left the IRS lodging unit. I've decided it's because he's *just weird*, and not that he's somehow peered into the depths of my soul.

I unsheathe my glowbeam. "She doesn't have a choice."

He waits on the landing. "We don't have to . . . blast anyone, right?"

I let out the longest sigh I can muster. I mean really. His reluctance is what got us into this plight in the first place. "I make no promises. If she resists, I'll take her down."

"She might give it back if we ask nicely."

"We will not ask nicely. We will demand that she—" I clench my jaw and lead us down the stretch of unit doors. "*Why* am I even arguing with you about this? Come on."

"All I'm saying is that sometimes people surprise us when we're patient."

"Not on a mission with a time constraint," I say flatly, slowing at Units 80 – 90.

A dull yellow door with missing number plates ends up being what we're looking for. Most of the color has chipped away over time. All that's left is the suns-stained shadow of the number 88 that should be bolted above the peephole.

I cock my glowbeam. "Back away so I can break down the door."

"Break down the—*no*," Timber says. "Let's just knock."

I brush him aside. Who does this slug think he is?

I get ready to rear back and bust some bolts. But before I can, Timber reaches forward and triggers the bell console. I glare at him. He purses his lips, refusing to look at me.

"There are children here," he mutters.

"How do you know?" I say back.

179

He motions to the colorful array of floral and creature drawings taped to the curtained window. There can't be children here. The Hemisphere has a population mandate in place.

And if there are, the adults in charge are doing a horrible job of hiding it.

Still, on the third ring, the dingy door opens a crack, and a small child resembling the Threes that teeter around our village peers out at us. Her polka-dot bow sits lopsided in her mangled mess of black hair. She barely fits into the oversized sleeping clothes she wears.

Without warning, she steps out and clings to my leg.

"Nope. Nope. Not in the cosmic depths." I immediately lift her off me and usher her toward Timber. "*You* deal with this, oh kind one."

"Mars, she's just a child." Timber's careful not to touch her as he kneels to her level. "Where is whoever cares for you? Is Byatt here?"

The child guides him inside with excitement, and I keep my glowbeam out, ready. Finger heavy on the trigger. Children or not, looks can be deceiving. It's best to stay alert.

Unit 88 is small and cluttered with items I couldn't name even if I tried.

A bizarre orbiting bassinet rocks another baby midair in the corner. Next to it, a metal-barred sleeping crate looks more like a holding cell than a resting place. Risen chairs with restraints and feeding trays sit beside another tattered sleeping mat propped up on a frame.

What in the name of torturous planets is this?

A third child scurries into the front room, chasing holographic blocks projected from a metal cube, stumbling over himself like a toddling Two.

Rose and I met when we were Seventeens, married shortly after our Coming of Age ceremony. From the start, she'd always talk about how adorable village babies are, how she wanted one of her own. We had a similar debate when I found Ere as a cub in the South Woods, orphaned and tangled in a snare trap. Ere was small and darling, a compromise, but it took Rose a whole six full moons to warm up to the idea of keeping her instead of trying for an actual baby.

"Hello?" Timber calls out at the threshold of a sustenance chamber overflowing with dishes. One of the children waves at him. "Is anyone here with you? Can you tell me—"

"Ask them about the transporter," I harp. "We aren't here to be village caregivers."

"They don't know anything about my transporter. They're too young."

"I don't have it," someone announces behind us.

I whip around and gape at the girl standing in the open washroom doorway. She's wearing the vest Timber mentioned, holding *another* child wrapped up in linen.

"Are you Byatt?" Timber asks.

"What do you mean you don't have it?" I demand.

"Please don't arrest us," she begs. "They aren't all mine. They're babies of other zone workers. I keep them hidden and watch them in the evenings while their parents are at work."

"The children are your business. Where's our device?" I snap.

The girl sobs. "It isn't here. I brought it to a trade shop here in Zone 3. It's called Trinket Gears. He offers a lot of tokens for something like that, and we needed the nurturing supplies."

"You—you sold it?" Timber stammers.

Acutely aware of the scraggly black-haired child looking up at me with more interest than I'm comfortable with, I bite back my curse before it leaves my lips.

17: VAIDA

Planet Nevarnost: Year 3051

K evin's grip tightens on my arm.

Exo-slime floods the ground, consuming every inch of porous stone. There's nowhere to run. Nowhere to break through. Not without upsetting the natural order of the Hallow.

I raise my brother's hunting knife, and a vine lashes out, knocking it from my hand and out of sight. I listen for the clatter, but instead, there's another squelch.

It spirals around Kevin's leg, winding slowly up his body. He doesn't flinch. "It's best if we stay still."

My stomach drops. "Is it, though?"

Another vine wraps around his torso. A thick, oozing tendril slaps his neck, where his mask hangs. It falls away, crumpling into a slimy ball before the void devours it.

They slither over our connected arms. One skims toward me, then stops, avoiding my belly. A thicker one binds Kevin's wrists. It pulls, trying to separate us, but I don't let go.

Above us, strings of translucent light travel between the Specters.

Another tendril wriggles toward Kevin's neck.

"They think we're a threat," he whispers.

Of course. Zee said they're drawn to life, and like the Nost eggs suspended overhead, I'm carrying life too. The Specters don't think we're a threat.

They think *he's* a threat.

As the snares tighten beneath his ears, he says, "If I let go of you, they'll let you leave."

He's right. They probably would. And I should leave him. He's from the Hemisphere. He's a smart aleck. He's been a pain in my ass since the moment we met.

But when he loosens his hold on me, I don't let go.

Kevin stiffens. "What are you doing? *Go.*"

"Don't be a hero. There's nowhere *to* go." I dig my fingernails into his skin, resisting the snares that want so desperately to pull us apart. "Let me think. I can handle it."

"I don't doubt your capability—" He closes his eyes as a vine feels for his nose, smearing a viscous film across his cheek. "Unless we can convince them I'm harmless, we're done for."

His words settle like sand in my chest.

"Focus your mind," I tell him.

"What?"

"Just do it!"

Another slinks behind his ear. I bite back a wince.

Kevin steadies his breathing in slow counts of four, his shoulders slackening with each exhale. Exo-slime coats his hair. It drips down the sharp line of his jaw. He's ridiculously calm for someone on the verge of being strangled by an entire cavern of ethereal snares.

"Focus on the Specters. On their warmth." I glance up at the bursts of light sparkling above us. "They're seers. They read energy. You have to let them . . . read you."

A single tendril drops from above, snaking around his broad shoulders like the desert serpents we find anchored to our well lines. Another one smacks his mouth, silencing him. Only his eyes and hands still clenched in mine remain free.

If they squeeze any harder, they'll break him in half.

Still, our connection holds. The Specters descend, their radiant forms drifting around Kevin as his palms grow slick in mine. Fear finds his eyes. One pulls away from the rest, aims for his heart, and envelopes him in its light.

All Nost are born with Cassia's Gift. Nia once described it to me as the overwhelming sensation of experiencing another's raw, unfiltered truth. She says humans feel emotions ten times more intensely than the Nost. Our egos cloud our minds. Our worries dull our intuition.

But the images the gift reveals are vivid—sometimes painfully so.

I was not born with the Goddesses' gift. Yet, as the Specter slips into Kevin's heart center, visions fill my mind, and a gut-wrenching ache buckles my knees.

They're supposed to be reading him.

But somehow, I can read him too.

"While the solution cools, we can prep the sticks."
The voice belongs to Kevin's late uncle, Billy Hale. He looks just like Kevin, but with glasses and slightly longer hair. Beside him, a younger Kevin hovers at the stovetop. He can't be older than four or five.
Together, they retrieve wooden sticks from a soaking jar.
"Can I do it, Uncle Billy?" Young Kevin asks.

Billy grins and lifts his nephew so he can roll the damp sticks in the saucer of sugar. "In two weeks, we'll show Nana the rock candy we grew. How does that sound?"

Young Kevin's face falls. "Two weeks? That's so long!"

"You can keep a tally of how many days go by." Billy takes off his digiband and fastens it around Kevin's wrist. "Lux will keep track for you. That way, you'll know when it's time."

Kevin buries his face in Billy's chest. "I wish Mama was here."

Billy's expression softens. "Me too, buddy. Me too . . ."

Nine years old.

Kevin stands on the front step outside Earhart Residential, his eyes widening at the dark plumes twisting through the sky.

A resounding BOOM rips through the air.

The scene fractures. Kevin runs through the fallout in Unity Commons.

Searching and pushing his way through panicked crowds.

He screams until he's hoarse. "Uncle Billy! Uncle Billy!"

Fifteen.

A medic from Zone 4 slides a tablet across the table. "She'll need constant care. Fill this out, and we can discuss hospice options."

"And if I don't?" Kevin asks.

"You're too young to—"

"I want to do it." Kevin pushes the tablet back. "I'll be her caretaker."

Eighteen. *Sometime last year.*

Kevin hunches over a terrarium filled with roakes at a cluttered workstation.

Then, the scene evolves. Chancellor Bay emerges from the shadows.

He's everywhere. Watching. Controlling.

In the mechanism office, where Kevin works on tech matters. Special tasks for Nucleus. Sending regular updates to ISR in Billy Hale's name . . .

Chancellor Bay leans in, his whisper practically a hiss. "The Hemisphere needs a proper head of command. If they think Billy is still alive, they won't bother checking up on us, and I'm free to make the changes necessary for our project's survival."

Kevin's voice catches. "I'm not doing this anymore."

"You will. Or I'll send you and your nana into the Outskirts . . ."

Nineteen. *This morning at the irrigation grid.*

"Ahh, I know what this is about." Graham pulls himself up off the ground, a slimeball sneer plastered on his face. "You've got a crush on the commander's daughter."

"People of the Outskirts are human beings. They deserve respect like everyone else," Kevin says and turns to face him. "And so what if I do?"

"Whoa. Like actually? Like a 'hit it' kind of crush or a real crush?"

Kevin tenses. "Don't talk about women that way. Of course it's real. I think she's funny and interesting. Unlike you, I know what it's like to admire someone genuinely."

That's about as much as I can take.

I sever the connection, my gaze falling into Kevin's.

A single tear slips down his cheek. His breath turns ragged.

And around us, the vines, the exo-slime, the Specters—they dissolve. They retreat into the cavern above, where the Nost embryos churn inside their egg-like sacs.

The tunnel ahead is clear.

"I think it worked," Kevin says.

He shakily drags a sleeve across his eyes, nose, and mouth, but it doesn't help much. He's drenched head to toe. Goo clings to his hair as he pushes a hand through it.

With a sigh, he bends down to pick up his soiled carbon face mask.

"Guess this is useless now," he says, stuffing it into his pocket.

I didn't expect to see what I saw, or to feel the weight of Kevin's past cyclone its way through me. Chancellor Bay's wreaked havoc on his life, blackmailing him into doing unspeakable things. How can Kevin not want him dead for what he's done? What's wrong with me that I do? And he has a . . . crush on me? Like an honest, genuine crush?

Kevin clears his throat. Our eyes meet again.

Does he know I saw everything? I can't tell.

Then he forces a smile. "Are you okay?"

He doesn't know. "Yeah. I'm fine."

"You sure?"

"Mhmm."

His lips part like he wants to say something else, but the sudden splash above us stops him cold. One of the egg sacs splits open. The fetus pulses awake, tiny tentacles unfurling as a high-pitched ringing fills the air.

I bring my hands to my ears. Kevin does, too.

"They're hatching!" he shouts. "We need to leave. Now!"

I don't need any more convincing. More mature eggs rupture, spilling liquid onto the floor. Kevin grabs my arm with his slimy hand and pulls me toward the adjoining archway.

As we cross the threshold, we come face to face with Nia.

"The nurturers are on their way to collect the newly hatched," she hisses, body taut as she corrals us down the passage. "If they find you here, any trust you've earned will be gone."

She's not talking to me. She's talking to Kevin.

"And all the times I've told you to keep south down here," Nia says to me next, and I struggle to keep up with her as she moves through the passage. "You don't listen."

"I *do* listen. I had it under control."

"You most certainly did not."

Cut me some slack, I want to scream, but even if I did, the screeching around us would drown me out. The ringing pulses in my ears, pain spiking behind my temples. Soon the familiar smell of nectar permeates the air, and relief spreads through me.

We were close after all.

Nia guides us through another turn, and stops beneath a single glow orb fixed on the wall beside the ladder that leads to the Hemisphere.

Kevin climbs first, leaving a trail of gelatinous residue in his wake. I follow, fingers trembling as I grip the rungs. The ladder sags beneath our combined weight.

Then, at the far end of the corridor, a gathering of twinkling orbs takes shape.

"It's the nurturers," Nia says.

"Hurry. Open the hatch," I tell Kevin.

"I'm—I'm trying. It's stuck!"

I shove him aside and fumble for the wheel latch. Nia slinks up the ladder behind me. I manage to loosen the wheel, Kevin helps me turn it, and the hatch creaks open with a thud.

He pulls me up with him. Nia follows, letting the hatch slam shut behind her.

I roll onto the concrete of a side street, into the smoggy air, just long enough to catch my breath and secure my face rag. *We did it.* We made it out without being caught.

Kevin stifles a cough. "Wow. That was—"

"A close one," Nia finishes flatly.

I push myself off the ground, brushing bits of drying Nost-fluid off my satchel. "You wanted to come to the Hemisphere. We got you here. You're welcome."

"Thank you," he says.

He stays put, like he's waiting for something more. But what else does he want me to say? We traveled through Nost Territory together. That doesn't make us friends.

What I saw in the Hallow doesn't change anything either. A crush is just that—a crush. It means nothing if I don't feel the same way. And I don't. Besides, Kevin probably has crushes on loads of people. He's got *lover boy* written all over him.

I bet when he likes someone, he gets all romantic and gushy. Writes letters, brings them flowers made of metal instead of real ones so they won't wilt, and respects the hell out of them or something. You know—stupid lover boy, green-eyed, tech nerd, mechanism-specialist things.

"I should probably get going." Kevin's the one who finally breaks the silence. "Good luck with whatever it is you came here to do, and thanks again. It means a lot."

At my nod, he takes off in a jog towards Zone 1.

Nia watches me with a grin. "I'm sure if you opened up and let him pursue you properly, he would certainly do all the things you just imagined inside your head." She cuts me off before I can respond with my typical sarcasm by handing me my brother's hunting knife. "I found this on the ground outside the Hallow. I thought you might want it."

I shudder, realizing we've been elbow to tentacle this whole time.

"Thank you . . . but those thoughts were purely hypothetical." I snatch my knife, tuck it away, and put some much-needed distance between us.

"I'm worried you'll miss out on something good for you."

"Good for me? Sure." I walk on ahead to figure out which Zone we're in.

"Kevin Hale is a kind soul. He has honorable intentions. He is honest."

Honest. *Is he?* The way she spoke to him underground, it sounded like they already knew each other. That tells me Kevin's hiding something. And so is she.

I stop walking. "Did you know him before today?"

"I knew his uncle." Nia halts beside me. "I did not know him before this."

I take in her words, but her eyes tell a different story. The way she blinks, the way she suddenly busies herself, plucking a wrapper from the gutter and feeding it to a passing trash bot.

Nia's lying to me.

To be fair, I haven't exactly been truthful either. But I'm

191

human. I'm flawed by design, fueled by my ego, as she so lovingly puts it. Nost live with integrity. They don't lie.

At least, I never thought they did.

18: TIMBER

Planet Nevarnost: Year 3051

"T rinket Gears. This is it," Mars says.

I ogle at the crooked hole in the wall, wedged between a textile boutique and a supply market. Draped in black silk and strings of multi-colored beads that sway in the swirling dust.

"Are you . . . sure?"

"Are you seriously questioning my ability to read a holomap?" He retracts the holographic grid, adjusts the amethyst-plated bracelet around his wrist, and surveys the area.

Once he's sure we're alone, he begins testing the door and windows for an entry point.

I stifle a yawn and shake myself out of a blank stare. Waiting until after most shops closed to search for my transporter seemed like a good idea at the time. But it's 10:00 PM, the streets are quiet and desolate, and the suns still blaze as brightly as they did hours ago.

We might be on another planet, but my body is convinced it's golden hour on Violet Moon. If I were home, I'd be washing up for dinner and preparing to settle in for a quiet evening of reading and tea. The little rest I managed to get while slumped in a chair at the lodging unit hasn't helped either. Mars, on the other hand, had no trouble napping. The moment his head hit the pillow on the sleeping mat, he was out cold the whole two hours we spent there.

That was, of course, after he'd complained we were wasting time.

Anyone smart would have utilized the break. Instead, I spent it replaying what I'd heard and felt while I was stitching him up. Forget the pain brought on by his anger, which was touchy and turbulent like an explosive waiting for its spark.

It was the way his inner world shifted when the mines were mentioned.

I've heard the stories. But the torment, guilt, and overwhelming sense of unworthiness I felt weren't just passing thoughts. They were deeply-rooted wounds.

Mars punishes himself for whatever happened in the mines. I didn't see the events unfold fully, but the toll it's taken on him is now part of him, and he's right that it's not any of my business, but I'm not sure he understands the way it consumes him.

Or maybe he does, and he's just learned to push those parts of him away.

When the door is a dead end, Mars turns to the shop's only window—a small, barred opening with stained glass panels in shades of hot pink, yellow, purple, and teal.

He unscrews the first bar. As he jostles the lock, it pops open.

Leaning forward, he reaches around to unlatch the door from the inside. I follow him through the silky, draped entryway into the shadowy space beyond. The place is dark, dusty, and packed floor to ceiling with, well, trinkets. Thousands of devices, gears, and contraptions of all kinds clutter the shelves that surround us.

Without hesitation, Mars begins searching for my missing time device.

I'm not sure where to start. The silence is unnerving, but everywhere I look, something equally extravagant catches my eye. Father would love it here. He'd revel in the bells, whistles, and space contraptions that seem both far behind and beyond our time. I pick up a sparkling geode and admire its shine before moving on to a set of floating brass keys. After them sits a tank of iridescent hopping beetles and cosmic slugs that leave trails of glow-in-the-dark muck.

They make me think of Mars' ridiculous nickname for me, and I glance over my shoulder, catching him thumbing through a deck of hand-painted oracle cards.

He notices me staring and sets them down.

"Look for your transporter," he mumbles.

"I am," I say, reaching into a jar of purplish-blue rounds labeled *100% Authentic Vetra scales from planet Amavetra*. I quickly pull my hand back when I notice a bald old man in goggles and a reflective silver jumpsuit watching me from behind the front counter.

The Nevarnost manifest said all storefronts closed by 10:00 PM. He shouldn't be here, assuming he's even the shop's owner. I open my mouth to speak, but he pulls down his floral face mask, pressing a finger to his lips to silence me. Then he points to an odd miniature doll with bright pink hair and a jewel on its naked belly, hanging from a ceiling wire nearby.

"Pull it," he mouths.

I glance around, then I mouth back, *"Me?"*

He nods his head, urging me again with a toothy grin full of silver fillings.

My eyes find Mars again, busy sorting through a bin of devices that seem to be made of the same material as our transporters. He swears to himself and examines each machine closely.

I return my attention to the man, my heart skipping a beat.

"Pull the troll doll," he whispers.

"No," I whisper back quickly. "Why do you—"

"*Who* are you talking to?" Mars snaps behind me.

"*I'll* pull it then!" the old man exclaims.

He hops over the counter with surprising agility, catching the troll doll and pulling it.

In response, a blinding light show of all colors and sounds erupts as the shop comes to life around us. "Now we're cooking. Let me show you around, kid!"

"What in the black void is going on!" Mars shouts, dropping the device in his hands.

He unsheathes his glowbeam, accidentally knocking into a digimag display as he tries to make his way to me.

The old man rips off his space goggles. "The name is Alden James," he says, attempting to put an arm around me, but I dodge it and trip over a trunk, overflowing with plastic cubes called Rubik. "Are you boys looking for a rare find? We have only the best at Trinket Gears."

As I pick myself up, my eyes adjust to the brightness of the shop. Everything in here is so disorienting, I don't know what's going on. "We're, uh, we're actually looking for a—"

"How about a crystal ball?" Alden gestures at a line of crystal spheres on display. "Smokey quartz. Guaranteed a direct prophecy 35% of the time. Or how about a pair of gamer specs to go with them pretty blue eyes of yours?"

"That's very kind, but I don't think—"

"Here, have a season globe." He places a glass bubble in my hands filled with bits of white dust and a sloshing liquid. "I've also got that in fall, spring, and summer."

The globe nearly slips through my fingers. "What—what does it do?"

"Careful there. You don't want to drop that in here. This shop will go from a hoarder's dreamscape to an artificial winter wonderland."

Mars snatches the globe from me and thrust it at Alden with a sneer. "Enough of this charade, you rambling, eccentric salesman."

Alden strokes his chin. "You know, you look like the kind of guy who could use one of these floral face coverings, circa Old Earth 2020. They go like hot cakes on the intergalactic market. And if you're into Old Earth mementos, I've got a Furby with your name on it."

"Enough. We are not interested in your merchandise!" Mars roars, shoving Alden into a rack of spinning meteorites.

They smash to the floor and disintegrate into dust.

Alden's eyes go wide. "Young man, those were authentic fallen stars caught in the interdimensional Celestial Canyons of planet Lark!"

"I don't care," Mars gripes. "We're looking for one thing and one thing only." He pulls his own transporter out of his pack. "It looks like this. A girl sold it to you. We need it back."

"*Gasp!* Another one," Alden says with a twinkle in his eye.

He tries to touch it, and Mars slaps him away. "Not so fast, space swindler. I'm giving you two seconds to return what's ours or I'll launch you so far into the galaxy, you'll spend your last moments *kissing* authentic Lark stars."

Alden's gleeful expression twists. He straightens his collar. "Unfortunately, I've already sent your, uh . . . device to a buyer. I sent it out in the Gallivant moments before you arrived."

Mars fires up his glowbeam. "I don't think so."

Alden raises a brow. "Unless of course you've got the moolah."

"The *what?*" I ask.

"The tokens. The tin. The change, crystal, sticks, or shells." Alden points to high-tech machine with slots across the shop. "Any form of currency works. I've got a converter."

Mars growls, "You just told us you sent it away."

"Yes, but perhaps the buyer will reconsider for a fair price."

I take off my backpack and pull out the sack of tokens Father packed for us. "We've got tokens. How much do you think the buyer would take? I think there's some crystal in here, too."

Alden wiggles himself away from Mars. "We'll give him all you've got. Maybe he'll change his mind." He skips away, his quirky persona back on. "I'll go fire up the Gallivant!"

"You're daft if you think he isn't haggling with us," Mars warns me, kicking over a barrel of plushies. "The transporter is more than likely here in this shop somewhere. There's no buyer."

"Let's give him a chance," I say.

"This shop was built for gullible fools like you."

I choose to let his comment roll off my back. Because I know I messed up, and I know he's reeling with anger. And I don't think I'm gullible. I just want my transporter back.

Alden emerges from the back room, carrying a pink box.

He sets it on the counter. "Here she is."

Mars and I gather around the device, which up close isn't just a box. The words on the front read *Easy-Bake Oven.*

"What is this foolery?" Mars asks.

"This foolery lets me send and receive items all over the galaxy. Gallivants can be built out of just about anything. Hence the Old Earth memento. And—" He takes a pan tool out of his pocket and slides a saucer of brown cake out the other side. "—it still works. Brownie, anyone?"

Mars crosses his arms. "You'd better get to the point of this real fast."

"*Right.* Your device." Alden shoves the brownie into his mouth and wipes the crumbs on his sleeve. "Give me the tokens. I'll put them in and see if the buyer bites."

Mars furrows his brows. He doesn't stop me as I hand Alden the sack of currency.

Alden sets the tokens inside the remodeled hatch on the Easy-Bake Oven. "We've got these all over the galaxy. I've even got one in my shower! Helps us planet-bound vendors keep up with the trade and manage multiple locations, so my customers always get the best—"

"We don't care," Mars says.

"My family's been in this business for eons. Take my card—" Alden continues to me, pointing to the holder on the counter filled with paper squares. "We run cargo crafts to trading posts between planets and various locations on the ground. My grandchildren, Henry and Merik, they're teenagers now. Can you believe it!? They've been working with us, too. Our personal agents. You can call that code if you ever need anything. Personally, from me or them."

"Uh . . . thanks." I take the card to be polite and slip it into my backpack pocket.

"How long do we have to wait?" Mars asks, referring back to the Gallivant.

"We should know within seconds if the buyer will take your bid." Alden flips on a switch. A spark, and a puff of smoke, come from inside the Easy-Bake Oven. Then he opens the hatch and reveals an empty interior. "Yeah, looks like it's a no go on the swap."

"I had such high hopes for this," I say. "Should we try something else?"

"*Feaukere*," Mars swears, and his glowbeam surges with power. "I *know* the transporter is still here in the shop somewhere. There isn't any buyer at all, is there?"

Alden isn't listening. He's captivated by the amethyst-plated bracelet clamped tight around Mars' wrist. "What a unique band you've got there. That might interest my buyer."

"It isn't for sale," Mars says.

I observe the way Alden gapes at Mars' wrist some more. I don't know what significance his bracelet holds. Given how often Mars touches it, and the Head Elder spiral etched at the end, my guess is it belonged to his father. It might even be all he has left of him. I don't want Alden to think it's something he could, let alone should, potentially bargain with.

"Mars," I say softly.

"*What.*"

I gesture him away from the counter. He reluctantly follows.

I lean in closer. "We're wasting time. I don't want to cause unnecessary trouble. I think we should just move on. Don't worry about me. In less than a few days, I'll be sent to the mines anyway. My life isn't more important than anyone else's."

"*What* are you blubbering on about?"

"It's my fault I lost my transporter. If we have time after we've established a connection with Kevin Hale and Vaida Wardell, then so be it, but I think we should put the mission first."

A trace of emotion stirs in his gray eyes, but I can't place it. He knows I'm right. Why isn't he agreeing so we can move on?

"Go wait outside," he orders.

"What? I just said—"

"I'm dealing with this my way."

"But—"

"Get. Out."

"Fine," I mutter.

Alden offers me one last smile, and I exit the shop.

Outside on the steps, I sit and bask in the hot air and the stench coming from a nearby trash bot scrubbing the edge of a sidewalk. Nevarnost's short hours of darkness are approaching fast. Rays of light wrap the buildings around me, offering that subtle brilliance of golden hour that I love so much on Violet Moon. As the natural light fades, the air grows mildly cooler.

I brace myself for the chaotic sounds I might hear behind me. Or whatever happens when Mars does things *his* way. I suppress the image of Alden getting blasted like the boy on the hover swings and force myself to ignore the dread creeping in, imagining Mars tearing through the shop like a rogue flare.

Something no one could come back from.

The way he looked at me back there . . . I thought he'd be pleased I was taking full responsibility for my faults. I thought he'd say something like *'finally, you slug,'* or *'about time you realize what's at stake here.'* Instead, he seemed . . . worried. Or maybe I'm reading him wrong. All I know is we've wasted too much time, and it's officially my fault.

I tap my digiband to check the countdown, but it won't turn on. I flip it over and check the charge. It's full. Taking off my pack, I retrieve my tablet. It's dead, too.

I check my digiband once more just to make sure.

"Oh, no," I mutter.

If we aren't connected to the *Iris*, we won't have access to the database. If we don't have our countdown, we can't keep track of time.

Mars isn't going to like this.

I get up to go warn him, and one of the excessively large hovering monitors that seem fixed on every street corner buzzes next to me. It blinds me with the incoming broadcast.

A robotic sound echoes in the alleyway. *"A message from your chancellor, Ezra Bay."*

Their chancellor appears on the screen, his soothing voice almost mesmerizing. "Attention fellow inhabitants of the Hemisphere. As you might already be aware, there was a terrible acid storm in the Outskirts. I am here to assure you that we are taking every precaution necessary to keep those living beneath our dome safe from harm.

"Furthermore," the chancellor continues. "I am issuing a word of caution to stay within the confines of our Hemisphere until we can contact Outskirt officials and confirm that it's safe for us to travel into Zone 9. Any other concerns can be submitted to the number of patrol officers stationed along zone exit and entry points. Thank you, and have a good evening on Nevarnost."

The broadcast dies. An electric hum remains in the air.

Mars exits Trinket Gears moments later with a scowl on his face.

Is now a good time to tell him that our tech is down?

As if this mission couldn't get any worse.

"Uh, how did it go with—"

"Here." Mars tosses me my transporter and keeps walking. "Let's go find Kevin Hale."

A rush of relief spreads through me. I feel the device in my hands and glance back at the shop, then at Mars, who is already halfway down the street. "Wait. How did you—"

"I said, let's go." He checks his digiband, and I cringe, waiting for the delayed reaction of him also realizing we no longer have access to our tech.

It takes a moment.

"What did you do now?" he hisses under his breath.

In my silence, Mars rubs his temples. For a moment, it almost looks like he might cry or hit me. I can't tell which one. Something happened in that shop. This isn't just a reaction to glitching tech. Intuition-wise, I know I should reach out and ask him about it.

The only reason I don't is because he's already started walking again.

19: KEVIN

Planet Nevarnost: Year 3051

. . . digital to-do list currently unavailable . . .

"The Hallow seems to be some kind of memory bank," I say to myself under my breath. "I haven't figured out where they pull their information from yet, but there might be a spiritual connection. The memories, especially the emotions, were . . . difficult to relive . . ."

Lamps shudder awake around me in the musky street-way.

My steel-toed boots thud against gravel as I walk, ignoring the stares I get for talking to myself. That doesn't bother me. I have to speak aloud, or I'll forget.

"Aside from the experience being emotionally draining, I'd need to ask the Nost if I could collect samples and analyze the Specters to confirm—"

Gah. I miss Lux already. Verbal logs seem pointless without her.

Past Cabot, Vespucci, Drake . . . *faster* . . . Champlain, Dias, Hillary . . . Earhart Residential. My arm swings out as I round the back flight of stairs.

Up to the top floor. Unit #11.

The lights are off, which makes sense. If Lux is down, so are the automatics, and she won't respond to backup generators unless I manually reset her. The thought of Nana sitting in the dark this whole time, cuddling her baby doll alone, breaks my heart.

But I'll rewire the circuits after I wash up. I'm still covered in gunk, and the last thing I need is to get it between keys or all over the regulator.

What a nightmare that would be.

I unjam the keypad beneath the door handle, wiping away the layer of dust coating the buttons. 0 . . . 2 . . . 1 . . . 7 . . . 9 . . . 3 . . . *click.*

"Nana?"

I step onto the welcome mat inside the front hall and set down my backpack. My next inhale triggers a gag. Sweat beads on my brow as the pungent, stuffy air hits me. The cooling systems are down. Luxframe is offline. Sensors aren't responding.

But this is worse than I thought.

I suck in another breath too quickly and cough, stumbling into the bathroom.

Sometimes Nana makes a mess. It's happened before.

I feel around in the dark for the light switch. Aside from a missing cover on a jar of toothpaste tablets, a nearly spent shampoo bar, and a UV-C hand sanitizer knocked off its charging cell, the bathroom is clean.

So, where is that smell coming from?

"Nana!"

I light up the hall as I go, triggering the manual sensors for the kitchen and the AeroGarden up in the loft. Refrigerator secured. Not a single dish in the sink.

Not a tea mug or crumb on the table.

She forgot to eat.

This is *much* worse than I thought.

I've never had to wear a face covering inside the unit before, but between the stench and the heat, I unhook a new mask from the hanging hutch in the hall and head to Nana's bedroom.

The smell intensifies. My eyes water.

Baby Doll lies on the floor next to Nana's chair.

Nana's rigid hand dangles to one side.

I can't see her face, but I know she isn't sleeping.

'm in the bathroom again. Collapsed on the chipped gray tile, sitting in a pool of my own sick because I didn't make it in time.

One of the medics I paged steps into the room.

He doesn't flinch at the sight of me.

This is his job. He sees this kind of thing every day.

"We've put her in a preservation pod to delay composition and contain the smell," he says calmly, like he's speaking to a small child. "With everything happening in the Outskirts and the power outages here, it'll be a few hours before the mortuary staff can pick her up. They'll refer you to an honorary representative to plan her service—which, again, might be delayed."

Exo-slime stings my eyes, mixing with the salty tears streaming down my face.

"I was all she had left," I say, barely audible.

"Sorry for your loss." The medic tears a ticket from his

pad and sets it on the counter. "When they arrive, give them this ticket so we can update our population records."

As soon as he's gone, the sounds start.

They escape my throat, but they aren't mine.

They belong to another boy. I hear his screams. I feel the way his whole body shakes. The same way he did as a three-year-old the night his mother accidentally overdosed on roake venom. Or years later when the Unity Arch fell and his uncle wasn't among the survivors.

These sobs are his. Not mine.

If I'd been here, would things be different?

Would I be putting on a cup of green tea right now?

Or tucking her and Baby Doll into bed instead?

If I'd been here, would Nana still be alive?

I drag myself into the shower. The air filtration resets, and I slap the gauge sensor. Lukewarm water pours over me. My digiband can't get wet, but I don't care.

Peeling off my clothes, I leave them in a heap.

I squeeze my knees to my chest. Rest my head back against the wall. Water spills over me, rinsing away the sick, the exo-slime, and the dust.

Everything else remains.

I sit in the loft, dressed, my eyes on the orange heat lamps hanging over the terrarium.

The jar of roakes I gathered from No Man's Land rests in my lap. I grab the one with a curved telson, and it fights the tip of my tweezers.

Right now, they aren't as strong.

One sting wouldn't kill me.

I think of my mother. I never really knew her, but Nana would tell me stories. She fell in love with a trade worker from Zone 7: Industrial, which is why she chose Nevarnost after graduating the Academy on ISR's orbiting home base, *Ophelia*. One afternoon, eight months before I was born, they were out riding in a solar cart. It flipped, sending them both into a nest. My father was killed instantly. He was allergic to the venom. My mother survived, but she got stung.

After that, roakes became a part of her life.

I study the roake scrabbling on my arm now. Its tiny feet explore my bare skin. As it buzzes, my heart starts to pound. I think of Soren and all the pain he claims the high numbs away. But at what cost? Would it really be worth it in the long run?

A knock at the door on the lower level. Whoever it is can go away.

They wouldn't want to see what I'm about to do.

My deal with Soren started because he caught me and a few others in Unity Commons one night with posters and paint pods. I knew he'd tell Commander Bay unless I agreed to supply him with his fix. But with Nana gone, the commander finding out doesn't affect her anymore.

My forearm flexes, tempting the roake to hiss.

It arches its body and readies to sting.

At the last second, I pluck the roake with my tweezers and place it over a petri dish covered in a plastic film. Orange venom dribbles into the container. The roake dies shortly after.

I put on my goggles, gloves, and a fresh mask from the top drawer of my workstation. Then I grab my handheld titanium mister and load it with poison. I transfer the roakes

I collected into the terrarium and fasten the top so no air can escape.

I release the mist into the cage. Until the life in them fades away.

Roakes only face one natural predator in No Man's Land—themselves.

On the lower level, the front door rattles. Specifically, the locking mechanism.

My first thought is Soren, but he knows I'm supposed to be on assignment. And it's too soon for the mortuary team.

Someone's trying to break in. Right here. Right now.

With so many grid issues going on, we'll likely see a rise in desperate people taking advantage of the situation. If Uncle Billy were here, he'd tell me to pick my battles, to box breathe until I can't box breathe anymore before handling it.

On a good day, I would. But today isn't one of those days.

Moments later, I'm in the kitchen, gripping Nana's cane.

I hide behind the half-wall as two muffled male voices argue outside, maneuvering around the keypad.

"The acid rain must be interfering with tech," one voice says.

"Your father should have known that," a deeper, raspier voice snaps back.

The door bangs open. I raise Nana's cane.

The softer of the two says, "Mars, we should just wait until he gets home."

Until he gets home. Are they here for me?

I peek at them in the reflection of the hallway mirror as they pass. Brown skin, sharp jaw, and flashes of red-and-black hair on the first. The other one is pale and blonde, wearing a blue tunic shirt with some sort of neck embellishment.

Both wear a kind of advanced face mask I've never seen here beneath the Hemisphere. Certainly not in the Outskirts. *Who are these guys?*

The one called Mars glares at the softer one. "Clear the kitchen. I'll take the rest of the unit, then we'll circle back," he says, disappearing down the hall.

I closed Nana's bedroom door, but if anyone touches her, I swear I'll—

Tunic boy enters the kitchen, hands up like a kid with a zeroed-out token card caught sneaking rides on the solar train. I don't give him a chance to speak. With one swing, he drops to the floor in a writhing ball, and his groans carry across the housing unit.

"Timber?" Mars shouts. His footsteps pound toward us.

I step over Timber and get ready.

Mars shows up right on cue.

"Who the slug are you?" he shouts.

I answer with a swing of Nana's cane. But Mars is quicker than Timber. His reflexes are trained, practiced. He knocks me back and swipes the cane from my hand.

My stomach lurches. *That's it.*

"Aghhh!" I yell, launching myself at him.

The floor breaks our fall. His fingers strain for the gun-like device on his belt, and I knock it aside, punching him in the face. He doubles over and lunges for my neck.

One hit, and I choke. But I return the favor.

"Timber, get my glowbeam!" Mars orders.

I slam his head down. He huffs. Angrily pins me back around.

Now he's on top. Bending my arm. Crushing my windpipe.

Stars—Gah. All I see are stars.

"Hurry up! Beat the bugs out of him!" Mars roars.

Timber panics. "I—I don't know where it went!"

"Of course you don't! Do you ever know?"

"Unnecessary commentary!" Timber says.

Mars spots his glowbeam near the doorway and releases the pressure beneath my jaw. He dives for the weapon, tucking and rolling into the corner.

There's a loud thrum. I cover my head, flattening myself against the floor.

A blast of bright light explodes through the wall next to the kitchen. Dust rises in the fallout, along with chunks of drywall. Splinters of wood drift over us like ash.

Timber coughs and comes out from beneath the collapsed table. He searches the room with wide eyes. "What have you done?"

Mars reloads and pulls himself up off the ground.

As he stalks toward me, I try to get up, but I can't. I thought I could take them, but it's not a fair match. Not with their glowbeams and training.

"This could have been easy," Mars sneers, the barrel of his glowbeam pointed through the settling dust, directly at me. "But you chose violence. So, in turn, *I* will choose violence."

He cocks his weapon, revving it up for another shot.

Timber's eyes widen. "Wait! Are you—are you Kevin Hale?"

"Yes," I breathe. "Who the heck are you?"

Instinctively, Mars lowers his glowbeam. Not without a scowl.

I stare at both of them. A couple strangers who have broken in and destroyed what little sense of home I had left. On perhaps one of the worst days of my life.

"William Hale sent us," Mars says, letting the glowbeam dangle at his side.

"William Hale?" I echo. "My—my uncle?"

Timber says, "My father. Yes."

I shake my head at the absurdity of what I'm hearing. Uncle Billy. *Father.*

"That's impossible," I say. "He's dead."

20: TIMBER

Planet Nevarnost: Year 3051

I t doesn't matter how many times Mars and I tell Kevin what we know. He doesn't believe us.

"Uncle Billy wouldn't abandon me," he says, seated at his workstation with his back to us.

At this point, it's less a statement and more of a reflective question.

Mars looms over him, one hand leaning on the desk. "I don't know how else to phrase it so you'll understand. William Hale is *alive*. He lives on Violet Moon in the year 3083, thirty-two years from now, with a family. He sent us here to find you, and we don't have time for your sob story or your reluctance."

"Go easy on him. He's had a rough day," I say, remembering that in one of our earlier attempts to get Kevin to believe us, he mentioned he lost his grandmother not long before we showed up.

Mars shoots me a glare. "You. Quiet. And you—" He wags a finger at Kevin. "Our tech is down, so your job is to help us log into the network so we can contact ISR."

Kevin doesn't respond. His focus drifts to the giant fish tank across the cluttered loft, his eyes glossy like he's stuck

213

in a daymare. I notice the small gash on his lip and the bruising on his left cheek, likely a result from our brawl in his sustenance chamber.

Wow. Mars really slammed him, didn't he? I rub my own bruise. To be fair, that smack in the face with the cane didn't feel good either.

"You should really ice that," I tell Kevin, motioning to his cheek.

He sniffs in. "It's fine. I'm so numb, the pain feels good."

I step closer to Mars, as close as I can without touching him. "This isn't working. He needs a minute. How would you feel if someone showed up immediately after your only remaining family died and told you your parents were alive?"

A flush creeps up Mars' neck, his expression hardening. "What did you just say?"

"You heard me. We all need a minute to digest this."

Mars' body tenses. For a moment I think he's going to lash out, maybe even wring my neck, but I hold my ground and refuse to back down.

"For someone who won't fight or touch anyone, you sure ride a fine line," he mumbles under his breath, then kicks aside a box of poster-making supplies.

Without another word, he retreats to a lounge chair in the corner of the loft.

At first, I don't know what to think of his comment, but then a small smile tugs at my lips. Saying what's on my mind feels easier around Mars than it ever did with Raine, my parents, or even the Council of Elders. Maybe it's because he knows my deepest truth, or maybe it's because I don't care if he hates me.

Or maybe it's because, now that I see the human beneath

the walls he built up to protect himself, I feel like I'm in the company of someone who understands what it's like to be haunted by their own inner world. If he gets to speak his mind, why shouldn't I? Not that I'm about to start beating anyone up or blasting them, though.

With Kevin and Mars separated, silence settles in the loft.

I take a few deep breaths and start pacing, letting curiosity guide me as I explore. This was Father's home, after all—a part of his life I've always wondered about. Kevin isn't the only one adjusting to unexpected revelations and fresh faces. In just a few days, I've learned about a cousin I didn't know existed, that Father discovered a form of time travel, that he once lived on this planet, and that he was not only a mechanism specialist but an inventor and former chancellor, among other things.

So, yeah. We're all going to take a minute to let the situation soak in.

The loft itself reminds me of Father's mechanism pod back in the Dunes. Packed shelves circle around us, filled with heaps of research equipment. Vertical planters lean against the walls. A strange terrarium houses withered, unidentifiable creatures. In the corner, between the fish tank and a sliver of mirror on the wall, is a stack of posters and half-painted banners of trees.

The same trees I saw drawn on the tar in the recreational yard.

I pick at the edge of the poster, reading the title aloud. "*Unity*. Like the Arch?"

I glance back at Kevin, who's now sitting up at his workstation, fidgeting with a couple gears, something Father also does when he's trying to think or process.

Must run in the family.

"It was my uncle's peace movement. The 10-year anniversary of its eradication is tomorrow—I'm sorry, but are you sure it's the right William Hale we're talking about here? William 'Billy' Nash Hale?"

Mars groans. "For the love of bugs. Yes. How many times do we have to tell you?"

Kevin runs a hand through his hair. "I know. It's just . . . I can't wrap my head around it. The time travel part doesn't surprise me. I knew about that from his journals, but the rest of it doesn't make any sense. He didn't write. He didn't call. Instead he sends you? Why now?"

I look to Mars, who locks eyes with me. We've been so preoccupied with getting Kevin to believe his uncle really sent us here that we still haven't told him about the storm.

My mission partner rises from his chair and unsheathes his glowbeam. "How about you cooperate, get us into ISR's database, and then we'll tell you."

"You can trust us," I echo, though not sure it means much anymore.

Not with a glowbeam aimed between his eyes.

Kevin ponders a moment, glances between us once more, then plops down in one of the chairs in front of his main workstation. "For the record, I'm against unnecessary hacking."

"I'm not," Mars says. "And it isn't unnecessary."

I hover behind Kevin and watch him pull data up from multiple windows. He uses both his touchscreen and his hoverscreen to type code. His finger movements are swift as he navigates the system, just like Father's always are when I watch him work in his pod off the *Iris*.

"You're a mechanism specialist." My hand almost grazes Mars' accidentally on the back of the chair. He slides his hand away just in time, and I disregard the heat in my palms. "Father is, too."

"So weird to hear you call him that," Kevin mutters. "But that's interesting."

"Incredibly interesting," Mars mocks.

I've been ignoring the mood swings, but ever since we left Trinket Gears, Mars has gotten worse. Whatever happened there altered him in some way. I make a mental note to find the courage to ask him about it later, when it's appropriate and I'm sure he won't rough me up.

"It is interesting," I continue. "When I was little, he'd take me with him on his days off to tinker in his mechanism pod. I'd watch him log moon patterns and geographical sequences."

This time, Kevin speaks flatly. "Sounds like he was a really great dad."

On second thought, I probably shouldn't be talking about my childhood when the man that raised me left Kevin at such a young age.

It isn't fair.

"I'm sure he has a good explanation," I say, though it doesn't lighten the mood.

"Would you quit distracting him?" Mars bites.

Kevin's fingers remain glued to the keys. When he turns his head to glance at the other monitor, the one with the photo of him and someone who I assume is Father, because it looks like a younger version of him, his eyes grow misty.

"Maybe we should take another break," I suggest. "We could go put the sustenance chamber back together or pick up the shards of glass in the front hall—"

"*Feaukere*," Mars swears. "Do you *ever*—"

"I'm in." Kevin slaps his touchscreen pad.

We both huddle around him.

The familiar ISR logo blinks on the screen, alongside Father's old profile, daily pins, and boards. Mars urges Kevin out of the seat and takes control, clicking onto a message conversation between Father and ISR home base *Ophelia*.

My eyes follow the lengthy feed, which goes back for weeks and weeks. Monthly check-ins, updates, weather briefs—all dated recently, from this year, on *this* planet.

"You've been impersonating a high-profile ISR officer," Mars says before I can.

"I'm not proud of it," Kevin admits softly. "But I didn't have a choice. The chancellor practically forced my hand. When Uncle Billy died—I mean, left, I guess?—he didn't let ISR know. He disappeared, and it sounds like he wanted people to think he was gone."

Mars furrows his brows. "It's a serious crime."

"It doesn't matter anyway, right?" Kevin counters. "He's *alive*." Mars reaches out to click on a red facial icon in the upper corner of the screen, and Kevin stops him abruptly. "I don't recommend doing that. I don't have full access, and if you go any deeper, you start accessing classified files that require facial biometrics. I can't bypass those. I don't know his passcodes."

"He didn't give us any passcodes," I say.

Mars thinks for a moment. "We can't initiate a proper rescue if we can't submit high-profile requests. Are there any other living ISR recruits or contacts left on Nevarnost?"

"The chancellor," Kevin answers, stepping away from us. "But even if he were convinced to help, the nearest planet to Nevarnost is Pentron, and that's still a month out at light speed." He pauses. "And rescue? Look, you two need to fill me in. Why did my uncle really send you?"

"There's going to be a huge—"

Mars holds his hand up, silencing me. "Go get the dozing mist out of my pack."

"What? No. Why would I do that?"

"Because I can tell he's going to be difficult, and I don't have time for any more of it—" He motions to Kevin nonchalantly. "—we'll knock him out and carry him if we have to."

"I can hear you, you know," Kevin says.

I shake my head. "We are not knocking anyone out."

Mars throws open the hatch in the floor and descends. I follow him down, feeling bad he got hurt, feeling bad I lost my transporter.

In fact, I'd keep apologizing if he didn't get so annoyed by it.

But there's no way he's doing this to me again. "We'll find another way to send for a rescue ship. You heard Kevin. The chancellor is an ISR agent too. Surely, he'll help."

Mars jumps the ladder, skipping the rungs.

When his feet hit the floor, the hallway below us shakes. "You didn't read the whole briefing if you think the chancellor is going to help us."

He picks up his leather pack in the hall, where splinters of wood and other debris are scattered. I reach the bottom of the ladder. My face flushes, irritation rising in my chest.

"The Nevarnost Project was a touch-and-go settlement. They transferred a small population here from Old Earth, made other supply drop-offs, then left. Other than a few assignment contacts, ISR left the project to cultivate on its own. They had no intention of continuing regular contact or shipments," I state clearly, tired of him not giving me a lick of credit for knowing what I need to know. "I stayed up all night and read the material *you* gave me. Twice. I'm trying to be resourceful. You told me I'd be daft not to be."

"Enough." He scowls, retrieving his canister of dozing mist. He loads it into the barrel of his glowbeam. "You want to know something, Timber? I didn't even want you here. I wanted to come alone." He fires up his weapon, a hunger in his eyes. "You care too much. You don't know when to suck it up and accept that this mission is at risk of becoming unsalvageable. Now step aside, so I can put this guy to sleep."

Mars really is a flare that can't be tamed. Back at the ISR lodging unit, I only caught a glimpse of what haunts him from his time in the mines. But that's not what this is. I don't know what *this* is. He almost makes me want to reach out, grab him by the arm, and force it out of him.

As he advances up the ladder to the hatch, it's Kevin that urges him back down. Back on floor level, Mars whirls to face him, glowbeam up.

"I know you want to shoot me," Kevin says, raising his hand in front of him. "But you said you were looking for a rescue ship. I might know where you can find one."

Mars aims his barrel smack between Kevin's eyes. "There are no ships on Nevarnost."

Somehow, Kevin remains calm. "Yeah, I know. ISR abandoned the project, I get it. But I'm not talking about a transport ship. I'm talking about something smaller, more traditionally used for excursions." He pulls the tablet from under his arm and holds it out to Mars. "I mentioned earlier my uncle kept journals. In some, he mentions that whenever ISR sent him on assignments, he traveled via spacecraft. That means there might still be one here."

Mars' thumb hovers over the glowbeam's trigger.

"I can help you find it if you just tell me what's going on."

The glowbeam's hum grows louder, and I know Kevin is one mood swing away from being dozed. He'll be out for weeks on that stuff. And then, no matter what happens in the next thirty-something hours, he won't stand a chance.

I can't let it happen. I have to do something.

As Mars readies to fire, I step in between them and grab his wrist. His weapon wavers, mostly out of shock. I'm as surprised as he is that I'm doing this. Instead of the rage I expected, fear radiates from Mars. *I'm scared I'm going to fail again*, the whispers tell me for him.

I can't fail at this too. I have to make a difference. For me. For Rose. For—

"Enough," I say aloud, keeping my eyes closed.

I don't want to hear his thoughts right now, I tell myself.

Sweat forms on my forehead. I'm shaking, but I hold Mars steady, using him to keep myself stable as I try what he suggested in the lodging unit as a last effort. *Let his emotions flow through you instead of holding them in.* These are *his* emotions. These are *his* thoughts.

They are not mine. They are not mine. They are not mine. I can make space for his feelings, but I have to release them because they aren't mine to carry.

Let it go, I tell myself. *Let it all go.*

I manage to curl my trembling fingers. Mars lets me lower his arm so his glowbeam is down at his side again. He keeps his eyes on me the entire time, his fear quickly dissolving and passing through, even though we're still connected by touch.

"We aren't . . . going to fail," I finally say, because now Kevin is staring at me, too, and I can only imagine what this looks like to him. "Without our countdown, we don't know how much time we really have, but we have time to try and locate this aircraft."

Palm now sweaty, I release my hand and wipe it dry on my tunic.

The gray in Mars' irises softens. I'm hoping my words will reach him this time, deep within the fortress he's built up for himself, his flare cat, and maybe even Rose.

Finally, he says, "We'll look for the aircraft. But if this doesn't work, I'm holding you both personally responsible." As he turns, he adds, "Don't ever grab me like that again."

"Okay. I won't."

"So . . . are you going to tell me why you need a ship now?" Kevin asks.

"The acid storm they experienced in the Outskirts is only the beginning," I say, taking a step forward. "Your uncle sent us here because there's a bigger geographical storm coming."

Kevin stares at me blankly. "What do you mean?"

Mars shoves his glowbeam back onto his belt. "It means that in less than thirty-something hours, you're all going to die. Every last one of you."

21: VAIDA

Planet Nevarnost: Year 3051

"It is nearly 3:30 AM. What are we waiting for again?"

I ignore Nia's words, keeping my eyes locked on the Nucleus building ahead. Nothing like staking out in a back alley with a Nost in your ear like a second conscience.

"A provision worker from Zone 3 should be coming by in the next hour to deliver rations. We'll sneak in with him." I motion ahead to the lift doors on the backside of Nucleus, hugging the street corner. "The main building is locked for the night, and Dad's ID card won't work on the Bay's personal entrance, so we don't have any other choice."

"Perhaps the fact that the only other signs of life in this radius are the sounds of rats chittering is a sign we should go home," Nia says, leaning against the automated dumpster.

I fiddle with my knife. "You can go if you'd like. I'm fine here on my own."

Truth is, I was hoping my lack of conversation would've scared her away by now. If we start chatting too much, she'll bring up her conversation with Zee again, and that's the last thing I need on top of the nerves tightening around the idea of murdering a man in cold blood.

Nia tilts her head. "And how do we know for sure this delivery person is coming?"

Because the morning after my night with Soren, when Chancellor Bay led me through the back way to avoid attention, we stumbled upon a weekly delivery of aqua pods and other expensive beverage stock for their ridiculous server bot. But I can't tell her that, so I say, "I just know."

Imagine a world where Outskirter children are drowning in their own blood from lung sickness while plum-suited businessmen sit in conference rooms, being served refreshments from a heap of AI-programmed space metal on hover wheels.

I perk up when I spot Soren, of all people, crossing the street.

He enters the alleyway, triggering the motion sensor, and an exterior light blinks on above the lift. I expect him to reach for his scanner card, but instead he paces erratically.

"It's a bit early for a walk," Nia comments quietly.

I keep my head down. This is the first time I've seen Soren since it happened. He's not just the lonely boy in the courtyard anymore. He's the father of my unborn child. And the thought makes me more nauseated than any bout of morning sickness ever could.

Not to mention, I'm literally here to take out his dad.

Soren stops pacing. Nia and I creep closer, ducking behind a line of decaying solar scooters on dead charging docks. A sharp ping echoes from his digiband. We watch as he types message after message on the projected keyboard.

"What is he doing?" Nia whispers.

"I don't know," I whisper back.

Then, two men wearing tattered clothes approach. The kind of guys I've seen hijacking solar carts in the Outskirts or stealing supplies from the ration shed. Some say they live in No Man's Land. Others say they drift from place to place without a home.

Simply put, they're roake hunters.

A smirk spreads on Soren's face as they make a silent exchange—a bag of tokens for something small and orange, catching the hazy light.

After the two roake hunters leave, Soren heads for the lift and fumbles in his pocket for his ID card. The normal thing to do would be to walk up and politely ask him to let me in. But considering he hasn't returned a single one of my messages since that night, I'm going to do things my way instead. I put a hand on Nia's tentacle and fill her in on my next thoughts.

Sometimes the Nost's invasive gift does have its perks.

She nods, and together, we move in on Soren.

I take him from behind, whip him around, and lock down one of his arms. Nia pins the other. He thrashes between us, cursing, and the orange syringe tumbles from his hands.

It rolls across the stone alleyway.

As Soren groans, I shove him toward Nia and snatch it up.

"Vaida, what the fuck?" he spits.

"Don't move, or I'll smash this." I dangle the syringe in his face. The neon glow reflects off his sallow skin and into his bloodshot eyes. "You're going to let us in."

"Why the hell do you need to get in this early?"

I raise the syringe again, and he flinches. "Okay. Okay. Fine. I don't care. Just don't . . . smash it. Gods."

Nia gives him just enough slack to tap his ID. A green light flashes on the lift's control panel, granting us access. We all step inside. I press the penthouse button and steady my uneven breath as the lift lurches and begins to rise.

Soren sneers. "If you wanted to come play, you should've just asked."

I lift the syringe higher. "Don't patronize me."

"Fuck—I'm *sorry*." He jerks his head, his sweaty hair falling into his eyes, and continues to writhe in Nia's arms. "I see you brought your little Nost friend with you."

"I don't particularly care for you either," Nia says bluntly.

I glance at her. "See? Told you I had a plan."

"Yes. I can see it was well-thought out."

I smirk. Nia smirks back.

This is the version of her I want by my side.

Soren's eyes stay locked on the syringe. "Careful . . . with it."

I roll it between my fingers, watching the liquid bubble inside. "What is this, anyway?"

He drops his head. "Wouldn't you like to know."

"I would." I jab him with my elbow. "Enlighten me."

Soren's knees sway, and Nia stretches her tentacle to keep him steady. "It's a venom shot," he says. "Some science geek from Zone 1 collects roakes and modifies them so they're stronger. I pass them to the hunters. They extract the venom in exchange for a lot of tokens."

"If you take that shot, you will die," Nia says plainly.

I study the boy I once swooned over, my nausea deepening. I knew Soren had experimented with roakes once or twice, but this . . . this is an addiction. It's in the way he looks at the syringe, the way his fingers twitch for it.

"Wait." My mind wanders back to the memories I saw in

the Hallow. "Did you say some science geek from Zone 1? Is Kevin Hale your dealer?"

Soren forces a chuckle. "Hale's my *supplier*. Not my dealer. In fact, if you see him, tell him he owes me another batch. I've been trying to get ahold of him all day."

I scowl. "Yeah. Sure. I'll tell him."

The lift doors slide open, and we step into the foyer, where a fresh bouquet of green and gold chimeflowers sits in an antique clay vase on the decorative entry table. Their silky petals unfurl in our presence, offering us a sweet greeting lullaby that sounds like the tune my mother's old music box plays when I crank the lever.

I watch the vibrations of sound for a moment, playing between their fuzzy centers, then quickly look away. Significant time has passed since I've been here, but for some reason, it feels like I never left. The chimeflowers' song continues faintly in the background as we move into the entertaining room, which looks exactly like it did two months ago, too.

A moss-colored, U-shaped couch takes up the majority of the space. Two glittering bronze bar carts wait fully stocked for the chancellor's next gathering. The retractable projector screen, which Soren and I watched movies together on every night during my stay, was never rolled up and put away, so it still covers the floor-to-ceiling window overlooking the entire Hemisphere and the Outskirts beyond. I told myself I'd never give Soren another chance to lure me in, to manipulate me on his own terms. Yet here I am.

Only this time, he's here on *my* terms.

"If you're here to see my father, he's in his study suite down the hall. Probably combing his hair, whitening his fucking teeth, or whatever the hell he does this early in the morning." Soren twists in Nia's grip, lips curling. "Now let me go and give me the syringe."

Nia leans into me. "Vaida, you cannot give him that vial. He will overdose, die, and you will forever be haunted by your choice."

I'm already haunted.

But Nia's right.

Soren isn't who I came here for today. It isn't his blood that'll be spilled.

I force myself to look at him. Not the version he's become, not the version that lured me in, but the boy I once knew. I try to summon the same empathy I felt for Kevin in the Hallow.

A series of events shaped Soren into this mess. Do I blame him for the shitty cards life dealt him? No. Do I believe it's on him to make better choices here? Absolutely.

But I wouldn't wish a life of roakes on anyone.

Except . . . Chancellor Bay.

On second thought, maybe this venom shot will be of use to me.

"Well?" Soren says. "Give me the syringe, or I'll report you."

I don't need to tell Nia what I'm thinking this time. When I motion toward the massive storage cabinet on the far side of the room, she lights up, drags Soren over, and together, we shove him inside and lock him in.

He bangs. He yells.

But Nia and I are already gone.

I stow the syringe in my satchel for safekeeping, and a sudden surge rips through me. I've never been this close before. I'm about to face the chancellor. I'm finally going to tell the man who took everything from me exactly what he deserves.

And then I'm going to kill him.

The entrance to Chancellor Bay's study suite is a decontamination chamber.

Nia and I move to one side, triggering the system. I unsheathe my brother's knife, let it hang at my side, and lower my face rag. A sterile mist seeps from the ceiling grates, leaving a sticky film on my skin that reeks of antiseptics.

"How odd," Nia murmurs.

Once it's finished its cycle, the doors open, and we enter. The chancellor's study suite was off limits the last time I was here, and now I know why. Shiny white tiled floors. Smudge-free, reflective walls. A gallery lines the far left side, filled with various paintings. *Actual* paintings, stretched across canvases of every size. Everything is so pristine it hardly seems real.

At the center of a smooth, crescent moon-shaped desk, a holographic projection of the Hemisphere rotates midair. To the right, an archway leads into an alcove bursting with vivid greenery and flora hanging from baskets and sprouting from planter pots.

Nia wears the same perplexed expression I imagine I do.

I step further into the suite, and my boots sink into the springy floor. A sharp breath catches in my throat. *Grass.* Part of the floor is made of grass. So green. So alive. So *real.*

This can't be Nucleus.

"Ah, Miss Wardell."

I jerk my head up.

Chancellor Bay stands on a floating running track in the

corner beyond the alcove. An actual running track, and he's not even out of breath. I've never seen him out of uniform before. In plum joggers and a tight black T-shirt, he almost looks ordinary. Not like a monster at all.

I didn't expect him to seem so . . . human.

"Ah, you've brought Nia with you," he says, powering down his machine. He coasts on the last tug of the track before stepping off the hovering platform. Grabbing a towel, he dabs the sweat from the back of his neck. "And a weapon, I see."

My hand hitches at the hilt of my brother's blade.

He crosses into his study and sits at his desk, barely sparing me a glance as he gestures to the gray ottomans set up before his workstation. "Please, do sit."

"I'll stand."

"I know you think taking me out of the equation will solve all your problems and feed the raging fire inside you, but I can assure you, I'm not the answer. I'm merely a variable." He pulls a tray of aqua orbs forward and pops one into his mouth. The way he sucks it down makes my skin crawl. "That, and it wouldn't be your best interest. Can I offer you anything to drink?"

I shake my head. "You're wrong. Taking you out would be in my *very* best interest."

This time, he plucks a berry from a fruit bowl and bites into it. "How so?"

How can he be so calm? I'm standing here with a knife in my hand and he knows I want blood, but he's acting like we're meeting for tea and sugar crisp wafers.

It's because he doesn't see you as a threat.

A mist expels from a nearby diffuser, filling the air with lavender and the serene cadence of tranquil music. Fuck, this place is messing with me. *Think of all the suffering going on beyond these sterile walls. Remember why you came here.*

There are children suffering. He's living in luxury.

I exchange a glance with Nia and step forward, closing the gap between me and the chancellor's desk. If he wants a challenge, I'll give him one.

I'll show him what a threat I really am.

"Enough with the small talk, Ezra," I spit. "I know you're using the Outskirters to mend the Hemisphere and have no intention of helping us in return."

"Yes. That's exactly what I'm doing." He stands and returns to his plants, running his fingers through the colorful blooms as if we're discussing gardening tips and not the lives he's stolen. "Did you know that devil's ivy and chrysanthemums are natural air purifiers?"

That vein bulging on his neck. One swipe of my blade. That's all it would take.

"My father and Matron Nost Far spent years trying to get through to you. All the conferences and so-called alliances. Did those mean nothing to you?"

The chancellor plucks a dead leaf from a stem and lets it fall. "My position in this project has never been easy. I've made decisions that others weren't strong enough to make because they worried about upsetting the masses. Don't think my choices haven't come without guilt.

"You think I don't know what it's like to lose people I care about," he continues. "Or to hold a belief so different from everyone else's that it turns the people I love against me?" He hesitates, his finger spinning a fidget ring etched with an evil eye. "You know, you and I are not so different, Vaida. I, too, was once a rage-filled teen looking for my people and my purpose."

I tense my wrist. My blade casts back the artificial light.

This must be where Soren gets his manipulative, empathic charm from. Chancellor Bay wants me to feel sorry for him. He wants me to think he relates to people like me.

But there's no reality in which I feel sorry for a man who's damned so many.

As I take another step toward him, he says, "Our air quality is declining rapidly. In a few years, the air outside our dome won't be breathable at all. Now that your father's workers have reinforced the crack, our plans for dome-wide lockdown are right on schedule."

"A lockdown? Do you even know what's going on out there? People are dying. We're suffering. Innocent lives, with no choice in the matter . . . families . . . children . . . babies."

"Sometimes you have to sacrifice the few to save the many."

"No," I say, raising my knife. "You have to sacrifice one to save everyone else."

I lunge.

But before my knife finds flesh, Nia's tentacle wraps around me from behind and yanks me back, wrenching the weapon from my hand.

My brother's knife clatters to the floor.

My eyes go wide. "Nia, what are you—"

"Listen to what the chancellor has to say."

What the fuck? I thrash, but she holds me firm. I know Nia's stronger than me. Still, I claw at the slimy tendril around my waist, trying to pry her suction cups from my skin.

The chancellor watches, unfazed.

And somehow that irks me more.

232

"Let. Me. Go!" I yell.

"She's protecting you." The chancellor approaches with his hands tucked behind his back until he's standing just inches away. "You should consider yourself lucky you have a friend who cares enough to make sure you don't become a killer before you become a mother."

My shoulders sag. *Oh, no.*

"That's actually what I wanted to discuss with you today." He steps around me, retreating to the holographic display at his desk. "I don't know if you know this, but all medical records get sent to Nucleus, regardless of whether you see a Hub medic or a Nost healer."

He presses a button. The Hemisphere diagram fades into a new projection.

My profile.

My face.

My everything.

I know before he even says the two red words beneath my name. *"With child."*

Nia's gaze is like a sand serpent's bite. I can't look at her.

Chancellor Bay leans forward at his desk. "When a contraceptive implant fails beneath the Hemisphere and we know about it, we order an immediate termination."

My mouth goes dry. *Immediate termination.*

"It seems you and my son give me no choice," he continues smoothly. "You can kill me if you'd like, Miss Wardell, but my death will only make things worse for you and your child."

It's a good thing Nia's keeping me upright because my knees go weak. I don't know what I'm doing about my baby yet. I haven't known I'm pregnant for very long, but the more time that passes, the more protective I become of the

233

idea that there's a life relying on me, its mother, to keep it safe.

But I will *not* let someone else make that decision for me.

"You kill me," the chancellor repeats, "and all the people that are loyal to me will carry on my work, setting our plans into motion. But the alternative—" he refers to my diagnosis, still bolded red on the screen, "—is that I override the Hemisphere population rule and offer you and the child full immunity. You'll be allowed to live in the Hemisphere with us."

Full immunity.

My head spins. I can't even process it all.

The chancellor's tone turns soft. "I choose to look at this as another opportunity to give back. Access to cleaner air, water, and food. A bed to sleep in. A *real* one. And my protection, of course." He pauses and fiddles with his ring again. "You might also find some comfort in knowing you're not the first girl my son has . . . run into some trouble with."

A bitter taste coats my tongue. "I'm not the—there's someone else?"

"Another Outskirter. Poor girl. Came to us with an unfortunate dependence on roake venom. We took her in, had our best medics rehabilitate her, and now she lives here with her daughter." He tilts his head. "We gave her another chance. You could have the same."

I let out a laugh. Like, actually. He must be joking.

"You think taking in someone, letting her keep her baby, and giving her a roof over her head somehow makes this all better?" I shake my head. "And no, it doesn't give me comfort to know I'm just another one of your son's conquests. Another girl fell for this bullshit? Honestly, I'm embarrassed for us both. And how about you rehabilitate your own kid!"

Chancellor Bay's brow furrows. "I don't expect you to understand my decisions, nor my relationship with my son."

I mean, he's right. I don't understand. Any of this.

He speaks about my situation like it's casual, like I'm selecting my fate from some digital catalog. I could have the *same* life as the other girl Soren used.

Because that's completely normal, right?

But full immunity for my child . . .

They would never know the sufferings of scrounging for food or the pain of belly bloat from drinking murk water gone bad. They wouldn't have to earn a good night's rest or live in constant fear of poisonous beasts and other sand terrors.

It's an offer I'd be a fool not to consider.

But it goes against everything I believe in.

"Feel free to take some time to think it over." Chancellor Bay rounds his desk like a cave cat circling its prey, holding my stare, knowing he has me exactly where he wants me.

I hate him.

"Though don't wait too long," he adds, his expression hardening once more. "My plans to close off the Hemisphere are moving swiftly. The sooner we get you settled, the better."

Nia finally releases me, but I don't move. My feet stay firmly planted.

You could still do this. My hand drifts to my pocket. All I'd need to do is reach in, pull out the syringe of venom, remove the cover, and jab it into his neck.

The poison would take care of the rest.

"Shall I call a patrol officer to escort you out of Nucleus?" Chancellor Bay asks, opening the contamination chamber door for us. "Or is there something else you wish to dis-

cuss?"
  Without answering, I leave.
  Because I think we've discussed enough.

22: VAIDA

Planet Nevarnost: Year 3051

B ack on the streets of Zone 5, Nia keeps her eyes down as we slink through the dark.

I want to yell at her for the shit she pulled back there in the chancellor's study, but I've been an asshole here too, a lying one who hid my pregnancy from her best friend.

"I wanted to tell you," I say, "but I didn't think you'd understand."

An extra-large sweeper trudges by, buffering the edge of the sidewalk.

"I understand more than you think." Nia waits for the sweeper to pass before crossing the street. "And I suspected your pregnancy before Zee confirmed. I was waiting for your honesty."

We stop outside a newsstand, where projections of twenty different digimags flash simultaneously, an obnoxious tactic to gain new subscribers.

"I don't tell you things because you judge me," I say bluntly. If she wants to have this conversation, fine. Let's have it. "Everything I do—how I spend my tokens, my plans for the chancellor, the tunnels I choose underground, the way I *speak*—you have a problem with it."

"I aim to guide you, protect you, and keep you safe."

"That isn't your job!" I exclaim, loud enough that the newsstand attendant closes his cart and wheels away. "You're supposed to be my best friend, but sometimes you act like my—"

"Mother?" she finishes for me.

I never asked for this.

"Exactly," I say. "But you aren't."

"You are right. I am not your mother." Nia's voice shifts, distant. "I did, however, make a serious promise many years ago to keep you and the child you carry safe until this moment in time. And while we're being transparent with one another, you make it incredibly difficult to help you or get close to you."

"What are you talking about?" I ask.

Nia exhales and closes her eyes. When they open, they gloss over.

I recognize the look. I've seen it my entire life in people I thought I could trust.

Am I a liar? Yes. I'll own that. But so is she. *So is Nia.*

I swallow hard. "How could you possibly have known I would get pregnant?"

Her posture stills. "I'm not supposed to tell you—"

"I don't care what you're *supposed* to do. Tell me!"

There's hesitation. She glances around like someone might be watching. Then she says, "Before the Arch fell, Billy Hale asked me to. I owed him a favor."

"And how could he have possibly known?" I ask.

"I don't know. He just . . . knew."

I don't know what's worse—that a man ten years ago somehow predicted my future or that my entire friendship with Nia has been a lie.

All those days plotting my next infiltration. All the nights spent in the Hub, laughing over meals and playing scrap games. The way she always listened to me complain about Dad.

Was any of it real?

Since the explosion, Nia's never left my side. She's always there to rein me in when I go too far. Always making sure I don't plot too hard and fall flat on my face.

And yet I don't really know her. Not *really*.

She never talks about her past. Never mentions the other Nost. I don't even know where she goes after walking me to my hut at night—just that she disappears underground.

A tremor runs through me, and I force myself to breathe. *I need the truth*.

"If Billy Hale never asked you to keep an eye on me," I say slowly, "would we still be friends?

Nia's stare drifts as she thinks of a response.

And that's all I need to know.

Rage spikes through me. I kick a low-riding mini sweeper, sending it sputtering before it stabilizes and scuttles off. Without another word, I storm toward the solar train station.

"Vaida, wait!" Nia calls, but I don't stop.

It doesn't matter anymore. *Nothing* she says matters.

She catches up with me, breathless. "You are acting childish. You are upset and running away from your problems instead of facing them. Please, just slow—"

"I'm acting childish?" I whirl around. The platform thrums beneath us as the incoming train approaches. "You've been lying to me this whole time."

"You have been lying to me too. What is the difference?"

"I lied about Soren. About my pregnancy," I say. "You pretended to be my friend for ten years. Maybe you don't see the difference, but I do. For a species that reads emotions, you sure don't seem to have many."

She doesn't waver. "Of course we have emotions. We simply don't let them consume us the way humans do. It's why we find you so fascinating. It's one of the reasons why we signed up for this project in the first place. Your species is ruled by feeling. It drives you to war, to violence, to destruction. We Nost acknowledge emotion, but we do not let it dictate our actions. Instead, we forgive. We don't dwell. We release what doesn't serve us. We live in the *present*."

I shake my head. "People like Chancellor Bay don't deserve forgiveness."

"There will always be a Chancellor Bay in your life," Nia says. "People will always wrong you. They will lie. They will disappoint you. That is human nature. Some have the self-awareness to make things right. Some never will. But chasing closure or an apology from someone incapable of giving it only harms *you*. Let go of what you cannot change, Vaida. Move forward to make a greater difference. Find the people who will understand you, who will treat you with respect and care. *That* is the solution."

A tear slips down my cheek. My fists curl.

How can she say that? After everything I've lost. Having to say goodbye to my mother and brother after the Unity fallout. Being forced to leave from the only home I've ever known.

Letting go is the last thing I want to do.

There's a difference between forgiveness and letting people get away with wickedness. There's a line to draw between feeling remorse for our mistakes and choosing to hurt others on purpose. But Nia doesn't understand that. And I don't think she ever will.

A rush of people parts around me, boarding the solar train.

Nia joins them, grabbing the stabilizing bar. "Get on. You will miss your ride back to the Outskirts."

I back away from the platform. "I'll take the next train."

Sadness grazes her eyes. The doors close.

And then, just like that, my former best friend is gone.

23: MARS

Planet Nevarnost: Year 3051

I think if I read another journal entry, I might keel over on the sustenance chamber floor. Right next to the broken shards of precious Hale family dinnerware we smashed in our earlier scuffle.

Somehow I ended up with the parchment versions while Timber and Kevin get to skim the digital versions. And after reading leather-bound notebook after notebook, I can only conclude that Elder Hale is about as sane as the mineworkers who willingly volunteered to take the night shifts during peak beast-prowling hours. Worse, every time I try to tell them this is a dead end, they both look up at me with the same ingenuous expression and tell me to *trust the process*.

I know better than anyone that you can short-order trust like a sugary pan of star bars on Seventh Day. Those honey-coated, blackberry-centered, star-shaped pastries Rose always gets in the Makers Market when she claims she's delivering watcher reports. We trust they'll be fresh, but they never are. Rose insists she likes them stale. I say that's just wrong.

Kevin Hale is a lot like a tasteless star bar.

Looks promising on the outside. Talks the talk, knows his

stuff. But the minute you take a bite, he's two blackberries away from spoiled. And he throws punches like a spineless dock fish. I'm not a sore loser, I swear, but I get enough trouble from Elder Hale back in the Dunes. I don't need another hot-headed slug on my case.

"A geographical storm makes sense given the recent daily reports. Weather patterns are off. Dust levels are rising. Atmospheric suffocation is accelerating." Kevin continues scrolling through his tablet while simultaneously jotting down notes on a pad. "I can't believe I didn't think of this myself."

"This log is about Violet Moon," Timber realizes, holding up a second tablet. "He recorded some of our tide patterns."

Kevin sits forward, sneaking a glance at Timber's screen. "He spent some time there when he was our age. Everything he described was beautiful and serene, so I'm not surprised he ended up back there. I still don't understand why he cut off contact with me, though."

Timber's earlier question pesters me: *How would you feel if someone showed up and told you your parents were alive?* Considering a plague took my parent's lives, I'd probably call the ritual master and plead insubordinate resurrection. There's a reason for everything. Maybe Kevin's uncle wanted nothing to do with this place after it was all said and done.

Though I can't speak for him. Elder Hale's a great big pill.

Keeping a firm hand hovering over the trigger on my glowbeam, I set the journal I'm skimming on the counter and lean back against a silver cold box in Kevin's dingy mess. I watch the way he and Timber scour the research on the table. They've flipped it upright again. Chairs shoved aside, backs hunched, they swap discoveries like two old pals. Why wouldn't they? They're family. Long-lost cousins.

My fingers twitch, instinctively reaching for the comfort no longer on my wrist.

The Trinket Gears shop owner wasn't lying about the buyer. The moment we sent my bracelet through the Gallivant, Timber's transporter shot back faster than light. He can never know what I've done. Truth is, I did it for one reason only. I am responsible for his return.

At least, that's what I keep telling myself.

"He mentions the airship in multiple entries but nothing about a location," Timber says, showing Kevin his screen. "Do you think it's here, beneath the Hemisphere?"

Kevin runs a hand through his hair. "No. He wouldn't have risked keeping it here. The chancellor would've confiscated it if he'd known. They have a . . . complicated history."

"What kind of history?" Timber asks.

Kevin lets out a laugh. "Oh. They, uh, dated. Briefly. When they were both seniors at the Academy on *Ophelia*. That was a long time ago, though."

"Elder Hale just gets more interesting by the minute. Too bad he sucks at giving proper mission briefs." I kick a shard of glass across the tile, and it ricochets off Kevin's steel-toed boots.

His sharp green eyes flick up, throwing me shade.

Instead of giving me the satisfaction of a retort, he turns back to Timber and nudges him. "Is there something legitimately wrong with Mars? Or is he always like this?"

Timber smiles. Only for a second, because then he catches me staring.

I clench my fists. I'm not sure why Timber and Kevin joking like two old school buddies gets under my skin, but it does. Maybe it's because if anyone's going to mess around with that considerably attractive, doe-eyed dolt, it's me. I'm his partner on this mission. Not Kevin. *Me.*

I feel a jolt in my gut as I realize the direction of my thoughts. I meant gentle, I tell myself. He's *gentle*, not attractive.

"Maybe his ship is hidden in the desert somewhere." Kevin steps around me to grab a new graphite stick from a wooden cup on the counter, then rummages through a drawer for some more scrap parchment. "Before it became the Outskirts, it was just No Man's Land. Nobody ever left the Hemisphere. It would make sense for Uncle Billy to park an aircraft out there."

"What are you doing now?" I ask as he starts scribbling again.

Kevin doesn't look up. "Making a list."

"That's a good idea. Lists are a great way to stay organized," Timber adds, and I think I'm going to be sick. "Did you know your digiband has a virtual planner feature?"

"Yeah, I know," Kevin replies. "Unfortunately, my digiband is waterlogged and isn't working right now. But I can't seem to think properly unless I write it all down."

"Father does that a lot, too." Timber taps his own digiband, but his is useless as well. "I do wish our holomaps worked, though." He looks at me for the first time since we started this cuddly sesh. "Do you think there's another way to sync it with Kevin's tech?"

Of course, he wants to use *Kevin's* tech.

"Nope." I straighten and join them at the table, placing my palms down as I lean on the heap of their mess. "Our equipment that pulls from the *Iris'* mainframe doesn't work on Nevarnost anymore for some reason. Truth is, we don't know how much time we really have. At this rate we're looking at only a possibility that there's an airship in the Outskirts, and by the time we search, it might be too late. You can't save anyone if you can't get ahead of the storm. That's the one thing you two bloated moon worms seem to keep forgetting."

"You don't seem very determined to figure this out." Kevin crosses his arms, rounding the table so we're face to face. "At least Timber and I are trying to do something about it. What have you done this whole time besides complain under your breath?"

Mercy me. A striking pain rattles my jaw as I clench my teeth.

"What have *I* done?" I stop myself from spitting in his face. "I got us here. And when the time comes, I'm the one that's going to make sure you and Vaida Wardell make it off this planet before that storm hits." I take a step forward. "Though I'm starting to wonder if you're worth it."

"Vaida Wardell? My uncle told you to save her too?" Kevin asks.

"Sorry. We must've forgotten to mention that," Timber says.

Kevin rubs his eyes. "It's fine. My uncle was best friends with her mother, so I guess it makes sense, but good luck trying to convince her to go anywhere. She's stubborn . . . like someone *else* I know."

"Mars is head of this mission," Timber chimes in, quietly, because Universe forbid he speaks in my defense against his new pal. "He knows what he's doing. There are just certain protocols we normally follow, and because our tech is down, we're a little off track."

Timber's words seem to appease Kevin, which irks me

more.

The Nevarnost slug relents. "Okay. Maybe we don't know if the countdown is accurate, but I bet—" He grabs his tablet. "—yes, I knew it. Suffocation rate is the lowest I've ever seen. Judging by this, the air outside the Hemisphere will be unbreathable by tomorrow around 10:00 AM."

I nod. Finally, some useful information. "That must be when the storm hits."

Kevin sets down his tablet. "It also happens to be one of the biggest peace rallies in Nevarnost Project history. It's that ten-year anniversary I mentioned. We're standing up to the chancellor and taking back the Hemisphere."

"Forget about a peace rally," I snap. "You're all going to die."

"I've been working on this rally for months in honor of my uncle and all those that lost their lives in the explosion. There are hundreds involved. From the Hemisphere to the Outskirts. We even have the Nost on our side. People are dying in the Outskirts. We deserve a chance."

"A peace rally will make evacuating people harder," Timber points out.

"We don't even know if we have a ship yet. Mr. Peace-keeper here won't prioritize."

"I am prioritizing," Kevin says. "The rally is going to happen whether our world is ending or not." He gathers a few pieces of paper and stuffs them into a dust-encrusted workbag. "In the meantime, we find the airship and try to talk Vaida into believing all this."

"It's all we can do," Timber reminds me, and it's not the first time today he's been the little voice of reason in my ear.

I secure my glowbeam. "Let's pack up and go then."

"We've got about another hour of darkness outside," Kevin says. "I'll grab some beamers so we can see in the desert, and then there's something else I need to do. If you two want to wait outside, I can meet you when I'm done."

"Take care of what? We don't have time—"

"Sounds good," Timber says, cutting me off.

Once Kevin is gone, I throw him a sharp glare.

"I'm sorry. I know I spoke out of turn, but leave Kevin alone, okay?" I turn away so I don't have to look at Timber. But he doesn't back off. "Mars, I mean it. I don't know what's going on with you, but don't take it out on him. He's going through a lot."

"Going through a lot?" I throw my head back with a chuckle. "You barely even know him. I mean, this might be the daftest thing you've said yet."

"All I'm saying is that if you must be mean and spiteful, save it for me."

I spin so fast it catches Timber off guard. His soft blue eyes widen like two gaping whirlpools ready to suck me in.

"Are you okay?" he asks.

Gods, I can't take it. I wish he'd stop asking me that.

I head for the door. "Keep your senses and whatever you think I'm feeling or thinking to yourself. They're wrong, just like you're wrong for this mission."

I push past him and stomp on, halting in the entryway. Tempted to go all the way outside, so Timber can't read me or take in my energy—or whatever it is he does with everyone he meets, everything he touches—I exhale, ready my glowbeam, and adjust my breather.

Minutes pass with no sound or movement in the residential unit.

What is taking them so long?

As I go to secure my pack, my fingers brush the transparent sphere Rose packed for me last-minute before sendoff. It rolls onto the floor and splits open, releasing the Confess Me Moth fluttering around inside. My throat thickens. *Oh, come on. Not now.*

I call it back toward me, and it lands on my shoulder.

Rose's voice drifts off its antenna and into my ear: *"Ah, so you needed my encouragement after all."*

My lips quirk ever so slightly. Regardless of our nontraditional situation, she is one of my people, and I do miss her.

"This is not going to be what you want to hear. In fact, it'll probably upset you. You'll probably scoff or roll your eyes or slam your hand against some wall somewhere, but you'd better listen anyway. It's okay to need someone. You don't have to do this alone."

I suck in a breath and hold it. *Gods, Rose,* I think.

"Let him in, Mars," her voice continues. *"Let Timber in. I know you want to. He understands what you're going through. I hear Raine talk about him in the woods when we're on watch. You two are more alike than you think. Timber can handle you. All of you. Even the parts you refuse to let me see. Even the parts you think aren't loveable or worthy."*

I exhale deeply and pinch the bridge of my nose, closing my eyes so the burning sensation will go away faster.

"All my love. Kick some cosmic butt."

The Confess Me Moth rises in the air, and I snap out of it.

I pick up the transparent sphere and search for the moth to stow it away. It flies down the hall, and I follow it around the corner. The Confess Me Moth hovers in front of a door that sits slightly ajar. As I capture it and place it safely back in my pack, I catch sight of Timber and Kevin through the gap. They kneel beside a kind of expiry box, a hand-woven blanket draped over the top.

It takes me a second to realize what's going on.

A makeshift Ceremony of Rebirth.

Timber speaks the traditional invocations in Vio softly. Kevin listens, his head bowed. I make out most of it, but they keep their conversation faint. This is a moment I'm not meant to be a part of. Just like the last Ceremony of Rebirth I attended from the comfort of a shadow.

I wasn't welcome there, either. Because I was the one who caused it.

When a miner dies beneath the surface, they call the watchers even if there's no body to haul back up and bury. I remember standing outside the base of the mineshaft lift, frantically wiping my bloodstained hands on a rag, while the response team rushed in to clean up my mess. And when the brother of the dead miner came barreling down the tunnel in tears, every other miner knelt and took on his mourning as their own.

Just like Timber does for Kevin now.

I carry my burdens because I deserve the weight of it all. Timber carries burdens because his capacity to understand the suffering of others is so immense, he can't always control it. He avoids others because of it. Yet he cares so much about people he doesn't even know.

Why does he put so much care into *everything* he does without fail? Like wanting to help the boy in the recreation yard. Or with the children back in Unit 88. Or when he begged me to let him die in Trinket Gears because he didn't want anyone else to suffer.

He's too good, that's why. There's a goodness in him I'll never know.

"Then we wish them safe passage," Timber says quietly.

"We say *'ruetere u ethere.'* It means *'Return to Ether.'* Typically, we'd light some herbs. I don't have any with me. But her soul will cross over now. She'll be reborn. Into her next life. Everything will be okay."

"*Ruetere u ethere,*" Kevin repeats even softer.

I shouldn't be watching this. Intruding on someone's personal grief like a strange voyager. But I can't bring myself to look away. Timber just knew Kevin needed comfort, company, and the acknowledgement that someone cares. He keeps saying his sixth sense is a curse, but I think it might be a gift he has yet to understand.

I wonder what it's like for someone to offer such compassion. I know he's technically read me, but does Timber sense other things about me too? Does he *actually* know what happened in the mines with that miner? Does he know how much I regret it? How it keeps me up at night? How I might spend the rest of my life punishing myself for it?

Timber did say I was subconsciously scared of something.

I just assumed I was afraid of hurting people. Of being too much, too angry, or too toxic for others to form a decent relationship with. But having someone accept me, be there for me, or see the dark parts of me that even I can't bring myself to face sometimes—that's terrifying.

A fluttering movement catches my periphery, and I manage to capture Rose's Confess Me Moth. I consider her words again as I secure the sphere in my bag. Was she right? Should I be upset by her words or should I embrace them?

I rub my naked wrist, puzzled again by the choice I made. If I were to confide in Timber, would he tell me, like he did with Kevin, that everything was going to be okay?

Would he care for me in a way that I'm slowly realizing I'm beginning to care for him?

24: VAIDA

Planet Nevarnost: Year 3051

Billowing dark clouds hang in the night sky like an omen.

The acid rain has stopped for now, but that doesn't mean it won't be back. I descend the winding steps outside the Emergence Tunnel with dragging feet. Hard to give a shit when all the solar carts are either out of commission because acid has eaten away at their frames or because they've already been taken from the port. Either way, I'm walking home.

It's only a couple miles back to the Hub, but in this heat, it might as well be ten.

And I really need a hole in the ground. Turns out being pregnant comes with delightful perks: pelvic pressure, the constant need to pee, hormones I can't control. Every confrontation feels like the end of the world. My best friend lying to me for the entire duration of our friendship and telling me to get over every hardship in my life is like a stab in the back.

The back of my throat starts to burn. I blink back the waterworks forming in my eyes before they have a chance to become something more and reach into my pocket for a glowstick with half its juice left. I flip it on, casting a greenish glower over the few feet ahead of me.

There's no real path to follow out here. Especially in the dark.

Dust picks up and wipes everything clean. The next gale reveals a beaten path at my feet, one with divots and crooked tire grooves. *Someone had a joyride recently.* Can't say I blame them, though. Drifting is about the only fun left on this desolate planet.

I shield my eyes from a singing wind that howls like it's mocking me. A rickety grind comes up on my left, followed by headlights and the dull roar of an engine having just barely escaped corrosion. I dart aside as a solar cart zooms past, kicking up a cruddy cloud. Moments later, the cart reemerges in reverse, slowing as it pulls up beside me.

Through the settling grime, familiar green eyes come into focus.

"Need a lift?" Kevin asks, and I swear I've never been more thankful for this face rag hiding my enormous grin. It's easy to brush off the emotion I'm feeling as relief that I don't have to walk anymore. I mean, it definitely doesn't have anything to do with seeing him specifically.

Two boys about our age are with him. One scowls at me from the passenger seat while the other smiles shyly from the back. Kevin nudges Mr. Grumpy to scoot over, and Mr. Grumpy scoffs but moves to make room for me.

Once I'm in, we take off in another bout of dust, picking up speed along the sand.

By the light of my glowstick, I glance at Kevin and notice the glassy sheen in his eyes. A trace of redness. There's something different about him. Usually he jumps right into conversation, grinning at me or spouting some nerdy fact about *something*.

"Did you see your nana?" I ask.

His knuckles tighten around the wheel. He keeps his eyes trained on the path ahead. Not a *'pay attention to the road'* kind of stare, but a *'you asked the wrong question'* kind of stare.

Something definitely happened.

"Um." I shift in my seat, eyeing our guests through the rearview mirror. "Who are they?"

The blonde-haired boy leans forward. "I'm Timber. This is Mars. Kevin is helping us."

I quirk a brow. "Cool . . . I guess?"

"We've got business in No Man's Land," Kevin says flatly, eyes still locked on the road ahead. "And I need to talk to you later. After I meet with your father about irrigation grids. Where do you want me to drop you off?"

His tone is so . . . *blah.* It's like he's here, but his mind is somewhere else.

Either that, or he's decided I'm not worth getting to know anymore.

Do crushes fade that quickly? Maybe I was too sassy. Too unkind. Or maybe he knows I know his secrets.

It probably isn't that serious, Vaida. Why do you care so much anyway?

"I should be free later, and you can drop me off anywhere," I say. "Outside the Hub. On the way. If you want to slow a little, I could even tuck and roll out right here."

The faintest hint of a smile rises in his eyes. It's small, but it tells me he hasn't fully cut me out yet. And considering what happened with Nia, I won't push it.

"I think we have enough time to safely stop the vehicle," he says.

"I beg to differ," a voice snaps behind us.

I do a double-take over my shoulder and glare at the boy called Mars.

Kevin seems to ignore the blunt comment entirely and pulls over outside what's left of a line of Outskirt dwellings. Caved in and sunken, they aren't livable anymore. It's sad. There'll be a lot of rebuilding to do after this—when resources and materials are already scarce.

"Thanks for the ride," I say, hopping out and rounding the solar cart.

"Hey, Vaida?" Kevin calls.

My ears perk up at the sound of my name.

I approach his side of the cart. "Yeah?"

"Can you just, uh, tell your father I'm going to be late for our meeting? I have to take care of some things, but I should be there soon."

"Very important things," Mars interjects. Timber attempts to silence him but fails miserably and gets cursed at in a language I don't understand.

"Well?" Kevin continues. "Would you mind doing that for me?"

I want to ask him what's wrong. He isn't acting right.

We've been in each other's presence for a solid twenty minutes now, and I don't have the urge to slap him over the head or argue with him out of sheer annoyance.

"I'll tell him," I say. "But, hey, you know—"

"Thank you so much," Kevin cuts me off. "I'll see you later."

Dammit. Lost my chance. The cart roars to life again and they disappear into the distance, their headlights devoured whole by the endless void that is No Man's Land.

When I enter the Hub, I'm surprised by how much progress we've made in healing and mending those who suffered the worst of the acid rain. The Nost work along-side our few medics, distributing whatever supplies and reserves they have. All the mess tables have been pushed to one side, and a resting area has been set up with old mattresses and cots.

It's organized chaos, but it'll do for now.

Dad must be around here somewhere.

I won't be able to look him in the eye and tell him I'm pregnant, let alone that I've been invited to live in the Hemisphere. It's a decision that still weighs heavily on me. And as I glance around at the few remaining Outskirters, I realize it's them I'd be betraying. They look up to my father, their leader. What would they think if I ran off and joined the man who put them here?

Even if the Nost help them rebuild, some of these people lost partners, children, and friends. I know I can't only think about myself anymore. There's an innocent child, with no say in the matter, who's counting on me to do the right thing.

But what *is* the right thing?

I join the guards stationed in the back of the Hub, gathered around an array of radios and parts they've salvaged.

"Have you seen my dad?" I ask them.

One points toward the back storage room.

I continue on, embracing the uneasiness in my bones. *At least tell him you're pregnant.* I don't have to tell him who the baby's father is. I'm just hoping his reaction will help me decide what I should do next. Not that I need his permission, but I think it'll help.

He's either going to be pissed, supportive, or both.

Thirty or more pairs of eyes fall on me when I open the door. Worse is I don't recognize half of them. Some are Nost, Matron Nost Far among them. A lot of them are Outskirters, although that isn't the issue, either. The issue is that the rest of the people in this room are wearing carbon face masks. There are Hemisphere people here.

What the hell did I just walk into?

"Excuse me, Far. I'll just be a second." Dad appears and gently takes me by the shoulders, blocking my view of what's going on beyond him. "Vaida, let's go out—"

I shrug away from him, duck under his arm, and enter the room fully.

I get a better look at the poorly crafted Hemisphere model in the center. Next to it is an even worse-off version of Nost Territory complete with various labels, markings, and maps. Hand-sewn banners hang overhead, drying. Buckets of multicolored pigment pellets are being sorted. And the one thing I keep seeing over and over again is the Unity symbol, the unmistakable tree of life, plastered everywhere.

"What is this?" I ask Dad.

"This is a project we've been working on." He reaches out again in another attempt to draw me in, but I keep my distance. "I've been meaning to talk to you about it."

My fists clench at my side. I throw dagger eyes at every single one of them. All this time, and nobody ever told me what was going on. The secrets. The lies. The deceit. Is this the meeting Kevin was going to be late to attend? More importantly, how *long* have they been working on this?

Then I spot Nia in the back, helping a Hemisphere girl with a rally poster. We lock gazes for a second, surprise splattered all over her face.

Fuck Nia, and fuck telling Dad anything about me. *I'm leaving.*

I spin on my heels and rush out of the storage room, back into the mess hall where Cook and his breakfast crew have begun prepping for the morning meal.

"We need to talk about this," Dad says, hurrying after me.

I make it all the way to the shack we share. It's still standing for the most part, aside from a collapsed half-wall. Along with the public toilet holes and shower stalls, most of our meals are served in the Hub. So there isn't much to think about when it comes to packing up.

I grab the holey canvas sack hanging on a hook by the side of my hammock, which is a disheveled mess as per usual. Whatever clothes I have go into the bag. Another pair of green cargo pants. Remembrances of Mom like her purple miniature ceramic elephant and her bronze music box with the mermaid figurine on top. My brother's jacket, tucked under my pillow. I pulled it off him before they took him away after the Unity Arch fell all those years ago, and I haven't slept without it since. I double-check my sleeve for his knife too, finding it safely there.

That's all I need. There's nothing else left.

"I wish you would let me explain," Dad says from the doorway.

I work around him, fumbling through old boxes and metal tins for anything else I might have missed. "You've been working with Hemisphere people. There's nothing else to explain."

"Yes, I have been. It's been a slow process, but we're making a difference."

Heat rushes through me. "Chancellor Bay isn't going to let us back into the Hemisphere," I spit, grabbing my cracked hairbrush off a hammock-side crate. "That alliance you and Matron Nost Far spent so long building together? He just wanted your laborers to fix the crack over Zone 7. He's planning on closing off the Hemisphere and leaving us out here to rot."

A heavy silence settles between us. I feel horrible being the bearer of bad news, but Dad's been under this peaceful illusion long enough.

He needs to know the truth.

"I didn't know about him closing off the Hemisphere. That might make things more difficult. Certainly not enough to call the whole rally off, but, Vaida," Dad says gently. "Far and I knew Ezra would betray us in the merger. We've had a contact on the inside this whole time, relaying messages back and forth—"

"What do you mean by a contact?"

"The mechanism specialist, Kevin Hale. He's been working with us for months now, helping us gather willing Hemisphere people." Dad takes a step forward, a hopeful light in his eyes. "We're going to show Chancellor Bay that so many of us want to be together again. We're taking back the Hemisphere. We'll do it cordially, and we'll make a statement while we do it."

There were more people crammed into that back closet than I expected, but not as many as Dad makes it seem. All I can think of is them waltzing into Nucleus waving Unity banners, only to be met by Chancellor Bay's patrol officers and their weapons. They think they're going to make a difference by coming together and asking . . . nicely?

They'll start a war. There *will* be casualties.

"Your mother, Billy Hale, and everyone in the old Unity group believed we could get through anything if we worked together," Dad continues. "That is why we're doing this."

The weight pressing on me since I first set foot outside

the Nost healer's tent continues to build in my chest. "Mom and Ethan lost their lives because of Billy Hale," I choke out, swiping at the dampness in my eyes. "Now Chancellor Bay is going to do the same to you."

His eyes flick to me at the mention of my older brother. We don't talk about Ethan or Mom much. Sometimes I wish we would, but most of the time I'm glad we don't. My brother was eleven when the Arch fell. He'd begged Dad to let him rally with Unity that day. I know the reason Dad won't admit that Billy Hale is to blame for the tragedy is because he blames himself.

But I was there too, and I survived.

I shake my head. "Don't do this."

"It's already done," he says proudly, and this time I let him keep his hands on my shoulders when he places them there. "We want you to join us. I see so much of your mother in you. You have her drive, her voice, and her sense of leadership. She'd be so . . . proud of you."

A tear slips down my cheek. *No, she wouldn't be.* Not if she knew I was pregnant with the enemy's son's baby and seriously considering running off to live with him.

"You're just saying that so I'll let go of the past, grab a Unity flag, and follow behind you tomorrow," I say, my voice breaking. "You don't know anything about who I am."

He lowers his face rag, revealing his reddened nose and the graying scruff on his round chin. "Of course I do. You are my very . . . stubborn . . . but strong-willed daughter. You are sure of yourself. You aren't afraid to speak your mind, and you'd do anything for our people."

I start to tug away, swallowing the phlegm forming in the back of my throat, but he only pulls me closer. "And our people need you *here*. Rallying alongside them."

I blink, and more tears streak my cheek. I've just lost my best friend, and a boy I thought could be a friend or maybe even more—I can't lose Dad, too. But I also can't stand by him and watch the chancellor obliterate them all.

"I'm leaving," I say. "I don't want any part in this."

Dad follows me to the exit of our shack, where I push open the tattered piece of cloth covering the hole, letting in what little daylight has risen in the otherwise dull amber-green sky.

As I glance back at him one last time, I see glimpses of myself and my brother in his hazel eyes. This is the man who raised me. I love him, but I don't like him right now. I don't like that he's willing to risk his life or the lives of our people. I don't like that he thinks bringing harmony to a battlefield is the way to gain the upper hand.

"We'll be here if you change your mind," he says.

I don't reply. I slip under the cloth, pull up my face rag, and head into the morning haze. As I do, a rumble of thunder echoes in the distance. I stare up at the sky, watching the clouds shift and move with urgency. I might not be able to stop the rally, but I can finish what I started once and for all. No more impractical attempts. No more messing around.

Chancellor Bay's threats don't scare me anymore.

If he's dead, then maybe Dad and the others have a chance.

25: KEVIN

Planet Nevarnost: Year 3051

~~handwrite a to-do list~~
~~pack beamers~~
~~take a solar cart~~
~~ignore mars' attitude~~
find the iris
attend the rally meeting
tell vaida everything

A head of us lies the endless expanse of No Man's Land.

A harsh wind sweeps through the desertscape, kicking up dirt and tumbleweeds as far as the solar cart's headlights can reach. We're less than an hour from sunrise, but something tells me I might never see the two suns fully again. Even if visibility does improve, it won't matter.

Not with the storm clouds waiting on the horizon.

Timber and I lean against the parked solar cart, our beamers on full blast, while Mars sits hunched in the passenger's seat scrolling through Uncle Billy's old logs on one of my tablets.

"He must've been seriously enlightened back then," Mars says. "Because I've never heard Elder Hale talk about 'metaphysics' or 'reincarnation theory'—what even is this garbage?"

"He studied abstract philosophy in his free time," I say, reaching over to yank the tablet from his hands and earning one of his infamous death glares. "According to his later logs, there should be a canyon up ahead. Or maybe it's around the bend. Hard to tell right now."

"Everything looks the same." Timber sighs, adjusting his breather gauge. "Mars, is your breather struggling to filter the air, or is it just me?"

Mars flips on his beamer. "Mine's fine. It's the heat."

"It's the humidity," I correct him. "The air's denser now, and the temperature's rising. It'll cool off just before the storm touches down."

Timber loosens the sweat-soaked collar of his tunic. "We need to stay hydrated."

I nod slightly but don't answer, too busy scanning entries for anything we might've missed. Normally, navigating these sand dunes is second nature. After countless mornings hunting roakes in the dark, I've learned to find my way out here.

But right now, I don't feel like myself.

"Let's keep going," Timber says as he pushes away from the solar cart. "The ship is out here. I know it."

My attention shifts back to them while my mind struggles to make sense of everything else: time-traveling blood relatives, the peace rally tomorrow, the mortuary team likely picking up Nana by now, and whether Vaida made it back to the Hub okay.

Oh, and the storm that's supposed to wipe us off the

map.

Nana can't be dead. Uncle Billy can't be alive. I can't reconcile the idea that he abandoned me—left me and Nana here alone—just to run away and start a family on another planet. It doesn't make sense. None of it does.

I move to join Timber, who is staring at the barren horizon. "I don't think it's out here. If my uncle really did leave Nevarnost back in 3041, he would have needed a ship to get off the planet because they stopped sending transport ships long before that."

Mars grumbles under his breath from the passenger's seat. Ignoring him, I climb back into the driver's seat and press the starter button, letting the engine hum to life. Timber stays where he is, the warm gusts of wind stirring dust through his flitting blonde hair.

I survey the back of his head, then the slope of his shoulders and the rest of his lean frame. My mind drifts to an image Nana once showed me of Grandpa. Like I'm the spitting image of Billy, he was the mirror of his own father when it came to physical features.

But Timber? Timber doesn't look anything like my uncle.

Hale genes are strong. We're olive-skinned, dark-haired, and green-eyed. Timber is the complete opposite. Yet he reminds me of someone. I just can't place it.

The humidity is getting to me.

"Who did he marry?" I ask aloud, but Timber doesn't budge.

He tilts his head, staring northeast, where a small sliver of sunlight breaks through the clouds and illuminates a formation of rocks curved into a half-moon.

"Why does it matter who your uncle married?" Mars asks.

"Because according to his journals, finding a life partner

who aligned with him was important. He was dead set on finding his soulmate, and to him, it was a divine process."

"*Divine process*?" Mars blinks. "I swear we aren't talking about the same person."

"He committed to a Vio woman. Her name is Blithe, and they're very much in love," Timber says, then points to the rocks. "Right there! See how the sunslight hits that edge?"

Blithe. Vaida's mother's name was Blithe.

But they found her body in the rubble.

Mars is right. Something isn't adding up.

I stand and grab the overhead rail. I don't see what Timber's referring to at first, but when I squint—a glint. It's subtle, but it's there.

"Shiny like . . . metal," I say.

Timber nods.

I hop out of the solar cart, boots sinking into the sand.

Mars follows, and the three of us descend the slant toward the half-moon cluster, stepping into the cove it forms. As we near, I notice the squiggly marks in the sand.

Roake prints.

I've never hunted this far out, but it makes sense.

"If you see any rocks or divots covered with webs, step over them," I say, directing them to stay at the edge of the gorge.

As we round the corner, a structure takes shape in the shadows.

Sleek titanium alloy panels. Massive space thrusters. My chest tightens, and I grab my shirt above my heart, stifling an involuntary laugh.

There, half-buried in the sand, glistens Uncle Billy's aircraft.

"I can't believe it," I say. "It's been here all this time."

Timber's breather whirls. "The *Iris*. Thank the Gods."

"*Feaukere*. It'll take hours to dig it out," Mars grumbles.

With trembling fingers, I trace the smooth surface of the craft's tip where it juts from the sand. Even half-buried, it's better than I imagined from Uncle Billy's descriptions. There's an elegance about it I can't shake.

Timber climbs over a mound of sand, landing on the top half of the entry ramp.

He studies the keypad that controls the hatch lock. "This must be it," he says. "How you and Vaida Wardell escape the storm. How the *Iris* later ends up on Violet Moon."

"One little problem." Mars joins Timber on the ramp. "Other than the obvious dig job we've got on our hands, this ship is small. It isn't built to carry hundreds."

"We can dig it out," Timber says. "And try to save as many as we can."

Mars spits on the ground. "You want to tell everyone they have to decide who lives and who dies? Be my guest. I guarantee you'll start an uprising bigger than any rally. And don't even get me started on rations. That is if there are any and they haven't spoiled from sitting too long."

My fingers graze against the exposed hull of the ship. Mars and Timber are concentrated on logistics, as we should be, but I'm still stuck on the *Iris* being here. "If his ship is here, how did Billy leave Nevarnost the year the Arch fell?"

Both Mars and Timber gape at me. The weight of my question settles between us, thick as the layer of sand lodged in the left thruster. A whistle of wind fills the silence.

Finally, Mars says, "There was a transporter missing from the main docking box."

"He . . . time-traveled his way out?"

"Maybe. Dunno. As much as I'd *love* to sit here and dissect your uncle's disappearance, there's a mission at stake. We don't have a countdown anymore. But my guess is the storm hits tomorrow sometime during your rally. You still need to convince Vaida she's coming with us."

I chew the inside of my cheek. How do I even begin to explain any of this to her?

"You're right. I can process this . . . later." I drag a hand through my hair. "For now, I'll head back to the Hub, speak with Vaida, and attend the rally meeting. If you two want to start digging the *Iris* out and do an inventory to see how many people we could potentially take, I'll do my best to come back as quickly as I can. We're sneaking into the Hemisphere at midnight."

L ess than twenty minutes later, I'm back in the Outskirts.

As I approach the Hub, thunder rumbles in the dull amber-green sky.

The dark clouds are creeping closer. They'll be on top of us before we know it.

Even though I'm holding the physical list I made before we left my housing unit, I keep glancing at my wrist, expecting to see my digiband and Lux—only to remember she's waterlogged and tucked away somewhere in my pack.

I cross 'find the iris' off the list using a graphite stick, skip over 'attend the rally meeting,' and run my finger over the last task.

I have to tell Vaida everything.

And somehow not sound like I'm short a circuit when I do it.

Time travel doesn't sound crazy to me because I grew up reading about Uncle Billy's time-traveling adventures in his journals, but to anyone else, it'll sound like a folk tale.

When I spot Vaida walking away from a half-fallen shack, I tuck the graphite stick behind my ear, shove the scrap of paper into my pocket, and brace myself for her disbelief.

She adjusts a canvas bag that's much too small for the load she's trying to hold inside over her shoulder and takes off toward the Hemisphere.

A moment later, Commander Wardell steps out of the same shack.

His eyes are watery behind his mask as he watches his daughter go.

"Sir?" I say.

"Ah, Mr. Hale. We're all waiting for you in the Hub." I glance after Vaida again. He must notice because he adds, "It seems my daughter is leaving. She won't be joining us, I'm afraid."

What? *No.* I need to talk to her. She can't leave.

"I apologize for my lateness," I tell him. "But do you mind if I—"

"Be my guest." He steps aside, gesturing after her. "Though I'll tell you that once Vaida sets her mind on something, she's hard to persuade otherwise."

Trust me. I know.

We head in opposite directions. Commander Wardell toward the Hub, me breaking into a light jog. I catch up with Vaida just as she passes the ration shed.

"Turn around, Hale. You're the last person I want to talk to right now."

I chuckle. "I'm seriously convinced you have eyes in the back of your head."

269

She spins around, her swollen eyes brimming with tears. "When were you planning on telling me? Or were you just hoping I wouldn't catch on?"

Not what I was expecting. "I have no idea what you're—"

"Don't act oblivious. I know you're part of the Unity revival. You're working with my father. That's what this whole thing has been about. Not some stupid merger."

I take a beat. Close my eyes. Let out a breath.

"It's complicated, okay? I promise it isn't—"

"You *lied* to me. You let me think I could trust you."

"I never lied. You never asked me if I was working with him."

"Why would I ask you something like that?" She tosses her bag on the ground. "I don't get you, Kevin. You know exactly what the chancellor is capable of. He uses you, takes advantage of you, forces you to impersonate your uncle, and holds it over your head to get what he wants. How could you think a peaceful approach is going to accomplish anything? The minute he sees you coming, he'll sic his patrol officers on you like it's nothing."

How does she know all that?

"I'm not sure what you're referring to, and I get that you're upset, but—"

"You know what I'm referring to." She cuts me off and lowers her face rag. "I saw your memories in the Hallow. I felt your emotions through the Specters. I know what Chancellor Bay's done to you."

I swallow hard. "You . . . saw all that?"

"Yes."

I search my mind for another explanation, but nothing comes. I don't even know what to say. There were . . . personal details revealed in those memories.

Including how I feel about her.

"Like *everything*?"

"Don't be weird about it." Her tone softens. "I wasn't going to say anything, and honestly, I don't care, but you know he'll go after you, right? Chancellor Bay will go after my father. He'll punish the Outskirters. He might even go after your nana."

I wasn't going to tell her about Nana either.

But I won't lie.

"My, uh . . . nana passed away last night," I mumble. "I went to check on her, and she'd gone in her sleep. The medics put in the order to have the mortuary pick her up."

Another tear slips down Vaida's cheek. She dabs it away. "I'm sorry."

I fight the urge to break down too. Right now I have to tell her about the storm.

"How can you not hate the chancellor for what he's put you through?" she asks, searching my eyes as if she's trying to understand. "How can you not want him dead?"

I don't have an answer for her. Not one that will satisfy her.

"Come back to the Hub with me," I say. "Let me show you what we've been working on. I can show you the maps, the plans, and the list of all the people who are joining us."

Her voice breaks. "I can't, Kevin."

She's crying now. For real.

If I reach out and attempt to comfort her, she'll slap me away.

I take the chance anyway. To my surprise, she lets me wrap my arms around her. As her head rests against my chest, my pulse thrums. It feels right, and I don't want to let go.

"Hey, it's going to be okay," I whisper, running my hand gently over her hair. "And of course I . . . hate him. I just decided, a long time ago, I won't *be* like him."

She lifts her head. "Somebody has to stop him."

"Ezra will get what he deserves." I watch the way she takes me in. "But we have to be better than him. Using wickedness to stop wickedness is like trying to force two magnets with the same poles together. They just repel each other. It's up to us to break the pattern."

Vaida lowers her face again and murmurs something against my chest.

"Come again?" I say softly, tilting her chin until she looks at me.

"Please don't judge me," she repeats.

"I never have. And I never will."

"I don't need a lecture." She pulls away, taking her warmth with her. "Dad won't listen, Nia and I aren't talking, and I don't have anyone else to tell."

"No lectures. Got it."

"I'm pregnant," she says. "It's Soren Bay's."

She's pregnant. "I didn't know you and Soren were—"

"We're not," she says. "It was a one-time thing. Don't worry."

My face goes hot. "Oh, I wasn't . . . worried."

"Yeah. Well. I'll bet it makes you think different of me."

Why would she think that? "Uh, no. It doesn't. I'm not really someone who judges others for their past, so all good there. Are you—are you okay? Do you need anything?"

Vaida stares at me. "I'm pregnant, and you still like me?"

The heat returns, this time down my neck, into my chest.

"I mean, yeah, Vaida. I *like* you. I thought we already established that." I let out a laugh to stop myself from stumbling on my words. "I've been keeping my distance because I can't read you that well, and I didn't want to make you uncomfortable or upset."

"No, I get it." She picks up her bag and dusts it off. "It probably wouldn't have worked anyway. I think we both want different things."

"I'd disagree, actually, with that statement." I force myself to be bold because I think she's just making up excuses now, and she hasn't looked me in the eye since she admitted to being pregnant. "We both want the truth. We both want to make things right, and we both want what's best for our people."

"Maybe . . . It still wouldn't work, though."

I shove my hands in my pockets. "I'd say I disagree again, but someone once told me I should work on taking rejection, so I'll just say I understand and respect your decision."

Her lips curve into a smile.

She glances over her shoulder, making a motion toward the Hemisphere. "Thanks for listening, but I have to go. Chancellor Bay offered me a place. I'm going to make him think I'm taking him up on his offer, and then I'm going to find some way to . . . bring him down."

Why does it feel like 'bring him down' is code for something much worse?

My mouth sours as Vaida begins walking again. Given what Mars and Timber have opened my eyes to, I don't even know if we'll even be around this time tomorrow.

I'd hate for her to do something she might seriously regret.

"Wait," I call out, catching up with her.

"Kevin . . ." She lets out a sigh. "I've already decided. You can't stop me."

"Trust me, I know. But you need to know there's a storm coming."

"Yes. Your peace rally. I already know."

I shake my head. "Much worse."

She stops again, this time with her lips pressed in a line.

"Tomorrow, a massive storm will touch down and wipe us all out. The Outskirts. The Hemisphere. Everything," I say quickly. "I know it sounds crazy. I didn't believe it either at first, but these boys, they showed up from the future—"

"Stop," she says.

"I'm being serious!"

"No. You're just making things up now to try to get me to stay." She pulls up her face rag, but it doesn't hide the fresh tears welling in her eyes. "For a second, I thought you . . . understood me. I guess I was wrong."

Sadness rolls into me like a shockwave. "I do understand you."

She thinks I'm making it all up. *She doesn't believe me.*

"I'm telling the truth. Nevarnost was never meant to sustain human life long-term. We have an aircraft in No Man's Land. There might be a way off this planet."

I reach for her.

She pulls back, hurt and anger etched in her features.

"Don't follow me."

". . . Alright."

Even though it kills me on the inside, I let her go.

There's nothing I can say or do that'll change her mind now. For a split second, I'd gained Vaida Wardell's trust. I'd held her in my arms, and it was the only thing that felt remotely right in this whirlwind of a few days.

Now I've lost it all again.

I don't think I'll ever get it back.

26: TIMBER

Planet Nevarnost: Year 3051

M y arms shake as I drive my tactical shovel into the sand surrounding the *Iris* once more.

The impact causes my hands to slip, and a patch of skin, the size of a small sand dollar, peels from my palm. I wince at the sting, release my hold on the smooth metal handle of my shovel, and let my body slump against the mound of sand next to me.

Sweat drips down my face. My hair is soaked.

A searing headache pounds behind my eyes.

And it's *hot*.

My breather works overtime. Every half hour or so, I have to swap out the filters or the back of my throat fills with the taste of dirt. The sand in No Man's Land is finer than the glittering grit in the Dunes back home, but when it cakes together, it's heavier, as confirmed by how tightly packed it is around the *Iris'* structure.

Mars and I have been digging for hours, and Kevin still hasn't come back.

I expected Mars to be angrier about his absence, but it seems he's preoccupied, laboring his way through his side of the aircraft.

As I catch my breath, I watch him fling another shovelful of sand over his shoulder.

When he's done clearing out the bottom half of the right wing, he grabs his tactical kit, unscrews the shovel head, and replaces it with the pickaxe attachment.

The tip of his tool strikes solid rock. Its sharp clang makes me flinch.

Once the rocks come loose, Mars sets the pickaxe down, shrugs his jacket off his shoulders, and tosses it into the sand. Using the top half of his shirt, he catches the sweat streaming into his eyes before picking up a rock and throwing it aside.

That's when he notices me standing idly.

"The *Iris* isn't going to dig itself out," he grumbles. "Keep digging."

He picks up the tool again, strikes a larger chunk of rock, splits it in half, and hauls the pieces away. Then he grabs his pack, pulls out a canteen, and takes a long drink of water.

I set down my shovel and reach into my bag for my healing kit. "I'll continue digging after I tend to my blister."

"Better get used to it." He tosses his canteen aside before returning to his work. "You'll get a whole lot worse than that down in the mines."

I unroll some gauze and wrap my palm. I'd gone a solid stretch of hours without thinking about what awaits me when we return home.

Now the reality starts to sink in again.

Mars keeps swinging, chopping through rock after rock with barely any strain. I watch his form, the way his muscles flex with each movement. I glance down at my own arms, which are tingly and numb from the excavation and nothing compared to his.

"You don't get breaks either," Mars adds without looking at me.

He removes another boulder, then wipes more sweat from his hairline onto his shirt. As he does, his shirt rides up, revealing his abdomen—which is also defined.

I try not to stare. But I can't help it. Mars is built like a soldier. I'm lucky if I outrun the lemurs on my early morning walks through the North Wood.

The mines are going to eat me alive.

"Is it really that bad?" I ask.

Mars grabs his tactical kit again, swapping the pickaxe out for the shovel attachment once more so he can finish digging out the thruster.

"Yep. It is."

When I don't move or say anything else, he lets out a long sigh and shakes the dirt off his breather. "What do you want me to tell you? That it'll be hard at first and get easier? Because it doesn't. It's bad when you get there, and it gets worse the longer you stay down there."

He scoops a heap of sand and sends it flying.

"Just pray the scouts give you a day shift so you're not running from man-eating cave beasts on top of pulling raw aura quartz slivers from the cuts on your knuckles every night."

I finish tying off my gauze. "Man-eating . . . cave beasts?"

"Loads of 'em. Especially when you start drilling in those deeper caverns or crawling on your hands and knees through holes just big enough for one miner." He glances at me. "How long will your sentence be?"

I shrug. "They didn't really tell me. Probably forever."

"Lifers get first dibs on pry bars, but I doubt you'll be down there that long," he says, hopping down into the trench he's dug. "Get yourself a good pair of gloves. Weigh your harvest regularly so they don't accuse you of packing your pockets—"

More sand lifts into the wind as he continues shoveling.

"When the shift assignments come out on First Day, be there early so you get one closer to the entrance shaft," he says. "And don't breathe too deeply when the luster dust is thick in the air. It'll stick to your lungs, and then you'll be hacking up iridescent slush for days. Do that too many times and your cavernmates will try suffocating you in your hammock at night." Mars pauses, looks at me. "You'll struggle. But it'll be good for you."

Good for me? How does any of that sound good for me?

"Thanks for the advice. That all sounds horrifying." I pick up my shovel again and approach the hole I've started, though it doesn't look like I've made much progress. "Why would you . . . choose something like that, if you don't mind me asking?"

"My reasons are none of your bugging business—" Mars huffs, struggling to clear the thruster's nozzle. The densely packed sand resists his strained effort, and he lets out another scoff before stopping altogether. "You know what? It's a little too convenient that your father packed us these tactical shovel kits. It's almost like he *knew* this would happen."

Mars abandons his shovel, grabs his pack, and stalks up the entry ramp.

"Wait. Where are you going?" I ask.

But he ignores me and disappears into the *Iris*.

I stand there for a moment, listening as the wind picks up around the aircraft. A scorpion-like creature scuttles across the sand, pincers up.

I grimace, leave my shovel behind, and head in after Mars.

Entering the *Iris* feels both familiar and foreign. It looks the same as our version of the aircraft back home, yet different somehow. Father's remodels and personal touches haven't been added yet. This version of the *Iris* still reflects his old life—a version of him that doesn't quite fit, at least not based on what I know of him now and the person Kevin tells me he once was.

I search for Mars on the upper level and find him in one of the walk-ins, changing into a clean shirt. As he pulls it down over his head, he kicks his dirty one aside and rummages through the crates of rations, tech, and other supplies as if he's looking for something.

"I think we should keep digging the *Iris* out," I say.

Again, without responding to me, he leaves the walk-in and triggers the motion sensor in the adjoining chamber, illuminating four cryopods lined up beside one another. They sit idle, like small white space shuttles with domed glass coverings. Their stillness is almost eerie.

I lower my breather. "If we don't finish the job, the ship won't be able to take off."

"Please," Mars says. "Don't act like you were doing much out there."

He bends down and picks up an empty wrapper at his feet. As he turns it over in his palm, the shiny package catches the overhead lights.

"Postcryo Serum," he reads off the label before running his fingers inside and smearing a liquid between them. "Someone's used these cryopods recently . . ."

He crosses the chamber and opens the rubbish receptacle in the wall.

279

"This version of the *Iris* has been sitting here in No Man's Land for 10 years or more at this point in time," I say. "Why would someone be using the cryopods?"

He brings up three more empty wrappers from the bin along with a few bottles of prep-juice, examines them, then shoves them back inside and approaches the pod in the middle. From between the leathery padding that lines the pod for comfort, he pulls out an earring. A mini abalone shell painted with traditional Vio symbols, attached to what looks like a flare cub claw.

"Someone from Violet Moon has been here recently, too, and it wasn't us," Mars says through gritted teeth. "Now tell me your father wasn't keeping information from us."

I shudder. "You think he lied?"

"I *know* he did. There are too many coincidences."

I focus my gaze on the earring, at the Vio markings hand-painted along the curve of the shell. Kevin said Father spent time on Violet Moon way back in the day. Maybe it's left over from then? The twinge in my gut tells me it isn't. And normally I wouldn't indulge in Mars' obvious disrespect towards an elder's authority, but he's made fair points thus far.

As events unfold and the more we uncover, things aren't adding up.

"What—what do we do then?" I ask shakily. "Do we keep going?"

Mars swears under his breath, shoves the earring into his pocket, and turns away. "Start the inventory," he says. "I'll finish digging the ship out myself. I need time alone to think."

"Are you—"

"Yes, I'm sure."

Then he exits the regulation chamber.

An array of supplies surrounds me in the walk-in.

I continue checking expiration dates on rations, carefully setting aside any cans or emergency meal pouches that expired years ago and logging the remaining numbers in the tablet I found on the shelf. Freeze-dried items seem to be fine, most with a shelf life of twenty to thirty years, but I do my best to organize them all into piles. Plant-based meals next to insect-dense proteins. Powdered milks and starches with dry staples like grains and legumes.

It's the least I can do since Mars is outside doing the bulk of the digging.

The whole time I'm working, the earring he found earlier lingers in my mind. I go back and forth between wondering if we really are missing something and telling myself Father wouldn't intentionally deceive us. Every time I think I come to a conclusion, I second-guess myself and spiral into overthinking everything all over again. None of it's helpful.

I finish inputting the last ration and review the stock chart. A graph with the projected numbers flashes on the screen. I hit compute, and the figures appear. *Ugh.* Even if the survivors eat the bare minimum, we only have enough for a few people.

Around 4:00 PM, the lift opens across the hall.

Mars steps out, drenched in sweat. Dirt and dust coats every inch of him from his hair to the laces of his boots. One of his palms is wrapped in the same gauze I wrapped mine in earlier. As he tosses his shovel aside, it clatters across the shiny metal floor.

He lets out a labored breath. "Only took nine bugging hours, but it's done. Liftoff should clear the remaining sand from the landing gear. Any word from Kevin?"

I set a can of root stew in the discard pile. "No. None."

"Great."

"He said he'd come back as quickly as he could."

"I *know* what he said," Mars snaps. "But if he's not here in the next few hours, I'm going looking for him. I don't care if he's planning his rally. I'm not letting him mess this up."

"I take it that means we're still moving forward with the original plan, then?"

"Your father is still a liar, but there's obviously a reason he wants us to save Kevin and Vaida." He shakes the sand from his hair. "We'll finish the mission and deal with the rest later."

"Alright," I say with a nod. "I trust your judgement."

With an eye roll, he grabs a set of fresh clothes from the heap of ISR gear I've separated from the sustenance inventory, then reaches for a ration pack from one of my other piles.

I straighten. "Hey, we need that. The provision numbers are low."

"I've just spent hours digging in the heat. The snacks your father packed us aren't enough." Mars tears into the ration pack with his teeth and spits out the plastic. "Besides, if there's enough for Kevin and Vaida, that's all that matters."

"I know. There is." I set the tablet down on a crate. "I just can't shake the thought of leaving everyone else here to die. I wish there was a way we could save more people."

"Not our problem. Take it up with your father when we get home. I'm going to turn on the water tanks and cleansing filters so I can wash up," Mars says, slinging the clean black shirt and pants he found over his shoulder.

As he walks away, I clench my fists. Maybe Father is a liar. Maybe he isn't. But I've had it with Mars taking his anger out on him. And I've had it with him acting like he doesn't care about anyone or anything. Especially when I know it's a coping mechanism, and a poor one at that.

"You're just looking for someone to blame," I say, following him.

Mars lets out a laugh and signals for the washroom to open. He sets his uneaten ration pack and clothes on the counter. "You're delusional, I swear."

He closes the door. My stomach tightens. If we're going to succeed at saving anyone, this conversation can't wait. If we're going to finish this, we have to work together.

I signal for the door to open.

Mars freezes, halfway through pulling his dirty shirt over his head.

He quickly yanks it back down. "*Feaukere.* What the—"

"I get that you're tired and frustrated, but you don't get to speak to me that way anymore." My tone sounds firmer than I expected. It feels good.

He glares at me. "What did you just say?"

Behind him, the cleansing stall faucet runs, its steam rising in the air. I step inside fully, unsure of where this courage comes from. I'm not backing down now. Not when I've managed to put my hands on him without crumbling into myself like a dying star.

"You've been horrible to me. You've been unnecessarily horrible to Kevin." I square my shoulders. "You can't keep treating people like this."

"I can't?" He grabs his glowbeam off the counter and aims

it directly between my eyes the way he did with Kevin back at Earhart Residential. "*Watch* me. Now get out."

"No. You'll have to shoot me."

As he revs up his weapon, I don't flinch.

He applies pressure to the barrel. "I oughta blast you into the wall."

"Okay. Do it," I say. "Get it over with."

For a split second, his expression settles.

A day ago, I would've backed down. Out of fear. A lack of confidence. Or because I didn't trust myself. But Mars isn't so scary anymore. I know his patterns. I've felt his touch.

If he was going to pull the trigger, he would've done it by now.

When he finally does speak, there's a surprising shakiness in his voice. "Don't you *ever* enter my washroom unannounced like that again. And don't you *ever* speak to me out of turn using that tone. I'm your superior on this mission."

"My—my superior?" My heart flutters at the word.

"Yeah. Me." Mars leans his head in and lowers his voice. "Not you. Certainly not that slug Kevin. *Me*. And quit acting like he's our savior, will you? It's exasperating."

I watch his eyes, his expression. The glossiness. The flush.

I don't even need to touch him to name it. This isn't just Mars losing his temper or unraveling like a loose suture thread with no anchor point.

This is jealousy.

Is that what this whole tough guy act is all about? Jealousy? And of who? *Kevin*? I might be wrong, but I don't think I am. It's written all over his face, and it would explain the instant aversion and mood swings. What I don't understand is why.

Mars has no reason to be jealous of anyone. He's . . . Mars.

As I step forward, he inches back, closer to the stream of hot water.

"A superior doesn't let his anger spiral out of control the way you do. A leader doesn't give up because details are misleading or because something doesn't go as planned."

I advance again, backing him against the inner stall wall so he can't run away or bull his way through. He glares at me over the barrel of his glowbeam.

Water pours over him as he chokes back a breath. "Anything else?"

"Yeah. There is," I say, keeping my body tight. "You might be the one calling all the shots. But *I'm* really the one holding it all together."

A sudden trill courses through me.

I prepare for a possible punch in the face, but I refuse to let the threat of connecting stop me from speaking my mind, from making myself small, or from standing up for myself anymore.

Surprisingly, Mars says nothing. Does nothing.

He lets the water pour over him while the steam continues to rise and swathe us both. I've hit his weakness. I know I have. I've triggered something in him, something dark, a pain only his flare cat can ease. Or perhaps the forced solitude of the mines.

Regret creeps in as I watch him process. *I never meant to hurt him.* I only wanted to understand him, to make my point clear. "I'm sorry," I say. "That was cruel."

We haven't looked away from one another.

We're so close now that I'm beneath the stream of water too.

If we moved another inch, our noses would brush. I can hear the thrum of his heart beating wildly in his chest. *Or maybe that's mine.* Sweat glistens on his skin, mixing with the oakmoss scent on his neck. It's the closest I've ever been to someone without shying away.

Mars lowers his glowbeam and lets it fall at our feet.

"You're right," he mutters. "I'm sorry—"

He shuts off the water and exits the washroom in a hurry, leaving a trail of puddles behind him. I stay where I am, dripping wet, the adrenaline of having finally mustered the courage to speak up for myself still tingling in my throat.

Did Mars just apologize to me? Did he just say he was sorry?

I head out onto the bridge in search of him, hearing him before I see him. His staggered breaths come from the walk-in. Soft gasps as he struggles to hold it together.

Gods. He's crying.

I start forward. "Hey—"

"Don't—" Mars holds up a hand. "What I'm feeling right now would send you into cardiac arrest, and then I'd have a dead slug on my hands. Give me a minute."

"Alright."

Mother always says that when someone is crying, sometimes they don't want to be fixed, or given a solution—they just want someone to hold space for them so they don't feel alone.

I *know* what it's like to feel alone. I don't want him to feel like that.

Then I notice his wrist is bare, and my heart sinks all over again.

"Mars, tell me you didn't trade your bracelet . . ."

He rests his forehead against the wall and lets out a long

exhale.

"Why?" I ease my tone. "Why would you do that?"

His eyes well. "You know why I did it."

I do know why. I would've done the same for him.

Mars faces me, his dripping hair half in his face.

"Let's just leave it at that," he says.

But I don't want to leave it at that.

As he swipes his wet hair from his eyes, the urge to feel his pain throbs inside me like a wound, begging for pressure to stop the burn. There have been times I've watched Raine go through struggles. Normally I'd listen to him vent from a distance. I've never wanted to purposely put myself at risk of mind-feeling his every thought as badly as I do right now.

I need to know what's going on inside Mars' head. "I'd like to hug you, if that's okay."

"You want to . . . hug me?" he mutters.

"If you're okay with it, I want to try."

"I'm covered in dirt. I reek—" He half-laughs through the sobs. "I'm a whole mess inside and out, Timber. It'll rip you apart . . ."

"I know," I say, "and I can handle it."

Mars wipes his nose on his sleeve and motions me forward. "Alright . . ."

He awkwardly makes space for me in the corner of the walk-in. I wrap my arms around his waist. At first he tenses, but when I rest my head against his chest, his body settles.

His damp, cold shirt sends a shiver through me. I ignore it, find my center, and close my eyes.

Then, I wait for the hit.

27: TIMBER

Planet Nevarnost: Year 3051

M ars' mind-space crashes into me like a wave.

He is the Vio ocean, and I am lost at sea.
All I can do now is let myself . . . sink.

I wish it were me he was comforting.

You're throwing your life away.

I love you so much, Mars.

We both want different things.

I'm the reason she's stuck.

You can't do this.

I'm going to kill you.

It's all my fault.

I endure the brine in the back of my throat.
"You're shaking, Timber," Mars whispers in my ear.
He tries pulling away. I tighten my hold.
And in return, he secures his embrace.
His emotions are one giant void. Navigating seems impossible at first, but when I choose a singular memory to latch onto, the others soon break into individual moments.

I wish it were me he was comforting. Mars was jealous watching me comfort Kevin at his grandmother's makeshift Ceremony of Rebirth.

You're throwing your life away. The Council of Elders shamed him the day he chose the mines instead of accepting a role on their council, but he did it because he wanted a choice.

I love you so much, Mars. Rose and Mars were in love the day they committed.

We both want different things. But they grew apart and fell out of alignment.

I'm the reason she's stuck. He carries the guilt of being the reason Rose will never be with someone who loves her properly because he's the one who asked her to commit first.

You can't do this. Mars caught another miner stealing crystal underground.

I'm going to kill you. The miner attacked him on a ledge, but then a cave beast came along, and the miner slipped and fell.

It's all my fault. Mars still blames himself for the miner's death.

A breath of fresh air finds my lungs as I break the surface.

I open my eyes, trembling hands still clamped at Mars' waist.

In the process of taking the totality of his inner world in, we've slid down the wall into a kneeling position. He swings his legs around so he's seated, and he keeps me upright, steady against his chest. Eventually my heart settles.

I slowly unclench. "You were right. You're a . . . mess."

He runs a gentle hand through my matted hair. "I tried warning you."

His deep slate-gray eyes water, and for a moment, it's like I can see the soul behind them. It's happened with Raine before. A moment where I feel like I know him in a way I can't explain. But with Mars, it's those hidden soft edges, just waiting to be explored.

"I wouldn't blame you if you ran the other way," he mumbles.

I look up, our faces inches apart. A heat rises between us from my palm against his chest. This has happened once before with Raine too, but it was an urge that came from him more than it did from me. At Kiki's dwelling, the day before I left for Nevarnost, his ever-persistent desire tingled on the surface of my skin.

What do you think Mars' kisses taste like? Voices of all the girls at the glowfish demonstration I attended all those years ago fill my brain. *I bet they taste like fire. Or the kind of venom that makes your tongue go numb. Gods, he's so handsome—*

Mars smirks. "You're blushing. You alright?"

Instead of words, my eyes fall to his lips. As I reach up and grab his cheek, his hand covers mine. Familiar desire rolls into me like a high-rising tide.

Only this time, it's mutual.

I draw him to my mouth, and his body quivers beneath my wandering hands. Our lips move in rhythm. Swirling tongues. Fingers weaving in wet hair. A shortness of breath.

He lifts himself up, shifts on top of me.

And the weight of him feeds the ravenous desire.

My fingers brush his navel as his lips rove tenderly along my jaw. Mars' kisses taste sweet. Not bitter. Something in between. I can't get enough of them.

"Dune skulls—" He huffs. "Are you *trying* to seduce me?"

I grip his forearm. "You don't like it?"

"Yes, I—*Like* isn't a strong enough word."

Pink creeps up my neck. "It felt like the right thing to do."

"Oh, it was," he says, sitting up. "But if I, uh, don't hold some semblance of self-control, we'll never finish inventory before Kevin returns. So . . . let's take it slow."

I force a laugh. "Right. We're on a mission."

Mars returns my chuckle, stands, and offers me a hand. Once we're both up, his hand lingers at my waist. "Don't think I didn't enjoy it, though. It was . . . mutual. Though you probably already know that from mind-feeling me."

"I do," I say with a nod. "And not to speak out of turn, but I think you should forgive yourself for all the other things I saw and felt while I was tapped in."

"You're kidding, right? You just defied your superior, practically seduced the living bugs out of him, and you're worried about speaking out of turn?"

I put my hand on his cheek, letting his warmth fill me up. The subtle vibrations of his pulse ripple through me, making me lightheaded, but I swallow the sensation, and it subsides after another self-soothing breath. "I'm serious, Mars. You can't blame yourself forever."

"I'll work on it." He gently shifts away from my hand and takes a step back. "In the meantime, I'm going to head to the lower level. There's another washroom down there and secondary walk-in to inventory. Stay up here and finish logging these supplies . . . Please."

"I think that's the first time you've asked me to do something nicely."

He keeps his gaze pinned in mine. "Well . . . yeah . . ."

As he steps into the lift, I say, "By the way, I'm a mess, too. If you could mind-read *me*, you'd probably run back into the mines without even thinking twice."

His lips curve. "Brutal analogy, Timber." Before the doors close, I hear him add, "But I know."

K evin never comes back.

By the time Mars and I finish taking inventory of the two walk-ins, change, take turns resting, and eat our rations, the brief sunslight of Nevarnost's daylight hours are long gone.

Now, night hours are closing in again, and all I can think about are the numbers.

Final calculations predict the *Iris* can sustain no more than 30 people for the month it would take to reach the nearest planet. That's with strict quantity regulations, carefully spaced living quarters, and accounting for all other emergencies.

There are thousands of people living on Nevarnost. How could we look any one of them in the eye and decide who deserves to live alongside Vaida and Kevin?

"We could load up the aircraft with extra supplies from the Hemisphere," I suggest, pacing the bridge for the hundredth time while Mars lounges on a pile of thermal blankets I'd organized earlier, a sketchbook of all things in his hands. "Or maybe from the Outskirts?"

Mars focuses on his shading, overlapping lines. "Still doesn't solve the space issue."

I stop by the bridge window, where in the distance, the Hemisphere gleams faintly amid the nearing black clouds. "Being in close quarters for a month beats dying in a massive storm."

"Too many people. Not enough time." He licks his thumb and cleans up the rough graphite edges of his sketch. "Imagine if Kevin were here . . ."

With a sigh, I join him on the thermal-blanket pile. "*Okay.* You were right. Maybe we should have gone looking for him. I just thought he'd come back on his own."

"Mhmm."

As he finishes the last bits of his drawing, my eyes drift to his side profile, lingering on his lips. Memories of us pressed together in the walk-in earlier this morning find their way into my head. My guess is that's the reason he's even indulging this conversation right now. Earlier he didn't seem to care, and in the many hours that have passed, there have been times I've questioned whether it even happened. Neither of us have brought it up again.

I did what he asked and stayed on the upper deck all the rest of the morning and afternoon so neither of us would be distracted. Even when I heard something crash down-level, I ignored it. He seems different overall, though. Calm. Renewed. And he hasn't called me a slug, dolt, or said "dune skulls" in hours. Not that I ever took his insults seriously.

Honestly, I'd grown to like them. Found them humorous even.

"Here." Mars tilts his sketchbook so I can see his finished piece. It's a sketch of me, standing by the window, looking out at the horizon.

"Wow," I say. "You're actually really good at that."

He rips the drawing from the pad and offers it to me. "If I give you this extremely thoughtful gift, will you stop obsessing over survivor numbers and let me go find Kevin?"

He's being sarcastic, but I take the sketch anyway because it *is* good and I do want to keep it. "As long as it doesn't involve dozing mist."

He clicks his tongue and gets up. "I make no promises."

"I'm sure he just got caught up somewhere."

Mars grabs his pack near the window. "*Or* something happened to him."

An uneasiness finds me. I hadn't let myself think about that.

"The rally isn't until later this morning," I say. "If we can't find him now, we know where he'll likely be. Almost every-one will be under the Hemisphere at that point."

Mars arches a brow at me, then stares at the dome on the horizon. He turns away abruptly. "That's it."

I scramble after him into the lift. "Wait. What is?"

The lift pings open. We walk down the entry ramp and into the dusty night air, where Mars' hard work becomes more apparent. Instead of having to climb over mounds of sand, we can now move freely around the aircraft.

I still don't know how he managed this alone.

"Oh, come on. Close your mouth or you'll choke on dust." Mars pulls out his breather and beamer, securing them both quickly. "It's not that impressive."

"Yes, it is." I go to do the same, keeping up as he strides all the way to the edge of the canyon to get a better look at the Hemisphere in the distance.

Then I freeze. "Shoot. I think I left my breather in the *Iris*."

"Don't worry. I have it." Mars pulls my breather from his other pocket. "You left it down-level earlier. I pocketed it so it wouldn't get lost. You're welcome."

As he hands it over, I slip it on.

Down-level? I never went down there.

Before I can question his comment, a puff of fast-moving dust and two unsteady headlights approach. A solar cart comes into view through the haze, skidding to a stop beside us.

Kevin jumps out. "I'm sorry it took me so long. Appar-ently the chancellor fast-tracked his plan to close off the Emergence Tunnel and block all the main entry points. Commander Wardell, Far, and I had to negotiate with Nost Territory to convince them to allow us to use their tunnel system. We're moving Unity's people in through Zone 7's old hatches."

Mars scoffs. "I don't need details. The *Iris* has a limited capacity. Timber said something just now that made me realize we can still get everyone to safety despite it."

I finish adjusting my breather settings. "How?"

As Mars points south, Kevin squints. "The Hemisphere," he says. "Makes sense. Most of us will be there anyway. Those of us participating in the rally, that is."

"Not just the ones at the rally," Mars corrects him. "*Everyone*. No one stays behind in the Outskirts. They'll suffocate out here. If we get them all beneath the Hemisphere, it won't just be you and Vaida surviving." He glances at me. "We can save more. Make a real impact."

Kevin's expression falls. "Yeah . . . so . . . Vaida isn't coming with me."

"What?" Mars snaps.

"I told you she was stubborn. She didn't believe me."

"Where is she?" I ask.

Kevin sighs. "The Hemisphere. She's going to live with the chancellor."

"Great. One more thing to deal with." Mars straightens his glowbeam in his holster. "But when we find her, we're doing it my way this time. She's going with you. That's final."

Kevin climbs back into his solar cart. "Good luck with that."

As Mars and I settle into the vehicle too, I turn to him. "How do we know the Hemisphere will hold? The briefing Father gave us said the planet was obliterated."

He buckles in. "It said the planet was obliterated. It said nothing about the Hemisphere.

"Commander Wardell sent laborers to mend the crack over Zone 7." Kevin throws the solar cart into reverse. "It should be patched by now, and the Hemisphere was built to withstand extreme weather—including acid rain. It could work. We just need to get everyone inside." He accelerates. "I'll have to access the central processing unit once we get there to make my broadcast. It should be in the comms center. I'll need to get past patrol and inside Nucleus."

Mars leans back. His beamer light joggles with every bump our solar cart takes in the sand. "Timber and I will get you into Nucleus. That's what we came here to do, right?"

He glances back at me, wind now whipping through his hair.

I call out over the noise with a sudden rush in my chest, "Yes. That's exactly what we came here to do!"

28: VAIDA

Planet Nevarnost: Year 3051

"Pass the nutrient pods, if you will," Chancellor Bay says from his seat at the head of the long green bioresin-and-wood table we're seated at.

I thought his study suite was immaculate. I hadn't seen his formal dining room. Same white glass floors. Glittering crystal chandeliers. Satin brass wall sconces and drapes of silk and other fine cloths. The elaborate breakfast spread was set out shortly after I woke up this morning. Dishes of plant-based meats, purée pouches, and protein oats with honey-glazed mealworms are the main course, but a blue spirulina smoothie bowl melts at my placemat.

I haven't really touched my breakfast. Not because it doesn't look good. Everything, except for an algae shot I've deemed inedible, *looks* good. And I know I'll need my strength if I'm going to outsmart the chancellor in any way, but when I woke up, my stomach was in knots, and I can't seem to shake it. So I settle for a sip of water and a bite of seeded toast.

One of Chancellor Bay's waitstaff scoops a spoonful of slimy, supplement-dense spheres onto his plate from a heaping platter balanced against her hip. Another tray of rehydrated fruit arrives, and across from me, Freya—the other girl Soren slept with—digs in. She wears the same plum-colored night clothes as the blonde-haired toddler sitting in her lap. Supposedly she comes from the Outskirts, but even if I'd known her back then, I wouldn't recognize her now.

I watch the chancellor lean over and hand his grand-daughter a pastry. As he makes her laugh with a foolish grin, I cross my arms tighter, keeping an extra-heavy hand on my sleeve where my brother's knife is safely tucked away.

When I arrived last night, I held my tongue and acted like I was grateful. I took the room key he gave me, sat on the comfortable, speckless bed, and waited patiently until everyone went to sleep. When I snuck out and approached his room, knife in hand, two patrol officers cut me off in the hall. I played clueless, told them I needed a latrine, and they believed me.

It didn't take long for me to realize that my one-on-one encounter in the study suite with the chancellor was a rare occurrence. He's always accompanied by *someone*. Whether it be one of his armed guards, the attendants that follow him around with digital planners and organizer bots, the array of council men and women he oversees, or his granddaughter—Ezra's never alone.

Which makes driving a knife into his chest really fucking hard.

If I want to stop him before the rally takes place, I need a new plan. Some way to single him out and get him by himself.

"Vaida, you've barely touched your meal," Chancellor Bay says, pulling me from thoughts of him bleeding out on the polished tile. "You'll need to keep your strength and start taking care of yourself properly, given you're with child."

There's that fancy term again. *With child.*

"When I was pregnant with Luna, I was hungry all the time," Freya says, lifting her daughter so she can grab another pastry from one of the many confection-filled baskets. "Of course, I was sick all the time, too. But that passed once I hit the second trimester."

I can relate to feeling sick right now. This whole charade is nauseating.

"Chancellor, would you be willing to accompany me to my appointment in Zone 4 this afternoon?" I ask as Luna pulls herself down from her mother and wanders over to him. "They might have something for my morning sickness, and I'd love your input on birthing options . . ."

I have to force the contents of my stomach back down when I realize what I've just said, but I need him to believe I'm all in. I need him to think we're one big happy family now.

He scoops Luna up and kisses her on the cheek.

"Unfortunately, I've got meetings all day. Freya's already agreed to go with you. She knows my preferences," he says and motions to the patrol officers by the door. "One of you go and tell Soren his breakfast is getting cold."

The taller one clears his throat. "He's under the weather, sir."

Chancellor Bay chuckles, helping Luna with the wrapper of her pastry. "Your daddy is *always* under the weather. What is wrong with him?"

"He's out of roakes. That's what's wrong with him," I say without thinking.

The air shifts. Both the chancellor and Freya glare at me

with distaste.

It's true.

"We prefer to have cordial conversations at the table, Miss. Wardell," the chancellor says in the fakest voice I've ever heard. "I do hope you understand."

I match his tone. "Of course. My apologizes."

As his forced smile fades, another patrol officer enters the dining room and approaches his place setting. "We have an update on zone closures. All hatches were boarded up successfully, and the Emergence Tunnel has been closed off as well."

"Good," Chancellor Bay says. "Let's see them rally now."

I sit up in my chair. "You know about the rally?"

Just his eyes flick to me. "I wasn't born yesteryear. It's the anniversary of one of the most controversial moments in the history of the Nevarnost Project. I'd expect nothing less."

I start to curl my fists but stop myself because he's still staring at me.

Inside, I'm screaming. I thought we'd have more time before he closed off the Hemisphere. I figured he'd do it over the course of weeks, not overnight. The reality of it all starts to set in.

Everything Dad, my fake best friend, and Kevin worked for—halted in a millisecond.

I tried to erase Kevin from my mind, but it was impossible. I haven't forgotten how he made up some storm to try and get me to stay, but I haven't forgotten how he comforted me, either. His nana had just died, and he was hugging *me*. Assuring me that everything was going to be okay. He didn't judge me when I told him about the baby. I'd been short with him, cold even, and still he tried to reach me. Is that what a crush does to a person? Or is he merely honest and well-intentioned like Nia described? More importantly, can two things be true at once?

Other than working with Dad behind my back, he's been all those things.

And when he acknowledged his affection for me, instead of facing the uncomfortableness the confession triggered inside me, I turned him down and pushed him further away.

My stomach twinges. People like Kevin don't let pain fester into rage. They harness it. They use it for good. Even if I could bring myself to open up to him, he deserves better than someone like me. I don't share his hopefulness. I don't believe peace wins wars.

Once I figure out how to get rid of the chancellor, I'll reopen the Emergence Tunnel and let my people back into the dome.

I will find a way to gain the upper hand here.

Across the table, the chancellor's digiband rings. He gives Luna once last kiss on the cheek before setting her down, wiping his hands on a cloth napkin, and rising.

"Daniels, I'm going to freshen up. Tell the team I'll be down to the conference room in five minutes," he tells the same patrol officer as before.

I crank my neck, tracking his movement. Chancellor Bay straightens his tie, mutters something to his waitstaff, and exits the dining room.

This might be my chance.

"Are you excited to be a mother?" Freya asks me as I push away from the table.

The cuff of my sleeve rides up, and I quickly grip the edge of my blade so she doesn't catch sight of it. "Sure. Can't wait."

"Well, *I* can't wait for our babies to grow up together." She picks Luna up and nuzzles her nose. "You're going to be the best big sister, aren't you? Yes, you are."

The toddler's giggles make my whole body twitch.

My window of opportunity is also closing.

Before Freya can chat me up some more, I rush out of the dining room and into the hall, picking up my pace toward the end where I know there's a latrine across from Soren's bedroom. It's where I sat the morning after and gaped at myself in the mirror, questioning everything that had happened the night before. Not a memory I want to relive by any means, but if watching the chancellor pass out on the bath mat is the event that replaces it in my mind, I welcome it.

As I near the end of the corridor, I unsheathe my blade and let it dangle at my side. Behind the closed door, the shower turns on. Chancellor Bay coughs. I tuck behind the half-wall that separates the latrine from the area outside Soren's bedroom door.

My grip is firm on the hilt of my knife.

One swipe. One stab.

Doesn't matter as long as it's deep.

At the creak in the hall behind me, I stiffen.

"Drop the knife, Miss. Wardell."

I deny him the satisfaction of me turning around. "Or what."

"It depends," Chancellor Bay says, taking a step closer. "I could send my patrol out on a hunt for your father and have him arrested for Unity affiliation . . . ."

In my peripheral vision, he circles me, stopping at my other side.

"Or I could open the Emergence Tunnel, let the rebels in, and send out patrol to manage the masses." The smell of peppermint rolls off his tongue as his hot breath hits my neck. "Of course, none of that *has* to happen. You could comply. Kick back your feet. Enjoy the stability."

A sharp chill makes the hairs on my arms stand still.

I refuse to be cowed by him.

With a growl, I whip around, knife up, and aim for his throat.

He catches my arm before my blade strikes and secures his hold hard enough to bruise. Using the force of my weight, I push, shakily, as hard as I can. As close as I can. Until the tip of my blade nicks him just beneath his chin.

Chancellor Bay grunts, straining from holding me off. "I'm not going to fight you while you're carrying my grand-child. But I have no reservations against snapping your wrist—drop it."

My lips curve. Knuckles red.

The latrine door next to us opens.

Soren exits, drying his damp hair with a towel. In the second I look at him, Chancellor Bay drags my arm down and uses the momentum to knock my blade from my hand. It clatters to the floor. He kicks it across the hall before Soren notices us both standing there.

The chancellor nods. "Good morning, son."

Soren just scoffs, pushes his way between us, and moves on into his bedroom. As his door shuts, I make for my knife, but Chancellor Bay is faster and swipes it from the floor.

"I think I'd better hold onto this for now," he says. "In the meantime, I suggest you find another outlet for your self-expression. Or in seven months, when the child is born, *it* will stay, and I'll have an escort return you to the

Outskirts empty-handed."

Bastard. "Knowing you, Ezra, you'll probably do that anyway."

He straightens his collar before stepping aside. "Remember your appointment this afternoon. You'll attend and be examined properly. None of that Nost nonsense."

Give me a break. The Nost have more sense than any of us do.

As he walks away, I slam a hand against the wall. *Mark my words, Bay. I'll get my blade back, and it will be the cause of your demise in the end.*

I fight the ever-persistent watering in my eyes and focus on Soren's bedroom door instead, which is ajar. Through the gap, I catch glimpses of him pacing erratically.

I push the door open all the way.

His face drops when he sees me.

I cross my arms and lean against the archway. There's no way I'm ever stepping foot into his quarters again. Not unless it's to hand over our screaming baby in the middle of the night so he can pull his weight for night feedings.

"Hey now, is that any way to greet the mother of your child?"

The dark circles under his eyes deepen as he nears.

"If you're just here to taunt me, then leave," he says. Doubling back to his bed, he flops onto his stomach and faces away from me.

He clings to his pillow, fingers pulling at a loose thread on the case. His hollow eyes fix on the window beside his desk. The room is exactly as I remember it. Dirty clothes scattered around the four-poster bed. A gaming system abandoned in a dust-covered crate. The old-school comics are still stacked in the corner from his weekly visit to Trinket

Gears.

It feels different now. *He* feels different.

"Do you even care?" I ask. "Are you even sorry?"

He chews the outer edge of his fingernails, then rolls over and yanks on his boots, struggling with the laces because his hands are shaking that much.

"Sorry about what?" he mumbles.

"Anything. Anything at all."

His silence is my answer. When he shoves past me, knocking my shoulder on his way out, it only confirms what I already knew. Once he's gone, my gaze drifts to the dresser by the door where, among an ashtray and leftover herbal smokes, something metallic catches the light.

A Holocube.

I pick it up. It's the same kind we used to play *Holoblocks* with in the courtyard as kids. Only this one is broken. Buttons missing. Holographic screen cracked. In working condition, it would project a multiplayer match with digital gameplay.

But this one looks neglected. Forgotten.

I turn it over in my palm, my thumb grazing the worn defense button. Sometimes you can restore Holocubes if you find the right tech specialist. This one seems too far gone.

Standing in this room, where I spent the night that changed my life, I realize Nia was right.

It's not that Soren doesn't care. Or that he used me.

It's that he's incapable of caring about anyone else. If it were me and my baby over a roake, he'd choose the temporary high. Soren can't take care of us. He can't even take care of himself. Because nobody's taking care of him. And I can't blame him for that anymore.

I can't keep holding onto hate for someone who doesn't even care about himself.

Game over, Soren. Nobody wins.

I set the Holocube down as a beeping noise sounds through the room. At first I think it's coming from the cube itself, but then I spot the flashing lights on the air gauge by the window. With a sigh, I cross the room and flip open the box.

The air quality bar fluctuates, then drops below red.

Thunder rumbles outside. Out the window, a streak of violet lightning flashes in the dark clouds orbiting the Hemisphere. *Weird.* I've never seen purple lightning before.

The air gauge displays red again, issuing another warning.

I don't know much about weather, air quality, or how any of this *really* works, but I know this isn't normal. Another burst of lightning slashes the sky. A single thought crosses my mind.

Could Kevin have been right about the storm?

29: MARS

Planet Nevarnost: Year 3051

I keep close to Timber, arms tucked at my side, as we travel a stretch of Nost tunnels lit by the lambent amethyst embedded in the rock. They form in clusters like the aura quartz does in the mines. I'm immediately transported back and have to remind myself I'm no longer there.

No cave beasts. No deep rifts. No raging miners.

Despite the harrowing unease, I don't regret my choices. The Council of Elders tried inducting me early on because a former Head Elder's child is considered a legacy.

They just *assumed* I'd step into my birthright.

But that's the problem with our archaic traditions. They expect us to know what we want to do with our whole lives when we become Eighteens. They expect us to choose placements or lovers without considering that some people and places are only meant for seasons, not lifetimes. People don't always need commitment ceremonies to signify deep connections. We might need to try out many different trades before we find our true vocation in life.

I didn't know what I wanted when I was an Eighteen, and I certainly didn't want to be forced into something I wasn't ready for. I chose the mines because I wanted a *choice*.

I didn't want others to choose for me.

It wasn't until my fellow miner Orion died that my choice became a possible life sentence. His death was an accident, but when I showed up for my trial, the elders told me it was karma for not following their guidance. Elder Hale was the only one who vouched for me.

It didn't matter how many times Rose told me it wasn't my fault; it never quite sank in, not until Timber saw everything inside my head.

I used to sit in the back of commitment lessons and laugh about the idea of soul connections and love and all that nonsense. I still don't know if I understand what I felt for Timber last night. I certainly haven't felt it before. But when he kissed me. Embraced me. Simply touched me . . .

An internal heat warms my core at the memories of it.

"They help us dream," a Nost says as she passes me, noticing my fixation on a larger point of amethyst jutting out of a low-hanging stalactite.

The Vio have theories about amethyst and dreams, too, which is why my father chose the material for his Head Elder bracelet. I rub my bare wrist now, because even the motion is comforting in this moment, and tell myself I will survive this, too.

As we continue down a slope of dirt, I anticipate iron tracks at my feet, or the coils of blast lines soaked in the explosive oil we harvest from temper trees. I've witnessed miners purposely blow off their own fingers to get out of digging in lower-level rifts.

My fingers find my wrist again.

Timber's hand grazes my shoulder. "It's okay to be anxious, you know," he says, leaning in. "And you don't have to talk yourself out of the feeling. You're safe. You aren't there."

"I know," I mutter. "This place just brings back . . . things."

Things he'll soon experience himself. Somehow that puts me more on edge, and I clench my jaw to ward off the stress sweat. I grew up rugged, became tough because I didn't think I had any other choice. The mines will ruin Timber. Any softness he has will be gone the first time he gets an infected sliver wound or witnesses a cave beast devour a miner in one giant-jawed bite.

Don't even get me started with the mind-feeling risks.

We slow in a passageway that smells faintly of spoiled sugar. Hundreds of bobbing glow orbs illuminate the space behind us, each held by an Outskirter acting in the hope they'll never have to live in the beyond again. Somewhere at the front of the assembly, Kevin is waiting with Commander Wardell and Matron Nost Far to give me their signal.

Next to me, Timber trembles so hard the zippers on his pack rattle. "Remember when I promised I wouldn't be scared? I think I made a promise I can't keep."

"It's alright. How are you doing, being around so many people right now?"

He inhales sharply through his nose, then exhales through his mouth. "I can't stop shaking," he whispers, and I reach out to steady him. "My chest feels like it's going to explode."

Dune skulls. Maybe he should stay here. Out of harm's way.

"Remember what I taught you. It's their fear. Not yours."

"It's mine too." He clutches his glow orb for comfort, squeezing mire between his fingers. "It's not going to work, Mars. Something horrible is going to happen today."

"Something horrible was always going to happen. That's why your father sent us here," I remind him, eyeing Kevin's gesture at the head. "Just stay close to me and watch your back."

Together we push through the crowd, up to where Kevin, Matron Nost Far, and the commander wait beneath a rope ladder with wooden rungs.

"We're lucky the chancellor didn't think of Zone 7 when he closed off the other tunnels," Commander Wardell remarks.

Far motions up the ladder with her staff. "Humans will go first. We'll follow after."

"Timber and I will take Kevin into Nucleus through one hatch," I say. "You two should go with others through another, so we aren't all coming from the same place."

Far nods. "We will gather within the confines of Zone 5 and wait for you there. My Nost are willing to hold off the patrol officers—or anyone—who try to stop you."

Timber reaches forward and takes my hand.

You're going to be okay, I think to him. I know he hears my thoughts when he gently squeezes his hand around mine.

Commander Wardell raises his glow orb in the air, sending a ripple of light throughout the passageway. The signal sets the masses into motion, and those going with Far and the commander veer left to find another entry point.

Passing orbs reflect faintly in Timber's eyes. The Nost that stride by study him, exchanging glances. I shrug them off and cough at the stir of dust kicked up by traveling feet. Timber might have a bad feeling about today, but this is what we came here for.

"What if I freeze up?" Timber asks.

I only let go of his hand long enough to take him firmly

by the shoulders.

"You're not going to freeze up." I search his face, then soften my tone because he *needs* to believe this too. "I thought of this earlier, but I never said it—I don't think you have a curse, Timber. I think you have a gift. One that, with practice, could make a huge difference. Don't fear your power. Harness it. *Own* it."

"You two ready?" Kevin calls from halfway up the ladder.

I give Timber a quick peck before nudging him forward.

"We're ready," I say, bringing up the rear and assessing my assets.

I've got a tech from the past and a gentle slug who's going to need a new nickname if we stick together long enough. This wasn't how I thought this mission would go, but a good leader learns to adapt in any given situation. I'll pull at their strengths and utilize their talents.

I'll make sure we finish this. Even if it kills me.

Opening the hatch releases an ear-piercing screech.

The noise echoes through an abandoned clinic, its floor flooded with acid rain residue. A streak of dim light stretches across the room. Soggy debris litters the floor. We carefully avoid a sinkhole, then Kevin and I drag an examination table out of the way of the exit.

A rustle sounds in the distance. Timber winces.

"It's nothing. Relax," I assure him.

We'll work on him not fearing his own shadow another time.

Outside the clinic, the streets of the forgotten Zone 7: Industrial are eerily peaceful. A massive barrier, constructed from a collection of raw materials, presents itself. Rotting planks, scrap metal, and jagged stones have all been haphazardly thrown together, keeping this zone isolated from the rest of the Hemisphere. It is the only thing that stands between us and the inside.

The mended crack rises overhead, dust still thick in the air. Sweat percolates on the back of my neck. I check my peripherals, adjust my breather, and together, we feel for any loose spots that we can squeeze through and pave way for the others coming.

Kevin splinters a board. "Found one."

I pull with him. We sever planks from their nails and shift enough rock to widen the gap.

Timber tugs on my arm. "Mars."

"Not now," I hiss.

As I peel off the last bolted metal plate in our way, a glimpse of Zone 6: Agriculture casts a faint light in our dark corner.

Timber shouts, "Watch out!"

I hear the static shock before it strikes. A growl escapes me. I dive, rolling, pulling Timber down and out of the way. Pouncing back up, I bring my glowbeam into position.

"Jolt stick! Patrol!" Kevin yells.

"I'm handling it," I bark.

I waste no time. Through the opening in the wall, I land with a soft thud on the browning grass below. Sparks fly. Plumes of purple and blue explode in the air. The patrol officer wielding the jolt stick cuts me off, and irritation curls through me.

Don't even think about it.

One shot. He's down.

Three more patrol officers round the corner, and adrenaline surges in my veins. I flip the setting on my release, cock it, and a vibrant orange light catapults from my barrel, enveloping all three of them into a thread-like, webbed

313

cocoon.

The blobs jerk sideways, shrinking smaller and smaller until they disappear altogether.

"If there's some, there's more," Kevin huffs, climbing out the hole in the wall. "Guess Bay didn't forget about Zone 7 after all."

Timber follows, wide-eyed and terrified. He kneels, groping the ground where the patrol officers once stood. All that remains now are orange splats. "There's—there's nothing left!"

"Let's just say they went poof." I pull him up by the collar of his tunic and steady him on his feet. *He's got some explaining to do.* "You knew they were out here," I say to him. "How? I thought you could only read and sense things if you're physically touching someone."

Timber shakes his head, his face still pale from shock. "I . . . I don't know. I got a really bad feeling and sensed them."

"Yeah?" I nudge him forward gently. "How about you use that gift a little more. I'll cover you." I give a small flick with my glowbeam. "You see or feel anything up ahead?"

"You . . . you want me to lead?" he stammers.

No, but the one thing I've learned about Timber in the short amount of time we've spent together is that his feelings are important. If he can sense the bad in others and the danger lurking around every corner, then lightning bugs—what has he been doing all this time?

Holding out on me, that's what. I push down the flash of irritation, reminding myself that opening up to others is just as new for him as it is for me.

"What do you feel now?" Kevin asks, pointing toward the streetway.

The flow of everyday foot traffic continues, oblivious to

our presence.

"I don't know," Timber says.

"Give him a minute." I shift forward, my glowbeam tucked against my cheek as I peer through my scope and survey the area. A few sweepers flying low. No patrol officers. "Looks like we're in the clear to cross Zone 6. Let's move quick before word gets back to Nucleus."

"I think it's okay," Timber agrees.

Kevin rolls his shoulders. "Zone 5. Here we come."

The ground beneath me becomes variations of littered sidewalks. We dodge the flow of people filling up the train platform, keeping our heads down to avoid drawing attention.

My glowbeam stays tight against my hip. At the threshold of our destination, Kevin pulls ahead and picks up his pace.

Timber stops short. "No. Wait."

We tuck away behind a stone pillar with spinning monitors. Their neon blaze orbits, casting flashes of color across the four patrol officers pacing the border between zones.

Going around the other side of the Hemisphere would take too long. Backtracking could waste time. Starting trouble could draw attention.

Think, Mars. "Timber, get me four muscle lock darts."

He presses against me without riposte, reaches into my pack, and slips them over my shoulder. One by one, I load them into my glowbeam.

"You'll cause a scene," Kevin warns.

"Hopefully." I aim my shot. *Fire.*

Across the street, the four patrol officers drop to the ground. Nearby spectators rush to their aid, crowding around them and freeing up the sidewalk for us.

Kevin pats me on the back before moving on. "Nice

touch."

Into Zone 5: Nucleus, we slog another block.

Timber offers us an expression at every turn. He doesn't have to speak. I know whether to continue on or not. Especially since distress and worry fit him like a crisp pair of leather boots.

That brings us right outside the Nucleus building.

"Six patrol officers up front," I report, eyeing the taut line of guard dressed in plum uniforms. "Another few at the bottom of the stairs. All on high alert."

Timber watches me browse glowbeam settings on the dial fixed to the barrel's outer edge.

"You'll need something with quick release," he comments. "Right?"

Right. I tilt my gaze up, into his. He smiles behind his breather.

Seems I've taught him something after all.

"Comms is on the seventh floor," Kevin says, stepping up next to me to show me the makeshift map he drew on a crumpled sheet of parchment. He trails the path with his finger. "That means if we enter through the lobby, we take the elevator up and then secure the floor long enough to hack into Hemisphere transmission system and send out the Unity broadcast."

"Hemisphere first. Broadcast second. Then we get you and Vaida out of here."

"If the dome holds that long," Kevin speculates, rolling up his map and shoving it into the side pocket of his backpack. "Commander Wardell and Far should be arriving with the others shortly. They'll spread out here and draw the chancellor out."

Behind me, Timber yelps.

I whip around so fast, my head spins.

Glowbeam up. Double-take. A boy has Timber locked in his arms, a shard of metal tucked tight against his neck. Between them, they share the same shade of sandy blonde hair. The same piercing blue eyes. That familiar arch of the brow.

"Who is this slug?" I yell.

"Soren." Kevin steps forward. "Let him go."

Kevin tries to get me to lower my glowbeam, but I'm not letting my guard down now. No way in the cosmic depths. *Because he's got Timber.* And we're so close to finishing this.

Be honest with yourself. Losing him would break you.

"I told you I would find you," Soren barks at Timber.

I raise a brow. "You know this guy?"

Timber shudders. "No, I don't know him!"

"Shut up! Shut up!" Soren points the metal shard at Kevin. "And you? You owe me roakes. I don't know what you or your uncle are up to, but I've had enough. I want them. Now."

"I have no idea what you're talking about." Kevin puts a hand out. "Let's stay calm."

Give me a break. "Let's rephrase this. If you don't let him go, I'll blast you."

"You aren't helping," Kevin mutters.

Soren jerks Timber back. "All of you be quiet." Timber's eyes meet mine, and I don't look away. "Where are they, Kevin? Huh? I feel—I feel crazy, man."

"What does he want? What is going on!" I spit.

"He's high on roake venom," Kevin says. "I don't have them, okay? I'm not doing that anymore. We aren't here to cause any harm. We're just trying to escape the storm."

"For the last time, I'm not *high*!" Soren lets out a yell. "And you're giving me those roakes, or I'll— I'll end him."

I fire up my glowbeam and point it straight between Soren's eyes. "I don't think so."

30: TIMBER

Planet Nevarnost: Year 3051

"**D**id you hear me?" Mars barks. Neither his gaze nor glowbeam wavers. "Let. Him. Go."

Kevin steps between him, Soren, and me, trying to diffuse the situation. Their argument escalates into a blur of shouting and swearing, while Soren's touch against my neck triggers the mind-feeling, as Mars called it, in my head. *Spiraling. Spiraling. Spiraling.*

My vision starts to fade in and out.

A heavy weight sits on my chest.

Turns out there is an emotion more famished than desire.

Addiction.

I blink back the tears welling in my eyes. Soren's need to exist in a constant state of numbness burns like a well-tended fire in my lungs. And as always, the pressure intensifies, relentless, like an unwanted friend.

Mother wasn't there the first time I experienced the whispers. She'd gone into the village to barter with a seamstress for fabric to sew Marlowe a new dress. It was Father that found me. Curled up like a dune snake on the beach. Hyperventilating so hard I thought I might die.

I couldn't catch my breath. I was a helpless Seven trapped inside his own body.

Father's tone was smooth. As gentle as he could manage. He hugged me. Held me. Rocked me like he does my younger brothers now. He told me to breathe.

"Box breathe, Timber," he said. *"In for four. Hold for four. Out for four."*

He meant well. But it only made it worse. I blacked out.

When I woke up, Mother was at my bedside.

She told me Father had carried me home, changed my sweat-soaked tunic, and placed a warm cloth on my forehead. We never spoke of it again. They never asked me why. Or how.

They just assumed it was an anxiety attack.

After that, I taught myself other ways to cope—practicing mindfulness, lavender under my pillow, avoiding others, recognizing that it's happening when it happens, and sinking barefoot into the dirt to connect with nature's gentle embrace as often as I can.

My anxious fits rarely became a problem after that.

Until they asked me to kill a moon worm.

Soren doesn't have the mind-feeling ability I have, but his anxiety begs for the same relief that mine does. My eyes water against the smell of his perspiration-soaked shirt. My insides churn at the welts up and down his arms. His addiction is a hollow ache, a yearning for relief.

Desire may burn. But addiction leaves my heart frost-cold.

It's Mars' voice that slashes through the ice. "His emotions and thoughts aren't yours, Timber!"

I close my eyes, utilizing the new skills I've learned. If it worked with Mars, it can work with those I don't willingly embrace too. As my chest deflates, my vision comes back into focus, on Mars in particular, shoving Kevin aside.

He trained me for this exact moment.

Watching him lock Rose into his grip.

"Free yourself, Timber!" Mars yells at me.

Kevin blocks another one of his attempts at obliterating Soren.

I grab onto Soren's arms, remembering the way Rose and Mars fought in the Dunes. Using the momentum of my weight, I whip myself around and knee Soren between the legs with as much force as I can. *When in doubt, knock 'em where it counts.*

Soren gasps. He stumbles back. Mars propels forward and punches him in the face, sending him twisting and falling face-first into a pile of street debris.

"Was the Derry Hook really necessary?" Kevin yells.

"He'll only follow us." Mars steps over Soren's unconscious form. He grabs me by the arm, pulls me into a quick hug, and ushers me onward. "Good work. Let's go."

His words are like the sudden warmth after a frigid season in the harbor.

"And wipe that smirk off your face, will you?" Mars spins on his heel and darts down the street, Kevin close behind him.

"I am—I'm not—I'm *sorry.*" I rush after them.

Mars wastes no time approaching the front steps of Nucleus. Like a whirlwind, he fires rounds, one after the other. None of the patrol officers stand a chance. They drop one by one in our wake, wrapped, stunned, and zapped, until we've made it to the double front doors.

Into the lobby, two more go down.

Mars is on fire, and for once, it doesn't fill me with dread or worry because I did something. I defended myself. And Mars thinks I did good.

We clamor into the lift off the lobby.

Kevin adjusts his pack. "I don't know how long we'll have, so while I'm hacking into the system, you two will need to keep guard."

"Got it," Mars says.

The doors spit us out into an empty hallway. Kevin takes the lead, searching until he finds the door he's looking for. A keypad comes up outside a comms entrance, revealing a set of digital numbers. Without hesitation, Kevin enters the correct code, and we're in.

He closes the door behind us. We enter into a circular room with an array of screens, monitors, and a strange-looking projector set up in the back.

"Chancellor Bay makes his broadcasts here." Kevin drops down into the first rolling chair, immediately getting to work. "As soon as I secure the Hemisphere, I'll make one of my own. Far and Commander Wardell will have gathered everyone outside Nucleus by then." He clicks and types, his eyes darting around the screen. "This might take a few minutes. Sit tight."

Mars nods and retreats to the entryway. I go to follow and accidentally stumble over Kevin's open backpack. A frilly pink ruffle sticks out the top.

"Hey," I say, pulling out a cloth baby doll. "My sister Marlowe had a doll like this growing up. Mother made it for her. What an odd coincidence."

"It was Nana's," Kevin says without looking away from his screen. "Please put it back where you found it, so I don't leave it behind."

I safely tuck it away. "Right. Sorry."

Mars watches me zip the pack back up. I join him in the entryway, leaning against the wall opposite him. "You tore your stitches," I say, reaching out for the wound on his shoulder. My fingers brush through the pool of blood. "I'll add another herbal adhesive really quick."

Digging into my pack, I retrieve another slimy bandage from its wrapping.

Mars doesn't fight me. He even holds out his arm for me to tend to him.

"Rose will be entertained that her little charade was the one thing you remembered."

"Yeah, I just . . ." Heat creeps up my neck. "It was the only thing I could think of."

"Like I said, you did good."

"*You* did good," I repeat. "The way you took out all the patrol officers, and then the way you punched Soren . . . Why did you do that, by the way? He was already down."

"He was . . . " Mars clenches his jaw, his expression softening. "Do you remember when you were a Fifteen and you attended my survival lesson?"

A flutter courses through me. "I was hoping we'd never speak about it again."

"Alright." He furrows his brows. "Well, I'd been teaching that class for a few seasons, and I'd never had anyone get hurt before. But *you* of all bugging people did. You got stung, nearly drowned, and for some reason that moment always stuck with me."

"Because I was a bloated moon worm with no hand-eye coordination, right?" I say, noticing Kevin listening to us out of the corner of my eye. "I ruined your entire presentation."

"You did indeed ruin it." Mars chuckles. "But no, that isn't why. It stuck with me because when you got hurt, it freaked me out. I went to see the Head Healer the next day to make sure you were okay. And—" He sighs, closing the gap between us. "I used to think I'd feel that way about anyone I was in charge of keeping safe, but just now when Soren had you, I realized it was because it was you. I like your soul, Timber, alright? I like *you*."

"You do?"

"Yep. I do."

Kevin glances at me from over the monitor, then adjusts the screen so he can't see us anymore, giving us a little privacy.

My dimples deepen. "I like your soul too, Mars."

He wraps an arm around my waist, tugs me in.

I lower my breather and kiss him.

31 VAIDA

Planet Nevarnost: Year 3051

I fly down the corridor, bursting into the room I slept in the night before.

I should've listened to Kevin Hale. I shouldn't have come here.

I yank my canvas bag off the hook and start stuffing my belongings inside. My heart hammers as my fingers touch something cold.

The roake venom syringe.

I roll it between my fingers. Chancellor Bay may have taken my brother's knife against my will, but I still have this. I could join Dad, Kevin, and the others. I could open the Emergence Tunnel before the worst of the storm hits. I could *still* go through with my original plan.

A slick layer of sweat soaks the back of my neck as I push forward out the door and toward the chancellor's study suite. Bag and satchel slung over one shoulder. Fingers coiled tightly around the syringe. A cold realization creeps across me as I think of my past failed attempts.

Nia was right. I'm not a killer.

But if the chancellor gets in my way, I'll do what I have to do. Not just for me and my unborn child, but for every child and Outskirter trapped in the growing storm.

The sterile chamber hisses as it seals me in.

Decontamination mist deems me clean.

I press the latch release and enter the sadistically tranquil suite. The fresh scent of grass hangs in the air. Soft instrumental music drifts through the room.

I round the blooming alcove and let out a scoff.

He's not here. Where else could Chancellor Bay be?

Past the crescent moon-shaped desk, the holographic Hemisphere display oscillates. I set the syringe down and take a seat, bringing his home screen up in front of me. I know nothing about the advanced technology they use here. Even when I was young, while all the other kids my age were coding, I was out in the courtyard with scuffed knees, playing recreational games.

I can read just fine, however, so when I spot a file labeled, 'Unity Arch: 3041,' I can't help myself. My click brings up a series of other folders: death records, elaborate project breakdowns, and Billy Hale's old remedial plans for tackling air quality and other environmental concerns. *None of it is new information.* When I go to exit, I see the 'Incident Report' file.

A detailed written investigation on the tragedy in front of me, I skim wildly for any mention of who or what caused the explosion, fully expecting Billy Hale's name to be there.

Patrol officers interviewed hundreds of people. They sent scientists, technicians, and an array of other professionals to analyze the scene of the crime. A mechanism specialist provided a detailed report on the origin of the explosion: *Faulty electrical transformer on the left side of the stage in Unity Commons. Likely due to an overloaded circuit or improper maintenance.*

I can barely keep myself upright. It was an . . . accident. Nobody blew up anything. All this time, I thought it was Billy Hale. I was convinced it was him. I *remember* him standing there.

Had I imagined it all? Was I truly too young to fully remember?

Or maybe I've been so dead set on looking for someone to blame for my mom and brother's death that blaming Billy Hale was easier than accepting the truth.

The chancellor's actions after the Arch fell don't exclude him—he's still the enemy in my eyes—but everyone else? They're just like me. They didn't have a say. They didn't ask for this.

Something shitty happened, and we all suffered in some way for it. Meanwhile, I took my anger out on everyone else. The Nost. Some Outskirters. Hemisphere people. Dad. *Kevin.*

Wiping the tears from my eyes, I quickly exit the folder and try my best to steady myself. *You came here to find the chancellor and potentially open the Emergence Tunnel, Vaida. Focus.*

There will be time to make this right. There has to be.

I click around, zooming in on Nucleus' mapping layout. The projection shifts. A navigation screen loads. An external feed comes online, directly overlooking a conference room.

The image sharpens: Chancellor Bay and his patrol team.

"Gotcha," I mutter under my breath.

"They've come in through Zone 7," a patrol officer reports. "Two entry points we missed. That zone was supposed to be closed off."

A smile spreads across my face. *They made it inside.*

"I told you to barricade every hatch." Chancellor Bay powers up his tablet. A dual message board linked to his study pops up in hologram form beside me. "Send a crew to Zone 7. Take everyone associated with Unity into custody and bring them here."

Another officer silences his digiband. "There's a lot of them, sir," he says. "We can't take them all. Once they got inside, others from the Hemisphere joined them. Including some members of the patrol team." He hesitates. "That's . . . our people out there."

Chancellor Bay slams a fist on the table. "I don't *care* who it is. If they're with them, they're against me, and that's all I need to know. Move forward with the plan."

"Kevin Hale was spotted recently," another officer points out.

Adrenaline spikes in my veins.

"He and two other boys fled after our officers were hit with body-numbing darts."

"Body-numbing darts?" Chancellor Bay sets down his tablet with a scowl. "Where would they have gotten those? We don't have access to those here."

"That's what the medics are saying, sir."

A rigid expression overtakes the chancellor.

"We might not be able to take down an entire rally," he says, straightening his tie. "But we can go after their fearless leader." He turns to his officers. "Forget what I said before. Bring me Kevin Hale. I don't care about anyone else."

A digiband chimes somewhere in the room.

An officer reports, "Alert says he's in Nucleus now."

I stow away the syringe.

I have to warn Kevin.

Moments later, I'm racing through the halls, breath ragged, lungs on fire. There are fifty stories in the Nucleus building, and Kevin could be anywhere—*too much ground to cover.*

I'm not a runner. My legs are short. I do brisk walks, not sprints.

All I have to do is find him before they do.

Freya cuts me off on the sixth-floor lift, and I *swear* she planned it.

She beams. "I was looking for you! I thought we could grab something to eat before your appointment this afternoon."

"Read the room, Freya." I sidestep her. "Out of my way!"

She doesn't move.

Fine. Forget the lift.

I shove through the stairwell doors. Here's hoping she doesn't follow.

Spoiler alert: She does.

Her annoying giggles echo behind me. "Didn't you hear me?" she calls.

I whip open the seventh-floor door. "I heard you. I'm choosing to ignore you."

We round the corner together and nearly stumble upon two boys making out in the comms room entryway. Rather passionately, I might add.

Freya bumps into me, gasping. "Oh my—"

"*Oh my* is right," I echo, grinning.

I couldn't have planned this better if I tried.

"Hey! Sorry," I say as the boys break apart. "Is Kevin here? I need to talk to him."

Timber flushes. Mars smirks.

"Vaida?" Kevin peers around a display monitor in back.

"What are you doing? Are you okay?"

I huff a laugh. "Naturally, the first thing you'd ask me is if I'm okay."

He stands and lowers his face mask. "Of course. Why wouldn't I?"

"You weren't kidding, were you? About the storm. About the—" I motion between Mars and Timber. "—boys from the future. It's happening, isn't it?"

"Yep," Mars says. "And from what I've heard, you're refusing to come along."

"Please tell me you changed your mind." Kevin retakes his seat, fingers flying across the keyboard.

"Yes. I'm sorry I didn't believe you." I glance between the boys once more before settling on Kevin. "The chancellor knows you're here. He's coming for you. He doesn't care about the rally."

Mars' hand tightens around his glowing, gun-like device. "When?"

"He could be on his way now."

"Vaida, your prenatal appointment?" Freya pipes up from the doorway.

Timber straightens next to Mars. "Oh, are you with child? Congratulations."

I groan. "Why does everyone keep saying it like that?"

"With the chancellor's son's child nonetheless," Freya says, crossing her arms. "Need I remind you how important it is to care for yourself in your position? What an honor it is to live here?"

Mars cocks a brow. "Wait, the chancellor's son?"

"Yeah." Kevin doesn't look up from the screen. "That boy you assaulted in the streetway? That would be Soren Bay. Relation to Chancellor Bay—the guy making this difficult."

Mars's nostrils flare. "He was going to *assault* Timber. I had to do something. You wanted to talk it out—that got us nowhere." Mars turns to me. "So . . Soren. He's the father?"

"Yes, *okay!* I slept with the chancellor's son, and it will forever haunt me. One of the worst decisions of my life. Can we drop it?"

A bitter silence falls. The only sound is the clack-clack-clack of Kevin's fingers on the keys.

Then Freya, of all people, speaks up. "Who are you all, anyway? Vaida isn't supposed to have guests unless they're authorized by the chancellor."

Dammit, Freya. Must you ruin everything?

"They're pre-approved," I say, ushering her out into the hallway.

Before she can protest, Mars slams the door in her face. Timber awkwardly locks it behind him.

Kevin finishes up at the control panel. "We don't have much time. I've secured the Hemisphere, deactivated the energy fields between zones, and baselined all regulation settings."

He steps over a tangled cord on the floor, then turns on the broadcast screen. "Mars and Timber, hold the door as long as you can. I'll start the transmission."

I step up onto the platform beside Kevin. "I want to help."

His green eyes light up like emeralds. "Then let's go live."

32: KEVIN

Planet Nevarnost: Year 3051

~~help everyone through tunnels~~
~~infiltrate nucleus~~
~~disarm the zone walls~~
~~escape soren~~
~~hack into the database~~
~~give mars and timber privacy~~
broadcast to the whole hemisphere

I've thought about this moment hundreds of times.

I've rehearsed these words in the mirror. Spoke them aloud before bed. Had full-on conversations with myself up in the loft—just me, the roakes, and Uncle Billy's pet glowfish. Logged countless attempts at speaking my truth via Lux.

I thought I'd be reading from a holographic prompter on my digiband. I thought Nana would be watching from our sitting room in Zone 1: Mechanisms.

I didn't think my uncle would be alive somewhere on another planet.

I didn't think Vaida would be here either.

Or that I'd grow to like her this much.

She becomes my visual anchor beyond the digital recorder. I drag a floating block to center stage and sit. The low, electronic hum of the broadcast fills the room. My eyes flick to Timber and Mars, standing guard by the door.

Then Vaida triggers the live signal.

My face appears on the wall monitor. As well as the external feed. The camera pans over the crowd outside Nucleus. Hundreds of people pack together onto the front steps, spilling into the streets, leaning over the solar train platform. Banners and flags ripple in the air.

Unity trees. Everywhere. In every human hand. In every Nost tentacle.

My eyes sting, thinking of Uncle Billy, how much he would've loved this.

All these people still believe in his mission. They still believe in him.

I take a deep breath. No script today. *Only my truth.*

"Two patrol officers coming this way," Mars reports, revving up his glowbeam.

He skirts around Timber, yanks open the door, and fires two searing rounds. Smoke curls in the air. I block the chaos out. Return my attention forward.

"You're live," Vaida tells me.

I steady my breath.

"Current inhabitants of the Hemisphere. Those from the Outskirts. And our Nost allies. My name is Kevin Hale. Some know me as the mechanism specialist from Zone 1. Others know me as the nephew of our former chancellor, Billy Hale, the man some of you believe caused this mess . . ."

I look up at Vaida, whose nod gives me strength to keep

333

going.

"I don't know what happened ten years ago. I don't know if the rumors are true. But I knew my uncle and what he stood for. He wouldn't have wanted us to let a tragedy divide us."

Mars unleashes round after round. Bright bursts split the air, slicing through smoke. The ground trembles beneath us. Lights stutter and glitch. Bodies hit the floor with thuds. Timber keeps his back tight against the wall.

Again, it's Vaida's encouraging hand that urges me on.

"Right now, there's a storm brewing outside. We face declining air quality at a rate we've never seen before. Resources are dwindling. People are dying. ISR isn't coming to save us. They're not bringing more supplies. What we have here is *all* we have.

"So many of us want change. We see the suffering of our loved ones and wish things were different, but fear holds us back. Chancellor Bay wants us to believe that banishing entire zones of people, sealing off hatches, and enforcing harsh restrictions is the answer. But time is . . ." I pause and swallow before continuing, ". . . precious. We can't change it. We can't get more of it once it's gone. But if we work together, we *can* slow the storm's impact. If we work together, the Hemisphere can sustain us all . . ."

I look up again, this time at Timber. He smiles.

"After today, leaving the dome won't be an option. Our survival depends on us overcoming our differences, facing our worst fears, and standing together. There are no 'Hemisphere people' and 'Outskirt people.' There are just . . . *people.* We *all* deserve kindness, empathy, and safety. This was supposed to be a news start. And it still can be—"

The monitors glitch out. *Fizz.* Fade to black.

Mars shuts the door, breath ragged. "What's going on?"

"We lost the broadcast," Vaida says. "There's no green light."

I spring up from the hovering block and check the recorder. It hums with promise. Then dies again. I dash to the wall of monitors, slamming switches on the darkened control board.

No. This can't be happening.

"If we lose internal power, the Hemisphere's atmospheric pressure will drop."

Vaida steps into a shadow. "What about the generators?"

"We were already running on generators," I say.

Darkness folds in around us. Every screen taps out. Silence creeps in, broken by the creaks of the building, settling and shifting.

The baying wind howls.

"The storm," Timber whispers.

I strap on my beamer and flip the switch. The headlamp falters, dim but steady.

Mars drops to one knee, yanking off his pack. "I think I packed a few strobes."

He digs through his gear and pulls out a strange tube swirling with neon-purple goop. A snap and a shake, and it flares to life, casting a radiant shine between us.

Mars passes three more out to the rest of us.

"They should keep their charge," he says.

I clutch mine tightly, guiding its glow over the controls. "Nothing. Not even a hum or a warm trill under the boards. Everything beneath the Hemisphere is dead."

"Will it hold?" Vaida asks.

Timber hesitates. "Let's hope."

A wicked crack of thunder rattles the walls. Through the

small window above the circuit box, the sky churns black and purple, split by craggy veins of lightning.

We huddle closer, watching the massive clouds close in.

"We have to get outside," I say, lifting my mask to my nose and slinging my backpack over my shoulder. "If this building falls, we're done for."

Timber winces. "The Hemisphere is supposed to hold."

I raise my strobe. "Staying clear of high-rises is smart—"

"Just in case it doesn't," Mars finishes for me.

W e race the pristine halls, our boots clamoring over the floor as we descend flight after flight of stairs.

The four of us burst into the front lobby and shove through the frozen maze of spectators huddled just inside the double doors.

"Stay close to me," Mars mumbles to Timber, reaching for his hand. "We can't miss the signal when our transporters activate to take us home."

Vaida leans in at my side. "What is everyone looking at?"

I exit the doors of Nucleus into the dimming dark.

A still, stale air hits my face. A few glow orbs, clutched in Nost tentacles, barely illuminate the space. The faint chatter of thousands blurs together across the expanse of Zone 5.

Banners clenched in fists. Signs discarded at their sides.

As though we never came here to rally at all.

Heads tilt upward at the plumes of smoke choking the sky, and we all watch twisted wraiths of black light slink through the glass arches and coil around the Hemisphere like a deadly serpent ready to strike.

Commander Wardell emerges from the crowd.

"Vaida." He pulls her toward him before she can resist. "Thank the Gods. I was so worried you were somewhere in the Outskirts."

"I'm fine, Dad," she says. "Where's Nia? Have you seen her?"

"She's with the children underground. She's safe."

Another electric crackle thrashes overhead. Commander Wardell releases Vaida as the strike slams into our dome, sending it reeling back with the force of the attack.

A shudder sweeps through me. I've never seen anything like this.

All at once, screams and shrieks muffle beneath the sharp *crack* that rises from the arch of our sanctuary. Dark masses jolt along the edges of the vaulted space above, aiming directly for the center. The Hemisphere's structure splinters, nearly splitting in half.

"*Feaukere*," Mars swears.

I drop my strobe. He and Timber knock into me, swept away by the pull of the horde.

A giant quake ripples beneath our feet. Buildings start to crumble. Walls collapse. Streetways split apart. The towering pillars, once connected by the hexagonal holographic screens separating each zone, careen. Behind us, the solar train lurches, swinging back on its tracks. And though it's barely visible, the remaining panels that contain us—the ones that shield us from the dangers beyond—spall. They fracture, spreading like pressure-pointed webs of shattered glass.

The Hemisphere isn't going to hold.

"Kevin!" Vaida screams.

I twist, catching sight of her as she's carried away in the

wailing mob behind me. Swatted and shoved, I let myself get sucked in too.

My hand catches hers. Tight. "We have to go!"

"Everyone underground!" Commander Wardell roars as he steps onto a stone ledge at the front of the Nucleus building. "Into Nost Territory! The hatches lead beneath the ground!"

His voice rises above the chaos, but it's not nearly enough.

Those who hear him scramble to follow. The Nost widen their stances, stretching their elastic bodies to pull in everyone they can reach. But the panic is too overbearing. Impossible to navigate. Most of the hatches are blocked. The two remaining in Zone 7: Industrial will be overrun.

It's complete pandemonium. A fight to the death.

We need another way underground.

"We'll never make it to a hatch," I yell, locking eyes with Vaida.

Timber and Mars break the crowd, finding us.

I huddle them all in. "I can't believe I'm saying this, but we have to get out of the Hemisphere. If we don't, we'll get caught in the fallout. Then nobody will make it to the *Iris*."

Timber dodges a mess of debris whipping through the air. "We can go underground from the Outskirt side. There are hatches there, right?"

Mars nods. "We'll get you there."

"The Emergence Tunnel is two zones that way." Vaida points over her shoulder, sweeping wisps of hair out of her face. "But it's blocked off, too."

My pulse quickens. "I might be able to trigger the release manually."

'**ve** never run this fast in my life.

Vaida's hand stays locked in mine as we weave through the disarray, tracking Mars and Timber ahead of us. Zone 4: Medical greets us with overturned medic carts and sparking diagnostic machines, their exposed panels lit up with electricity. A group of runners trip on the tangled wires. They stretch too far and snap, setting the machines ablaze.

Smoke billows around us. Coughing, I shield my eyes.

A wire whips around. I yank Vaida back just in time.

She clings to me. "Fuck. That was close."

Zone 3: Provisions comes into view, and for a moment, I believe we'll make it. We'll get out before the Hemisphere turns to dust.

Then a patrol officer spots me.

"There he is!" he shouts. "Kevin Hale! Stop!"

My eyes go wide as Mars leads us into an alleyway. His weapon surges, leaving a sparkling mist behind us. Another patrol officer steps into our path.

I duck, and Mars takes him out.

We're in the clear. Or so I think.

As the Hemisphere collapses, shards of paneled glass rain down. I hurl myself aside just in time. Mars pulls Timber with him, narrowly avoiding a fragment of glass that slices two men rushing from their streetway shops nearly in half.

Blood spills into the spurting water in the street, swirling as it drains into the steaming grates. Vaida covers her mouth in shock. I try not to look.

"My head . . . " Timber groans, blood trickling down his forehead.

"You're fine. You're fine," Mars says. "Get up. We can't stop."

Vaida screams, "Look out!"

My life flashes before my eyes.

Slivers of glass whizz past me, exploding on impact.

The gales whip harder, sucking in trash and loose debris.

Keep moving, Kevin. You are not dying today.

We push forward, using anything solid as cover. Shielding our eyes, we dodge rogue shards of metal prying loose from their binds. Mars paves the way, and the tip of the Emergence Tunnel comes into sight.

No need to override mechanisms after all.

There's nothing left.

We charge down the sandstone steps, slipping in the washout. My eyes lock on the solar cart port a short distance away. *So close.*

"Everyone get down!" Timber shouts.

Behind us, a vortex devours the Hemisphere.

Wind whips my hair. Dust chokes my lungs.

Our bodies slam into the ground and saw-edged shards of glass plummet, slicing through the air. Whatever was left of the dome's structure is gone now. No shelter. Nowhere to go.

We have to reach the *Iris* before it's swept up into the storm.

Mars crashes into the sand beside me, gasping as a shard slices deep into his calf. Violet blood pools beneath him. Another slashes my arm. Pain sears across my skin.

I look around for Vaida. But she's gone. No longer at my side.

I spit out the sand in my mouth. "Vaida!"

Mars tears off his pack, lifting it above us like a shield.

Thwack. A shard hits his pack, striking through canvas.

Another shard slams into his upper thigh.

"Mars!" I lunge for him, then a wooden shaft spears into my side.

A strained yell rips from my throat. With a shaking hand, I crack it in half, leaving the serrated end still lodged in my skin. "Gah—Mars, are you okay!?"

"Get. Us. Out of here," he growls, biting back the pain.

Timber scrambles toward us. "You've both been hit!"

I force myself up. "I'm okay. It's not that bad."

But when we try to move Mars, he howls.

A solar cart skids to a halt beside us. Vaida leans over the dash, frantically waving us in.

"One. Two. Three." Timber and I heave Mars off the ground, helping him into the back. Timber climbs in next to him.

I hoist myself into the passenger's seat.

"Drive," I tell Vaida.

She slams her foot on the pedal. Pushes the solar cart to its limit.

In the side-view mirror, the storm churns closer. My entire body locks up. I clutch the sidebar, holding on. Blood soaks my shirt. A sharp pain sears through my skull. The dust is so thick behind my mask, it scorches my lungs.

"You need a healer," Timber exclaims, trying to get a look at Mars.

"If you cry, then I'll cry, and none of that bugging helps."

Vaida slows near the Outskirts.

I jolt upright. "No! No! Head for No Man's Land!"

She doesn't hesitate. Hammering the accelerator, she

veers off-road. The cart dips hard, nearly losing control, and she cuts behind jagged rock formations.

We tip back and forth in the uneven sand.

Vaida wrestles the wheel. The cart drifts.

"What's in No Man's Land?" she shouts over the roar of the storm.

"My uncle's aircraft!" I yell back.

Knuckles bone-white on the wheel, her eyes flick to me as another solar cart appears out of nowhere and slams into us at full throttle.

33: TIMBER

Planet Nevarnost: Year 3051

Mars' entire body goes rigid in my arms as the rogue solar cart rams us.

His bloody cheek strikes my chest. My chin dips, and we curl inward, holding each other as the solar cart rolls. Straps digging into our waists. Whipping through the sky.

The air is beaten from my lungs. My vision blurs at the edges.

Will I ever see my parents again? Raine. Marlowe. Kiki. *Anyone?*

Flashes of the mission return. The first pulse of vibration from the transporter in my hand. Mars's look of dread when we were paired. Heated sand swirling around us, consuming us in a cyclone of space and time. In a blip, we'd crossed light years. We'd entered a time loop with no end in sight. Not knowing what we'd really find here.

I like your soul, Timber, alright? I like you.

I know we've stopped moving, but my body still reels, spinning like a tumbleweed across the sand. My breather's been ripped from my face. I choke on toxic air, lungs begging for breath.

I yank it back up over my mouth and lean against the

headrest, swallowing hard.

We made it. We're alive. We're upside down.

Then I feel it—warm, sticky blood pooling in my hands.

Fingers trembling, I grope for the release and free Mars first.

His head slumps forward. *He'll be okay. He'll be okay.*

Blood trickles from a cut above my brow, dripping into the sand.

The droplets swirl with warm violet, Mars' blood, and the pit in my stomach swells. Our bodies drop, one after the other, into the mound of sand where the solar cart crashed.

Grit covers my arms. A ringing fills my ears.

With one heave, I maneuver us both between the seats and pull us out into the open, beneath the churning dust and dark skies.

He's been hit more than once. Too many times.

How am I going to fix this? What can I do?

Father didn't pack me enough healing supplies for this.

Mars stirs. I pull him closer, my entire body shaking.

He's lost too much blood. His wounds are too deep.

I don't know what to do. I don't know what to do.

"Timber," he croaks.

"I'm here. You're bleeding. You need—"

"Dune skulls. Do you *ever* stop talking?"

Thank the Gods. *He's still Mars at least.*

Beside us, Kevin and Vaida are already on their feet.

They disappear around the front of the totaled cart. As I tug on Mars' jacket to gauge his injuries, Kevin rushes back, digging through the wreckage for his pack and Vaida's bag.

"It's Chancellor Bay," he pants. "We're making a run for the *Iris*."

Then he's gone.

Mars clutches the collar of my tunic.

He yanks me close. "You have to go after them, Timber. Get them on that aircraft. Make sure they survive."

I shake my head. "No. I'm not leaving you."

Mars winces at the slightest movement. "It's you," he says.

His pain lances through me as I steady him against a rock.

"You're—you're the baby Vaida Wardell is carrying." His voice shakes. "I don't know how he knew, but your father didn't just send us to save Vaida and Kevin. He sent us to make sure *you* make it off Nevarnost before the storm hits."

"What? How do you—"

"You need to go. Now."

He holds my stare.

I wipe the blood from the corner of his mouth. This isn't some double blade in a recreational yard kind of injury. This is much worse. I don't know if he'll survive this.

"*Go*, Timber." Trembling, he unsheathes his glowbeam and forces it into my hands. "Take this. Don't hold back. Make sure the chancellor doesn't interfere with them getting away."

My fingers curl around the weapon.

I back away slowly, unable to tear my eyes from the boy with the forbidden flare. The boy who sees me, understands me, and who taught me how to start seeing my curse as a gift.

Something in me aches to stay. Just for a second.

I press a soft, fleeting kiss to his lips. "This isn't goodbye. I won't let it be."

Mars lets out a breathy laugh. "You'd better come back. Or I'll wrestle you down."

"Promise?"

"I promise. Now, go!"

I take off in the sandy current, ignoring the thick dust seeping through my breather. The storm churns behind me, swelling to its peak beneath the wicked skies.

Kevin and Vaida come into view through the canyon.

So does the silver sheen of the *Iris*.

And Chancellor Bay—a mangled mess of ruffled hair, blackened eyes, and a bloody gash bulging on his left ear—stalks close behind them.

He powers up the jolt stick dangling in his left hand.

My body begs me to stop running. My lungs burn.

Mars told me to finish this. To make sure Kevin, Vaida, and the baby she's carrying—*somehow me*—get away. I don't know how he knows. Or how he figured it out. But I don't have time to question it. I'll process that truth later.

Right now, my life depends on this too.

Mars would complete this task without hesitation. With honor. Strength. Perseverance. He wouldn't back down. And I need him to be proud of me. To know I *did* learn something from him, from all of this, even after all the times I let fear consume me.

After all the times I told myself I couldn't do it.

"Hale!" Chancellor Bay yells over the roar of the wind.

He reaches the entry ramp just as they do. Vaida whips out a syringe from her pocket, but Kevin throws out a shaky hand, signaling her to stay back.

"Ezra, it's over," he says, gentle but steady. "It doesn't matter anymore. Come with us if you have to, but please—don't do this. We're running out of time."

Chancellor Bay forces a matted tress of hair from his face.

"You think it doesn't matter?" His ruddy cheeks glisten with sweat. "I sacrificed everything for this project. I saved it. I did what *nobody* else had the guts to do."

There's a limp in his step forward, likely from the shard of dome glass perforating the skin below his kneecap. The fact that he's standing at all is actually quite impressive.

Focus, Timber.

"Everyone worshiped Billy like he was a god," Bay continues, jolt stick swinging in hand. "But I was the one who came here after graduation while he was off gallivanting through time and space. I was the one who apprenticed, worked hard, and clawed my way to the top."

He advances up the ramp.

Kevin steps in front of Vaida, planting his feet.

"And in the end, they *still* made him chancellor," Bay spits. "All because your mother died, and Billy decided to step in and play Dad. ISR didn't even think twice about handing him the power because he was best friends with all the higher-ups." His jolt stick hums, electricity snapping at its end. "Even when I took over after he disappeared, no one respected me like they did him. They stayed loyal to a man who damned them all to hell."

"I've seen the incident report. The explosion was an accident," Vaida snaps. "You can't blame him anymore for what you've done here. Take responsibility for your actions."

As the chancellor laughs, Kevin looks to Vaida. He doesn't say anything more, but as she nods, confirming what she just said as truth, Kevin stands taller and clears his throat.

"I'm sorry things didn't work out between you and my uncle," he says. "Or that you didn't get the recognition you deserved. But that's the past, Ezra. I'm not him. Hurting me won't fix this. It won't make it right. It won't change anything."

A slow, cruel smile spreads across Chancellor Bay's face. "I admire your wisdom, Kevin. You and Billy both have that in common. But I'm not here to make amends. I'm here to destroy the one thing in this world your uncle cares about most."

Lightning crackles across the inky sky, mimicking the inhuman growl that rolls off the chancellor's lips. He whips his jolt stick around and lunges forward, driving Vaida and Kevin apart, sending them tumbling onto the slick, angled ramp.

I freeze.

Chancellor Bay tosses his jolt stick aside and hovers over Kevin, who's now flat on his back. He pins him with the weight of his steel-toed boots, pressing harder to keep him down.

No. No. No. Come on, Timber.

My heart hammers in my chest. Thunder echoes through the canyon.

I rush forward. Vaida is already up, her orange syringe clutched in her hand.

She clatters into me, and together we charge toward the chancellor and Kevin.

But as Vaida lunges, Chancellor Bay slaps her hand away, jerking her wrist and stopping her strike just inches from his jugular.

Kevin writhes beneath him, struggling to breathe.

Vaida winces as the chancellor wrenches the syringe from her hand, then tosses her aside as if she's weightless. "You stay out of it," he hisses.

He analyzes the syringe. The look of recognition lights his eyes as he wedges the cap between his teeth, bites it off, and spits it out. Kevin retaliates with every shred of energy he has left, but it's no use. The chancellor yanks down his sleeve and claws off his mask.

"No!" Vaida cries. "It'll kill him!"

Do something, Timber.

My glowbeam whirls to life in my hands. I steady myself, my thumb hovering over the trigger. "Don't move," I say in a tone that doesn't feel like mine.

I aim my barrel directly between the chancellor's dull blue eyes.

Setting at stun. Power is maxed. Potency is at 100%.

"Don't make me use this," I warn.

The chancellor chuckles. "Please. You're harmless."

Two things happen next. The chancellor injects Kevin, and I pull the trigger.

A blast of light erupts from my glowbeam, sending the tyrant flying through the air in a motionless heap. *I just stunned the chancellor. I just stunned the chancellor. I just—*

"Kevin!" Vaida rushes to his side.

I collapse to my knees across from her, both of us staring down at his unconscious body between us. Kevin's cheeks are pale and his body is trembling, burning with a feverish heat.

The healer in me springs into action.

"What was in the syringe?" My words are surprisingly calm.

"Roake venom," Vaida answers shakily.

Roake venom. Father prepared me for this moment.

He knew the chancellor would inject Kevin with venom.

I reach into my tunic and pull out the antique brass

column locket on waxen cord. Father's knowing begs a thousand questions, but I don't have time to hesitate. I unscrew the top of the locket and let the purple pill, the venom neutralizer, fall into my palm.

"Sit him up. This will help him," I tell Vaida.

Together we gently tilt Kevin's head.

He starts to shake in our arms, but we hold him steady. Breaking the pill in half, I deposit the liquid into his mouth. A drop dribbles off his lips. It stains the collar of his shirt.

But he takes it down.

And I didn't hesitate.

34: KEVIN

Planet Nevarnost: Year 3051

I'm sinking.
Mother. Father. Nana. They're here.
Venom laces my blood, rattling my bones.
Down. Into the void. Drowning.
They surround me. Bind me.
Claim me as their own.
The inferno splits me half.
Sucks the breath from my lungs.
Hot iron in my veins.
Everything is cold.

I'm shivering.

"Kevin."

Wisps of brown-and-purple hair. Her galaxy-print face rag slips down. Warm lips graze my cheek, pressing into my clammy skin. Energy rushes through me.

"You're alive. Breathe."

Saltwater stains my eyes. Blinking burns.

Disorientation claims me as I'm pulled upright.

"We have to go. We're leaving Nevarnost."

I can't speak. Not yet. This world feels too far away.

But I've returned. I've escaped the void. My body smothers the flame. The venom retreats, washing away. A bitter taste coats my tongue. *He—He saved me.*

Arms lock around me. Timber and Vaida guide me up the ramp.

How did he save me?

"I have to get back to Mars!" Timber shouts over the storm.

Vaida reaches for him, and he hesitates, then accepts a hug.

I touch the place where her lips brushed my skin. My other hand grasps for the antique necklace hanging from Timber's neck. The waxen cord breaks. It falls into my palm.

He doesn't notice. He takes off into the dust.

The locket rolls between my fingers.

I tremble at the engraving.

To Quinn. Love, Billy.

35: MARS

Planet Nevarnost: Year 3051

In my fading consciousness, I fixate on the flutter of iridescent wings cupped in my hands. . .

Rosanna, you love me more than I could ever love myself. You've given me endless chances, even after all I've done is make life difficult for you. You keep asking me to let you in, to tell you why I'm so miserable all the time. And I've punished you for it.

I've never told you how . . . sorry I am for that . . .

My breath hitches. I can no longer speak.

Shakily, I guide Rose's Confess Me Moth back into its sphere and set it down next to me, away from the pool of violet blood gushing from beneath my jacket.

As I tug at the zipper and peel away the sticky fabric, the sliver of glass impaled above my rib cage tugs, sending fresh waves of pain through me. I breathe through each sway, shaking the heaviness in my head. I try not to think about the cracked transporter in my other hand.

It broke with the slam of the shards against my pack. It's dead now, its biometric scanners unable to read me or take me home.

My fate has been decided for me.

I will never get to apologize to Rose in person. I won't get to explore a life I'd only just begun to imagine. I will die here, with the rest of them. I will suffer here, like the worst of them.

And I should be thinking of Rose, but I'm only thinking of *him.*

I don't know if I'll see Timber again. I loathe my stubbornness for resisting letting down my guard for so long. Because we could have had more time. But I'm so glad we came here together.

I spit blood onto the sand. *Stay awake, Mars. You have to stay awake.*

At that moment, a shadow crosses the sky, cutting through the thick swirl of air.

A thrumming noise builds around me. I force my chin up and catch sight of the *Iris,* taking off in the dusty red cloud. The Unity tree painted on its underbelly glistens in the wind, picking up the golden streaks from an otherwise blackening mass.

Vaida Wardell and Kevin Hale will live.

And that means Timber Hale will, too.

I knew it first when I saw the photo of Kevin and his uncle in the loft—how similar the two of them looked, and how blatantly unsimilar Timber appeared. Elder Hale's lack of detail going into this mission. The *Iris* being here. Or how we would have noticed Kevin and Vaida on Violet Moon all those years later as elders, had they made it in the way Elder Hale said they did.

Timber made a connection between Kevin's grandmother's baby doll and the one his sister had growing up. And come to think of it, I don't think I've ever spoken to ISR directly. It was always relayed messages and briefings from

Elder Hale. It wasn't until Soren Bay grabbed hold of Timber in the alleyway that I saw the true resemblance between them. Like Kevin and his uncle, Timber is the spitting image of his biological father, too.

And after spending time with Kevin, after watching how easily Timber fell in line with him, I'll admit I was jealous at first. But then it became obvious.

I don't know if the real William "Billy" Hale is alive or what happened to him after that rch fell in the year 3041. But I do know Kevin pretended to be him all those years after he disappeared, so it would have been easy to continue the charade. Almost like second nature.

Elder Hale *is* a Hale. But Elder Hale isn't Billy Hale.

He's . . . Kevin Hale all grown up.

And Timber? His entire life depended on this mission. His mother is Vaida Wardell. He's the child she's carrying. That's why Elder Hale bargained with the Council of Elders.

We weren't sent here to save a dying planet.

We were sent here to save Timber and his parents.

And if Timber were here right now, he'd panic. He'd worry about me. Tears would stream from those bright blue eyes of his—Gods, they're beautiful.

I swear I'm looking into them . . . right . . . now.

My body is lifted off the ground.

Rose's voice says, *"You're okay, Mars."*

"Watch his head," Timber's voice says next. Then, a hand that feels like his intertwines with mine tight. *"I'm right here with you. I'm not going to leave you again."*

Other voices I don't know, can't place, join the disorientation.

"Press his thumbs into the transporter," a young man commands.

"We're down to one minute," a younger girl adds.

A mirage of colors and shapes whirl around me.

My mind is messing with me. I know they aren't real.

Given how much blood I've lost, I feel as though I'm floating.

Dune skulls. Timber would have admired me without fault in these final moments. Traditional Vio would have been spoken. We had a soul connection that could have maybe been—would have been—me loving to be loved.

. . . Rose, you will find someone. Someone who treats you right. Someone who will hold you when you're upset. Who doesn't forget your birthing day or forget to pick up the wash on washing afternoon. You will find someone who laughs at your jokes, and who wakes up every morning with a longing for romance and mutual affection, just like you do.

Someone who will kiss you like . . . he kissed me.

But it's not me. It never was. It never will be.

—Mars

36: TIMBER

Planet Nevarnost: Year 3051

Sand kicks back as I sprint across the desert, heading to the wreckage of the solar cart.

I keep my eyes on the tree of life, reaching into the horizon.

They made it. Vaida and Kevin made it. We did it.

I come to a skidding halt outside the wreck. My lungs constrict, and I clutch my chest, whipping around, searching in all directions for Mars.

He was right here. *Why isn't he here?*

"Mars!" I shout into the roar of the storm.

He was right here. He was right here.

"Mars!" I scream again.

The heel of my boot nudges something round, resting in the dirt at my feet. I bend over and pick up a Confess Me Moth, of all things, in a transparent sphere.

But that's it. The only sign of life around me.

Black swirls of winds rise in the sky, and the ground beneath me quakes. Cylinders of dust whorl without remorse.

Gripping the sphere, I gasp and double back, moving as fast as I can.

Back toward the canyons. Back toward where the *Iris*

took off with Vaida and Kevin safely inside. They got away. I did what Mars asked me to.

Gods and Goddesses, he would be proud.

From my pocket, a light seeps through.

The soft vibrations of my transporter escalate, beckoning me home. But I can't leave yet. I can't leave without him. It wasn't supposed to be this way.

"Mars!" I yell, growing hoarse.

I search every which way, running, not daring to glance over my shoulder at the storm. A divot in the sand trips me up, but I scramble back to my feet quickly.

I spot a form behind a mass of rock to my left, boots sticking out.

Mars.

As I round the formation, my heart leaps in my chest. Not my mission partner. It's Chancellor Bay, barely conscious, his body shaking from the massive stun he endured.

"Please," he rasps, reaching forward with a blood-soaked hand.

His body quivers in my presence. I drop down next to him, pressing my back against the rock, while the dust swirls in the air on either side of us.

My mind goes foggy. I space out, listening to the trill of my transporter.

Deep breath, Timber. Mars is okay. He has to be okay.

"He's alive," the chancellor says, barely audible.

"What?" I lean in closer. "Who? Mars?"

He struggles to shake his head. "B—Billy. He was—he was here . . ."

I glance down at the tyrant who's caused so much pain. He's lost a lot of blood and is now, apparently, hallucinating the image of his former comrade. I close my eyes and feel for the biometric scanner on my transporter, ready to press the pull that will take me back home.

Because that's the only choice I have now. There's no more time.

Hovering over the heat of the device, the chancellor's next words will me to wait a moment longer. "You look . . . just like him . . . like . . . Soren . . ."

My eyes spring open. He's talking about his son.

Which, if Mars is right, makes him my . . .

"If you have any sense of . . . mercy. The storm is a slow, tortuous death. Please . . ."

Then I notice the cold shine of metal—an old hunting knife, quaking in his hand.

Absolutely not. I shake my head. The confusion surges through me, but somehow, something deeper than confusion starts to sink in.

"I'm sorry," I stammer, realigning my transporter. "I can't. I won't—"

Wind strikes the air, whooshing into the vortex.

I shield my face, and my transporter is knocked from my hand. I fumble through the sand, finally feeling its weight settle in my palm again.

But the chancellor would suffer, Timber.

I can't let him suffer. Even if he deserves to.

A force, not my own, takes the knife from the dying man's hands.

My other hand anchors against his back for leverage. Our connection triggers the gift I was born with, and almost immediately I am overwhelmed with his agony and grief.

"You—you loved him," I say softly, noticing the sting of regret pouring out of him, mingled with the resentment and shame of his life's twisted path.

"Of course I did." Chancellor Bay's blue eyes fall into mine. "If you met Billy Hale, you'd . . . love him, too. He was . . . extraordinary . . . the . . . one that got away . . ."

A tear falls down my cheek as I see the human beneath the monster.

All the emotions Vaida never thought he had. All the feeling, hurt, and pain no one ever knew he'd endured. He's done unforgivable things. None of which can be justified by his pain.

But they weren't done for nothing.

Like anyone, he's a man with a history, a father that did the best he could with the tools he had. A man who felt betrayed and misunderstood by those who promised to protect him. A man who chose violence over healing because he couldn't escape the expectations that had been thrust upon him following his birth.

The choking wind fills my lungs. My fingers go numb.

A lull of Vio invocations pour out of me, like ritual.

I press my thumbs into my transporter, so it'll take me home. But not before the final phrase—the one that seals the fate of souls, the one that binds life to the cycle it must follow.

"*Ruetere u aethere*," I say, guiding the knife into my grand-father's chest, and watch with wet eyes as he breathes his last breath.

37: VAIDA

Galaxy 22Minor: Year 3051

There is nothing left of the Nevarnost Project.

Everything we built is gone. The Hemisphere, the Zones, the Outskirts.

From the bridge of the *Iris*, I watch massive black clouds devour the barren dust planet below. The weight of our decision to flee settles heavy in my heart. Some might call it cowardice. Some might call it fucking reckless. But I stand by it.

I chose the best possible future for my baby.

The Nost will survive. They lived underground long before we humans arrived. Nevarnost, in all its unforgiving forms, was theirs first.

I'd like to think there are human survivors. Maybe Dad found shelter. Maybe Soren disappeared underground. *May Goddess Cassia spare them like she spared us.*

But the devastation is too much to process.

I take the lift to the main deck, where Kevin sits at the control board, double-checking thrusters and running diagnostics, ensuring our course is set.

For a moment, I thought I'd lost him, too.

361

Watching him succumb to roake venom made me realize something. The day we first met, it wasn't hatred that filled me up when I looked at him. It was something else.

Something warm.

Something steady.

It feels strange, standing beside Kevin without a face mask or layers of rags. For the first time, I can see him fully—every line, every smile, every shadow.

I rest a hand on his shoulder. "You really should rest after what you've been through. Your wounds need cleaning. You deserve a break."

"I know. And I will." His voice is distant, his expression grim. "But right now, the system won't let me set landing coordinates."

I frown. "What do you mean?"

"They've already been locked in."

"Locked in? By who?"

Beads of sweat form on his temple. "I don't know. Someone manually set them . . . and the cryopods were recently used. Two of them have been reprogrammed. For us."

I sink into the seat beside him. "Do you think Timber and Mars did it?"

Kevin shakes his head. "I don't think so. The coordinates and pods were programmed on Thursday, July 3rd. I think . . . somebody else was here." He looks at me. "And I think Timber and Mars coming back in time was part of something *much* bigger than they even knew."

Something bigger.

I think back to what Nia said outside Nucleus. "Your uncle knew I'd get pregnant with Soren's baby. He asked Nia to watch over me all these years."

"What? How would he have—"

"I don't know." I press a hand against my stomach.

He leans back in his chair. "It's all a matter of time . . ."

"What is?"

"My uncle was a deeply spiritual person. In his journals, he wrote that time isn't linear. He believed everything that has happened, or will happen, has already happened. That it's all happening at once," Kevin says, tapping his fingers on the console. "Versions of us could be traveling through time right now, leaving us pieces of a puzzle we won't understand until we're meant to. For all I know, an older version of *me* was here days ago and set these coordinates . . . but I won't know that until I *become* that version of me and do it."

My mind spirals. "So . . . Timber and Mars were always going to come here? You and I were always going to make it out alive?"

"I think so—"

His eyes suddenly light up. He sits up straight and yanks open a drawer beneath the control panel. I step aside as he rifles through files and scattered equipment.

He stops.

In his hands is something wrapped in burlap and tied with twine. Kevin looks at me, then slowly unwraps it. A pair of glasses falls into his hands, along with a folded bit of parchment.

"How did you know?" I ask.

"I didn't." Kevin beams. "I would've torn apart this whole ship until I found something. I just got lucky on the first try."

He unfolds the parchment, and over his shoulder, I read the words in faded ink:

I didn't abandon you, Kevin. Wear them well. — Billy

A chill rides my spine.

363

Kevin's eyes lift to meet mine.

Before either of us can speak, the console hums to life. A video conference invite box flashes on the screen.

Incoming Call: ISR

"Something in the Hemisphere must have triggered a warning when it collapsed." Kevin leans forward and hovers over the answer button. "Biometrics have been overridden too . . . that's weird. I didn't do that . . . I couldn't have done that."

I squeeze the back of his chair to steady myself. "We should answer. Just tell ISR the Nevarnost Project is gone. Tell them your uncle is alive somewhere, and we need help."

"I . . . . can't." His jaw goes slack. "Think about it. Even if Billy is still out there, he's led everyone to believe he's dead. There must be a reason. Not to mention, I've been lying to ISR for *ten years* pretending to be him through messages and distant contact."

"They'll understand."

"I'm over eighteen, Vaida. They're the highest-ranking authority. If they find out I've been impersonating him and lying, they'll arrest me." He looks at the glasses in his hands once more. "I think he *was* here. On Nevarnost. A few days ago. Somehow, he left these for me and set everything up for us. Who else could've programmed the *Iris* or overridden the biometrics?"

"Kevin . . ."

There's hope in his voice, and I'd hate to see him disappointed.

"I'm serious," he says. "I know you think it's crazy. But this note proves it."

"I don't think you're crazy—"

The console rings again.

"Wear them well." He smooths his thumb over the glasses. "I think I have to keep up the lie. At least until we get to our destination and I can figure out where he is. We look alike. Given his rounds of cryosleep in the past, we can say I recently traveled if they question it."

"You want to trick ISR into thinking you're Billy?"

"It might be the only way we get anywhere safely."

"But is that what you want?" I search his face, willing him to look at me. "You've spent your whole life taking care of everyone else. Nobody is forcing you to. What do *you* want?"

"All I wanted was to make my uncle proud."

"I think Billy would be very proud of you."

Tension releases in his shoulders.

"I suppose you're right," he says.

"Of course I'm right. I'm *always* right."

He laughs. "Sure you are."

He puts on the glasses, and they automatically adjust to his eyes. After a deep breath, Kevin answers the call from ISR. A robotic female voice echoes from the machine: *"Welcome back to Luxframe. Please state your full name for log in preference and confirmation to accept the call."*

"William Nash Hale," Kevin says.

"Welcome back, Mr. Hale."

Before he can talk himself out of it, I reach over his shoulder and press *"accept video conference."* Kevin and I are a team now. Working together means honesty and forgiveness, but it also means lifting each other up when doubt creeps in.

Nia taught me that.

A woman in her late twenties materializes on the screen.

Her silver uniform contrasts with the ivory tones of her skin, and her long red hair falls in waves around her face. A polished gold ISR pin rests proudly on her chest.

"Commander Derry. *Kathryn*." Kevin says her name like he's known her forever.

He really does know everything about his uncle.

"Agent Hale. *Billy*." Her smile is genuine. "I was beginning to worry. We lost communication with Ezra in Nucleus. Gods—do you ever age?"

Kevin chuckles. "Did some traveling recently. You know me."

I step out of the frame, keeping close enough to listen.

"The storm hit at 1100 hours."

"How many survivors?" she asks.

"Three humans. Ezra didn't make it."

Commander Derry's expression softens. "I'm sorry to hear the Nevarnost Project ended like this. I know how hard you and Ezra worked. Given everything you went through."

Kevin nods. "I wish we could've saved more. We just ran out of time in the end."

"I understand," she says somberly. "Your lab is waiting for you here on *Ophelia*, exactly how you left it, should you wish to return here. Beachum and I are actually heading out on a scouting voyage of our own, so I won't be here if you decide to come home."

"I'm actually set to go somewhere else," Kevin says.

"Oh? Where were you thinking? I can authorize landing clearance."

"Uh . . ." He scrolls through a side screen, finding a directory of planets. He brings up the screen that tells us our locked-in coordinates, and I grin. "Violet Moon," he tells Commander Derry. "We're headed to Violet Moon."

"Alright. I'll send in the landing approval now." Commander Derry straightens in her chair and starts typing. "There's no permanent command posted there for ISR, but Gregorius Mars is still the Head Elder. You can touch base with him when you arrive. I'll also need a full incident report and analysis of everything that happened on Nevarnost once you're settled."

"Will do. Promise or—"

"Perish? Hell yeah, Hale."

She winks. Then the screen goes black.

F our vertical cryopods wait for us in the regulation chamber.

I remember learning about them in primary school during our interplanetary travel unit. Thick curved panels of glass, their padded interiors bathed in a greenish-blue. They were built to lower our body temperatures and stop biological time.

When we wake up, we'll be the same age we are now.

That's about all I paid attention to.

Kevin and I have both changed into the simple black cotton pants and long-sleeved shirts we found in the supply unit on the bridge. He offers his hand and I take it, climbing into my pod.

While he checks my vitals on the control screen, I drink the prep-liquid from the vial he gives me. It's tasteless, yet thick, and coats the back of my throat with a thin film.

"Electrolytes. Pulse. Both heartbeats look good," he says.

I try to find a comfortable position. "Why four cryopods if it's just Billy's ship?"

Kevin dims the screen and steps in front of my pod, bringing us inches apart.

"One for Billy. One for my mother. One for Nana." He pauses a moment. "I guess the other was for my grandpa, but he chose working for ISR over coming to Nevarnost."

"Nana was lucky to have you, you know."

"I know," he says softly.

I find myself scanning every inch of his face. The brown waves of hair that reach just below his ears, the sharpness of his jaw, the little dimple at the corner of his mouth. His eyes remind me of the vibrant green flora in Nost Territory. But it's what's behind them that matters most—genuine kindness, heart, and honesty.

We're about to go into cryosleep for more than a decade.

Nia would really want me to make this moment count.

"What," he says. "Why are you staring at me like that?"

"I just realized that I never gave *you* a compliment underground."

"Oh?" He leans in a bit closer.

"Yes. You called me beautiful—which is an obvious compliment—so I meant to tell you that you're objectively handsome and too smart for your own good."

His smile widens. "So you *do* think I'm smart, then?"

I roll my eyes. "Don't let it go to your head."

"Too late. My ego has now doubled in size."

Our laughter fades, but neither of us looks away.

There's something else I want to say, but the words tangle on my tongue. The thought of it makes my heart beat so fast that my vitals screen lets out a noise.

Kevin raises a brow. "You alright? Baby alright?"

"Yes. I just—I want to say something."

He nods. "Okay."

I swallow hard. "I was wrong about you. And I'm looking forward to getting to know you more when we land on Violet Moon—Why are you smirking at me like that?"

"I knew I would grow on you."

I jab his arm. "Shut up. You did not."

"Mhmm. I did. I just knew."

He leans in. I tilt my head as our noses brush.

"Can I kiss you now?" he asks gently.

Instead of answering, I press my lips to his.

His hand finds my cheek, anchoring me to him. My fingers weave through his hair. It's gentle, and the corners of my mouth rise as he deepens the movements of his lips. The cryopod around us disappears in these moments. There's nothing else but him. But this.

Kevin's affection is patient. It doesn't demand or take like the last time I was kissed by a Hemisphere boy. It's just enough to let me know he cares.

When we break apart, his cheeks are redder than mine.

I laugh. He nods, then steps back to the vital screen one last time to start the countdown of my pod. "Billy set our travel time for thirteen years, even though Violet Moon is much closer. I don't know why, but I'm choosing to trust his reasons."

I rest my head back. "It's okay. For us, it'll just feel like a day."

"I've also been trying to wrap my head around this idea that if I'm pretending to be him, and we're going to Violet Moon, and 'Billy' sent Timber and Mars, it means—"

"I know . . ." I look down at my stomach. "I've thought about that, too."

"As long as we're on the same page," he says as the countdown sounds. "Have a good sleep, Vaida. I'll be here

369

when you wake up. It'll be a fresh new start for us both."

Yes. It will be.

The cryopod closes, blocking him from view. Cool air seeps over me from the edges of my pod, and the icy finish creeps up the glass. My brain grows fuzzy. My eyes are heavy.

We are going to Violet Moon.

When I wake, my baby will have a home.

It doesn't matter how he came to be, because together, we will build something new. He'll know all sorts of things. Instead of dusty lungs, he'll know fresh air. Instead of hate, he'll know love. Instead of anger, he'll know forgiveness. There will be no Hemisphere or Outskirts—only one community, a place where everyone lives together peacefully.

More importantly, my son will know a man with a gentleness in his heart.

38: TIMBER

Planet Violet Moon: Year 3083

My knees slam down into iridescent black sand.

Thumbs throbbing from the heat of my transporter.

Everything blurs. My lungs can't take it.

Somebody yanks at my breather.

A gust of crisp, clean Violet Moon air rushes in.

Silver and purple twilight spills over me, shimmering across the *Iris* where it sits less than a mile away. Father wraps his arms around me so tight it hurts, but the pain and ache of his emotion feels good. So good I hope it knocks me out again. Because I can't process any of this.

I can't lift my head either. If I do, I'll have to look into Father's eyes.

I know who he really is now. He's Kevin Hale. All grown up.

And Mother, her voice is a dream. "Timber, you have to breathe."

She cuts in and out. The edge of consciousness sweeps me under.

"Let me help him." Then louder. "*Kevin—out of the way!*"

My body falls limp as he releases me. Mother is there, running her hand through my blood-caked hair. "It's okay. It's okay," she whispers to me. "You're okay."

Her face comes into view. Those familiar hazel eyes, touched with gold.

Breathe, Timber, they say. "In and out. In and out. In and out."

Mother's voice is the last thing I hear.

Vaida's voice is the last thing I remember.

"He wasn't where I left him," I mutter before I slip under.

W aves crash against the rocks outside my sleeping room window.

A salty taste lingers in the back of my throat.

My body is rock. Heavy. Lifeless in mounds of sweaty cotton linens and goose-feather pillows. When I open my eyes, I brace for a burst of violet and thick clouds of sand.

But everything is calm.

My soft pale skin. My clean tunic and undergarments. The walls of my sleeping room, white against the driftwood floor. Even the vitamins resting still in the tray by my side.

A streak of morning light slips off the tide, catching the sea glass mobile above me.

The glass pieces clatter together in a gentle song.

I sit up slowly. Pressure surges in my temples.

Maybe it was all a dream. My Coming of Age ceremony. The time travel. All of it.

Maybe Raine is waiting for me in the South Woods. Maybe Father is busy working in his mechanism pod near the hull. Maybe Mother is in the sitting room, nursing the babies while Marlowe plays with our brothers. And I—I am a healer. That is who I am. That is what I do.

The linens tucked around me crinkle as I pull my knees to my chest and rest my head. I know none of it is true, but if I imagine the best instead of the worst, then Mars isn't gone.

A gentle lull pulls me back. "You're awake."

My eyes flick to Mother standing in the doorway, then drift to the glowfish splashing in the cove outside my window. She crosses the room on quiet, bare feet and sinks onto the edge of my sleeping mat so softly I barely feel the shift.

"How are you feeling?" she asks.

I can't answer her. I have never felt so much all at once before.

I was taught to forgive, to find the best in everyone. Part of me seethes with anger at her presence. My love for her outweighs it—but it's still there.

All the things I never knew about her. About the man I call Father. About my birth father. My history. She even changed her name. Was that supposed to make Father feel better about changing his, too? *And how did I not recognize her?* Vaida's face was covered most of the time with her face rag. I suppose it wouldn't have been as clear.

The thought of Mars out there somewhere invades my mind, and my heart cracks.

I should have looked harder for him. People don't just disappear. They can't.

Not to mention, I've done the worst thing a person can do. I've taken a life. And not a mindless moon worm. An actual human life. One that begged me to, but still, I cannot fathom forgiveness in a greater sense for any of us.

Not yet. Not even close.

Mother's words are careful. "I want you to know that everything we did, we did for a reason. If we told you too much about your future, it might have changed. Then we wouldn't be here. Everything had to happen exactly as it did, or the time loop might have been incomplete."

She tries to grasp my hand, but I pull it back and turn away from her.

I stare at the ocean, embracing the tears welling in my eyes.

"Am I the worst decision of your life?" I ask.

"Why would you say something like that?"

"In Nucleus comms . . . you said being with Soren was the worst decision of your life." I glance at her. She attempts to wipe away the water pooling beneath my eyes, but I retreat, keeping a distance between us on the sleeping mat. "That must mean you think of me as something—"

"Timber, you're the best thing that's *ever* happened to me. I didn't know it then. I was young and confused, and there was a lot going on, but I don't regret you. Not even close."

"Tell me what happened to Mars," I snap. "Where did he go?"

"I don't know." She reaches for me once more. Again, I jerk away. "Your father has been reworking the transporters all night to track his location."

I chew the inside of my cheek. "That's not good enough."

"I know you're filled with too many emotions to process right now. But please . . . please know we love you. We are here for you. *Both* of us." Mother reaches into her pocket and places my wooden talisman and a folded-up piece of parchment on the sleeping mat next to me. "Whatever you decide to do at your second trial tonight, we support you, and we think you should have your talisman after everything you've been through regardless."

I don't move. I don't touch it. I don't care about Vio tradition right now.

Mother's warmth fades, and the sleeping mat shifts as she rises. I hear the soft creak of the floor as she lingers in the doorway.

I keep my eyes on the glowfish in the cove.

"I killed him, you know."

"You killed who, Timber?"

I glance back at her.

"The chancellor. I killed him with a hunting knife so he wouldn't suffer."

For a moment there's a glint of light in Mother's eyes. An expression that almost unsettles me. "Do you revel in that, Vaida? You seem . . . pleased by my actions."

Her expression falls. "I revel in nothing of the sort."

A t dusk, it rains.

A soft pitter-patter against our thatched roof. A clean, steady stream that will soak the garden flowers and make the fruit in the South Woods glisten like polished crystal. Our sun will set for hours, offering its charade of colors in the sky.

Now, I just wish it would end.

I remove my white tunic, crumpling it in my hands before letting it fall to the floor. I tug open my armoire, its door groaning in protest. My mind races as I search for a navy-blue tunic with decorative neck adornments, purple day pants, and leather boots—proof of what happened and where I've been. But they aren't here. I'll never see them again.

I settle for a brown tunic and gray day pants, figuring it's what's best, given I'll be facing the Council of Elders tonight for the second and final time. Before I dress, I smooth the talisman Mother left for me in my palm. It's simple, a spiral sun carved in its center.

We spend our whole young lives waiting for this moment.

A symbol of completion, marking the beginning of our adulthood.

But all it is, is a hunk of wood. A symbol that looks familiar, but I can't place it. It's not one I've ever seen here on Violet Moon. I set it away. I won't need it. Not where I'm going.

But the folded page of parchment with Mars' drawing of me from our night on the *Iris*—I tuck that into my pocket to keep with me. It'll give me strength underground when I have nothing else.

As I finish tying my plain belt, I notice Raine coming up the path through the window. Everything that happened between us seems insignificant now. I was only gone a few hours by Violet Moon time, but like Mother and Father, he too feels like a stranger. The Timber he came to say goodbye to at the Dunes yesterday morning is gone. I'm still trying to figure out who came back in his place.

This version of me doesn't know how to be around Raine.

I dash from my sleeping room to the sustenance chamber before he makes it to our front step. My sister eyes me from the counter where she preps the evening meal, chopping an array of root vegetables near a simmering pot.

"Mother said you were sick," Marlowe says, moving the

bouquet of metal roses Father welded for Mother on their last commitment anniversary so she can pull her crust dough closer. "I'm making you soup and your favorite mango tart. I don't care what you say, we're sitting for a family meal to celebrate your birthing day properly before your trial tonight."

They told her I was sick. Of course; they wanted to keep this between us.

I've never looked at my sister and felt such envy as I do now. How could she not know? It's unfair she's been spared from all of this. But as unjust as it is that she is rightfully our father's daughter, and he will always hold that true in his heart, this isn't Marlowe's fault. She has nothing to do with this.

I close my eyes and lean back against the front door. "I'm not sick."

"You look it." She drops a heap of sweet potatoes into the pot. With one hand, she grabs a rag. With the other, she draws her sharpest knife from the cutting block. My mind swarms with images, visualizing it covered in blood and plunging into a man's chest, a dying plea in his eyes.

If you have any sense of mercy. Please.

"I think Raine's outside." Marlowe sets down her tools. With a swish of her long skirt, she joins me at the door. "Why aren't you letting him in? He's looking in the window."

She reaches around me, and I recoil as she opens the door.

It knocks me forward. Marlowe giggles. "Sorry about that, Rainey. Timber's feeling ill, and it seems his sickness has taken away his sense of proper hospitality."

"That's alright." Raine peers inside. "Can I come in?"

He smiles warmly while Marlow returns to her place at

the counter.

I can't look him in the eye. "Probably shouldn't. I might be contagious."

"I'll take that risk." He steps a little closer. "I just wanted to check in before your trial tonight . . . and apologize for how I acted at the Dunes yesterday. I clearly had a lot to say, and it wasn't the right time for any of it. I'm really sorry."

"No . . . you're right. I haven't been great at communicating or being honest."

The air grows heavy with tension, but he doesn't budge from the doorway. Raindrops splatter his watcher uniform, dotting his full cheeks and dampening his long hair.

He puts his hands in his pockets, and I avoid his gaze, focusing on his lips instead. They part slightly, and I'm suddenly reminded of kisses. Just not his.

Marlowe gives her soup another stir. "I'm going to go pick some carrots from the garden." She nudges me as she passes. "*Talk* to him, you goon."

When she's gone, Raine steps fully inside and shuts the door behind him.

"Well," he begins, "I've been thinking, and I guess the abrasiveness in my tone was more about my feelings. I promise I'm not saying this as some last-ditch attempt to change your mind about your ceremony, but I . . . I support you in whatever you choose. Even if I have to visit you in the mines." He pauses, his eyes meeting mine. "Because I love you, Timber. Or, I guess, I have feelings for you, and it's been on my mind for a while. And I decided that even if you don't feel the same, I had to say it. This might be my last chance—"

"Raine. Please stop," I say quickly. "I can't—I can't do this right now."

His cheeks turn pink. "Oh. I'm—"

"You don't have to apologize. I'm not mad." I take a step toward him. I have to be honest now. *Even if it hurts.* "I'm going through a lot right now. It's not you, I just . . . I'm not in a place where I can be open like you need me to be. I appreciate your flattery, and anyone would be lucky to be with you or to have you as a friend, but I'm not there right now, okay?"

I don't want to hurt him. Raine has been more patient than anyone with me, but this is possibly the worst timing in history—and I just traveled through actual time.

That, and how do I even begin to explain any of this to him?

"Is there anything I can do to support you?" he asks.

I shake my head. "No. I just need a break from this. Please."

He steps back toward the door, giving me a single nod before leaving. He's out the door and running through the downpour with his hands over his head moments later.

My heart tightens in my chest, breaking into pieces I'm not sure I'll ever be able to put back together. I can't deny I've felt something for Raine in the past. I just didn't know what it was, and then Mars happened. Even though he isn't here, and might never be, a part of me still clings to the idea of him. If I indulge in feelings for Raine now, I might destroy whatever is left of us—or any chance of what we could be in the future, if that's even our fate.

Raine deserves better than that. We both do.

39: TIMBER

Planet Violet Moon: Year 3083

The *Iris* entry ramp illuminates me in the darkness.

The cool silver finish of the incline sends shivers up my spine. A sensor flashes, letting me into the living quarters, and the floor lights flicker to life in the small sustenance chamber off the sleeping room. Everything is clean and still: a thriving plant on the butcher block, fresh linens near the water basin.

An aircraft converted into a home, the warmth pulled from every inch of it.

Shadows move behind the opaque divider. My heart jumps, preparing for the worst.

When Rose rounds the corner, I feel silly for thinking such a thing. She raises her brows, clearly not surprised to see me. She must have known I'd end up here before heading over to the Council of Elders' hut for my trial. Her hair hangs in knotted clumps around her face. Her eyes are swollen and puffy. I think I'm haunted, but she must be heartbroken.

"Excuse me." She pushes by, gathering her belongings. Stacks of pressed cotton dresses and worn leather-bound books. Tales from the village library—*A Galaxy of Love, Neptune's Daughter, Warrior of Stars*. Undemanding romantic stories to pass the days, a fantasist's escape; I've even read a few myself. As she stuffs them into the bag set outside the washroom, it dawns on me she's leaving.

"Mars' Ceremony of Rebirth will be on Fourth Day." She fastens the buttons on her bag, folding in a decorative headband. "That is, if you're not in the mines by then."

"We can't be certain he's dead. He might still be out there."

She sighs, pushing a tangled tress from her face. "Timber, do you honestly think that's the truth? After all this, you must learn to accept that nothing comes without consequence."

"He wasn't there when I went back for him, Rose," I say, biting back the urge to break down. Now is not the time to cry. *Because she's right.* "He was gone. I don't know how."

She picks up her bag, sets it on the counter in the mess, and carefully places her potted jungle plant beside it. "You know, I always thought I put on a brave face because that's what you do when you're committed to someone, but I cared about him deeply."

"I know," I tell her, reaching into my pocket. I feel for the transparent sphere containing her Confess Me Moth and hand it to her. "He cared about you, too. This was lying in the sand near the solar cart wreck."

She takes it, her bright umber eyes focusing on me.

"Do you think terribly of me? Can you—could you—forgive me?"

I've only ever known Rose through the eyes of Mars. Through Raine, when he would run with her at dawn. She doesn't seem like the grudge-bearing type. But I could be wrong.

"I think the greater question is, can you forgive yourself?" She slings her bag over her shoulder, her plant cradled under her other arm. As she does, her dress shifts, and I catch a glimpse of the inked planet Mars above her heart. "By the way," she says, pressing the scanner beside the door, "Ere is up on the bridge. I'm not messing with her. Good luck."

Gee. Thanks.

"You don't have to go." Her energy starts to fade as her feet graze the threshold of the ramp, heading down the incline. "You can stay here. This is your home."

"Mars was what made this ship a home," she says. "Besides, after his Ceremony of Rebirth, our commitment will be broken, and I'll be free to find soulship in another if I wish. I'll be staying with the watchers until then. We have a communal treehouse in the South Woods."

I hang my head, thinking she's gone, but then she adds, "Mars was my best friend. He was my platonic soulmate, and I wanted him to be happy. He liked you, you know. He acted like he didn't, but that's what Mars did. He pushed away anything good for him and acted like he was above it, hoping it would go away before it got too real."

Yeah. All too real.

Rose disappears down the ramp, her matted tresses bouncing behind her.

Across the mess, I call the lift. Avoiding the bridge would be wise. Letting Ere have her way with the *Iris* would be in my best interest. But danger calls to me now. I crave the rush that surges through me when I face my fears head-on.

Her growl beckons me as I rise.

When the lift settles and the doors open, Ere is waiting, stalking beneath the control board. Sharp teeth exposed, claws curled, her eyes flashing crimson. Her white fur bristles up the arch of her back, and the hairs on my arms stand on end.

I widen my stance. *"U wooe beacke deree."*

I won't back down. I won't.

Ere's foaming mouth hisses and opens with a great roar.

I give it right back. A scream which writhes from beneath my ribs, a gut-wrenching roar of my own. Ere hesitates, slinking her tail around herself. Sitting, she tilts her head in my direction. Her eyes fade to violet, and a wave of relief settles inside me.

There, her eyes seem to tell me. *You are not the coward I thought you were.*

A clatter of noise and disgruntled chatter carries from the walk-in.

I enter and am immediately drawn to the corner. The last time I was here, thirty-two years ago, Mars bared his soul, and we kissed. My mind swiftly moves on from that thought, focusing instead on Father—well, Kevin—hunched over a spread of transporters in the docking unit.

Some are disassembled. Gears and regulators attached to others.

One zaps his fingers. *"Crap.* Lux, log attempt 45 as a fail," he says into his digiband. "Can't seem to get the time to regulate properly. Can't return to the same year more than once. I'll try again and tap into the continuum on another channel."

"Attempt 45 is recorded."

It takes him a second to notice me. When he does, he sets

down the device in his hand and pulls up a second stool, which I don't take.

"I'm bringing Mars' proposal to the council tonight. If I can convince them to change village rule, maybe they won't send you to the mines when you refuse to kill the worm."

"I don't care about the mines. That's where I'm going, and I've made peace with it," I say to the man I once begged to blaze across a dying planet with me. "Did you know?"

Only a day ago, I was comforting a teenage version of him at his nana's bedside, performing a makeshift Ceremony of Rebirth in her honor. But the wrinkles around his emerald eyes remind me that he is still the man who raised me.

"Did you know Mars would disappear?" I repeat, watching him tinker with another mechanism, his movements precise. "Kevin—" My voice is no longer mine. "Did. You. *Know*?"

He slams the transporter down on the bench.

"I am still your father, and you will treat me as such." His expression softens, and for the first time, I see him blush. This is perhaps the hardest conversation we'll ever have.

I wonder if I'm the only person, other than Mother, to have ever seen him cry.

"No, I didn't know," he says, running a hand through his hair. "I knew you'd both probably need a healer, him especially, which is why I told Kiki everything and had her waiting on standby. But when Mars' transporter went offline while you were gone, I assumed the worst. I didn't know beforehand." He meets my gaze. "I've been trying to rewire the mechanism so we can—"

"You knew this whole time what you were sending us into, though," I say, and he sets down the transporter and finally gives me his full attention. "All those lies about the transporters appearing outside your lab and notes from your future self—How could you do that? If you'd told us *everything*, maybe Mars would be here."

"It wasn't all a lie. A case of transporters really did show up outside Billy's lab all those years ago. I just fabricated the contents of the note." He swallows hard. "Because if I'd told you the truth, *we* might not have made it here."

"I don't care," I say briskly. "It was a selfish thing to do. It was the *wrong* thing to do." I rub my temples. "All those people at the rally beneath the Hemisphere . . . Commander Wardell . . . the Nost . . . Mars . . . they all died *just* to save you and Mother?"

"The Nost sought solace underground. And we can go back and check for human survivors, I'm sure of it—" He wipes his hands on his pants frantically, a bead of sweat trickling across his forehead. "And you know what, Timber? Your mother saved the lives of countless babies during an outbreak of violet fever the year we landed here, okay? *Including* Mars. We also made a difference. Don't think I haven't carried the guilt of what we did. I haven't forgotten."

"You didn't have to become your uncle."

"Billy didn't give me a choice." He pushes his glasses up his nose, which I now find to be an irksome habit because he doesn't even need them. "I thought for sure he'd be here when we landed or show up shortly after to help make sense of this, but he didn't. Someone had to make sure you went back. So, yeah, I took matters into my own hands and picked up the pieces. I never meant for anyone to get hurt in the process."

"You're just spewing words to make yourself feel better, Kevin," I spit.

"For the last time, I'm your—"

"But you aren't!" I exclaim, stepping to the opposite side

of the hovering bench, where his mess of space metal sits between us. "Soren Bay is my father. You kept that from me, too."

Father clenches a transporter with white-knuckled fingers. "You think your words hurt me, but I will never stop caring for you as my own. No matter what toll this takes on us, on our family, on how you see us." He flicks his gaze to mine. "I'm sorry, alright? I'm sorry I thought controlling the situation meticulously would make this easier for you."

I know he wants me to accept his apology. To move past this. And I should want to, but I can't. All I want is to hold onto this sinking feeling, this anger, and let it take me like high tide.

I cross my arms. "Maybe you should have just gone back and saved your uncle the year the Unity Arch fell or stopped the explosion. At least nobody else would have suffered for it."

Father averts his gaze from the transporter unit in front of him, his eyes true and kind like the Kevin I once knew. "Your mother and I talked about it."

"Then what? Why didn't you?"

He lets out a sigh. "Because, Timber, we knew if we went back and stopped the Unity Arch from falling, it would alter our future. If we'd gone back and saved Billy, Blithe, and Ethan, maybe you wouldn't exist. In the end, we chose *you*." His words soften me, dulling the biting cold clouding in my chest, but only a little. "I've been trying to wrap my mind around my uncle's disappearance since the day you and Mars showed up in my housing unit and attacked me like a couple of rogue flares—"

Out on the bridge, there's a crash.

Father leaves my side. I rush with him out of the walk-in.

We enter the refuse room, where a shelf of linens and clothing has tipped over in a heap. Ere hisses at the mess of black-and-teal ringlet curls sticking out from the pile. A young girl, no older than a village Seventeen, pokes up between two plush pillows and offers the great flare cat a treat of seasoned squid.

"*Relere Ere,*" she says. "*Yere grere sofere.*"

Father and I exchange a glance, stepping back as the girl rises completely, brushing dust off her ISR-issued black leggings and matching sleeveless shirt. From the backpack she wears, which is hand-painted with colorful toadstools and moths, pops up a much smaller flare cat. A cub, with sparkly magenta eyes and soot-covered fur.

It purrs at the sight of me, and as the girl scratches behind the cub's ears, I notice her ears and the earrings she wears. They are a match to the earring Mars pulled out of the regulation chamber: small abalone shells with decorative Vio markings and a flare tooth charm.

What in the galaxies is going on?

"Told you you'd get to see Father," she tells the flare cub.

My heart nearly skips a beat. I'm not sure if I heard her correctly.

She speaks into her digiband. "Lux, send a message to Elder Father that Jet and I made it to the year 3083, safe and sound."

"*Message sent, Iris. You're all set.*"

Nope. I definitely heard her correctly.

I clutch my chest. "Did you just say—"

"Grandfather," she says to Father as she pulls up a holographic scanner that floats off her wrist and projects it onto the wall behind us. "You'll want to get him a chair. I can't remember if my briefing says he passes out or upchucks all over the floor."

My knees wobble. "Maybe it's both."

Iris—I mean my . . . daughter? . . . well, her name is Iris—moves between us and positions herself before a panel in the aircraft's interior.

"This is interesting," Father mutters.

"That's one word for it," I mutter back.

"It's not that interesting," Iris adds, setting down her backpack. Her flare cub, Jet, scampers out, pulling the pack aside. "In fact, it's perfectly uninteresting."

I shield my eyes as her laser beam slices into the wall, cutting out a compartment.

She reaches in and pulls out a square item covered in burlap. "If my calculations are correct, we have about thirty seconds before—" She pulls away the covering, revealing the Easy-Bake Oven Gallivant from Trinket Gears. "—a very special delivery."

My heart starts to pound again. *How did that get there?*

Iris waves us out onto the bridge and back into the walk-in, setting the Gallivant on the hovering bench next to the transporter docking unit.

She double-checks her digiband. "Wait for it."

"Dare I wonder what we're waiting for?" Father asks, careful not to step on Jet, who sits patiently at Iris' feet. "I assume this is time travel-related, and you're from the future."

"Your assumptions would be correct."

I swallow hard. I think I need a glass of water.

From inside the Gallivant, a flash of light bursts.

Iris opens the front, clears the smoke, and reaches for the item inside.

My eyes go wide as she slips her newly delivered treasure

on her wrist alongside her digiband. "Is that Mars'—"

"Elder Father's bracelet?" Iris interrupts. "Why yes, yes it is. I'm supposed to also tell you that you are such a cosmic slug for being the reason he gave it up in the first place."

I chew the inside of my cheek. "Got it. Thanks."

"Are you going to tell us why you're here?" Father asks. "How Mars is alive?"

Iris smiles, scooping Jet up in her arms. With her free hand, she moves the Gallivant out of the way and brings the transporter dock close.

"My mission is very clear. Very straightforward." She points to a single blinking light in the charging cell that wasn't there before, beneath the Alpha transporter's empty slot. "Arrive. Retrieve delivery. Make sure Father doesn't pass out. Establish a connection with my contact."

I raise a brow. "Transporter Alpha is online. How is that possible?"

Father spins the docking unit toward him and messes with the light plate. "Charge is at 5%," he says under his breath. "Online sensor is green for go. It's not—it's not possible."

"Yes, it is," Iris says. "That would be my contact waking up from cryosleep."

"Who's your contact?" I ask, though I already have a guess.

Father's hand trembles as he runs his fingers over the blinking light plate. His voice comes out smooth, answering for her, realization dawning in his eyes.

"Her contact is Billy Hale," he says.

END OF BOOK ONE

VIOLET MOON

KAYLA MAURAIS

THE DIVINE UNFOLDING OF VIOLET MOON

Some of you may be surprised to know that *Violet Moon* was written before *Soul Sucker*. I intended for it to be my debut and was even devastated when I realized it wouldn't be. Late 2018/early 2019, a character popped into my head whom I would frequently refer to as "the boy lost in time and space." I didn't know his name or who he was, but I knew he was a character begging for his story to be told. Later, at a late-night domino game with my out-of-state cousins at my Memere's house, they asked me about my writing. I told them I was trying to think of a name with a nickname for a main character, and my cousin Carrie threw out William/Billy.

Everyone else at the table disagreed that it was a good combination, but to me, it felt right immediately, and it stuck. After that, the boy lost in time and space became the infamous Billy Hale, and if you haven't guessed already, this book, at its core, is really the start of *his* story. From there, the original drafting process began. I completed my draft, had beta readers look at it, revised it more than once, and tried pitching it to agents, hoping they'd like it as much as

I did. But as the rejections kept coming in, I felt defeated. Because it felt like a really *big* story for me. And I couldn't let it go. Not yet.

As a last attempt to give the manuscript a chance, I submitted it to RevPit, which is an online Twitter contest where the winning submissions receive a full developmental edit from professional editors in the industry. I'd submitted another manuscript a year earlier and didn't get accepted, but I figured if they wanted *Violet Moon*, it would be a sign that it still had a chance.

Only a handful of editors participate in RevPit each year, and each one only chooses one writer to work with, so my chances were slim but not impossible. Once you submit, editors can request the full manuscript to see if it's something they want to work on, and within hours of submitting to the contest, *Violet Moon* got a full request. It didn't mean I was chosen, but it meant my sample pages drew someone in enough to consider taking me on, and a few weeks later, when the final contest winner list dropped, I felt this overwhelming sense of alignment inside me. *Violet Moon* had been chosen, an actual industry editor wanted to work with *me*, and I had been given another chance at strengthening the story to hopefully someday see it in print.

After the news sank in, I cried. Because I'd prayed about it heavily, and it was my sign from the Universe above that Billy Hale, and the story that took up way too much headspace in my mind, was worth it. *I* was worth it. And for the next few months, I worked with my editor, Natasha, on the manuscript, which included a near full rewrite of the plot and storyline. This was also right around the time the pandemic hit and the world went on full lockdown mode. My external world stopped, but my inner world kept me going. And by the time the RevPit agent showcase rolled around—the final piece of the RevPit contest, where you put all your hard work on display for agents to view—I was ready to take *Violet Moon* to the next level. I thought to myself, it's finally time for me to get an agent, become a serious author, and see my book in stores.

Reality set in when nothing resulted from the showcase. I watched fellow RevPit 2020 mentees get requests and offers of representation, and while I was ecstatic for them, it was discouraging. Still, I knew the bright side of having just worked with a professional editor meant that my manuscript was ready to query to agents outside of the RevPit contest, too, so I quickly got to work preparing all my submission materials and kept going. In total, I probably sent close to 80+ query emails to agents. There were a couple full requests, a few told me I was a good writer but that the genre was oversaturated, and some even asked for more—but all of them ended up in rejection. *All* of them. That's over 80 rejection emails ping-ponging around in my head.

If you're someone trying to face a fear of rejection, I suggest becoming a writer and pitching to agents. It will test you, but it will also teach you a lot about yourself and your writing. This was also a time when general morale was at an all-time low due to pandemic fatigue, and stories with characters required to wear face masks hit differently than it would have a year or two before.

So I accepted defeat and shelved *Violet Moon*. But that didn't mean the story left me alone. It didn't. It kept pushing and prodding the inner corners of my mind. It would seep in when I'd hear certain songs I'd choreographed scenes to, come in waves when I watched movies about time travel, or fill me with melancholy when I saw anything neon-purple or space-like.

I wanted to give up on writing altogether, but I knew that wasn't the answer. Because the reality is sometimes it takes several books and years before an author catches their big break, but it didn't mean I wasn't sad about it. I wrote *Soul Sucker* shortly after that, fully intending for it to be a standalone. In fact, up until about a month before *Soul Sucker* released, I thought it was a standalone book. I never intended for it to be a trilogy. But then during one of my final edits before sending it to print and celebrating the debut of my publishing career, I realized that not only was *Soul Sucker* a trilogy set in the same world as *Violet Moon*, but they were connected.

I wish you could've seen the smile on my face when I finally outlined the trilogy and realized that despite having to shelve the story, my time with *Violet Moon* and Billy Hale wasn't actually over. **It was all just a matter of . . . time.** Which brings us to the present day. Six years after *Violet Moon* was originally written, revised with an industry professional, rejected over 80 times, and—despite my reluctance—left on a virtual shelf to collect whatever the digitized equivalent to dust is.

After I released *Soul Sucker* in February 2023, I intended on releasing *Violet Moon* next, but then life happened, and I didn't feel the pull to write any more. I was overwhelmed with a new job, spiraling into bouts of depression, and really feeling the pressure of life all at once. It wasn't until late 2024/early 2025 that *Violet Moon* called to me like a Jumanji board. Yes, that's the only analogy I can think to use because it feels like that moment when Alan Parrish discovers the game board after hearing its drumming through the construction site walls. Mind you, Billy Hale and all the other characters stayed with me all this time, but they were finally back in the forefront of my mind space, begging and urging me to pick up my laptop and get to work.

Only it had been years since I'd looked at it. I knew if I was going to publish, I'd need to revise, edit, and take it back through the manuscript preparation process. I told myself over Christmas break 2024, I would do it. Even if it took every ounce of energy in me. Once school got out, I locked myself in my room, and I revised. I did nothing but eat, nap, comb over words, edit, and rewrite passages that needed it. And when the holidays ended, I was *still* revising, so I would juggle work and writing like my life depended on it. I would nap after work, stay up all night writing, take a short nap between the hours of 2-4 AM, and go right back to work. There were some nights/days where I didn't sleep at all. I would be in the middle of a scene and slowly watch the sun rise as I scrambled from my laptop to get ready for school. I was exhausted, it wasn't healthy, and I often felt like I was going crazy, but I was determined to make it happen.

I finally finished the revision, and then the manuscript went to one last group of beta readers. Once they were done with it, I revised again based on their feedback, and then the book went to my copy editor, Jen, for its final polish before publication. When her notes came back with some last-minute concerns about some loose plot threads, though I agreed and found value in her feedback, I felt the overwhelming sense of dread fill me up that the manuscript *still* wasn't ready.

If you aren't familiar with the publishing process, it can be a very intricate and layered experience, so I encourage you to think of how many hands and revisions go into your favorite books. It's a labor of love, and *Violet Moon* certainly was testing me in more ways than one.

After spiraling with emotions, I pulled myself together and geared up for *one* last revision. It took about a week, the book went to a proofreader to catch any final mistakes as a result of this last-minute addition of words, and then the book was off to formatting and print. As I hit send that night, I realized a major core memory of mine was about to come full circle.

Two very different versions of me co-created *Violet Moon*. Six years ago, a younger me came up with the idea, wrote it, took it through RevPit, queried, revised more times than she could count, endured 80+ rejections, and ultimately made the hard but right decision to shelve it—despite the story demanding space in her mind. But it was an older, present me who picked up where she left off, reshaped the story in all the best ways while staying true to its core, and now it's out in the world, where I know it will find its fanbase and readers. So many versions of me exist between the girl who started this journey and the woman who's finishing it, but I think of younger me often. I picture her hunched at her desk, making timelines, sketching character profiles, researching, and feeling defeated when she did all this work only to be told it wasn't time yet for Billy Hale to make his debut.

I think of her awe when the realization hit that *Soul Sucker* had to come first, not because she and *Violet Moon* weren't good enough, but because each and every story is another piece to a greater puzzle that will inevitably all unfold in their own time. I wish I could tell her how deeply I appreciate her trust and surrender to all that is. Because she let go of this story six years ago, not knowing if it would ever be picked up again. Not knowing that she was sending it into the folds of time and space so present me could catch it, shape it, and give it the release it deserves.

If you're still reading at this point, kudos to you, because I bet you didn't think you'd get a full publication story in addition to an acknowledgements section here. But I had to share. People always ask me what it's like to be an author or what the process is like, and I always fight the urge to say something sarcastic like, *"Well, do you have hours and hours, or do you want the cookie-cutter version?"* The truth is that writing is hard work, like everything else is. Sometimes the act of it sets your heart on fire, and you need it as much as you need your next breath. Sometimes it takes so much from you that you feel like an empty shell of a human at the end when the finished product hits the shelves. And sometimes, when the dust clears and you look back at how far you've come, you see how transformative the process is.

I know there will be people and writers alike who have gone through something similar or who have given up on a dream because they were rejected, it was too mentally taxing, or they didn't think they were good enough. But I'm here to tell you that sometimes the reason things don't work out or the reason things are harder than you anticipated is because it simply isn't time *yet*, because you're meant to find your own strength in the process, and because it's meant to turn out bigger and better than you realized it ever could.

ACKNOWLEDGEMENTS

How do I even go about thanking all the people that supported me, helped me, or had their hand in the unfolding of this process? I'm going to try my best. I'll start by thanking my parents, Phil and Stacie Maurais, my siblings, and grandparents. And thank you to my cousin, Carrie, for helping me give the "boy lost in time and space" a name. To all the beta readers, alpha readers, and sensitivity readers that helped me ready *Violet Moon* to be submitted to RevPit back in 2019: Jessica, Chelsea, Josie, Dani, Elli, Aimee, Sarah, Noreen, Efsane, Rachel, Meghan, Amelia, Sarah Mae, Jessica P, Katia, Alive, Ash, Amber, Brooke, Geraldine, and Vanessa.

Thank you to Natasha Hanova, the editor who took on *Violet Moon* in RevPit 2020. You don't realize how important that milestone was for me. I hope the version you hold in your hands today makes you as proud, if not more, as the original version you read did all those years ago.

To my copy editor, Jennifer Lindsay, for being honest, genuine, and nurturing in your delivery of feedback and edits. Even though I don't always want to hear my areas that need improvement, sometimes those are the comments that help strengthen the manuscript most. Your time and care with me and my work is always a welcomed gift. And to my proofreader, Claire Olivia Golden, and her sweet cat Persephone for being the little sprinkle of pixie dust at the very end of the whole process. You were patient, supportive, and made sure my manuscript was polished and ready for eager readers' eyes before I sent it off to print.

To my cover artist, Allison Li, whom I met many years ago on Wattpad of all places. For some reason, when I was searching for *Violet Moon's* cover artist, her name popped into my head, and I was lucky that she was willing to take this project on all these years later. She even held a space for me for an entire year after I thought I was going to release *Violet Moon* and then stalled.

I can't continue without thanking all the other talented artists that contributed to this project as well: thank you to Shepengul (@shepengul) for being an outstandingly patient mapmaker, Laras Bek (@larasbek) for the beautiful book-themed bookmark and transporter sticker, Nikkita Bell (@nikkitabell) for designing the playlist page featured at the beginning of the book, Jasmina Belarbi (@artofmina) for the flare cat sticker, Kristina Becker (@witchkart) for the Confess Me Moth sticker, Pantonia (@pantoniaworld) for the glowbeam sticker, and Mariah (@spredgey_books) for taking on the task of spraying thirty exclusive paperbacks for my launch.

Thank you to my best friend, Bri Rodriguez, for being an endless support system in my life. You are always eager to read my work, and please know how much it means to me. And to my other friends Brian Loveless and Jessica Renwick for always cheering me on with vigor.

To my alpha readers and original street team members: Martha Cottle, Tatiana Reams, and Phoebe Matthews. Blade Bailey, you're also an alpha reader, but you have also been a great support system behind the scenes in those final months before publication. I value your wisdom and the delicacy you give to creative people and just people in general. Thank you for being you.

To my newer pool of beta readers that read the version I spent Christmas break 2024 and beyond revising—Lyn Gagnon, Lily Gagnon, Ali Williams, Sarah Malinowski, Cassandra Young, Kathy White, Amber Myers, Lewis Hughes, Kelsey S, Leslie Morgan, and Katherine Brito. Darian Reid, thank you for not only being a beta reader but for becoming a great confidant and friend.

To all those that supported and backed my Kickstarter campaign. I wasn't sure how it would go given I'd never done it before, but you all came through and exceeded my expectations: Amy Chung, Nana and Grampa, Nikkita Bell, C. Erik Orjiako, Rebelle Roberts, Kristen Illarmo, Brent Loon, Danielle Malinowski, Jim S, Diane Vallere, Erica Rue, Claire Olivia, Alexandra Corrsin, Donna Oberton, Marisa Cohen, Sara Massery, Jeremy Hayes, Samantha, Bri, Jessica, Joey Hedrick, Aimee Deblaiso, Rachel Simpson, Tricia Flowers, Caroline Fowler Davis, Mariah McKenna, Ashley Cilenti, Grace Hoffman, Jeanette LeBlanc, Valerie A. Sizemore, Danielle B, Catie O'Neill, Jimmy Yauch, Leah Johnson, Kate McShane, Alexis Maurais, and Kristie Bessey.

Thank you to Emma T. Fink for not only beta reading and supporting my Kickstarter but for being my temporary virtual assistant. You helped me with a lot of tedious behind-the-scenes research that helped make the book's launch all that much easier. In addition, thank you to Laura

Williams and Jessica Renwick for editing my blurbs and to H Khan over on Fiverr for creating my Kickstarter campaign video trailer. Because of all of you, my Kickstarter was a success!

Thank you to all my coworkers I saw on a day-to-day basis who helped me survive the process of putting a book out and juggling a full-time job while I was also navigating the tough but right-for-me decision to leave the teaching career-space. To my former teaching team—Tracy Remington, Ben Redstone, Crystal Cloutier, and Andrew Oliver. You all accepted me for who I was, quirks and all, and I wouldn't have survived half as long without you. You really are the *dream team*, and I'm grateful I got to be a part of it, if only for two short years.

To Sean Whalen, my next-door classroom neighbor; I appreciated your enthusiasm when I'd ramble on about writing and anything else I was thinking on a daily basis. We started teaching together, you were an anchor for me on the days I struggled most, and you always seemed to know how to make those days brighter. Though I won't be there anymore to pop my head in to say, "Morning, Sean!" know I'll be cheering you on from afar. Garrett Whitten, I don't think you realize how special it was to me that you would check in about my writing progress during our morning hallway duty. Your genuine kindness didn't go unnoticed—thank you.

Toni Hart, I appreciate you! Your little moments of support throughout the process made a lasting impression. Megan Anderson, thank you for not only backing my Kickstarter, but for being my personal cheerleader. You eagerly supported *Soul Sucker*, and you championed the support for *Violet Moon* in a way that fills my heart with so much joy. I appreciate you so much.

MaKayla Stevens, you gem of a human. Not only were you an amazing principal, but you cared about my writing and knew how important it was to me. I've never had a boss take the time to support and show the enthusiasm you did when I mentioned my love of writing. It meant a lot to me, and I'll never forget it. I will also miss you more than you know.

Tracy Remington—I know I already thanked you above when I mentioned our team, but you deserve a second acknowledgement for being one of the best mentors I've ever had the pleasure of growing and learning under. You were assigned to me as a teaching mentor in 2023, but I've gained so much more in our two years working together. I couldn't have survived without you, and your continued belief in me both as a writer and as a human being are part of the reason why I was able to find the strength to finish this book and see my plans through. I can be my quirky, messy, and authentic self around you, and you've come to admire my flaws as your favorite parts of me. Our paths crossed for a reason, and I thank the Universe every day for you. I hope you know the impact you leave on people, and I look forward to seeing where our journeys take us in life.

Though this is less a writing thank you and more a "thanks for helping me survive the last two years while I also put out a book" thank you, I also want to thank Jen Waterman, Brian Daniels, and Michael Jack for supporting me in this career. I learned firsthand how monumental the fundamentals of writing and literature can be to young minds, and though my teaching career was short-lived and I will be pursuing other career ventures, your support, respect, and the environment you fostered while I was working under your care mean a lot to me.

I know some of you might be reading this and thinking, "Why is she thanking all these people if it doesn't have anything to do with *Violet Moon*?" But you see, it does. Six years is how long it took me to put *Violet Moon* out from first draft to publication. And six years is exactly how long I've been in education. From starting out as a sub/tutor and education technician to working as a full-on classroom teacher, I started this book when I entered education and I'm finishing it as I leave. It's symbolic in all the best ways, each step mirroring my growth as a writer and the unfolding of *Violet Moon's* timeline, so, yes—I must give thanks where thanks are due. Because the process of teaching also influenced the creation and follow-through of this book.

With that said, I can't forget to thank the two 8th grade classes I had the pleasure of teaching in the last two years. You taught me a lot about myself, about education, and about how important writing is to me. Even though my time in teaching is over, I hope you all remember how capable you are. It was a trial by fire in some ways and the greatest gift in others. I wish you all success in your future endeavors. And for my fellow writers, don't give up! If anything, let my journey remind you that just because it takes time, doesn't mean it isn't happening or worth it.

— Kayla

1: SHEA

If Dash screws this up, we're dead.

A gust of wind billows around me. I lean back against a jagged rock tall enough to block the chill. My tight-fitting breather mask constricts my face, but it's necessary. Like all planets in the Realm of Souls, air quality on Lark is thin. Without my breather, it'd be like sucking noxious oxygen through a straw. My lung tissue would rupture. My chest cavity would expand.

I'd black out before the air bubbles infiltrated my bloodstream.

I'd be completely brain-dead in three minutes flat.

The thought makes me chuckle. As if I'd ever get myself in such a predicament to begin with. I'd have to be negligent enough to forget to secure my straps.

Which would never happen.

My little brother, on the other hand, attracts life-threatening situations like stale cronuts attract baby crumb lizards in the heat of summer. The digiband clamped around my wrist beeps. I check the notification. User offline. *Shit.* He's turned off his tracker. Again.

I press comms. "Dash, report."

My gaze narrows in on the notification bar, empty save for a check-in message I'd sent to Headquarters earlier. Dad expects us home in an hour, and I've never missed a deadline in my entire life. I certainly don't plan on it now.

I ping Dash again. "Status. Location. Anything?"

Nothing. Notification: *Undelivered.*

I'm going to kill him.

Wait here, Shea. I'll steal the spirit-creature thingy alone, Shea. It'll draw less attention. I'll be in and out in ten minutes tops.

Yeah. Right. We never should've split up.

I pull back my hood and peer around the rocks at a cluster of canvas dwellings in the distance. They stretch for miles in the shadow-laden desertscape, floating inches above the ground like the Star Spirits which inhabit them. The transparent, faceless beings loiter around their dwellings. Their long, silver cloaks glisten in the starlight. They don't speak, rather they communicate via telepathic thought. Or that was what the Universal Database said when I looked them up.

I bet the Board of Galactic Studies would revel in a sight like this. If the authorities knew the things I've seen or the places I've been in the past eighteen years, their skin would crawl. If I were to submit even a smidge of the classified research I've gathered, an Intergalactic Space Relations agent would come knocking on our door, launching a full-on investigation into my family's operation.

Regardless, I'll write a study worthy of publication in the Universal Database. I will make sure the name Shea-Lynn James is known across the galaxies, like the revolutionaries before me.

Unfortunately, today is not that day.

I abandon my hiding spot. Darting between rock clusters, I stick to the shadows and keep a close eye on the Star Spirits nearby. Mom used to tell us stories about them. Born from the fallen stars of Lark, they have the power to rise and walk among us in human form. Some venture off and integrate with other populations until they become middle-aged. When it's time, they return home to Lark so they don't risk losing their spark or die out completely.

We're not supposed to be here without an invitation. If those Star Spirits catch my brother or me, they could alter our existence with one bolt of raw celestial power, marking our souls for eternity. Forever branded an Enforcer and a Thief.

Sweat pools on the base of my neck. I take off toward the outer edge of dwellings in search of my brother. Damp sand cakes in the grooves of my water-resistant boots. I quicken my strides, tear my way through a canvas tent, and clamber over bronze carts of medicinal herbs. Then I'm back into the open air once again.

It's been about eight years since I joined James Co. On my tenth birthday, Mom showed up with a homemade citrus cake, as any loving mother would. Dad, however, tossed a couple of beat-up weapons we call glowbeams on the table and told me I was old enough to join the family business. We steal and sell for profit. It isn't an honest living, but it becomes second nature when you've been doing it for as long as we have.

At least, to me. This is the fourth time Dash has been late on the retrieval this month.

I wait for a Star Spirit to pass before I burst into another dwelling, this one home to a devotional altar piled high with crystals. As I turn, my arm knocks over an amethyst cluster. My chest constricts, and though I manage to tip the cluster upright, the irritation pressing against my diaphragm doesn't lessen. I mean, how hard is it to locate a tutelary, lure it in, and return to our meeting spot anyway? They're soul-protecting constructs created by Star Spirits. This place is crawling with them. Yes, one can only view them with interdimensional goggles.

But Dash is currently in possession of our only pair.

The howling wind picks up. Another empty dwelling. And another. In the next, I let out a yell, kick over a suspended cot draped in silk. He always does this to me—takes his sweet ole time as if we haven't got other places to be. Must be nice to dance through life without a care in the world.

We're going to be late. I'm out of breath, at the end of the line. The final tent presents itself, a flickering glow radiating between the gaps. I swear, if he isn't in here—

I burst inside.

Dash lifts his head. "Aye, Shea, I knew you'd come."

For someone tied to a center post, he's stupidly cheerful. Glowbeam up, I square my shoulders and scan the tent, ready to face any Star Spirits that might get in my way. "How many are there? What did they do to you?"

"Whoa, you need to—"

I throw a sharp glare.

A lock of shaggy, dark brown hair slips from the band of wide-lens goggles slapped on Dash's head. "I'm cool. My soul is cool. And like, uh... two Star Spirits?"

"You better have it." I step over a basket of moon worm silk, knitting itself into a ceremonial cloth near the hearth. Tipping the barrel of my glowbeam into an armoire, I make sure we haven't got any company. The ancient symbols adorning the door catch my eye. I fight the urge to take out my travel journal and trace them for further research. *They're stunning.*

"Now, now," Dash says. "I'm hurt you'd question my capabilities."

I kneel next to my brother and whip out my blade.

Once his wrists are free, he pulls back the right side of his vest and pats his hidden pocket. His hazel eyes glint in the floating candlelight. Whatever he's got tucked away purrs.

Touché. "How'd you get it?"

"Plucked it off a Star Spirit when they escorted me in. James Co.'s infamous interdimensional goggles worked like a charm."

I roll my eyes. "At least tell me you put up a fight this time."

Dash purses his lips and looks at the floor. He fiddles with the industrial piercing in his left ear. "Yeah. About that... "

I close my eyes. "Dashiel. Tell me you did not get caught on purpose." He tries to walk away. I grab him by his goggle strap and let it snap against his skull. He yelps. "You told me you wouldn't do this anymore. We're partners. How am I supposed to rely on you if I can't trust you?"

"It's easier if I get caught. They don't suspect a thing!"

"That's bullshit. You're better than that, and you know it." His excuses for laziness are growing old. "You realize every time you do this, we take twice as long to finish a job."

He crosses his arms. "This reprimanding is taking just as long."

With another eye roll, I reach into my vest and pull out a brass portal key. I've worn it since Dash pickpocketed it off a mage during a gig on planet Verve years ago. "I'm done letting your negligence interfere with jobs. We'll finish this conversation later."

"Ohhhkay. If you say so."

Biting back a retort takes every bit of willpower I have. It's impossible to make a point when he never understands. At seventeen, Dash has already been captured, kidnapped, taken—you name it—more times than I can count. Yet, he forgets I'm the one who must come to his rescue. *I'm* the one that must explain to Dad why we're late. Every. Single. Time.

He massages the red marks on his wrist. They've calloused. "I did my part, okay? Who cares how I do it?"

"*I* care. And stop switching off your tracker."

He snorts. "I will when you stop trying to micromanage me."

"We don't have time for this, Dash!"

"I don't appreciate you raising your voice."

"I'm *not*."

I keep my stance firm. He blinks wildly. The wavering expression on his face is priceless. He'll cave first. Always does. That'll be the Thief in him. Enforcers are trained to stick it out.

That includes meaningless quarrels.

After a few more moments of tense silence, my brother sighs. "Fine. Let's go home."

That's what I thought. I relax my shoulders, hold back a smirk, and grip my portal key. Summoning a Door takes concentration. The first time I tried, I called forth half an entryway with no clear view of the other side, and Dash nearly lost an arm. Dad was less than pleased because Dash had mastered the art of theft, stealth, and hacking in a few days. For months, I studied and practiced skills expected of an Enforcer. Meanwhile, my brother kicked back, drank Fizzies milkshakes, and played Holoblocks on the console. When

I questioned the balance of responsibility, Dad reminded me that someday this business will be mine.

A flash of light glimmers outside our tent, catching my peripheral as I ready to summon our Door out of here.

Dash takes two steps away and peers through a window flap. His shoulders tense, and I immediately shiver. I already know we won't be taking the easy way out before he says, "Star Spirits headed this way."

Moments later, we slip out the back. Our little quarrel is now a blip in the past. My brother and I are partners again. I'm at his heels. Boots pummeling the sand, battering slick patches of desert rock. Dash is faster than I am. Always has been. When it comes to speed, my heavier set frame is no match for his athletic build, but I know he'd never leave me behind.

Pinpricks of electric light shatter the dark. Hot wind bites my cheeks. Another gust of oxygen filters through my breather, stinging the back of my throat. I glance over my shoulder. My eyes grow wide. A dozen Star Spirits glide across the sand at great speed. They gain on us, wielding lightning in their translucent hands.

Dash cuts right. "Head for the canyons!"

I skid in the sand, falling into pace with my brother. Our path brings us near the Celestial Canyons, where an array of metallic, open-top spheres sit idly on a pulley system meant to suspend them across the gorge. *This is where the Star Spirits come to catch the stars.* Images from books in our home library fill my head. I shove Dash into the nearest sphere, eager to press all the buttons.

Star Spirits zing blades of light at us in retort.

Dash ducks. "Tell me you know what you're doing!"

Ignoring him, I try the many dials, gears, and levers.

"Shea-Lynn, tell me—"

"I know what I'm doing!"

As if I'm staring at one of the labeled diagrams in my research books, I skim the control panel in search of the lever that will release our sphere.

Dash hovers by my ear. "Hurry up."

"Don't rush me."

Focus, Shea. It's your job to get us home.

Another luster explodes overhead. Our sphere jolts, sending us to our knees. I flip the switch. We zip out into the canyon. The suspension cables tug taut. Disregarding the airiness in my stomach, I close my eyes and begin the summons. *This is it.*

Our sphere sways. Dash keeps me steady.

"They're trying to pull us back in," he says.

"I need a second."

Light blazes through the dark. My eyes spring open.

What now? I pop up. Before, the Star Spirits were waiting at the edge of the canyon like a pack of angelic wolves. Now, they're gone. The only Star Spirit in sight sits stationed in a sphere suspended a few yards from us.

An eerie silence claims the sky. A sky on fire.

The first meteor plummets. The remaining Star Spirit catches hold and throws it back, allowing the fallen star to gather momentum. It accelerates and gets sucked back up into the atmosphere. Dash hangs out the side of the sphere to get a better look.

I turn to my portal key. *"Imagine you are standing at a Door. This Door is oval with wood panels and wrought iron locks. This Door leads to planet—"*

Another jolt sends our pod careening wildly from side to side.

My knees bounce off the floor.

Dash knocks into me.

Bullets of light continue to plunge in the space around the pod. They collide with the void like rain, detonating upon impact. One spark catches our control board. Another zips up the wiring. Those sparks meet and short-circuit the release lever keeping us midair. One of our four suspension cables snaps, tilting us off-center. I gasp, bracing my feet against the sphere's edge before we slide along the incline to our untimely deaths. My brother slams into me from behind. I hold my ground. My portal key dangles before me, flitting among the meteor ash.

Adapt. Think fast. Remember what Dad taught you.

The pounding silence in my head breaks, and noise floods back in like a rogue Skyway train running off its tracks. Dash screaming my name. Plummeting stars zinging around us. Our sphere groans in protest, clinging to its remaining support cables. I dig my fingers into the metal bindings and curl my toes into the soles of my boots, slipping another inch.

"Stop moving," I hiss at my brother. Our way out is hanging around my neck, right in front of my face, but both my hands are occupied. "Do something! I'm holding us both up!"

"We're going to dieee! We're going to—"

Not today. We're not dying today.

Our second suspension cord snaps.

I squint. The sweat from my forehead burns my eyes. The heaviness in my gut sinks deeper, and our sphere tips back, sending us sailing across the canyon like a pendulum.

As the canyon wall nears, the remaining two cords detach. Brisk air whips my hair and tattered bits of my vest.

My portal key necklace slips between my fingers. The force of free fall tears Dash's breather off his face like it's nothing, and it disappears into the abyss. *Fantastic.* Now, I've got less than a minute before he blacks out. Less than forty seconds before the canyon floor claims us. Thirty seconds before we're absolute toast.

My little brother falls silent, his head hanging forward. *There's still time. I can still do this.* I wrap my body around his. The fiery stars blur. We spiral through the air, destined to become sibling splats. I reach above my head, wedging my fingers beneath the taut chain. Tug it down. Grip it tight. Palms sweaty. Key secured.

If I don't get us out of here in time, we're both dead, and then Dad will really think I'm unfit to take over the family business.

"Imagine you are standing at a Door. This Door is oval with wood panels and wrought iron locks. This Door leads to planet Diggs."

Bits of the Door I summoned materialize into thin air. Splintered wood, rounded at the corners. A wrought iron lock. The familiar glow pours in from its cracks. I fumble for the frame. Before we crash into the canyon, I pull us through, and the Door slams shut behind us.

Somewhere nearby, Dash groans, telling me he's still alive. Good because I'm going to kill him. Thanks to his refusal to follow protocol, I've got murk water in places I'd rather not discuss. Leaves soak my unruly locks of brown hair, and my ass is bruised, but at least we're not stains on the canyon floor.

As I trudge toward the bank, I adjust the levels of my breather to check the air. Planet Diggs is in the First Realm, like our home planet, Sarasing. Air quality is thick. Breathable. I remove my breather. Take a few breaths to acclimate. Scanning the surrounding area for Dash, I spot him in a sludge puddle, coughing and clutching his head.

I hover over him. "Are you alright?"

He untangles a spiked toad, desperately trying to escape from his goggle straps. It croaks, and he croaks back, "I think I just saw my whole life flash before my eyes."

"You blacked out from lack of oxygen." I tap my digiband to check the clock. Nearly falling to our deaths put us behind schedule, but we can still make it back to Headquarters in time. "Luckily, I got us out before your lungs collapsed. Take it easy until you get used to the atmosphere. I'm going to scope it out, see if I can find the buyer's location."

I step over my brother's outstretched legs and follow the road. His coughs echo around me, allowing me to keep track of him. We're in the middle of nowhere. Which is exactly where we want to be. A crescent moon hangs in the sky, its rays streaming through the wrought iron streetlamps. At the end of a dirt path is a small, rundown cottage puffing wood smoke, just as the brief said there would be.

Dash appears at my side with the toad cradled in his arm. "Is that the client's house? Also, do you think Dad would be mad if I took this home and kept it as a pet? I named him Arnold."

"No. Get that out of here—" I knock the toad out of his hands. It flops onto the path and hops away into the shadowy thicket. "Seriously? We're on a *job*. We have five minutes."

"Well, sorry. But that reminds me." Dash puts on his interdimensional goggles, which stayed firmly on his head despite his useless breather. "Gotta make sure the other little guy survived the trip."

A flutter of excitement takes over me. I keep my composure, though. My brother unzips the compartment in his vest, cups his hand, and allows the unseen being to crawl into his palm. On my end, he's holding air. On his end, I know he's holding something extraordinary.

Tutelaries usually are. However, I've only ever read about them.

"Dearest sister, I can feel you hovering over my shoulder." Dash glances back, and I pretend to fiddle with my digiband. "Admit you're dying to see it."

I purse my lips. "I don't know what you're talking about."

"Take a peek." He offers me his goggles. "Come on. For research?"

My gaze narrows on his empty, cupped palm. I *am* dying to see it.

"A quick peek for research." I put the goggles on.

The rose-colored lenses shift, bringing me into the ethereal realm of view. Dash urges me to hold out my hand. I do, and a white wisp of a creature appears. A lizard with glimmering geometric markings wriggles up my arm. I've never seen anything like it. A toothy smile spreads on its tiny, oblong head. It glares at me with bold emerald eyes. As it rolls onto its back, I notice the spiral on its fleshy underside. An engraved spiritual mark all tutelaries have.

Dash nudges me. "Smile any wider, and your face might freeze like that."

"Oh, shut up." I nudge him back.

"I believe that beloved creature belongs to me," a drab

voice says behind us.

Okay. Play times over. Dash and I whip around back-to-back. Goggles off. Our glowbeams up and ready. As the hooded figure emerges, the pungent smell of metal and myrrh carries in the wind.

"Mathias Burgess," I say as the newcomer lowers his hood.

Archaic First Realm lore gets things wrong. Folk stories aren't facts. The majority of vampires aren't bloodthirsty, violent heathens. Those I've encountered are, at most, humble cowards with an iridescent light allergy. And Mathias fits the profile. Sullen eyes, one missing an iris altogether. Dirt caked under his brittle fingernails. A sickliness hangs about him in the wrinkle of his pale, leathery skin.

He holds out a skeletal hand. "Miss James."

I refuse to shake it. "Cut the small talk. You owe us hefty coin."

"I—I already paid your father." Mathias stumbles, slowing his movement each time he nears the warmth radiating off a nearby streetlamp.

And here we go. "You're lying."

"I'm—I'm not. I swear."

I aim my glowbeam at the vampire. He raises both hands and blinks, stunned by the warning flash. "You have two seconds to deliver your end of the bargain, or we take this tutelary back where it came from."

Mathias cringes. "NO—I mean, *okay*, I don't have it. I don't have the coin."

"Knew it." I prod Dash and give him a wink. "Let's go. I'm sure Dad can sell this elsewhere for double the price."

Dash grins. "Triple even."

This usually works in situations like this. Buyer thinks

we're going to leave. Buyer panics and begs. Buyer makes up for their own negligence.

Because let's face it. People suck. Creatures suck. Trusting anyone to hold to their own promises SUCKS. My mother would give the clothes off her back to any stranger. No skepticism or questions asked. She'd trust them. And I wish I could be like her. I really do. But I've seen the cost too many times to be that foolish.

Dash pretends to stuff the tutelary back in his vest as we walk away. We're halfway down the road, getting ready to summon a Door home, when I hear a wavering, "Please. I'll—I'll do anything."

There it is. I put my hand up and side-glance my brother. We backtrack, meeting Mathias at the outer edge of his streetlamp safety-net.

I cross my arms. "What do you have to offer me?"

"I'll give you a vial of my blood." He wrings his trembling hands. "Or a fang from my adolescence. They're all in a jar tucked beneath my sleeping crate."

Dash chortles. "You keep all your baby teeth in a jar?"

"They sell," Mathias insists. "I've seen it."

"Not for enough," I reply.

Dash leans in. "Aye, offer her something better!"

The old vampire alternates his gaze between us. A bead of sweat forms on his brow. I know the look. Hell, I know it. And it kills me every time. This is going to get messy.

"Well?" I say again, handing my glowbeam off to Dash so I can grip the knife hanging on my belt with both hands.

"I—I don't—"

I leave my brother's side, grab a fistful of Mathias's cloak, and yank him into the light. A cry escapes the vampire, his pale skin sizzling in the artificial heat.

He falls to his knees, shaking. "I need this tutelary."

"You buyers are always the same." Pulling him closer, I whisper in his ear, "Lucky for you, I'm feeling generous. I'll finish this deal with you, but not without taking a payment of some sort in return."

I glance back at Dash. He nods without hesitation. A Thief will stand by their Enforcer because we make the rules. Even if it's gruesome. Even if it doesn't go as planned. This outcome is on me and me alone. I'm the one who must face our father if we don't deliver the product and collect some kind of payment in return. Dash did his part back on planet Lark. Now it's time to do mine.

"What—what will you take?" the powerless vampire cries.

I roll up the sleeve of his cloak and wipe my blade. In the tiniest moment, the Board of Galactic Studies comes to mind. If they could see me now. I can only imagine what they'd think. "A finger or two," I say. "A finger or two will do."

2: DASH

I'm in a love-hate relationship with stealing.

A deep-rooted sense of control settles inside me when I take something that isn't mine. I'll admit it. I know what I do is wrong. It doesn't mean I wanna stop. The stealing, that is. I could, however, live without all the near-death situations. The phantom trapped in the washroom mirror at the Hover Rink is tiring of hearing my resignation speech. Yet, I still haven't worked up the courage to tell my sister or Dad that I want nothing more to do with James Co.

I'd tell all the phantoms trapped in ALL the mirrors on Sarasing before telling them.

I let my hands wander in search of something to fill my pockets as Shea and I walk along the array of vendor carts crowding Spinners Pier. The ocean waves rage beneath the worn boardwalk at our feet. Bursts of briny air dissipate in the sweaty rush of intergalactic citizens. I pocket a bag of custard chips off one cart, juice-filled pods off another, and a roll of spice zingers from the last. By the end of the line, my pockets sag with plenty of snacks for later. I can't remember which rom-com is playing on the late-night channel tonight, but they're all binge-worthy.

I unwrap two sizzling cinnamon candies and shove them into my mouth.

Shea checks her digiband. "I'll never understand why you like those things."

"Because they make my mouth feel numb," I say, licking sugar off my fingers.

She scrunches her nose, falling deeper into her usual obsession with the tech strapped to her wrist. A giant velociraptor from Old Earth could plunge from the sky and wipe out the entire Vacationeer District, yet she'd still make it home on time.

I pop the last spice zinger into my mouth, savoring the after-kick. Shea crosses the boardwalk toward the storefronts. Does she ever stop and enjoy the moment? I keep at her heels, occasionally pocketing last-minute items like game tokens and holo-point cards. As we cross into the west side, relief spreads through me. We're finally home.

Spinners Pier is the 11th stop on the Skyway Silver Line. As a glorified tourist attraction, the Vacationeer District is one heck of a cover-up for our family business.

The line outside Palms is a mile long today. Eager out-of-realmers wait to pay hundreds for the latest novelty psychic scams. I run my hands along the new spools of sheer fabric on the loading dock at Grimm's Garbs. Retro beats fill my ears, ping-ponging between neighboring nightclubs lit up in neon, and as we stroll past Bay's Baubles, my belly flutters. The life-size Holoblocks capsule simulator is now on sale.

Our motion triggers the digital advertisement posted over the shop.

"Play Holoblocks: Holocity—the game of strategy and strength—from the comfort of your home," I say along with the chipper AI. "Collect those multi-colored holographic blocks like a gaming ninja and defeat as many levels as possible before the clock runs out!"

I moonwalk around Shea in the same synchronized manner as the entertainment AIs do on the screen.

She side-eyes me. "Stop it."

"Youuu love it. Don't lie."

"Love is a strong word," she says.

I stumble into a trash bot picking up stale fries, brush myself off, and catch up with her in the crowd. "I put the console on my birthday list. It's too big to steal on my own. They've got tons of theft droids."

"Uh-huh."

I catch a whiff of fryer grease from Tee Tee's Tentacle Shack, and my entire body thrums. The digital sign on the teal-blue shack says the wait time is less than ten minutes. This never happens. I step up to its order kiosk and scan my eyeball.

Shea reaches over my shoulder and deletes the entry. "No. I've got two rotting bloodsucker thumbs in my vest pocket. We need to get them on ice and to Dad."

Tee Tee, the massive, mucus-green space slug roasting a batch of steaming tentacles over an open flame beckons to me. My mouth waters in anticipation of those warm, herbed hopper-flour tortillas they always come in. The sweet and tangy sauce drizzled on top... It doesn't matter that I forgot my Universal Comms earpiece at home, Tee Tee knows my order by heart.

Shea's still glaring at me, boot tapping the walkway and body tensed up like it's all she can do to keep herself from grabbing me by the wrist and dragging me home like she did when we were kids.

"Look, Shea, you made me get rid of Arnold—which was a devastating loss I can't even talk about right now—so I'm getting my Tee Tee's taco if it's the last thing I do." I re-scan my eyeball, blinking past the retinal burn. "You can go home, though. I'll bring you back a side of squid nachos with that savory honey sauce you like."

My beautiful sister sighs. "Ugh. I'll wait for you. It's fine."

I hold back a smirk. Fine. What a word. We didn't make bank on planet Diggs, which is why she doesn't want to go home alone. She did everything she could have done. It wasn't her fault that bloodsucking vamp didn't have the coin he'd promised Dad.

A pair of thumbs will sell. We'll find some eager potions master, space witch, or other being that prowls the Underweb to buy them off us. For the same amount we were bilked, even. But Shea didn't do exactly what Dad asked. We both know what that means. Better if I'm there to soften the Henry James guilt trip blow.

Sticking annoying close to me, Shea continues to fiddle with her digiband while we wait for my turn to order. A couple of giant mosquito creatures with lacey-pink wings and telsons squeeze by. They sip cherry heart slushies from Pup's Slush Shack through extra-long straws. One knocks an arm with Shea, and I hold my breath for a second, fearing she might pluck off their wings. Instead, she ogles, a familiar glint in her eye—the one she gets when she discovers something she hasn't seen or heard of before.

Something worth logging in her travel journal.

I watch her contemplate the thought, a hand hitched at the pocket in which I know she keeps her journal. When she catches me staring, she clears her throat and returns to her tech. My sister's a curious lil' bean. One that refuses to overindulge in her guilty pleasures, unlike us regular teenagers. Lucky for her, guilty and pleasure are two of my favorite words.

I use my shoulder to break through the rush. "Hold my spot. If you must order for me, don't you dare let Tee Tee add dehydrated meal worms to the spread."

"Wha—Dashiel. *No.* Get back here."

Too late. I'm gone.

I follow the winged creatures to a boutique cart and wait while they try on Spinners Pier swag. As they browse hats, I slip behind them and dip my fingers into the taller one's satchel. Shea will appreciate this. Doing a bit of research for her will make her feel better. I pull up a passport card, wedge myself between the mannequins, and glance at the profile. Looks like we got a couple of Mees on holiday from planet Monsoon. And they're staying in the Fancy Schmancy District. Very fancy indeed.

One Mee slips the vendor three coins for a holographic visor. Before they walk off, I return the passport card and keep the cherry heart slushie they left behind on the counter. Shea said she needed to keep the bloodsucker thumbs fresh, right? Nothing cooler than a slushie.

"Did you just steal that?"

I turn, almost dropping the cup. Two familiar faces have me cornered between a mannequin and the sun googles display. Zena's glacier-blue gaze freezes me to the spot as heat creeps up my chest. Behind her, Chip fishes a pack of herbal smokes from the pocket of his green Sarasing Academy Holoblocks team jacket.

"Zena! Hey! What are you two doing here on Spinners Pier this fine afternoon?" I tuck the slushie under one arm, wiping a streak of syrup on my pants so I can lean in and kiss her. Chip's husky frame blocks me. So close, his sweat and pinewood cologne overpowers the fryer grease aroma in my nose. "Whoa, Chip. I can't quite get around ya if you stand—"

"Are you going to answer her question?" he asks.

I glance from the slushie to Zena, the heat in my palms making it slippery. "I didn't steal anything from this cart. At least not today. The Mee left it behind, and my sister needs it for something, so I figured I'd recycle because you know how important rec—"

"Okay. Um, Dash. We should talk." Zena brushes a blonde curl behind her ear. The globe light off a nearby club glints pink on her cheeks. I've never seen someone so beautiful. I should write her a poem about that later. "For a moment, maybe... uh, privately?"

Chip takes a drag of his herbal smoke. "Make it quick, Z. Dinner's at seven."

Dinner? Why would Zena go to dinner with Chip? She doesn't even like Chip. She told me he was the rudest guy on the Holoblocks team.

"You at least got the flowers I sent you the other night, right?" I ask her.

"Did a Mee leave those behind too?" Chip mutters.

I glare at him. "No. They were from Pinkie's Floral."

"That high-end place off the Purple Line?" He scoffs. "Yeah, okay."

The sudden urge to pickpocket Chip's zonecard so he can't pay for his dinner later crosses my mind. Zena grabs my arm and drags me off to the side before I can get close enough.

"Yes. I got the flowers. They were lovely." She hugs herself. "I—I don't think we're going to work out, Dash. Chip and I are kind of a thing now. I'm sorry."

My heart gives a wretched tug. "I thought we worked well together. I really like you."

"I know. We did. And I like you too." Zena sucks her teeth. "You're always so busy with work." She glances at Chip for a moment, and my tender heart splits. Dinner, huh. "I want someone who can go to Academy events with me. Someone who isn't afraid to be intimate. You understand what I'm saying, right?"

"Zena, I'm not afraid to be intimate. I told you I wanted to get to know you better. What are your hopes and dreams? What makes you happy? In an ideal world, we'd read poetry together and star in Academy plays. You know that kind of bonding before we—"

Chip steps between us. "I'm hungry. Let's go, Z."

"I'm sorry, Dash," she says, and they take off into the crowd.

I hang my head. Single again. Without even a love letter farewell, or a kiss to remember her by.

Behind me, Shea-Lynn clears her throat. I don't move. Of course, my big sister would show up now.

"That's why I don't date." She holds out my steaming tentacle taco. "Zena was definitely cheating on you this whole time. You can't trust anyone these days."

"Some of us want to date." I'm still watching Chip and Zena. He grabs her hand. Soon they become specks in a trail of herbal haze. "Chip didn't believe I got her flowers from Pinkie's Floral."

"He thinks we're poor," Shea says. "Here. Take your food."

"Why would he think we're poor? We aren't poor." As we walk, I chow down on my tray of tacos. Through a large mouthful, I add, "Besides, why would that matter? Love is about the person and who they are on the inside. Not riches. Not looks. Not anything else."

"How optimistic of you. If only it were that simple." Shea checks her digiband again and quickens her pace. "Look, we don't have time for this. I'm sure that someday you'll make someone very happy. Sadly, that someone will not be Zena O'Hair. You just have to deal with it."

That's her answer to everything. You just have to deal with it.

"For your information, Zena doesn't even like Chip. He talks badly about all the girls. Including her and the rest of the Holoblocks cheerleading team." I reach into Shea's pocket and take the vamp thumbs and her travel journal without her noticing. "Which I wanted to try out for, but you wouldn't—"

"I didn't realize you were interested in cheerleading. You need to forget about Chip and focus."

"No, no. I don't think I need to focus on the job—and not the cheerleading team, though that would be cool, the actual team!"

I plop the thumbs in the cherry heart slushie and make a messy note in her journal about Mees with the ink stick stuck between the pages. Shea's so preoccupied with her brief, she doesn't notice when I slip the journal back. "There's another tryout next week. They're looking for a new captain for the varsity squad. The old one graduated and went on to play for the major leagues. I gave Dad the sign-up brochure."

"You don't have time for sports, relationships, or friends. We have an overflow of runs coming up. Hours of prepping to do."

Heinous Hades. She needs to give it a rest. We almost died this morning, and she's already worried about the next gig.

I imagine myself saying something confident like—dearest sister, I'm quitting the family biz so I can lead a normal teenage life—but all that comes out is a monotonous, "Yeah, yeah."

Shea guides us across the busy streetway towards Fizzies, the confection shop whose basement we also call our humble abode. Its pastel blue and purple sign is a welcome home that never gets old. Mom always says it makes our home smell sweet. I pocket her favorite Fizz-tarts as we pass through the shop on the way to the back whenever I can.

Upon entering Fizzies, Shea nudges me, bringing my attention to the three broad-shouldered men sitting at the fountain counter. Intergalactic Space Relation agents, otherwise known as ISR dipsticks. They're hard to miss in their sleek, slate-gray government-issued uniforms. Brand-spanking new glowbeams hang on their belts. I make eye contact with the one making love to a frosted cookie and wink at him before we duck under a curtained archway toward the lift.

"Second time this week they've come hanging around here." My sister presses the call button on the far concrete wall. "I saw in the Daily Report they busted an underground market ring in the Remedial District a few weeks ago."

"Welp. Can't trust the Sicky Place."

"The ring was selling stolen spacecraft parts. I bet you anything ISR is making their rounds looking for similar illegal trades."

"Guess it's a good thing we aren't part of an illegal trade," I say, and she throws me a look that would win a prize for the least impressed sister in the galaxy.

The lift doors split open and deliver us into the front hall of our living quarters. We stop and kick off our boots at the mat. Shea hangs up her vest, then flips her long brown hair over her shoulder and searches her pockets.

I hold up the slushie. "Looking for these?"

"No, I'm looking for the thumbs." She pulls her pockets inside out and double-checks the hidden compartments. "Maybe they fell out when we were walking? I can't find them."

"Yeah, because they're in the slush."

My sister's eyes gloss over.

"What did you just say?"

"I put them in the slush to keep them cold." She swipes the drink cup out of my hand, and a dribble sloshes onto the hardwood. "Whoa, take it easy. I thought you'd be happy."

She groans. "Dash, you didn't. Tell me you didn't."

She marches down the hall of our windowless basement accommodations. Past our closet-sized bathroom and into our drab kitchenette. She pushes aside an overflowing heap of Spinners Pier takeout containers in the sink and tries to wash the thumbs under the automated tap. The icy chunks rinse off. The cherry-pink hue doesn't. She bites back a wince.

I throw my hands out. "I don't see what the big deal is!"

I keep at her heels all the way around the maze of hallways, past Mom's hospice library, to the double doors leading to Headquarters.

Shea triggers the motion sensor. The biometric scanner light blinks green, confirming her identity before allowing us entry. Hints of cigar smoke lingers. As the air thins, Dad's many half-human-half-AI hirelings take form, hustling about the multitude of inventory in organized chaos.

Between stock swaps and off-planet runs, Headquarters is ever-changing. The space is wide, like a warehouse, making it nearly impossible to see through to the other side. Someone stuffed the metal shelves, from the floor-to-ceiling, with every bell, whistle, odd, and end you can think of. Siren scales and squiggles. Season globes and trinket gears. Items take up every inch of free space—technical, supernatural, antique, or plain extraordinary.

Shea and I enter the whirl of commotion, ducking and weaving to avoid knocking into hirelings. Some rise up and down the wrought iron spiral staircases leading to the lower levels. Others slide along ladders that run the length of the shelves, passing items back and forth to be sent out through our collection of Gallivants. These tricky devices ship products to the outer galaxies, realms, and to any of our space cargo crafts.

We craft Gallivants out of anything.

Great-grandfather Alden invented them in the year 2955. He'd created one out of an old Easy Bake Oven. He had a thing for vintage Earth mementos. You simply put an object inside to transport it and wait for the spark. A glittering sulfur smoke means it went through.

We pass my favorite Gallivant in Headquarters to date—a corroded treasure trunk Shea and I scavenged from the depths of an outer realm ocean.

My sister fiddles with her portal key. "Let *me* break the news about the thumbs."

Tucked away on a wooden platform awaits Dad's workstation. We climb the steps. A hireling catches a cylindrical container from a chute directly above our heads. They set it on Dad's massive desk. It slides open to reveal two cheeseburgers and a side of curly potatoes.

"Mouthwatering," I comment as Dad takes a bite. "Is that Lippy's or Grand Sam's?"

Dad chokes through a mouthful. "Oh, good. You're back." He sets down his cheeseburger, adjusts his glasses that are way too hipster for his middle age, and wipes ketchup off his bristly chin. "Neither. I ordered out of galaxy."

Shea clears her throat. "Sorry it took us so long, Dad. Dashiel got taken by a Star Spirit, and by the time we got to planet—"

"Taken is one word for it." Dad opens the thick leather-bound ledger on his desk and raises his salt-and-pepper brows. I roll my eyes. We get it, Henry. You think I'm a shameful excuse for a son. "Let's get to the coin. Our liaison in the Residential District is demanding the advances we took in extraterrestrial stock last month."

My sister's line of sight falls to the dried-up, syrup-stained vamp thumbs in her hands.

This won't be good. Maybe I really did screw this up.

Dad clears his throat. "Well? Let's have it. I haven't got all day." I put a hand on Shea's shoulder. She shrugs me off and sets the thumbs on Dad's desk. He narrows his stone-cold gaze at them. He picks one up and rotates it under his lamp. "What is this?"

To her credit, Shea doesn't flinch. "Mathias didn't have the coin. You taught us to always finish deals. Vampire fingers will sell to make enough profit."

Dad alternates his gawking stare between us. "Is this some kind of joke?"

Shea shakes her head. "We put the appendages in slush to keep them... fresh."

Dad snatches the other crusty thumb from his desk and

chucks them across the platform like nobody's business. They narrowly miss a hireling's head.

"What can I do with appendages soaked in sugar and artificial dye?" Dad tousles his short curls of graying-brown hair. "This is beyond irresponsible. Do you have any idea what this does to our profit base?" Dad's gaze flicks to me for a second. He rounds his desk to face Shea head-on. "I expect better from you two. Especially you, Shea."

Back in the day, I used to get into yelling fights with Dad. I'd call him out on his ruthless moves and demeaning words. Every single time it resulted in him being harder on her than me. Shea's the real reason I've stayed this long. I stopped taking Dad's distaste for me to heart a long time ago. He knows as well as I do, she'll carry the burden of his reprimanding to her grave. I don't care if he's our father, our boss, or the criminal living beneath Fizzies—Dad's a bully. One that pathetically feeds on the fear of others.

It's better if I keep my mouth shut. Sometimes I can't help it. I'd rather he yelled at me right now. This isn't even her fault. None of this is in her control. Not the thumbs or the coin.

"The slushie was my idea, Dad," I say. "Also, I got dumped today, if you care."

Shea slaps her forehead. "I told you to stay out of it."

"No. I will not stay out of it."

My sister elbows me in the side so hard I think I might shut up, but my refusal to let Dad belittle her takes over. I match him stare for stare.

"Maybe you should start vetting buyers or taking a deposit before you send us out."

Dad doesn't answer me. He just sits there, a smug look on his face. It's killing him, I know it. I know he's itching to knock me in the teeth whenever I mouth off.

"Did you hear me?" I approach his desk.

Shea grits her teeth. "Dashiel."

I don't care anymore. I'm gonna say what I wanna say. I was going to tell my sister on her own. Now it feels pointless. "Your clients are all sketch balls. I'm leaving this—"

"ENOUGH!" Dad smashes a fist on the desk so hard it sends a heap of folders flying. I swallow the sudden lump in my throat. Even the hirelings startle. He points at me. "You watch your mouth. And you—" He motions to Shea, a vein bulging in his forehead. "This should never have happened. You're the leader of this team. You prep for the job, handle the heckling, and ensure the job gets done right, no matter what. Understood?"

Now my sister's voice is small. "Understood."

"Wonderful." He slams down in his desk chair and brushes aside his now lukewarm cheeseburger. One of his file folders splits open. He catches me staring and slaps it shut. "Now, let's talk about your next assignment."

The contents of my gut swirl, making me queasy. The Hover Rink phantom would've been so proud—I was *this* close to quitting. But at what cost? Would it have been the right time to leave when Dad's on a power trip? On second thought, when isn't he on a power trip?

A hireling raises a hand from the other side of the warehouse. "Incoming!"

Stepping back in line with my sister, we catch the tubes that drop above us in sync. Compliant Shea opens hers immediately and starts reading. I wait, staring at the bobbing head of our dear father, the supposed ringleader in this sadistic operation.

He's going to brush this one aside, isn't he? Nice.

"A medicine run for Mom?" Shea reads out, looking up from the digital scroll in her hands. "I don't understand. This isn't an assignment. It's an errand."

Uh, what now? I unscrew the capsule in my own hands and tap the glowing scroll inside. It unravels holographically, summarizing a job on Ominous, a planet in the Realm of Shadows.

"Mine must be a misprint." Shea reaches over my shoulder for a better look at my scrolling brief. "Okay. So, it looks like we're going to drop off a classified—"

"It is not"—Dad's eyes don't lift from his ledger—"a misprint."

"You're sending us on separate assignments?" I ask.

"That isn't standard protocol." The slight waver in Shea's voice has returned. "A Thief and an Enforcer always work together."

Dad snaps his fingers, and two hirelings appear at his side. He hands them an envelope. "Put out this message in the comms Gallivant to trading post 188 in Galaxy LDV17."

Once the hirelings are off, Shea says, "I think we should stick together. After we go to planet Ominous, we can double back to the Ornate District to pick up the medicine."

I nod. "I agree. Together is better."

I sometimes seem like a space case, but I'm grounded, I swear. I will always stand by the ones I love. Besides, the Realm of Shadows sounds like a tricky place. I've never been to planet Ominous before. I don't want to be left alone with all things that go bump in the night. I sleep with a nightlight for Goddess' sake. This is too much.

"My word is final." Dad focuses on the ink scrawl before him. "Oh, and Shea—Dash will need the portal key for his travels. Hand it over to him before you go."

My sister hesitates, tugs at her key all the same, and a shudder courses through me. That key is her nightlight. As she hands it to me, I try making eye contact. She avoids my gaze.

"You're dismissed now," Dad says without glancing up from his work. "I need to talk with your brother alone regarding his assignment."

Wow. I don't even know what to say.

Shea saunters out of Headquarters a little pink-faced. As the door shuts, a noise escapes her that could almost pass for a sniffle. I want to run after her and hug her.

Dad shuts his ledger. "I'm sure you're wondering why it's you."

I keep my fists curled at my side. "I'm sure you're going to tell me."

"The client requested a one-person transport." He plucks a leather-bound box with a tiny gold lock off his desk. That's when I notice the Sarasing Academy Holoblocks sign-up brochure crumpled among the other clutter on his desk. Stained with watermarks, it's become a well-loved coaster. I bet he hasn't even looked at it. "Unfortunately, Shea is not a Thief."

"What, the client requested a Thief?"

"Not exactly." Dad looks at me for the first time today. "I need a Thief."

I swallow hard. "According to the brief, it's a delivery."

"This is the item you'll be dropping off to the client." He slides the leather-bound box toward me. I catch it with ease, a simple flick of my wrist and palm. "You meet with him, give him the box, and then I need you to take something for me without him knowing."

"What's in it?" I shake the box against my ear. Like I do

every year around the holidays with the gifts Shea wraps a month early and sets beneath our decorated Yule log stack.

Dad leans back, kicks his feet up. "Doesn't matter what it is."

I shove the box into my pocket. "I think I deserve to know."

"The client is working on a creation of sorts." Dad messes with the tip of his quill. His fingers stain, and he wipes them clean on my Holoblocks brochure. "I can't disclose further details, but it's small, probably in a vial or a tube—I need you to steal one of them."

This monster is up to something. He shuffled those folders extra quick earlier.

"You're to be discreet," Dad continues, sitting up. "It's a simple job, and they've already paid, so all you have to do is deliver and pull. It's important that you get this item for me."

My throat goes dry. I stare at my feet, wishing I could tell him I refuse to help him.

"I'm not daft, Dashiel. You want to leave this business.

I lift my gaze to his. "How did you—"

"I've known for a while now," he says. "You and I know I can't run this business without you. An Enforcer is nothing without her Thief."

Well, I wasn't expecting this. "If I do this for you, you'll let me out?"

"Oh, no." He chuckles. "You're doing this for me because it's your duty. I know it hurts you when Shea takes the brunt of the blame between the two of you. So, if you pull what you tried to pull earlier, try to leave, or disrupt this operation, I will make both your lives, but mostly hers, a living hell."

"You mon—"

"That'll be all, Dashiel."

Dad rises. He stalks off across the warehouse, leaving me with a mysterious box in my pocket, a mission that makes zero sense, and a rising heat inside my chest.

What kind of father blackmails his children? Shea wouldn't even believe me if I told her. As much as I hate it, I'm stuck. But I won't give up. Henry James will not decide my life for me. While an Enforcer is nothing without her Thief, a monster is nothing without his lackeys.

I'm going to have to convince my sister he's up to no good, more no good than James Co. usually entails. How? I don't know. Shea's whole life revolves around this business. She eats, breathes, and sleeps the job. There's no way I can leave now.

Not unless she quits with me.

KAYLA MAURAIS is a young adult and new adult sci-fi/fantasy author from New England. She first started writing creatively when she was thirteen. Since then, she's gone on to get a master's degree in screenwriting. Her publishing imprint, Wraith's Fate Press, was established in April 2024. When she isn't writing, Kayla enjoys spending time by the ocean, visiting theme parks she wishes were haunted, and going on road trips to discover new places. She is also an educator, birth doula, developmental editor, and tarot reader. For more on Kayla and her offerings, visit kaylamaurais.com or connect with her on social media at @authorkaylamaurais.